Entanglement *of* Revenge

CHRIS BROOKES

A SCHNAUZER PUBLICATION

First published in 2014 by Schnauzer Publications

Design by Spiffing Covers Ltd

A CIP catalogue record for this title is available from the British Library.

All enquiries to: **enquiries@chrisbrookes.info**

ABOUT THE AUTHOR

Chris Brookes lives in Sheffield, England.

After working for several years on creating the characters for a mystery series, based on the registers of a police court missionary, he wrote several scripts intended for screen production. However, in 2012, he was persuaded to write the storylines as distinct novels, and in 2013, Schnauzer Publications released *Fate*, the first story in the entanglement series. For the last twelve months, Chris has been busy writing this, the second book, *Revenge*. The third book in the series, *Deceit*, is planned for release in Autumn 2015.

Other projects the author is currently working on include a short radio play, *The Road*, and the development of a TV series adapting the Jacques Futrelle mysteries. In addition, after many evenings spent discussing the concept of a sitcom with his good friend over a bottle or two of Pineau des Charentes, finally, the time is right to start capturing these ideas into scripts.

Away from writing, Chris has always loved to sketch and, over the years, has produced numerous limited editions of his work. With more time now available, he hopes to once more pick up his pastels.

ACKNOWLEDGEMENTS

James Bond has Miss Moneypenny, I have Miss Redpen! She is my editor, Helen Hancock, to whom I am deeply indebted. There are few I trust to re-craft my work more than Helen. My sincere thanks to her hardly seems enough for all the time, skill and effort spent editing this book.

When first starting *Revenge*, I discovered the composer, Adrian Munsey. Adrian's compositions drew me deep into a world of most emotions, and meant I could create the book's mood and atmosphere. To appreciate how much his music influenced this author, I can only urge you to listen to his albums: *Requiem* and *Incognito*. Thank you, Adrian.

A small army of test readers from around the world agreed to read the book as it developed, and fed back their opinions and comments – some good, some bad, and just occasionally, some ugly. Their criticisms, though, were always constructive and allowed me to better understand the reader's point of view.

My thanks to Jan "should be a comma" Chatterton for her help and contribution towards this book.

Robert Bradley gave me vital help to guide me through the fascinating world of mining, and checked for any technical facts.

The lovely Leonie Byrne allowed me to borrow her looks and, I think, some of her personality, when developing Louise. The story of Louise, however, is not entirely mine. On occasion, I have merely adapted to my setting, details and supposed events relating to the ex Crown Princess of Tuscany. I must, therefore, acknowledge the author, Henry W. Fischer as the originator of that story.

To James and his team at Spiffing Covers, thank you for your patience, professionalism and brilliant creative designs.

Last, but certainly not least, my biggest thanks have to go to my wife, Kate, and my family and friends, without whose love, support and encouragement I would not be able to live my writing dreams.

Chapter 1

Treeton Colliery, 1916

There had been ten people in the descending cage that night: 187 years of pit experience between them, and all could tell a story of the hell of working in this mine – should anyone want to listen. All, that is, except for a boy of 14, who was eagerly awaiting his first shift in the brutal conditions of the Lorimer pit district. And Dr Robertson. The doctor had been requested at the pit bottom to administer morphine to a ganger who had slipped whilst illegally riding the crank between the pony and tubs. His leg was trapped, and so badly crushed that he would be lucky if it survived.

Quite why Robert Elliott was also in the cage it was hard to imagine. Particularly as he was dressed in his everyday suit with a crisp starched white shirt, the collar pinned together tight at his neck and serving as a constant reminder that his weight was gradually creeping upwards. He didn't speak, and indeed wasn't spoken to. He was simply there. In his head he heard music – a violin playing a lovely melody. But why would a court missionary be in a pit cage, standing with his trademark cane in hand?

The banksman clicked the steel bar safely into place and signalled with three rings of the bell to the engine room. The cage then began its descent down the narrow shaft to the coalface some 500 yards below.

One hundred yards down, a terrible straining sound started to be heard. It was angry and stressed, like a ship straining at its mooring in a swelling sea, and followed by random clicking. 'What the bloody hell is that?' called one of the men.

The cage suddenly stopped. The banksman had signalled an emergency. He knew there was definitely something wrong! Although safety checks on the wire rope had only been carried out six hours earlier, the men's safety was his primary responsibility. He knew his actions would mean lost productivity and, for that alone, he'd get no less than a Spanish inquisition by the deputy manager. Also, to delay bringing an injured man up to the surface would need some justification.

The young boy in the cage became nervous, calling out, 'What's wrong?' Elliott also couldn't feel entirely at ease. He'd been down mines before, but never had the cage stopped abruptly. Dr Robertson seemed unconcerned.

'Don't thee get frettin', lad. It's always nowt,' came a reassuring miner's voice as the cage finally stopped bouncing.

'Shine thee torch up. See if tha can see weear it's cummin from,' called one miner to the other. He was the only one positioned to see upwards through a slit hole in the cage roof, where the inspection hatch hadn't been sited properly.

'Fuckin' hell!' he shrieked.

Neither the doctor nor Elliott cared for those words, although Elliott was never surprised by bad language: in his probation work it was all too commonly heard. Nevertheless, these days it seemed as if the returning soldiers from the front couldn't finish a sentence without the f-word. He frowned at the miner, wanting to remind him there was a boy present, although he knew the lad would, no doubt, be using the word freely within days.

What the man had seen was the source of the pinging sound and the wire straining – the 'V' cut in the wire rope. It was now clearly visible and began to open up right in front of his eyes, exposing more and more bright raw metal. He went rigid with fear.

'What is it?' a voice asked. But his colleague just continued to stare in fear above him.

'For Christ's sake, what?' another voice howled.

They all struggled furiously to see the problem, but with ten men crammed in so tightly, it was near impossible to move.

Another ring of the bell meant the cage was being

brought back up the shaft. But, no sooner had it started to ascend again, than the cage suddenly listed over 10 degrees. A high-pitched scraping began as the cage violently dragged up along the brickwork.

Peering down the shaft, the banksman could now see the cage approaching. Sparks were flying off the bricks, as the metal began carving through them like butter. What should he do? Signal to stop the cage again? Suddenly, he saw the wire rope come into view, still taking the strain but hanging on with literally only a dozen threads. 'Jesus Christ!' he cried out, trying to think quickly. If the cage stopped now, how much longer could the rope last? Should he request the winder to overwind and hope the cage could make it through to the locking safety device in the headgear? He realised there just wasn't time!

It was agonising to watch – 30, 20, 10 yards to go to the landing stage, then he could get them all out safely. All he could do was pray, 'Our Father, which art in heaven, hallowed be thy name …'

For the occupants of the cage it was nothing short of a living hell. Petrified, they clung for dear life onto anything that felt static. Elliott, still hearing the violin playing its soulful tune, stretched out his hand to the boy, who was trembling with fear.

'Are we going to die, Mr Elliott?' wobbled his voice.

'And lead us not into temptation, but deliver us from

evil.' The banksman's words could now clearly be heard by the men below.

Elliott pulled the boy tight into him and allowed the music in his head to drown out his thoughts as the cage slowed virtually to a stop. It inched upwards, still scraping the bricks like a nail on a blackboard.

Seven, six yards …

Five never came!

The almighty cracking sound of the wire rope snapping filled the shaft. A rush of air came volleying up and threw the banksman backwards. He lay there and knew what was going to happen. All he could do was wait and hope that, if he too were to perish, it would be over quickly.

The roaring noise on the brickwork was deafening. He closed his eyes tightly. Like a serpent, the rope finally flicked out of the shaft and flayed around. Anything in its path was lashed unmercifully, as it sliced through metal casings and tore apart wood as easily as a lion rips at another wild beast.

'For thine is the kingdom, the power and the glory.'

The weight of the cage could wedge it no longer against the shaft wall. Bricks began to give way and crumble. Eventually, it slowly righted itself. Then, the three tons of cast iron and steel, along with its occupants, finally plummeted.

'Forever and ever. Amen.'

At the edge of exhaustion, she stood bewildered – tortured by her thoughts. But nothing existed in those thoughts that made any sense to her. She had no idea why she was there, no perception of her surroundings, nobody to help her. A face so dirty, gaunt and lifeless. A pathetic figure wearing a once-attractive dress, now soaking wet and ravaged by the filth of her environment.

Rain continually lashed down. She felt cold and numb, drops of water falling from her hair into the blackened puddles at her feet. Lifting her head, she looked out at the dark, bleak landscape around her. As far as she could see, there was only the colour black. The wet, slimy black of a coalfield's spoil heap.

The noise of the pit hooter carried on the wind. Tonight, it was a long haunting sound. Soon, curtains in the village would twitch, lights would come on and, in the harsh early hours of morning, people would gather for news at the pit gates.

Meanwhile, on the heap, the figure trudged forward until she could walk no further. She fell to her knees. Her hand slowly opened and allowed the big hacksaw to fall to the ground.

Chapter 2

'Aargh! Aargh! Aarghhhhhhh,' Elliott screamed and shot forward into an upright position, his eyes instantly wide open, the pupils fully dilated. He gasped furiously to get air into his lungs. It was the third nightmare he'd had this week.

The sudden and violent force of his jolting movement and the screaming instantly woke Ann, his wife.

'What? What?' she screamed in terror and jumped out of bed, more from an instinct that she was in danger than anything else. A blind panic came over her as she tried to make sense of what was happening. Eventually she calmed down enough to recognize where she was and leant over to touch her husband. 'Robert, what on earth is it?'

Elliott was sitting up in a trance, his hair, face and pyjamas soaking wet with sweat.

'Robert, Robert, speak to me. Are you all right?' Ann was shocked as she cupped his clammy face in her hands. 'You're absolutely wet through!' She realised that he had had another awful dream.

Elliott wasn't a man to show his emotions but, at this moment, all he wanted to do was cling on tightly to her –

to someone who was real. The noise and commotion had woken the whole household and, within minutes, their two sons, Henry and Cecil, entered the room holding a lamp.

'Mother,' called out Cecil in concern and ran towards her. She cradled him for comfort as he began to sob.

'Shh now! It's all right. Everything is fine. Father has just had a bad dream, that's all.'

'Father!' said Henry, holding up the lamp to reveal Elliott, still sitting rigid. They had never seen their father in a state of distress before and it frightened them. In fact, Ann too had never seen him looking so traumatised. Her husband was normally never one to suffer from bad dreams. All she ever witnessed of him in his sleep was his loud snoring. She could write a book about that!

At last Elliott shook himself and puffed out his cheeks. 'Phew!' was the best he could manage as he wiped his brow. 'I'm all right. Don't worry!' he said, bringing his hands down calmly. To everyone's relief, it seemed that Father, with a smile on his face, was back to normal.

By now the dog downstairs was barking and Lily, the housemaid, had arrived on the scene, followed shortly after by their house guests, Tom and Mary Sharpe. All stood rather awkwardly, only slightly inside the bedroom. Somehow going right in didn't quite seem appropriate.

'Is everything all right, Mrs Elliott? It's just I heard

all the commotion and —'

'Yes, everything's fine, Lily. We've just been watching Mr Elliott rehearsing for his part in the church play that's all. He was very good!' Ann's dry humour was never far away. Tom gave a hearty laugh, in tune as ever with his hostess's wit. Mary gave him a nudge, in embarrassment.

Lily, totally perplexed and never fully sure how to take her mistress, could only give a wry smile. 'I'll go down and calm Bessie.'

Elliott looked over to Ann and gave her a frown at her teasing.

'Don't worry, dear. I will remember to tell her I was only joking!'

She then turned her attention to Henry and Cecil. 'Right boys, drama over. Come on, back to bed. Let's all try and get back to sleep.' She went to escort them back to their rooms.

Mary offered her assistance. 'I can do that, Ann,' she said, holding out her hand to Cecil. But before she could set off, baby Lucinda's cries were heard from her and Tom's room.

'Oh, Mary, I'm so sorry. Here, you go and attend to Lucinda. I'll look after the boys,' Ann said.

Elliott could only offer a culpable smile.

Tom felt obliged to ask, 'Are you quite all right now, Robert?'

'Yes, I'm fine. Thank you. Just a silly nightmare that seems to have brought the whole household to life suddenly. I'm sorry to have awoken you all, Tom. Things aren't normally as eventful of an evening, I can assure you,' replied Elliott, acutely aware his guest must think he was spending a night in some sort of mad house.

'Oh, what a shame,' Tom quipped. 'Well, I'll bid you goodnight again,' and he began to exit, just as Ann returned. 'Young master Cecil is settled once more, I assume?' he enquired.

'Yes. Bless him, he just needed a bit of reassurance.' She paused, then had to say, 'I'm so sorry, Tom, to have disturbed your sleep.'

'It's not a problem.'

She wasn't convinced, and gave him a dubious look.

'No, really. We weren't asleep anyway,' he lied, not wanting to make an issue of the matter. Secretly though, he would have given anything not to have been woken up. It was only in the last week that the baby had begun to sleep for more than a couple of hours at a time during the night.

Tom bade his hosts goodnight and returned to his room.

Elliott took off his pyjama top and lay back. Ann climbed back into bed and cuddled up to him. 'Better now? I wonder what's bringing this on all of a sudden?

What was it about?'

After taking a deep breath in preparation for the onslaught, he began to replay the scene. 'It was truly awful …'

Looking over to the clock, Ann realised she might regret asking. How could she have forgotten her husband's love of telling a story! She had been hoping they could just kiss and cuddle for a while but she snuggled in closer, listening attentively.

'… and you know that moment, Ann, when you sense something is going to happen?'

But there was no response. He glanced down to see her eyes firmly closed. 'Oh!' he said, with slight disappointment, although he should have been content that she had lasted a good ten minutes before falling fast asleep. He gently laid her back on her side of the bed.

During what was left of the night, Elliott drifted in and out of sleep until, eventually, he was wide awake again – or at least he believed he was. Once more, he pondered the dream, trying to understand the relevance of it all. He could see the look on those men's faces so clearly. The true look of fear. Grimacing and contorted faces, with eyes wide open yet empty of life. He would always remember that look, and the nauseous sensation that went with it – a hollowness that finds its way through the bones like damp through a stone. He knew all but two of the men, although none of them were what he would call friends.

As he lay in the dark, the music he remembered returned to his head – a violin playing the same melody, although this time it was much softer, still beautiful but slightly more mournful, even haunting. Half an hour later, Elliott was once again asleep and dreaming.

Suddenly, a voice spoke. 'Don't you just wish it all could have had a happy ending? But I do so adore a tragedy, don't you?'

Elliott recognised the voice instantly. It came from the man sitting in the chair in his study.

'We meet again, Robert.'

Elliott didn't say anything, just stared.

'Every time you dream, I'll be there with you. You can see my hell,' he carried on, calmly and softly. Then, his voice changed, becoming angry and bitter. 'Why did you have to meddle, Robert? Why?'

The man sitting in his chair was the now deceased Canon Charles Brockwell, Elliott's one time friend whom he'd exposed a year earlier for his evil acts and, consequently, had watched take his own life.

Chapter 3

Two weeks earlier.

Quite why Sister Agnes chose to alight at Sheffield railway station with Marion would perhaps never be known. Was it intentional and planned in detail? Or was it just out of sheer panic that they had boarded the first train which arrived at York station that afternoon? Whichever it was probably wasn't important. What was important was the fact that they had escaped. The nun didn't know what the future would hold for Marion. All she knew beyond a doubt was her own future. The pain, and her experience, told her she only had weeks, if that, before her lord would take her.

Stepping out of the train and standing on the platform was almost too much for Marion to cope with. She looked around, eyes wide open in amazement, gawping at the different people who passed her by. She was like a little girl lost, suddenly thrust into a whole new world. But Marion was no girl: she was a grown woman. Putting her lips together in a pout, she began to blow bubbles. Harder and harder she blew, until they dribbled down her chin. A woman passing by gave her a look of deep disdain. For Marion, this wasn't normal. Normal was to be given a smile and kind words, such as, 'Yes, very clever of you, Marion.' And why were all these men not dressed in white coats? Why were the women not adorned in habits? Overcome by anxiety, she rushed back to the train door, clutching at the handle and shaking her head. Her world was suddenly violated by strangeness – new noises, sounds, light and smells. Her mind was overloaded, so that she couldn't filter new things and place them where they should be. Marion wanted to go back to normal. To the environment of the asylum. To what she had been used to.

Sister Agnes put down the single case and went over to her companion. She placed her hands to each side of Marion's eyes, forming blinkers, and made her look straight at her. 'It's me, Sister Agnes. Hold my hand.' Marion seemed to calm a little at the familiar voice and the touch of hands.

'I want to go back,' said her bewildered voice, '… Back … Back.'

'Marion! You're safe. Everything is all right. I'm here.'

'No! Go back.'

'Listen to me.' The sister looked deeply into Marion's frightened eyes. 'We have to go somewhere new for a while … just you and me.'

'New?'

'Yes. Somewhere different for a while.'

'Then go back?'

'Perhaps.'

Sister Agnes couldn't help but feel guilty. What had she done? How was Marion going to manage when she was gone? At least back at the asylum she had routine and order – her pills to take, her treatments, and a sense of belonging. However, the sister was pragmatic. She had to be with what she'd discovered. It was going to be unbearably hard but, with the little time she had left, she had to try. If there was any justice, her lord would intervene and help.

'We're going to take a ride in a taxi now, Marion. Go to our new place, with a room just for us. Would you like that?'

'Just us?'

'Yes, after we take a ride in the taxi, then it will be just us.'

Marion smiled. It was sincere. Her world centred around Sister Agnes and she trusted her. 'The new room has a table?'

'Oh, I should think so.'

Marion's expression drooped. 'Buzzzzzz!' she acted, with her hands to her head, referring to the electrodes associated with a table.

'No, no, my dear. All that has finished now,' the

sister replied, gently cupping Marion's face to relieve her anguish.

Marion's smile returned. 'Then we shall go to a new room.'

They walked out onto the station forecourt. Marion clutched hard onto the sister's arm as another new set of sensations assaulted her. The sister flagged a taxi.

'Perhaps you would be good enough to take us to some reasonably priced rooms, young man. Quite near to the centre, but preferably away from too much noise.'

The driver scratched his head. Not too much noise and Sheffield, with all its industry working to full capacity, didn't really go together. But he thought he knew a place that might fit the bill.

The place where they did end up was, in fact, ideal. It was a small room upstairs in a terraced house and at the top of a hill. Beyond, there was only open scrubland, formerly an old iron works. Although only a mile and a short tram ride away from the city centre, any foundry noise seemed to be diffused by three large hoardings. The elderly landlady explained to Sister Agnes that it had been unoccupied for some time. The young man who'd rented it previously had gone away but paid her a whole pound, asking if she would keep the room available for him for when he returned. Then, he had said, he would bring his new bride. That was many months ago. It had never occurred to her till recently that he'd signed up for war duties and was now lost, presumed dead.

The first couple of days were fine. Sister Agnes was able to think and work out what she was going to do, whilst Marion mused away the time looking out of the window. She felt safe and contented. Most importantly, she had her pills. The sister knew though, that by the third day they would all have gone, and then it would start. In her time at the asylum, she had witnessed many times the consequences of taking patients off their medication, and she knew, therefore, that the next week was going to be horrific. She prayed that the lord would help Marion through it. What lasting damage the drugs had done, she could only guess at; and all she could do was hope.

Aware of a convent out in Derbyshire, she eventually decided that after the next week, when, she hoped, Marion would be through the worst, they would pay a visit there. Then she could explain everything to Mother Amberhill. She would surely help.

She sat back in the chair and looked over to Marion, asleep on the bed. Now she could say her prayers.

~~~

In all her time at Rosterhay Asylum, Sister Agnes had never pried, never looked at any patient's notes unless
~~~

told to do so, never asked questions. Her duty as a nun was only to God, and she was satisfied in her work, a path of helping the mentally ill that her lord had chosen for her. Always it was hard work, and heart-breaking to see but she carried out the tasks assigned by the doctors without query. That is until the night she was instructed to fetch Dr Robertson's bag from the office.

The sister had first met Marion on the night she was brought in. She had obviously been heavily sedated and was put into a private room close to Dr Robertson's office. Not that he used it very much, being seldom at the asylum. He would visit and do a clinic once a fortnight, perhaps twice. However, that night he was to stay and sleep in his office. The sister was instructed to sit with the patient, who was now strapped down to the bed, and to wake the doctor if the patient came round. It was at about 4 in the morning when Marion did stir. Sister Agnes, who had dozed into a half sleep, awoke immediately as Marion became hysterical and thrashed about trying to release herself.

Dr Robertson was soon at the scene. Marion was now wild with rage, bordering on hysterical. She continually hurled abuse at him. As he fumbled for his syringe, the sister remembered Marion saying to her, 'You have to help me! They're trying to silence me … kill me.' Then the solution of chloryl hydrate was injected and calm was immediately restored. Marion's head slumped back onto the bed. The sister asked no questions.

In the following weeks she couldn't believe that somebody could sleep almost continuously, but then she was never there when Marion was pumped full of a host of different bromides, barbiturates and opium. Eventually, Sister Agnes became Marion's primary carer, and never, in all the time she looked after her, did she hear Marion refer to her past life, family or anything associated with normality.

Dr Robertson never seemed to visit any more. Still, all carried on as normal, not least since Marion was given her daily dose of pills. The sister sometimes wondered why Marion was never included in the new therapy trials. This new 'psychoanalysis' treatment, as the doctors were calling it, seemed, to Sister Agnes at any rate, to be far less harsh than the constant use of drugs. Also, she had observed a definite improvement in some of the other patients.

Then, one day, Dr Robertson turned up unexpectedly. He went to Marion's bed and, as had been usual, he assessed her state. He reached for his bag but realised he'd left it in the office. The sister was instructed to fetch it.

In the office, she reached over to pull it off the table. Two files, half hanging out, suddenly spilled papers onto the floor. She scrambled to scoop them up and couldn't help but notice the name label on the front of one of the files: MARION.

Had it been any other name she would, undoubtedly, have just put the file back in the bag. But by now she had become so attached to Marion and the mystery of her, that even her good lord couldn't stop her curiosity. She opened the file. Inside there weren't any personal details, such as she had seen in other patient files, no drug control forms, no analysis of treatment sheets, no notes or opinions. All that was there was a single sheet stating: SEDATIVE TREATMENT ONLY. MUST ALWAYS HAVE A DAILY DOSE OF ...

It then listed a surprising number of drugs, prescribed in varying strengths, and for different time periods, most of which were abbreviated and meant little to the sister. At the bottom, it simply read: NO VISITORS, LETTERS OR TELEPHONE CALLS. ALL QUERIES ABOUT THIS PATIENT MUST BE REFERRED TO DR. A. P. ROBERTSON

In the other file were technical drawings and plans for a building. The attached photograph, labelled 'Front Elevation', would have been of no interest to Sister Agnes, except that there was a woman posed in the foreground. She recognised her immediately: it was Marion. As she looked up, she took notice of the address of the property, and a terrible realisation came over her.

<center>~~~</center>

With each day that passed, Marion seemed to get worse. She was now having acute withdrawal symptoms. There was nothing the sister could do, other than mop her brow and hold her. But Marion began to have outbursts of shouting and screaming, unable to understand what was happening to her. Only when she had no more strength to fight and collapsed with exhaustion, could the sister cradle her like a baby and hum gently to her.

Marion's outbursts soon attracted the attention of the landlady, and even the neighbours. The sister knew it would only be a matter of time before they were asked to leave. She had to make the trip to the convent as soon as possible. However, time was not on her side. Her own pain was becoming intolerable. Sister Agnes was suffering from stomach cancer.

Then, one day, the sister's prayers seemed to be answered: she wasn't awoken by Marion screaming. Instead, she simply awoke naturally to find Marion calmly sitting by the window, looking out and rocking herself.

As each subsequent day passed, Marion steadily improved, slowly becoming her normal self, or as normal as she ever had been back in the asylum. For her to be normal again, in the true sense of the word, was a hope too far, even for Sister Agnes. However, at least now the sister felt she could take Marion on a journey to the convent without attracting undue attention.

Unfortunately, that journey never came.

Marion sat patiently at the end of the sister's bed, waiting for her to wake. She waited and waited, not understanding why Sister Agnes didn't answer her. Why, today, was the routine different? Perhaps it was because she wasn't sitting by the window. She went to assume her position at the windowsill, where she rocked gently. Again she waited … and waited. In fact, she waited for two days.

What prompted Marion to eventually venture outside the room was probably hunger. Even in her state of utter confusion, she knew she had to eat. It was as if, suddenly, an instinct for survival had taken over. She could plainly remember where the sister had hidden the key to the door, even though she couldn't comprehend that she was dead. Every hour or so, it became a ritual for Marion to check on the sister. Always she was lying motionless, and now she was blue and stiff, but Marion just tucked the blankets in a little more tightly.

The time came to unlock the door. She went down the stairs, opened the front door and walked onto the street. Now it was a whole new world she faced, full of strangeness, confusion and danger. But her fear had gone. She began to walk down the street, not knowing where she was going or what she was going to do. She just walked. By four o'clock in the afternoon she had entered the city centre. The streets bustled with activity. She stopped abruptly and strained to listen, then looked upwards. There was nothing other than a pair of pigeons cooing loudly, yet it was a sound that triggered a reaction: a sound she associated with the asylum.

'Back … back,' she mumbled. Then, with determination, she walked on. Rounding the corner, she saw a familiar sight and there she headed. It was the railway station.

Reaching the platform she looked left and right. Was it that one? Or this one? Perhaps the one over there? She gazed at the trains and began to become anxious.

'Are you all right, luv? Need any help?' asked a kind voice.

'Back … back,' Marion said.

'Back where?'

'Buzzzzzz!'

The kindly man realised the woman before him was somewhat confused, and just smiled in recognition of this. 'Perhaps it's that one you want,' he said, pointing up the platform, and moved hastily away.

Marion walked down the platform as far as it went, and eventually she found herself on the tracks. There she continued to walk, oblivious of the danger, until she disappeared into the distance.

The following morning, a couple of young boys saw a yellow bundle on one of the pit spoil heaps at Treeton Colliery. As they approached, it became obvious what it was: it was a body. With trepidation, they rolled it over. Marion gave the faintest of moans.

Chapter 4

Elliott felt utterly drained. In total, he reckoned he couldn't have had more than an hour's sleep. Constantly tossing and turning in bed had taken its toll. He hadn't been able to get the nightmare out of his mind, thinking endlessly about the terrifying sequence of events. It had affected him more than he would admit. His head thumped.

In the bathroom, with forefinger and thumb, he forced his heavy eyelids open wider and looked in the mirror. He had to admit he wasn't a good sight. Eventually he dragged himself down to breakfast, where Lily only added to his misery by presenting him with a plate of kippers. He tried hard to show his appreciation.

'Oh dear,' remarked Tom, who was sitting at the table and looking quite the opposite of Elliott, even though he also had only slept for an hour or so.

'Good morning,' Elliott managed, pushing his plate to one side.

'Morning old chap.' Tom laughed, clearly remembering that the last time he had sat at this table for breakfast, he was the one who was bleary-eyed and couldn't face cooked fish.

Elliott had not forgotten either. 'Yes, I remember,' he sighed.

Tom looked over to Bessie, the dog. 'Just as I predicted, girl. It's going to be your lucky morning.'

Bessie's ears pricked up in anticipation.

Watching Elliott slide his hands down over his face, Tom commented, 'I thought you might be feeling somewhat bleary. One usually does after a bad nightmare … Suffer from them often?'

'Until recently, no, never. And why this time I should have dreamt about the disaster, and being there, I'll never know.'

'The disaster, and being there?' Tom asked, always intrigued by the content of dreams, and thinking that perhaps this would be a good example to give his students to analyse.

Elliott explained. 'Two weeks ago there was a tragic accident at the pit not far from here. Eight men, one boy and a doctor plummeted to their deaths in the cage. From all accounts, it appears the wire rope had been deliberately cut!'

'And your part?'

'My part?' said Elliott indignantly.

'In the dream, Robert.'

'Oh, I see. Well … I don't know why but I was just there, observing it all happen.'

'How dreadful … And how bizarre!' Tom frowned. This was something quite different to ponder.

Tom and Elliott's relationship was always a meeting of minds, since each was interested in the other's profession. More so nowadays, for Tom was engaged in research with a colleague on the working of the criminal mind: from petty thieves to murders, he relished the prospect of carrying out criminal case studies. That was where Elliott came in. Who better than he to introduce Tom into the world of the criminal classes? And for Elliott, who better than Tom to help him further understand the psychology of the many men, women and young lads who crossed his path through the courts. No sooner had Tom mentioned his research than a short stay in Sheffield with the Elliotts was being arranged.

Meantime, Ann was hatching her own plans. For weeks Elliott had dithered about holidaying with her parents in Scarborough, using all manner of excuses for delaying the visit. The real reason for his reluctance, however, was that he hardly ever saw eye to eye with her father on anything. Ann didn't relish being the peacemaker again either – the consequences of one war were quite enough to deal with. She cleverly suggested, 'If you're busy with work, dear, then I'm sure Mary would welcome a break and come with me. It would do her and baby good to get some fresh sea air. And the boys would love her being there.'

How could he disagree!

'So, what delights have you in store today, Robert?' enquired Tom, whilst handing over a kipper to the patient and now grateful Bessie. He sat and watched as Elliott pushed back his hair and studied his hairline in the mirror.

'Oh, yes. Sorry … Well, I thought …'

Luckily for Elliott, that morning was not very busy and didn't tax his sluggish mind too much. There were just a few reports to look over in preparation for his next court visit. By 11 o'clock, with the aid of several cups of tea, each containing the customary five spoonfuls of sugar, Elliott was feeling his normal self again. The afternoon seemed a much better prospect for Tom – a long walk for the pair, in the brisk air, to visit Haddington Hall. It was here that the owner of Treeton Colliery resided.

Elliott had visited the Hall before, but hadn't been inside the house or indeed met its owner, the Earl of Ranskill. He'd simply walked in the grounds near to the house with the groundsman, discussing exactly what was required of the boys: the boys being the latest set of delinquents handed over for Elliott's supervision following their appearances before the bench. As always, he would endeavour to find them suitable work, with the hope of a fresh start in life. On this occasion, he had secured labouring duties for half a dozen of the young men, digging out foundations for a new and ornate fountain structure. He was though, quite unprepared for his reception on this visit.

On arrival, Elliott was informed that the earl sought a meeting with him: no reason given; he was simply to be escorted to the library. Escorted indeed, thought Elliott, not sure whether he should feel like someone of importance or merely a criminal summoned before the judge. Both he and Tom stood looking around the impressive room with its huge collection of books. Tom mused over the rows of tomes with their decorative covers, eventually running his fingers over a line of titles. He then stopped and gave that look. It was like watching a set of cogs clicking into place, then being released. His brow tightened, creating a multitude of tramlines as he analysed his thoughts. 'Umm! Interesting.'

What Tom was referring to, Elliott had no idea.

'I wonder if any actually get read?' Elliott puzzled.

'Oh! Some of them, I've absolutely no doubt!' Tom commented, placing a book back in its logical position.

Elliott studied each large oil painting adorning the walls. He gave particular attention to the horse study. Eventually, he decided on his opening line for when his host appeared, 'A fine example of a Stubbs, Lord Ranskill.' Then, he reconsidered: what if it wasn't a Stubbs? After all he couldn't see a signature, and what did he know about fine art anyway? Perhaps it would be best to just open with, 'You wished to see me, Lord Ranskill?'

After what seemed an eternity of being kept waiting, the doors were flung open and in walked a man, rather short yet stocky, and dressed in a fine tailored suit. He strode straight past Elliott, not once looking at him. 'These men you've sent me. Best you could manage, is it?' he scolded, gesticulating at the lads through the window, as if they were all at a cattle market.

Elliott was stunned.

'I'll need more labourers. You'll provide me with a few more,' continued Ranskill.

Elliott raised his eyebrows. 'Will I now?'

'Yes, you will.' Finally, he looked over to Elliott. 'Have them start on Monday.' With that, he was off towards the door.

To say Elliott was livid would be an understatement. He seldom met with the gentry outside the courts, and those he'd met before, he didn't speak highly of. The earl's arrogance and bad manners merely confirmed his opinion. 'And whom, exactly, do you think you are addressing, sir?'

Ranskill stopped and gave a surprised look before responding, 'Well you, of course! Oh, yes, before I forget. The crippled one, see him?' Again, he gestured with his hand towards the window. 'We'll send him back.' It was if he were talking about a herd of pigs he'd just taken delivery of.

It seemed as if Ranskill hadn't noticed the presence of Tom at all. Eventually though, his eyes did turn towards him. It was a look nothing short of confusion. 'And who might you be?' he blasted.

'My name is Professor Thomas Sharpe.'

Ranskill just looked him up and down before walking on. He then stopped abruptly and turned around. 'You could look at some loading calculations for me,' he cried, almost insisting.

'I'm a professor of general surgery, sir,' Tom replied with equal insistence.

Ranskill thought for a moment. 'Then you're no use to me,' he said and duly turned and strutted out of the library.

Tom calmly commented, 'Obviously not! … What a strange man!'

Elliott was simply dumbfounded and left the Hall seething with rage at the pomposity of its owner.

~~~

The Earl of Ranskill was the third generation of the Warsop family to reside at Haddington Hall, a beautiful
~~~

sandstone building erected in the 1700s. The house had known much happiness and jollity over the centuries but not any more: for the last thirty years of the family's ownership, it had reeked of scandal, mystery and tragedy. Above all, it begged for love again.

Unlike his father, George Warsop was a very successful businessman. He had been brought up in the family tradition of military schooling and, at eighteen years old, he had been made a lieutenant. Not long after, he was unleashed on his own corps of men, or as he preferred to call them in private, his cannon fodder. After eight years of service, he turned his back on the army, following an altercation with a general over tactics in the Anglo-Zulu war. He wouldn't accept his superior's instructions not to advance his battalion further because of the fear that too many of his men would be lost.

On returning to Haddington, he soon became bored and was not prepared to simply play the heir apparent, ambling around the estate with no real purpose, like his father. Instead, he saw the future in coal, which was plentiful under the land they owned in South Yorkshire. In 1880 he established the Warsop Mining Company, and by 1890 the company was mining in six collieries across the region. By the time his father died, some three years later, the wealth of the family and Haddington's future was assured.

The earl's success made him the talk of society, but he shunned his fellow gentry whenever possible. There were hardly ever any dinner parties, shooting days or indeed any lavishness at Haddington. All Ranskill was interested in was his work and making money. Certainly he had little interest in the opposite sex. However, he was vain enough to know that the Warsop name needed perpetuating, and so attending society dinners became a necessary evil. To him, the endless round of polite small talk was always excruciating. Although a confident tyrant within his own world, Ranskill was socially inept among his peers. Just occasionally, he would drink a little too much wine and show some of the more alluring traits of his personality to a potential wife. But the earl always had an advantage that was admired by many a female dinner guest and their families: wealth. Poor Isabelle Dutton-Flowers, the daughter of Baron Benjamin Flowers, was soon chosen as the prize cow.

Any thought of bringing anything to Haddington other than a son was very soon dispelled for Isabelle. Her position in the household could, at best, be described as one of sufferance. The only light in her tunnel of gloom was that her husband was rarely there. To her, he was a disaster in all aspects of their life together, especially the bedroom; although at least he was fertile. Two sons, Frederick and David, were produced to fulfil her duties, but Isabelle was anything but maternal. Soon it became commonplace for her to go for days without seeing them. One nanny, who was dismissed from service, was quite open with her comments in the village. 'If I swapped him for a monkey, I doubt whether she'd notice,' she said.

After only four years of marriage, Isabelle finally left Ranskill. It was a scandal that rocked the upper echelons of Yorkshire society. Rumour and speculation raged and filled the column inches of the local newssheets for several weeks. The most favoured piece of gossip was that she had eloped to America with a secret lover.

The stony-faced earl banned all newspapers from the house and forbade even the slightest mention of Isabelle. She became the evil that no one could speak of. He couldn't stop the caricatures of his domestic life in the press, but he certainly had no intention of suffering any malicious talk at home. Above all, he was determined that the two boys would never see their mother again.

~~~

Elliott had at last calmed down, although he vowed that, if he had to talk with Lord Ranskill in future, he would be prepared and, rest assured, next time, he would have plenty to say to him. As Tom and he walked through the entrance hall back towards the large outer doors, they
~~~

heard the sound of a violin. It was playing the same tune Elliott had heard in his dream and now couldn't get out of his mind. Intrigued, they went towards a door that Elliott noticed was slightly ajar and gently pulled on the handle. Inside was a man with a violin pressed lovingly under his chin. With each stroke of the bow across the strings, a beautiful sound filled the room. Elliott stood there admiring the talent of the player. Slowly, he closed his eyes and allowed the music to seep into his soul.

As the music finished, Elliott opened his eyes and began clapping. 'That was absolutely beautiful, young man.'

The man looked terrified at seeing the two strangers and immediately fled.

Elliott looked over to Tom. 'You'd expect to be taken aback if you didn't know somebody was there watching you, but that was most odd!'

Tom's forehead tightened to display the deep tramlines again. It meant only one thing – he was thinking. What he was thinking about, nobody could have the slightest clue – yet!

'Don't worry, sir. It's nothing you've done.' The voice that suddenly came from behind them was that of the butler, Dowling.

'Oh, hello … Well, thank goodness for that,' said Elliott.

'He's the earl's younger son, Master David. A bit affected, I'm afraid. We don't get many visitors these days, so he easily gets scared by a stranger,' explained Dowling.

'Well, I'm sorry to hear that,' answered Elliott.

The professor added his observation. 'And yet he has confidence to play the violin like that.'

'Better than any professional, I've heard, sir.'

'Indeed,' agreed Tom.

Just then, the young musician, David, reappeared cautiously.

'Hello, young man,' Elliott offered in a reassuring voice, but there was no response.

'He won't speak, sir,' Dowling offered.

'I see.' Elliott was all too familiar with mute behaviour through his experience with Walter Stanford. He signed, 'Well done!' which was a short phrase he thought he remembered Mary signing, all that time ago.

'I doubt he understands that either,' suggested Dowling.

The musician grabbed at the sheets of music on the stand and fled once more.

As the two guests were led back to the outer doors, Elliott looked around and couldn't help remarking to Dowling, 'I hope you don't mind me saying, but the house seems so lifeless. Not a criticism of the standards you keep. Please don't think that. It's just, well … I don't sense any soul to the place.'

Dowling was far too professional to offer critical comments on his master, although his face suggested he might have wanted to. For over twenty years he'd been in charge at Haddington and he'd certainly seen and heard more than he should have during that time. He did, however, look at Elliott and say, 'There was a time, sir, with Louise, when the house had hope!' Tom tilted his head and then looked back to the house. He looked puzzled and indeed he was.

Elliott walked with marked disappointment towards the crippled man in the grounds. He put his arm around him as they walked on and then broke the bad news. Jonny Pearson stopped and put his hands towards his face and sobbed.

'How has it all come to this, Mr Elliott? Me now a cripple and can't even get work to feed the wife and bairns.' The once proud man, who had volunteered to serve King and country, turned to look back at the house and threw down his pick in anger at the earl. 'Bastard!'

On the way back, Tom was quite quiet. He was still contemplating something. But where was the logic? In his world, puzzles could only be solved through logic.

Chapter 5

Tom hoped today would be all it promised to be as he waited with Elliott to be led to the cells.

'Prepare yourself, Tom,' Elliott advised, and handed him a handkerchief. He remembered how Mary had reacted when Sergeant Drake had opened the door. Things hadn't changed much since the two of them had visited Walter Stanford there four years ago.

Drake duly arrived with his bunch of keys and pulled back the door. The stench leaked out, like a stagnant mill pond suddenly disturbed with a stick. Tom didn't bat an eyelid: no grimace; not even a faint snarl of disapproval. He simply handed the handkerchief back to Elliott and said quite nonchalantly, 'Quite an aroma.' With all the horrible stenches he'd experienced whilst amputating limbs on the front line in France, nothing could offend his sense of smell anymore.

'This is a friend of mine, Sergeant Drake. He'll be accompanying me on my rounds today,' Elliott offered by way of introduction.

Tom held out his hand. 'Professor Thomas Sharpe, Director of Surgery, St Thomas', London.' He was becoming very fond of the ring of his new title.

Drake didn't quite know what to say, other than, 'Sergeant Sidney Drake … erm … well, just Sergeant Drake.' He shook Tom's hand firmly.

Elliott just smiled.

First on the list of detainees to see was a habitual drinker, a man in his mid thirties.

Drake opened the cell and they all proceeded to enter.

'Good day, Mr Hawkins,' Elliott started, and got straight to the point. 'I thought we agreed all this drunkenness was going to stop!'

'Ah well, you see, I promised I would try, but then —'

'Save it for the magistrates, Mr Hawkins,' interrupted Elliott. 'I'm sure they'll relish every word of your fable.

Hawkins forced a smile, with a hint of confusion, not really sure he understood the word 'fable'.

'If we can keep you out of prison, I'm going to send you to work at a racehorse stable.'

'But I know nowt about riding 'orses, Mr Elliott!'

'I rather think the work will be a little more menial, Mr Hawkins.'

'What! No, you don't mean shovelling sh—'

Elliott stopped him. 'I'm told only that the duties will be varied.'

Once Hawkins had finished sighing with disappointment, Elliott continued. 'This gentleman here is doing some hospital research and needs to ask you some questions.'

'Oh, I'm not often ill, Mister,' Hawkins explained.

Tom realised it was going to be an arduous interview!

~~~

The next cell held a young boy, wilfully kicking at the flaking paint on the wall. Elliott knew him well from his visits to Rotherham police station. The lad started when the cell door suddenly opened. 'Bloody 'ell, yer frightened me 'alf to death.'

Elliott looked down at the flakes of paint all over the floor. He took a while to pass comment. 'Master William Doherty here is going to be a tradesman, Professor Sharpe.'

The boy looked rather perplexed.

'… Or at least he will be, once I've set him repainting this cell!'

'How old are you, lad?' Tom wanted to know.

'What's it to you?' came the sarcastic response.

Elliott blasted at the boy, 'Why would you like to know, sir?' followed by a glare that left him in no doubt that any further cheek wouldn't be tolerated.

'Fifteen, sir,' the boy mumbled towards Tom.

'And on what charge are you held?'
~~~

'Nickin' … I mean … taking sacks of coal, sir.'

Drake chirped up from the door, 'Might I have a word, gentlemen,' and gestured to the corridor outside the cell.

There he explained the situation.

'I'm afraid it isn't as simple as just stealing coal. The lad was arrested on the spoil heap of Treeton Colliery, the night of the pit disaster. And with him – a large hacksaw!'

Elliott immediately reacted. 'Why wasn't I informed earlier, Sergeant Drake?'

'He was only transferred here yesterday – from Rotherham.'

'I see. To be charged at a higher court, I assume?' Elliott asked, becoming composed again.

Drake nodded in agreement. 'I'll see if I can let you borrow his file.'

Tom's eyes lit up. Now things were getting interesting! 'Can I interview him further?'

'Probably best if Detective Hollins authorises that, sir,' Drake concluded.

~~~

Visits to further cells revealed nothing of great concern to Elliott. There was merely routine questioning of further drunks, two women who had brawled over some
~~~

potato starch, of all things, and a rather anxious man of some obvious social standing, who had been caught in a compromising position with a woman in a back alley.

Tom had gleaned what information he needed for his studies and seemed quite happy with his haul for analysis, although, inside the final cell, he found what perhaps intrigued him most of all.

'Not sure what we're going to do with this one, Mr Elliott,' Drake announced, fiddling with his bunch of keys until, at last, he found the correct one. 'Either a dangerous accomplice or a fruitcake.' Having delivered his opinion, he began to unlock the door.

'By that, do I assume you mean deranged in some way, Sergeant Drake?' asked Tom.

'Whatever term you prefer, Professor. All I know is, it means a lot more work for me.'

'Your compassion for the afflicted touches me,' was Tom's caustic comment, but it received no reaction from Drake, other than a slight shrug of his shoulders.

Elliott's question to Drake deflected further tension. 'I'm not sure I follow you. "Dangerous accomplice?"'

Drake swung open the door. Inside, sitting on the wooden bench, was a woman. She rocked back and forth, cooing like a pigeon. It was Marion.

'The morning following the disaster, she was found half dead on the same spoil heap as the boy,' explained the sergeant.

Elliott paused, looking at Marion with concern. Although she had been cleaned up, she still looked awfully bedraggled.

'Her name?' he enquired.

'No idea. Can't get an ounce of sense out of her. No reason for being there, no possessions, nothing. I'm hoping you'll be able to come up with something.'

'Well, let's see what we can do,' offered the ever optimistic Elliott.

Tom followed Elliott into the cell and watched, somewhat agog, as enquiries started.

'Hello, Miss. My name is Robert Elliott. I'm a police court missionary.'

After several questions which Marion showed no interest in answering, it was all too obvious to Tom, with his in-depth knowledge of psychology, that he needed to take control of matters. He began cooing. Elliott could only stare at him in utter bewilderment.

'Coo, coo … coo, coo,' the voice projected.

Suddenly, Marion turned and responded, 'Coo.'

Soon they were acting out a bird's courtship ritual. Eventually the pair began to laugh. Through the laughter Tom said, 'I'm Bertie, the pride of all the flock.'

'I'm Marion,' she gushed, with nothing but innocence.

Elliott's eyes were wide open in confusion.

'Do you like pigeons, Marion?' asked Tom.

'Yes.'

'Do you have them at home?' A nod confirmed so. 'And where is home?'

Marion stopped to think. It was plain to see she was struggling with her thoughts. Her expression was pitiful as she wrestled with trying to remember. Eventually she gave in and returned to gently rocking. All calm returned.

'Well! That was interesting, if nothing else,' commented Elliott, before asking, 'What do you think?'

Tom didn't answer immediately. Instead, he went over to Marion and knelt down in front of her and spoke softly. 'Would you show me your arms?' She held them out without objection. What he thought might be there, wasn't. 'I need to feel your head. Will you let me do that?' Eventually she nodded. Gently, he felt her skull.

'Buzzzzz!' she called out, making them both jump.

Tom reached out and touched her hand. 'I'll come back and see you soon.'

Marion looked at him. His words triggered her memory. 'Back … back,' she started to say, over and over.

Outside the cell, Tom gave his assessment. 'She could be an opium addict or similar, although normally I would expect needle marks. As there is nothing evident, it would have to be tablets or laudanum. I would need a blood test to know for sure. It might be a case of her suffering amnesia, but I can't see any obvious blows to the head.' The lines on his forehead were now deep furrows as he deliberated. 'Of course, it may just be a case of there being a mental problem. I'm afraid that five minutes with her reveals very little. I need to think about it.'

'What do you suggest in the interim?' asked Elliott.

'Mmmm …,' followed by that look. Then a pause. 'She seems settled enough. Tell Drake to keep her warm and well fed. And she must be absolutely alone. She is not to be housed with any other prisoner.'

'You don't think she is —?'

'I only think that we need more facts, and some logic, Robert,' Tom interrupted.

Chapter 6

Spring 1912

The entrance to the grounds of Haddington Hall couldn't be considered spectacular. In fact, to anyone unfamiliar with the area, it looked like nothing more than two small sandstone pillars which led into open pasture. However, rounding a corner, a quarter of a mile further on, the drive opened into an avenue lined with the most glorious oak trees and leading upwards towards the summit of a hill. Beyond, and down in a dip, was the Hall. From the summit of the hill, it was hard not to be impressed by the Hall's splendour: its stone front with the sweeping semi-circular stairway designed to draw the eye up to the grand façade. And draw her eye it did, as the carriage passed through a charming archway, before skirting round a baroque fountain in the pebbled courtyard.

The carriage came to a halt in front of the great entrance. Louise stepped out. She came to Haddington as a new bride, the wife of Frederick, first born and heir to the Warsop family estate and fortune. Standing and looking at the splendour of the Georgian architecture, she sincerely hoped this would be a loving home, where she would be happy and able to raise a family. But little did she realise just how much her arrival was detested by her new father-in-law. Equally, little did her new father-in-law know just how spirited and determined Louise Corberwell was!

Louise, at twenty-six, was far from an obvious choice of wife for an earl's son; but circumstances meant that her new family's alternatives were limited. She was two months pregnant. Doggedly she had remained resolute that she would not abort her baby, as she understood her father-in-law had demanded; and, likewise, she would not conveniently disappear with payment for her silence. If marriage was not an option, then scandal would have to be the order of the day. What made the whole affair even more unbearable was the fact she did love her husband very much: or at least she had before they came to Haddington.

Louise was pretty, and never failed to turn a head or two when she entered a room. She had long red hair, and whilst her figure was slightly plump, she carried herself with grace and an air of sophistication. Her upbringing, until the age of fourteen, had been in Scotland, where her parents owned a very successful livestock business. The younger of two children, she had been sent to boarding school in London and thereafter to finishing school in Switzerland. In every sense but financial, Louise, at the age of twenty, was very much independent, and had no intention of returning to her roots. The prospect of adventure in Europe was always infinitely more appealing than life back home, even though she would have been a 'lady of leisure' there. As long as her father would support her, she would continue her studies, live life to the full, and drink in the wisdom of the scholars she found herself surrounded by. Soon she was writing travel journals and sending them to a company in England for publication. It was a time that was wonderful and precious to her.

Louise had not always known happiness though. Her mother had been a severe disciplinarian, and had it not been for her husband's desire to educate his daughter, she would doubtless have steered Louise toward a life of nothing but obedience. Mrs Corberwell had an all-consuming dedication to the Catholic Church. Yet her actions were always a contradiction of her faith. She was harsh in the extreme and never shy of taking a hand to her children: a bony hand, with a large diamond ring turned inward towards the palm, was the cause of many wounds for Louise and her brother, invariably around their heads. What the mother also possessed was an unstinting confidence in the priesthood and particularly in one priest, Father Mackintosh, who could do no wrong. She never hesitated to doubt her children's honesty, but regarded all that Father Mackintosh said as the complete truth.

The incident that eventually broke any bond that remained between Louise and her mother occurred just before the young girl left for boarding school. At fourteen, she was beginning to blossom into womanhood, and this soon attracted the attention of Father Mackintosh at Sunday school. His strictness towards her in class was suddenly replaced by an ever-increasing leniency. Now, he would often pat her on the head, and let his hand drift down over her hair and onto her shoulders. He would brush past her when strutting about the small room, and give her a meaningful smile. Always he seemed to be looking at her. As a young, innocent girl, she didn't see the true significance of his actions; but she knew enough to feel uncomfortable.

Confiding her concerns to her mother, she asked to be excused lessons in future. This brought a swift response.

'You malicious little creature,' hissed the mother, gripping Louise's face. 'How dare you throw suspicion on such a holy man? I will not hear your evil thoughts. No, you shall not be excused lessons. In fact, this Sunday I will lock you in the room alone with Father Mackintosh, just to prove the strength of my trust.'

The fanatical mother carried out her threat a week later.

At first, the priest kept his distance, and wandered

the room preaching at her relentlessly. '… and he said unto her, watch out for false prophets. They come to you in sheep's clothing, but inwardly they are ferocious wolves.' He turned and leered at her, then smiled with a cloying sweetness. 'You do understand my meaning, dear girl?'

Louise nodded, her eyes full of fear.

'Fear not, Louise,' he said softly, and walked towards her.

She seized the burning kerosene lamp. 'One step more,' she cried, 'and I will throw the lamp in your face.'

The coward stopped in his tracks and began muttering, expressing his desire in words that she couldn't fully understand. She kept a rigid hold of the lamp.

'I warn you, Father, I will dowse you with it, should you take a step nearer to me.'

Eventually, the eternity of that hour was over and the door opened. Louise, so relieved that the fiend would now leave, nearly fainted. She never forgave her mother for the episode, and stood quite emotionless at her funeral some seven years later.

Her father continued to support her financially until his death, when the Corberwell estate passed to her brother. Unfortunately, the brother did not share his father's view on the enlightenment of women through education, and stopped the monthly allowance that had been paid to Louise. With only the meagre earnings from her writing to sustain her, she was eventually forced to return to Scotland. A bitter legal battle with her brother followed, in which she staked a claim to a share of the family fortune: a battle she eventually won, but at the cost of never speaking to her brother again.

Louise was never one to live life without splendour. With her inheritance, she purchased a fine house in Salisbury and played the desirable and well-to-do lady. There were frequent visits to the opera, lectures and concerts. Most of all, she relished an invitation to a ball, where many a society wife would stare at her with unconcealed spite, as she took their husband by the arm and engaged him in talk about the excitement of life and politics in Europe. It was at a ball given by the Clements to celebrate the entrance of their daughter into society that Louise caught sight of him. He was young, tall, handsome, and in his military garb, looked most appealing. It wasn't long before she had engineered it so that the pair were in conversation.

'Lord Frederick Warsop, son of the Earl of Ranskill, Miss Coberwell,' Major Romsey introduced them.

Frederick was on a twelve-month posting with his regiment in Salisbury, and through his family's name and standing was quite often invited to society functions. Unlike his father, he was totally at ease in such gatherings.

He was pleasant, openly friendly and confident. In addition, he was an accomplished conversationalist, a fact Louise couldn't help but notice as she debated the European situation with him. For someone eight years her junior, he seemed knowledgeable beyond his years.

Only when Major Romsey asked to take her hand and lead her to the dance floor did she realise they had been standing talking for a good half an hour. The old major was anything but a dancer, but she smiled politely when, for the umpteenth time, he stepped on her toes. All the while, as she danced, she kept glancing over to Frederick. Although he was now engaged in conversation elsewhere, he couldn't help but take the occasional look over to Louise. Her flaming red hair, those sparkling green eyes – he was smitten. She too was curious and needed to know more.

'You will forgive me, Major Romsey, but I really must sit down. There is only so much a woman can take of your fine waltzing,' she explained demurely.

'Of course, my dear.' He bowed graciously and led her to a chair on the edge of the dancing. The old dog knew the truth.

Louise was soon on her feet again, and there was only one direction in which she wanted to head.

Frederick picked a glass of champagne off the tray of a passing waiter and handed it over to her. 'Hello again!'

For the next six months, their time together was blissful: the opera, the galas, the endless concerts, the strolls by the lake, the visits to art galleries, it was all perfect. Now she was no longer just curious and needing to know more – she wanted more. On the eve of his departure for a month of regimental manoeuvres, she finally discovered the act of love. Gently he held her chin in his hand and kissed her. Not even the scholars with whom she had flirted all those years before could make her heart skip quite as it did at this moment. Finally, they lay on the bed and pushed together as one.

<p style="text-align:center">~~~</p>

The reception of the happy couple at Haddington surprised Louise. Even allowing for the delicate social situation her condition put them in, she had expected that some family members would be there to greet them. Instead, on the steps of the house, there stood only the butler, Dowling, and a footman. Upstairs, watching through a window, was her new father-in-law, accompanied by Dr Robertson.

'The prodigal son returns, dear Anthony, and with him the strutting strumpet!' the earl sarcastically remarked.

'Indeed,' replied the equally sour and unimpressed

doctor.

'Well, I suppose we ought to make an appearance,' Ranskill suggested.

As Frederick alighted from the carriage, a horse and rider trotted through the archway and pulled up by the entrance. A woman, finely dressed in riding attire, dismounted from her beast and walked over.

'Aunt Matilda!' Frederick cried, and proceeded to give her four kisses, two on each cheek. Four kisses was the family tradition and meant the recipient was in favour. This was a gesture that the Earl of Ranskill had adopted in his military days, following his observation of the way royalty greeted each other.

'Frederick! My favourite nephew. How are you? I saw the carriage from the meadow and knew it would be you.'

Frederick then held out his hand to Louise and helped her down from the carriage. 'This is Louise, Aunt Matilda.'

The aunt's face suddenly looked as though she'd sucked on a lemon. 'Louise,' she managed.

There were no kisses, no warmth. Just a brief nod of her head, which Louise surmised was an attempt at a welcome.

In the ensuing silence, Louise looked over to her husband, thinking he would say something further but he didn't. Instead, he just stood looking as though there was nothing amiss. 'And this must be?' she nodded towards the man on the steps, trying to ignore the coldness of her welcome from the aunt.

'Dowling, ma'am. I'm the butler,' came the friendly reply. 'And this is Bennett, our footman.'

'Just the one!' exclaimed Louise.

'No, there are several more.' He coughed with some embarrassment, '… Just not today, ma'am. They have the day off.'

'I see. Well, better their welfare than ours, eh, Dowling.' Her comment was clearly directed to the aunt.

Finally, her new father-in-law made his entrance. Dr Robertson held back, half in, half out of the doorway.

After the aunt's coldness, Louise could be forgiven for expecting nothing but an icy welcome from the man, but he did have the decency to extend a much warmer greeting than his sister.

'Well, welcome to Haddington, daughter-in-law. I hope you'll be very happy here.' Unfortunately, the insincerity of his words couldn't really be disguised. Only one kiss on the cheek followed. As yet, she didn't realise the significance. However, Frederick was more than aware. He attempted the traditional gesture with his father, only for the father to draw away. No kisses at all meant displeasure of the highest order.

Frederick looked to be in absolute fear of his father – something Louise couldn't help but notice. Where had the dependable and fearless man she loved and married suddenly gone?

Whilst the earl's greeting might have given Louise some hope she could become part of the family, his sarcasm soon showed her otherwise.

Out of the second carriage jumped her beloved King Charles spaniel, which began sniffing at each person in turn.

'What … is that?' bellowed Ranskill.

'It's my dog, Millie, Lord Ranskill,' she replied and watched, somewhat embarrassed, as the dog squatted down to relieve herself. Ranskill turned to his son and remarked, 'I see you've inherited a bitch, Frederick!'

If ever a woman needed to don a robe of steel, this was the time.

'A very clever and loyal bitch, I might say,' Louise commented crisply.

Their eyes met. The fierce battle of wills had commenced.

~~~

The first few weeks of their married life at Haddington seemed to pass off without great incident. All was as
~~~

cordial as could be expected in the dining room, and hostilities seemed to abate whenever the family gathered together. But Louise had already begun to despise the place. The stark interior of the hall betrayed its beautiful exterior. It was always cold and dark, and the decor was beyond anything Louise could find kind words for. Even her bedroom, despite the many furnishings she'd brought with her, appeared lifeless and drab.

Still, at least she had Frederick, who seemed to have regained his charming attentiveness: at least when they were alone. She didn't quiz him on his relationship with his father and family, not wanting to fight another battle.

She also had Crecia, her Italian maid. Dear Crecia! What would she do without her? The little ball of Latin fire was even less impressed with Haddington than Louise, and was never shy of telling her mistress so. 'This place it not a-right, Miss Louise,' she'd say in her broken English. Their relationship was more one of friendship than an employer-employee one. If all else failed, she had Crecia to make her laugh. 'The cook know nothing. I no like her. But the penguin, he, I like,' was Crecia referring, of course, to Dowling.

The days for Louise were dreary and long-drawn-out. Frederick had returned to Salisbury to finish his tour of duty and hence there was nothing really to do. The bleak weather and her ever-increasing bump made it difficult to get out much, and this added to her misery. Oh how she longed for the opera or the theatre.

The worst days were those when she had to suffer Aunt Matilda and her society friends. 'Four hours! Four hours, I had to put up with their whining and drivelling,' she told Crecia, before collapsing exhausted on the bed. 'Could they not at least play bridge … in silence?'

At one of these social gatherings, Louise experienced the sarcasm of Matilda – a sarcasm every bit as cutting as that of her brother. But, she didn't go down without a fight.

'Shameful, I quite agree. What do you think Louise? … Louise!' asked Matilda.

Louise had long since switched off and was staring aimlessly out of the window. Eventually she heard her name. 'I'm sorry?'

'The miners striking again,' Matilda sighed.

'What about them?'

'Louise! You haven't been listening to a word … We were saying how shameful the strike is and what damage it does to the earl's profits.'

'I'm led to believe the men strike because of the lack of safety in the pit. They are merely expressing their worries by striking. Maybe if Lord Ranskill were to listen more to their concerns, it could be avoided.'

The ladies gasped. Matilda looked with hatred at Louise.

'Concerns you share no doubt, dear Louise?

'Perhaps you would prefer for us to return to the palmy days of the Inquisition; to have a daily auto-da-fe until all the heretics are burned!'

The gasps became even louder, before Lady Melrose politely suggested, 'Perhaps we could take a stroll to the library, Lady Usher?'

With the ladies gone, Aunt Matilda allowed her bile to overflow.

'Really, Louise! What must they think? That you're a socialist? You are most vulgar at times.'

'You asked for my opinion and I gave it. I'm sorry if it doesn't meet with your or your guests' expectations. But the situation is quite clear to me.'

Matilda glared at her with rage. 'It is unfortunate that you came into our family, because you will never be one of us!'

Louise watched Matilda stride off in disgust. What a pity, she thought, that she didn't slip and fall on that horsy rump of hers. Then she leant back in her chair and caressed her bump. 'Dear child, just what sort of life am I about to subject you to?'

The following day, all hell broke loose. Ranskill came storming into the library, with only one riding boot on. 'Louise!' he demanded.

'What is it?'

'Your … your …' He was so enraged he struggled to find the appropriate word, 'Your ruddy animal,' he eventually blurted out. 'It's done its business in the garden and I've just trodden in it!'

'Well, where else would you expect her to do it?' Louise replied, quite logically.

'Not in my garden. Take her to the meadow.'

'The meadow is a mile away. But perhaps I could get Dowling to follow her with his shovel – just in case.'

'I didn't ask for sarcasm, young lady.'

'Then don't be ridiculous, sir. The poor thing has to do it somewhere, and better outside than in.'

'Oh, ridiculous, am I?' mocked Ranskill. 'I wondered how long it would take before your respect wore off.'

'I merely speak as I see fit, sir.'

'Evidently,' the earl huffed. 'And I would prefer you address me correctly.'

'I'm supposed to be family. I will not go around calling you Lord in private.'

'I insist.'

Louise had had enough. 'Then I insist on you calling me Louise, Henrietta, Emma, Elizabeth, Heather!'

Ranskill gave another guffaw before looking away. He glanced around the room. Was there something different? His eyes finally settled on the strange, brightly coloured picture above the mantelpiece. 'What the …?

Where is my grandfather's portrait?'

'I thought the place was in need of cheering up, needed some colour. So I've had him moved to the dining room.'

He bowed his head and shook it in disbelief. 'You've done what! That picture has been there for as long as I've been alive. It serves to remind me of my history.'

Louise couldn't resist, although she knew how much displeasure would be heaped on her and Frederick. 'As I said, sir, I thought the place needed cheering up.'

She wasn't wrong. Ranskill hissed maliciously, 'I tolerate you, Madam, because you carry my grandchild. But trust me, I will see you out of this family as quickly as you came in.' Then, he stormed off, bellowing, 'Dowling! Dowling!'

Louise once more held onto her bump and talked to her unborn child, 'That was the roar of Grandpapa, the mighty lion. But alas, now with a face as red as a baboon's backside.'

Chapter 7

'And you will remember to move the …,' Ann started to say, but stopped on seeing that her husband wasn't paying the slightest bit of attention. She looked over to Mary and cast her eyes upwards, 'Men!'

It was worth a try, she thought. 'So, it's agreed, dear. When I get back you'll take me to buy that new dress?'

'Yes,' replied Elliott, oblivious to anything other than where he'd put down his pipe tobacco.

'Perhaps we could stretch to those shoes as well?' she attempted.

'Yes, dear.'

Ann looked again towards Mary. 'Unbelievable. Is Tom the same?'

Mary gave a smile. 'Well, not quite as bad.'

Elliott turned over the newspaper on the bureau. 'Ah, there it is. Right. Sorry, dear, what were you saying?'

Both women laughed.

'It doesn't matter, Robert. Just have a chat with your wallet. Prepare it for an outing next Saturday.'

'What?'

'Yes. And I'll remind you that I now have a witness!'

Elliott could only give a frown of confusion.

Meantime, Ann was thankful that she had Lily, the housemaid, on hand to see that her husband and Tom survived the week, whilst she, Mary and the children were away.

Tom entered the room holding baby Lucinda but promptly handed her over to her mother. Mary then sniffed and gave Tom one of her 'not very impressed' glares. 'Why, thank you, Tom.'

Tom just looked at her, with every bit of innocence he could find, followed by a skilful diversion. 'So, are you all ready for the off?'

'Well, we were. But it appears Lucinda has done something and now needs changing.'

'Oh dear!' he said, watching Mary turn and take the baby upstairs.

They were all assembled waiting for Mary's return when the taxi arrived. Eventually she appeared as the horn sounded for the third time. She looked rather embarrassed and indicated with a nod to Tom that she wanted a quiet word.

'The bucket's gone and I can't find Lily. You'll have to deal with it!' she said as low as possible.

'Deal with what?' Tom asked.

Mary looked down to the bundle wedged under her arm. 'I can't just leave it in the bedroom.'

His eyes opened wide in alarm. 'Mary, I can't —'

Mary interrupted, and through clenched teeth, said sternly, 'Tom. Just find Lily and deal with it, please!' He knew when his wife meant business, and gingerly he took the bundle and held it behind his back.

With the boys excitedly pulling the suitcases to the waiting cab, the adults made their final farewells. It had been a while since the partners in either couple had been separated. Tom's anxiety showed.

'Have a lovely time now and take care, Mary,' he said, giving her a peck on the cheek, before kissing the baby. 'And you, young lady. You look after mother, do you hear.' But Lucinda had fallen fast asleep. He kissed them both one last time. 'And remember what I said, about the — '

'Tom, I'm going to Scarborough for a week, not back to Mesopotamia,' Mary sighed.

Just then Cecil bounded back into the hallway, hardly able to contain his excitement. 'It's a Wolseley 16/20 and it's got 20.3HP, the driver says!'

In his excitement, Cecil had entirely forgotten to say goodbye to his father, until prompted by his mother. He quickly gave him a hug and rattled, 'Bye, father.' He then went to Tom and attempted to do the same, only to draw back and ask, 'Phew, what's that smell?'

Mary came to the rescue. 'Well, we'd better see how well a Wolseley 16/20 compares with an Austin 25,' she remarked, which took Cecil totally by surprise.

Mary knowing about engines: now that impressed him. Of course Mary didn't know more than the odd model name, but she would go along with things and throw in a few more engine terms as required.

Cecil began to drag Mary down the path. 'How do you know about engines, Mary?'

'Well …'

The adults laughed, for Mary had started a conversation she might well regret.

Elliott kissed Ann. 'Ring me. Let me know you've arrived safely.'

Ann then walked over to Tom and kissed him on the cheek. 'Bye, Tom,' she said, followed by a whisper in his ear. 'Leave it by the outbuilding and tell Lily. She'll sort it out for you.'

Tom gave her a desperate look of appreciation.

~~~

That afternoon, Elliott and Tom settled down in the parlour. It was finally peaceful, yet both men couldn't help but feel the strangeness of the house without their loved ones there. Elliott thumbed through the file on William Doherty, the lad held on suspicion of involvement in the mining cage disaster. As always, he made notes, knowing he could be asked to give an opinion in court. Tom tried
~~~

to read some medical notes he had brought with him from London, but kept reading the same page over and over. He was pre-occupied with his wife and daughter's safety. He looked at his pocket watch and strained to listen. Was that the telephone ringing? The ball of his foot began to pump furiously, shaking his leg.

Elliott looked up with some frustration. 'Have you got St Vitus dance?'

'I'm sorry, Robert. It's just I'll not settle until I know they've arrived safely.'

'They'll be fine. Stop worrying.'

However, it was another hour before the phone did finally ring and Tom could stop his fretting. After a ten-minute chat with Mary, he re-entered the room a different man. Elliott simply gave him that omniscient look of his.

Elliott took to reading his file again. It seemed inconceivable to him that the young lad, Doherty, could be considered guilty of involvement in murder. There was no doubt the lad was a rogue, but in all his encounters with him over the years, there had never been anything to suggest to Elliott that the boy had sinister motives. Still, the evidence seemed damning enough. He read on, diligently going through Doherty's statement, which had been captured verbatim.

'*... Then, I decided to head back home. I can't remember the time – reckon it would be after midnight* *though. Coming over the top spoil I tried to keep my footing, but I suddenly stumbled and fell. When I looked down, I saw what had caused me to fall. My foot had caught in summut heavy. I picked it up and found it was a hacksaw, the kind I'd seen used by shaftsman. I thought I'd take it … not to keep, but to hand it in at the pit office when I passed next. It puzzled me as to how it got there. Reckon it must have accidently dropped into a tub and came out when it got emptied on the spoils. I wandered a bit and then, suddenly, there they were in front of me – the police.'*

Elliott flicked through the rest of the file, stopping at some photographs. The top one was chilling, showing the cage, or what was left of it, at the bottom of the shaft. He took a deep breath, recalling his dream, and shuddered before moving on to the next photo. This was a close-up of the cut on the sabotaged wire rope and of the hacksaw. Next came photos of the bodies. He quickly passed over them and let out a sigh.

'Everything all right?' Tom asked.

Elliott took a moment to answer. He snapped the file shut and offered it to Tom. 'Details about Doherty and the pit cage disaster. Not exactly pleasant viewing.' He lumbered out of his chair and stretched his legs. 'I'll find Lily and get her to make us a pot of tea.'

Tom opened the file and began reading. Eventually, he too came to the photos; but they were nothing to the horrors he'd witnessed in the makeshift field hospitals in France. He studied the close-up of the wire rope and hacksaw. Then something occurred to him.

Elliott came back into the parlour. 'I've no idea where Lily is,' he announced. 'So you'll just have to sample the delights of my brew,' he added and started to pour. 'Sugar?'

Tom looked over, fearing the obligatory five spoonfuls. 'Erm, it's all right, Robert. I'll do it!'

Having rescued himself from tea tasting like syrup, Tom offered a question. 'Can you recall if the lad was right or left-handed?'

Elliott considered the question for a moment but couldn't give an accurate answer. 'No, I can't say that I noticed. Why?'

'It's just … well, I believe whoever cut the wire was left-handed.'

'Interesting observation. What makes you think that?'

Tom passed Elliott the photo of the wire rope and hacksaw. 'Look at the handle.'

'Looks normal to me.'

'Ah, but is it?'

Elliott looked confused but was equally intrigued. Tom began to enlighten him. 'The thumb housing on the left has been scooped out to make it a forefinger guide.

You'd only do that if you were left-handed.'

'Very good!' Elliott acknowledged.

'Furthermore, I doubt you'll find Doherty is left handed.' Tom began to stroll about the room like an excited schoolboy who'd solved the ultimate puzzle in a chemistry lesson ahead of anybody else. 'You see … in the cell, the lad kicked the paint off the wall with his right foot. I remember that distinctly. And most people who kick with their right leg favour their right hand.'

Whilst the observation was a good one, and Elliott was happy to give credit where it was due, by the same token he liked nothing more than to play devil's advocate. However, he decided not to punch too many holes in his friend's theory and simply suggested, 'But surely if the hacksaw handle was originally intended for a right hander, the forefinger guide would still be there on the right. So why wouldn't a right handed person still use it?'

Until now, Tom had delighted in playing the brilliant detective on the verge of a major breakthrough. He gave Elliott a resigned look, accepting there were two sides to an argument. 'Just an observation.'

'And a very good one, Tom. There's no mistaking that.'

Just then Lily entered the room, looking quite poorly. 'Were you shouting me, Mr Elliott?' she asked in a husky voice, and stood pathetically before them, her face as white as the apron she was wearing. Above anything else, she hoped that her master didn't require anything that needed too much physical effort.

'My dear girl, you look positively ill. Come here, let me take a look at you,' Tom said, and felt in the inner pocket of his jacket. He took out his tongue depressor and asked Lily for the customary 'Aaah'. Next, he felt the glands in her neck.

'Looks like a nasty case of tonsillitis, girl. You need to gargle with some salt water and then go straight to bed. Mr Elliott will bring you a hot drink with honey.'

Elliott nearly dropped his tea in shock. While he wasn't a man without compassion, he couldn't quite agree with Tom's appraisal of his role in Lily's recovery.

'Now I understand your parents don't live too far away,' Tom continued.

'Yes, only a few miles, sir,' Lily croaked.

'Well, if you're no better tomorrow, you should return home and take to your bed for a few days.'

Elliott was now agog.

'Don't worry about your pay. I'm sure Mr Elliott will see things right,' Tom concluded.

Finally, the master found his words, 'Oh, I'm sure Lily feels comfort in your every word, Professor Sharpe.'

Dinner that evening was a sight to behold. Lily's comment that the rabbit stew was all prepared, hadn't meant quite what Elliott and Tom had assumed. The two men gawped at the skinned, uncooked carcass underneath the muslin before, eventually, Elliott gingerly gave it a prod. He then proceeded to lift the lid on the pan. Raw vegetables bobbed up and down in the water as he pushed them back and forth. He looked over at Tom. 'This is your fault!'

'Do you fancy getting some fish and chips? I'll pay,' was the best Tom could say as a peace offering.

~~~

The fish and chip shop was a good half a mile's walk, but with the weather being nice, a leisurely stroll provided a pleasant end to the evening. It also gave both men the opportunity to discuss what to do next with Marion. From Elliott's point of view, he was convinced she had nothing to do with the colliery disaster and she was nothing more than a sad case of a mentally disturbed woman. Quite why she was found on the spoil heap he couldn't fathom, but he was sure it was all coincidence. Why he should think this way was more down to instinct than anything else. What did bother him a little, however, was where she had come from. Through his work, he was aware of most of the characters in the area who were in need of help, and it seemed somewhat strange that she hadn't
~~~

come to his notice before now. Perhaps it was simply that she was from outside the area and, out of desperation, a struggling family had left her to fend for herself, in the hope that she would be picked up by the authorities and provided for.

This was the idea that Elliott ultimately decided was the most likely, being something he'd seen on occasions in the past, particularly when mental troubles set in with the elderly. He explained to Tom that in these hardened times, it was felt that the asylum would offer three meals a day and provide a greater degree of knowledge on how to deal with mental illness.

In the case of Marion though, she wasn't elderly, and Elliott was eager to learn Tom's opinion on how best to treat her.

'I would first like to go and visit her again and carry out a few tests. Would that be possible?' Tom enquired. 'If nothing else, it would tell us if she's using drugs.'

'I'm sure it can be arranged. We'll go down to the station again tomorrow,' Elliott declared. As the pair rounded the corner, to their horror, the sign on the shop window stated, 'No fish today – open again tomorrow'.

It was quite against Elliott's principles to frequent a public house, but if they were to eat tonight, then he had to relent.

Early the following morning both men were at the

station, waiting patiently for Sergeant Drake to conclude the release of the drunks, vagrants and others that had been detained for the night.

'Morning, Mr Elliott,' Drake finally found the chance to say. He then acknowledged Tom with a nod, 'Professor.'

'The professor would like to carry out a few tests on the woman found on the colliery spoils, Sergeant. We'll wait here until it's convenient,' Elliott said.

'Well, you'll have a long wait, sir,' Drake explained to Tom.

Elliott drew himself up to his full height, thinking the sergeant was being deliberately awkward. 'And why would that be, Sergeant?' he abruptly asked.

Drake simply smiled and stated calmly, 'Because she's not 'ere, that's why.'

Elliott looked at him with a bemused expression. 'I beg your pardon!'

'Not 'ere. She was released yesterday. Detective Hollins got a visit from a woman reporting to be family and after that, he was satisfied that there was no reason to detain her further.'

Tom looked over to Elliott. 'Erm, well, I guess that saves us finding a suitable solution for her.'

Walking back home that day, Tom stopped at a newspaper stand displaying the front page. On it were the photos of the ten casualties of the pit disaster. He was very surprised to see Dr Robertson's face amongst them. 'Good lord!' he exclaimed.

'What?' asked Elliott.

'This man, Dr Robertson,' explained Tom, pointing at the photo. 'I used to work with him.' He read the brief obituary before concluding, 'So! He ended up being a business partner to Lord Ranskill, did he? Quite a diversion.'

Tom began to explain to Elliott some of his and Robertson's turbulent past, but he stopped short, as he remembered the book that was out of sequence in the library when they'd visited Haddington Hall. The furrows appeared on his forehead once more, and he thought about the strangeness of the earl's second son, Master David. A chill went down his spine.

'What on earth is it, Tom?' Elliott asked.

'Do you think we could perhaps visit Haddington Hall again? There are a couple of things I'd like to check on. I'm probably wrong but, once I've got more information, I'll explain everything.'

Elliott hated suspense but agreed he would be patient.

Chapter 8

One o'clock came and went, then 1.30 am and eventually 2.00 am loomed. Elliott looked once more at the clock on the bedside table and watched the second finger slowly tick round the face for the final minute. He felt a strange kind of anxiety. Never before had sixty seconds taken so long. Then, as if dabbing tincture onto an aching tooth, he felt calm again as the new hour began. For such a small timepiece the ticks were very loud and cut through the silence of the room. The precision of the sound soon began to irritate him again. He turned his restless body over for what seemed the hundredth time, the rustle of the cotton sheet making only a brief interruption in the monotonous noise.

How odd it was for Ann not to be beside him. He felt uneasy. Moving to her side of the bed made everything feel even stranger. He moved back again to regain his sense of familiarity. With his eyes heavy and his head beginning to pound, he felt a wooziness like the first draw of nicotine made him feel when he lit his pipe in the morning. Perspiration began to bead on his forehead before, eventually, his eyes rolled shut.

It was soon 2.15 am, and Elliott had finally drifted

into a deep sleep – and into a nightmare that couldn't have felt more real. Canon Brockwell was again sitting in the chair in Elliott's study. He looked quite normal, until he turned his head. Then, the bullet wound, the cause of his death, was clearly evident. In his lap, he had the Doherty file and was looking at the photos. Studying the mangled cage remains, he sighed with a perverse sense of satisfaction. Elliott simply stood watching him.

'Such a mess!' Brockwell said, and viewed the photo from another angle. 'Do you think they died before reaching the bottom?' He paused and thought for a moment before answering his own question. 'I guess out of sheer terror, yes, some did. I really must find out.' He lifted his eyes and looked at Elliott. 'How are we, Robert?'

This time, Elliott spoke. 'What exactly is it you want?'

'Oh, it's so remiss of me not to have said earlier,' Brockwell replied with a sickening smugness in his voice. 'It's quite simple. I've come to seek revenge.' Brockwell then began a malevolent rant, his eyes showing all the hatred and frustration he felt.

'All this time, I've waited. Stuck in an infernal hell. I was God's own. He owed me peace, not this. Why should I suffer? He created me, nurtured me. It was he who gave me my frailty. And you, Robert. You deserted me. The one man who could have helped. Instead, you cornered me like a rat and gave me no option but to take my life.'

He touched his wound and a nervous shudder ran over the whole of his upper body.

'Don't you dare blame me. What you did was evil, and like all cowards you refused to face your punishment,' Elliott fired back.

'Punishment! This is my punishment, damn you. And for what? Not being able to resist temptation.'

'Perversion,' Elliott corrected him.

The two men glared at each other in silence. Elliott couldn't help but recall the happier times they had shared. Times of friendship, before any trace of Brockwell's vice was evident. Then, they had shared evenings of thought-provoking conversation as couples with their wives; shared days out with their families. It was all still a mystery to Elliott how his one-time friend had managed to hide his true way of life so well.

Brockwell suddenly spoke more calmly. 'Enough of our squabbles. Tonight, I'm going to show you just how imperfect we all are.' The next moment the two men were standing in the colliery engine room. It was the night of the disaster. They could see a man cutting a V in the wire rope with a large hacksaw. He had his back to them but Elliott recognised the man's figure. Turning towards Brockwell he gasped, 'That's —'

'Yes, it's Tom.'

As Tom turned around, Elliott saw his face was smug

and vengeful. The man looked pleased with his chilling work.

'No! No! It can't be so,' Elliott pleaded.

'Why? Because he's your friend? Well, so was I, Robert. So was I,' Brockwell spat out, before returning to his former calm. 'Nobody wanted to see Robertson killed more than Tom.'

Elliott stood looking bemused as suddenly he found himself in a public house observing a conversation between the two doctors. He recognised the place as being in Sheffield. The two men were sitting in a corner of the snug, the room being empty apart from them. Tom was angry and pointing a finger towards Dr Robertson. 'If this gets out, it will ruin me,' he said forcefully. In fact, with such venom as Elliott would never have believed Tom capable of.

'But there's no reason for things to get out, Tom. I can keep a secret,' Dr Robertson explained. 'That is, of course, if you'll have a word with the hospital board. Convince them that what I did was merely in the interest of advancing science.'

'Your work is sordid,' Tom replied.

'So is your use of prostitutes!'

Elliott's eyes opened wide in horror at the revelation and he watched as Tom lunged at Dr Robertson and held him by the throat.

In his nightmare, Elliott suddenly felt Brockwell's hands around his own neck. He struggled to get free, hearing only Tom and Brockwell's voices shouting in unison, 'I'll kill you! Do you hear? Kill you!'

Elliott gagged and spluttered and finally awoke holding his neck. As he opened his eyes, Tom was touching his shoulder.

'Easy now, Robert. Calm down. You're just having another nightmare.'

The following morning, Tom was first up again, although the time was gone 8.30 am. The whole thing completely confused Bessie, when she awoke to find nobody there. Normally, by 7.00 am Elliott had taken her for her walk and she'd be back in her basket, waiting patiently for the boys to come downstairs. This invariably meant the odd titbit came her way; though always, of course, out of sight of their father. However, this morning there was a bonus. Tom was sitting by the kitchen range feeding her endless bits of his toast.

Elliott finally appeared, looking as bleary-eyed as Tom recalled seeing him days earlier. The constant disturbance to his sleep made him quite grouchy. 'I would prefer you didn't feed her bits,' he growled.

Tom could feel a strained atmosphere was brewing, and had the uncomfortable feeling that he was being watched and analysed whenever he turned away from

Elliott. Eventually he had to say something. 'Robert, if I've upset you in any way, then please tell me. I'm sorry about feeding Bessie but I —'

Elliott cut across him. 'No, Tom. It's nothing to do with Bessie … Though we don't feed her scraps,' he added, for absolute clarity. Tom took his rebuke admirably. Elliott then wandered over to the mirror and put out his tongue. He grimaced at the yellow coating he saw on it. 'I'm sorry but it's these blasted nightmares. I feel like death warmed up this morning.'

'Umm, yes. I've been thinking about that,' Tom said, and watched Elliott yet again check the hair on his forehead.

Tom watched with interest as Elliott lifted up his fringe and pressed it back, asking, quite out of the blue, 'Do you think I'm receding?'

'Well … er, perhaps a little,' Tom agreed.

'Worrying, isn't it? Getting old!' Elliott philosophically remarked.

Tom thought the question rather pessimistic and attempted a little humour. 'Yes, I suppose it is. No matter, Robert. At least you still have all your own teeth. Or I assume you have.'

Elliott didn't quite see the funny side. 'Of course!' he grunted.

'So, these nightmares. Tell me about the one last

night,' Tom asked, changing the subject back to what he wanted to know.

'Oh, they're just very strange things and situations. Nothing in particular.'

'It didn't look like nothing when I woke you.'

'I can't honestly remember much.'

Tom could see that Elliott either didn't want to talk about it or was blatantly lying to save the embarrassment of explaining. He knew from his studies that some middle aged men would start to display signs of anguish about their lives and often appeared to dream about the most bizarre, and sometimes sexual, experiences: things they would otherwise never think of.

Of course, Elliott didn't want to tell his friend the truth, that, in his dream, it was Tom who was doing the most horrible things.

Later, Elliott asked, 'Everything is all right between you and Mary, isn't it, Tom?'

Again Tom was rather surprised as to why Elliott should ask him such a question out of the blue, but gave his answer nonetheless. 'Of course. Shouldn't it be?'

'Even in the … well, you know. In the …' Elliott enquired with excruciating unease.

'If you're referring to what I think you are, Robert: as much as a new baby allows.' He couldn't for the life of him understand why his friend should ask him such a question, but again, could only assume Elliott was passing through some kind of psychological crisis in his life. He did though, think it would be fun to turn the tables. 'How about you and Ann?' followed by a crafty look.

Elliott coughed unconvincingly. 'Goodness, is that the time? We ought to be getting a move on.'

Chapter 9

Autumn, 1912

It had been a good while since the cry of a baby had rung out through Haddington Hall, and longer still since the joy of such an event had been truly celebrated. Louise was determined that the birth of her child would bring changes to the household. The earl was resolute that the only change would be his daughter-in-law leaving his home – and alone!

Poor Louise suffered dreadfully in her last month of pregnancy, her agonising back pain being equalled only by the pain of birth itself: a feat which left her immobile for several days. Her trials brought her as much sympathy from her father-in-law as would be given to a sick miner in his collieries. Aunt Matilda's empathy was little better. As for husband Frederick, who had returned from his military duties a few days earlier, he had no real idea about comforting his wife and was more interested in telling her about the intolerable conditions of the officers' mess. The only member of the family to show her any real understanding was her brother-in-law, David. And he in turn was the only one of her new relations whom

Louise felt any sympathy with.

David, two years younger than his brother, was sensitive, caring and, unlike Frederick, did not seem to live in fear of his father. At least that was how it was in the days before tragedy befell him.

Louise also had to endure Dr Robertson, albeit never in a medical capacity. That much she insisted on, for she detested the man, probably even more than she detested her father-in-law. She felt the pain of giving birth would be a mere picnic compared with her dealings with this business partner of the earl. He was the most unpleasant, vindictive man she had ever encountered. She couldn't find anything positive to feel or say about him. His stooped body and ingratiating look only added to her disdain. Undoubtedly, Dr Robertson was always ready to do his master's bidding and the more unpleasant or downright cruel the task, the more he relished it.

As Louise's time drew near, the family and Dr Robertson congregated in a room beyond her suite. A begrudging Lord Ranskill sat in his chair, constantly taking out his pocket watch and studying it, as if labour should have a time limit. Whenever Louise's screams were heard, he let out an exasperated sigh. Aunt Matilda sat playing with the hem of her sleeve, clearly wishing she were out riding one of her horses, but occasionally she made the effort to try and give Frederick a comforting look, as he paced nervously from one end of the room to the other. Young David simply sat in silence and hoped that, for Louise's sake, it would all be over very soon.

Dr Piermont, the doctor whom Louise had insisted should be in charge of the birth, suddenly entered the room. He looked calm as he went over to his jacket lying on a chair in the corner. 'Sorry, forgot something,' he stated casually, whilst rifling through his pockets.

Another loud scream brought Frederick to a halt in his nervous marching back and forth. 'Is everything all right, Dr Piermont?' he asked anxiously.

'Everything is going to plan, m'lord,' reassured the doctor.

'It's just that my wife sounds in such distress.'

With a pleasant smile, Dr Piermont explained. 'Lady Warsop is well dilated and the baby isn't breached. All is as one would expect. We just need nature to take its course.'

Frederick went puce at the thought of it all. His father simply hated to hear Louise being referred to as 'Lady' and gave a contemptuous frown.

Dr Piermont could see Frederick was unconvinced by his assessment and offered him further comfort. 'Be assured, m'lord. Should it become necessary, I will administer chloroform.'

The earl rose from his chair in indignation and

squawked his opinion. One that, even for him, was heartless. 'You are aware of the Church's view on the use of chloroform in childbirth, Dr Piermont? Human intervention in the miracle of birth is a sin against the will of God. If God had wished labour to be painless, he would have made it so.'

As if waiting for instructions, Dr Piermont looked over to Frederick. But his father wasn't quite done yet. 'Don't look at him, man. I'll give instructions!'

From where he suddenly found his courage, Frederick didn't know. However, he managed to bring out his words quite firmly. 'Father, if Louise has instructed that chloroform should be used, then I will not object.'

The room fell silent for a moment. Ranskill gave the look of disapproval he always gave when Frederick attempted to affirm an opinion and breathed deeply. Dr Piermont was then treated to another example of his sarcasm. 'And I suppose you'll be advocating next that the father should be present at the birth!'

As much as Dr Piermont wanted to express his opinion, he decided to hold his tongue.

For Ranskill, the conversation needed ending. 'If the learned doctor has now found what he came for, then perhaps he should return to the work for which he is being so handsomely paid.'

In the bedroom, Louise was squeezing Crecia's hand

as hard as any man could have done. Crecia grimaced, but as always rose to the occasion. If ever Louise needed a loyal hand, it was now. Although, at the edge of sheer exhaustion, she could still laugh at her Italian maid's insistence to push. 'Pusha! Pusha! Like Papa pusha the mule when he no move …'

The midwife looked up in dismay from between Louise's legs. 'I rather think we need a little less pusha and a bit more relaxa, m'lady.'

Louise let out another half-laugh, half-scream. Crecia whispered in her ear, 'You still pusha, Miss Louise.'

Dr Piermont finally came to her aid. 'Would m'lady like me to give her a little chloroform to help with the pain?'

'I fear if you don't doctor, my language might not be ladylike for much longer.'

Placing his fetal scope carefully on Louise's stomach, Dr Piermont listened for a heartbeat. He smiled and confirmed, 'As strong as an ox. As is yours, m'lady.' Crecia couldn't have agreed more, and watched her fingertips go whiter and whiter as Louise continued to grip her hand ever more tightly. Ten minutes later, it was all over. Louise had given birth to a son. Finally, her suffering could turn to joy.

So too could Crecia's. The maid stood there shaking her hand, trying to get the blood back into it. 'Questa situazione mi ricorda di, Giovanni. Lui sempre spremuto me così stretto quando abbiamo fatto sesso passionale,' she stated jovially. In her joy, her words came out in her native tongue, which was just as well, for had they been understood, they would certainly have raised a few eyebrows.

In the room beyond Louise's suite, the baby's cry was suddenly heard. Frederick, in his excitement, barged into the bedroom, only to be greeted with the sight of the aftermath of the birth, as well as a look of horror from the midwife and nurse. 'Too early!' they cried. Feeling quite faint, he promptly turned to walk out again.

Once everything was cleaned up, the midwife asked, 'Shall I fetch his lordship now?'

'Yes, please do. That is, if you think his constitution will stand it.' Louise joked.

Frederick's eyes welled up on seeing Louise cuddling the small bundle. For all his recent performance as an uninterested husband, he now swooned over his wife and new son with pride. But, sure enough, his ability to demonstrate insensitivity wasn't far away. Taking the baby from Louise, he folded back the shawl to expose the bewildered little face half squinting at him and announced, 'How clever father is, producing you.' He then proceeded to take his prize in to the family and to hold the baby aloft. 'I give you a future earl,' he cried, to applause from everyone.

Louise should have been disappointed in her husband, but she was already more than aware that he now saw her as merely fulfilling a purpose. And, whilst she still had hope for their marriage, in her heart of hearts, she knew it was destined for emptiness. For now though, she would embrace the new joys of motherhood. Or at least she would if her father-in-law kept his distance and didn't interfere. Of course, there was little chance of that. If the earl was to win his battle, then he needed to strike when the enemy was most vulnerable. To Louise, however, vulnerability simply meant one needed to fight harder.

Two weeks after her accouchement, Frederick surprised her by suggesting a trip to the theatre. Yes! There was hope, she thought. But little did she know that he would use the outing to break the news of a six-month posting far away. Returning from the performance, Louise went straight upstairs and prepared to feed the baby. Crecia was waiting, and looking very agitated.

'I think I'll wear the white one, Crecia. It's so much more comfortable for feeding little Edward,' Louise stated. She then asked if the baby had been all right during her absence. She was gradually realising from her maid's expression that something was amiss.

'What is it, Crecia? What's wrong?'

Crecia knew exactly how her mistress would react, but there was no way to avoid telling her. 'Bambino already fed, Miss Louise.'

Louise suddenly stopped brushing her long hair, holding the brush in mid air. Her eyebrows squeezed together. 'What do you mean, already fed?' she asked, looking at Crecia in the mirror. But already she suspected her father-in-law would have had a part to play in it all. Crecia didn't want to answer.

'I asked you. What do you mean, already fed?' Louise repeated sternly.

'Hima! Lord Ranskill. He bring a wet nurse for bambino.'

Louise went red with rage, just as Crecia had suspected she would. She flung her hairbrush down on the bed and shouted, 'I might have known. That man's behaviour never ceases to astound me. Who does he think he is?' Grabbing her shawl, she burst out of the room and stormed down the stairs, oblivious of a footman carrying a tray, whom she nearly knocked clean over. At the bottom, she turned onto the corridor leading to the earl's study. She was fired up and ready to explode.

Walking the other way down the corridor came Frederick. He could see Louise's face was like thunder. 'Louise! What on earth is the matter?'

She passed him by before crying out, 'Your father!

That's what's the matter.'

'My father?'

'Yes, your father. Or should I say, that vile serpent. And I intend telling him so.'

Louise kept on down the corridor, leaving Frederick bemused. Suddenly, he went white with fear at the prospect of a confrontation between the pair. 'Wait! I'll come with you,' he pleaded, although the thought of the encounter filled him with panic.

'Yes, dear,' she muttered. 'If you have a pair, but somehow I doubt it.'

Louise flung open the door to Ranskill's study, swept in, and slammed the door shut behind her. Her father-in-law and Dr Robertson were standing over a map spread on a large desk. They looked up in amazement as Louise began her rant. 'How dare you? You evil man! What gives you the right to deny me my maternal right?'

The men were speechless as she stood waiting for an answer. Ranskill finally found his composure and retorted, 'I take it you are alluding to my instructions for the child.'

'The child, as you so delicately describe him, is mine! And I demand my right to nurse him as I see fit.'

The battle which, until now, had consisted mainly of jibes, sarcasm and tit-for-tat had suddenly erupted into something altogether different. Ranskill spat out his next volley. 'And you, dear daughter-in-law, forget my right to uphold traditions within this household.'

Louise rolled her eyes in disbelief.

Dr Robertson felt most uneasy with the predicament he found himself in. On the one hand, he wanted to give Louise a piece of his mind. On the other, he was a politician and knew that battles were won, not with words, but with devious actions. He tactfully suggested to the earl, 'Perhaps I should leave you. We can conclude our business tomorrow, George.'

However, Ranskill was never as adept as his partner at playing politics. Instead, he wore his emotions on his sleeve. This was a standoff, and he had no intention of backing down. 'No, Anthony, stay. Witness first hand my daughter-in-law's contempt for the Warsop name and all it stands for.'

Louise too had no intention of finishing things here. 'I have done my duty to this family. I have given you an heir. You ought to be grateful that I am helping to perpetuate your precious family name. Who would, if I didn't?'

By now, Frederick was outside the study with his ear to the door, straining to listen to the quarrel. He stood back and agonised over his dilemma. Fight or flight? He gingerly opened the door. All eyes were cast on him.

'Ah, Frederick! Do join us. You can enlighten me as

to your views. Do you support your wife?' Ranskill asked, with derision.

Just as Louise suspected would happen, her husband reacted like a lamb to the slaughter. He looked down and pathetically fumbled with his hands. She sighed in exasperation. What she'd hoped her husband would have behind his hands, in order to stand up to his father, was obviously missing.

'I'm sorry, father, but I don't have any idea what this is all about.'

'Your wife, man! Thinks all tradition and etiquette should be ignored in this house, in favour of continuing to feed the child herself.'

Frederick looked over to Louise with some astonishment. 'We agreed, dear.'

'No, Frederick. You agreed with yourself that the lord and master here would want it his way. And I said that since he's not the father, he'll have to just want.'

Frederick carried on looking at his wife with eyes wide open, unable to believe she was talking in this way. His father simply stood there, becoming redder and redder. Louise was taking delight in finally letting out all her frustrations.

'Oh come, Frederick. I'm doing what any mother naturally wants to do. You would think I'm proposing to become a wet nurse to a child from the slums. Stand up, for God's sake, and support me.'

But Frederick could only look over to his father and cast his eyes downward. Then he muttered, without taking his gaze away from the floor, 'If father has decided, then —'

The groan of disappointment from Louise was so audible to him.

'It's tradition. Ladies have a wet nurse,' was the best answer Frederick could come up with.

Louise gave her parting shot, before turning and leaving the room. 'Well, poor me! How could I forget? Our baby is to be an earl first and always, and my child only because he can't help it.' Feeling totally alone and utterly exhausted, she slowly trudged back down the corridor. David was standing there, looking forlorn. Louise smiled. 'I suppose you heard all that?' she said.

David nodded. 'Father is a bully, and so too, is the idiot with him.'

'Would that be Frederick or Dr Robertson?' Louise joked.

They both laughed.

'My battle with them is yet to come,' said David.

Louise didn't know exactly what David meant, but she had her suspicions. 'Then we'll have to become comrades in arms,' she said and cupped his sad face in her hand.

'They'll get their comeuppance, wait and see,' he insisted, with fire in his eyes.

Louise gently kissed him on the cheek. 'I hope you're right … Goodnight, David.' With that, she walked back up the stairs.

David watched her with interest and sighed, 'Goodnight. And I'm really sorry.'

She turned to ask. 'For what?'

'My father!'

Once in her bedroom, Louise collapsed on her bed and sobbed her heart out.

~~~

In the study, Frederick was getting the full force of his father's anger. 'I will not tolerate such outbursts from her,' his father barked, and so near his face that the fringe of his hair lifted upwards. Dr Robertson watched with a smile on his face, delighted to see the son squirming.

'Father, I will talk with her immediately and express your displeasure.'

Ranskill huffed and turned away. 'Talk to her indeed.'

'Yes. As soon as —,' Frederick attempted, until interrupted.

'Will you listen to him, Anthony. He will talk to her.' Ranskill mocked his son before again rounding on him
~~~

and blasting his words directly into Frederick's face, 'No. She needs a husband to take his hand to her. The insolent woman needs a sound beating.'

'Please, father. You know that is not my way with a woman.'

'Then perhaps it ought to be!'

'I'm sure her behaviour can be explained by the difficulty of the birth. I will consult the physician in the morning.'

'Yes you do that, Frederick. Maybe he will prescribe cutting out her tongue!'

Dr Robertson laughed hard. Frederick couldn't have felt more belittled. Still, he just took it all, standing in silence. His father eventually slumped into a chair, his fat belly protruding over his belt. 'Go Frederick! I am weary of your presence. I do not wish Dr Robertson to suffer any more of your sentimentality,' he said, smirking at the doctor. In return, the doctor gave a snarled smile in recognition of a job well done. Frederick feebly dropped his head and left with no more to say other than, 'Father.'

The two men continued with their character assassination of Frederick as the door closed behind him. 'No finer specimen for the future of Haddington, eh, Anthony? Thank God I will be dead.' The father carried on with his contemptuous words about his son. To Ranskill, Frederick was a son who always fell short of his expectations. Support, love and encouragement were words that were very much alien to him.

Dr Robertson gave his vicious assessment of the situation. 'A future earl we can work on. But evidently the future countess appears to be the problem.'

Ranskill spun round in his chair, hardly able to get his words out fast enough. 'That woman will never be the Countess of Ranskill, Anthony! By fair or foul means I will see to that.'

Dr Robertson was very pleased to hear it, but had his own ideas for how this could be achieved. He gave one of his toadying looks, his upper body stooping down low, like a cowering dog. 'If you'll permit my opinion?'

'Go on.'

'Louise is like a cow —'

The earl had to interrupt. 'Well! That much we agree on.'

'… or like a broodmare. She exists to breed from, to deliver offspring. She is young and lives to perform.'

Wondering where his partner was going with the conversation, Ranskill gave a confused frown. 'Your analogies are most entertaining, Anthony. But your point is?'

The doctor was happy to explain. 'A cow eventually outlives its usefulness. Only then can you slaughter it. I'm merely suggesting to you that, right now, Louise has the upper hand.'

It was then as if they were discussing a contingency plan for the colliery. There was no emotion, just facts.

'I think I understand your meaning,' Ranskill said. But he wasn't totally sure he did. He thought for a further moment, then pointed out. 'But I now have a grandson. She has produced a future heir for Haddington.'

'Indeed. But think about it, George. What if the new puppy proves to be the runt? Doesn't survive. A litter or at least a couple of pups are preferable, are they not?'

Ranskill was now on the same page as his friend. However, he stated his terms for continuing to tolerate his daughter-in-law. 'Preserving a line for Haddington is one thing. But I will not be ridiculed in the process.'

Dr Robertson's final words were chilling. 'We simply ruin her, George. But we ruin her slowly. And then …'

Chapter 10

The woman handed over a bag to Mrs Broadbent and smiled. 'Everything she'll need for now is in here. And, as soon as I'm able, I'll bring her some more clothes.' Mrs Broadbent took the bag and placed it on the floor in the little dining room. 'Oh, I nearly forgot,' the woman continued, and produced some notes from her purse. 'This should cover most things until I return.'

'How long do you think you'll be away?'

'Oh, not long, I'm sure,' replied the woman.

Mrs Broadbent gave another warm smile and asked, 'What's her name?' referring to the second woman, who so far had said nothing.

'Marion. My name's Marion,' came the woman's answer, as she looked around the room and through the window onto the quaint little garden. Beyond could be seen the rolling hills of Derbyshire.

'Well, you're most welcome here, Marion. I'll show you to your room shortly,' Mrs Broadbent said. But Marion didn't really appear interested. Instead, she was more curious about the dovecote in the garden. Watching the doves fly in and out made her eyes light up. 'Coo, coo,' she murmured.

'Marion has had a frightful time of late, Mrs Broadbent. You will be mindful of that, won't you?' the woman urged.

'Of course. You can rest assured that Marion will be most comfortable here, and that I will treat her with the utmost understanding.'

'This is so kind of you. To take her in for me … Now, I really ought to be going.' The woman then called, 'Bye, Marion. Mrs Broadbent here will look after you whilst I'm away.'

Marion's expression was impassive. 'Bye.'

'Thank you again. I'll be in touch,' said the woman to her hostess, and promptly turned to leave.

'Yes, goodbye, Mrs Ridgeway.'

The woman in question though, wasn't Mrs Ridgeway at all. She simply liked the sound of the name, and it was fit for purpose in carrying out her business. Business that had only one motive – revenge!

Marion hadn't been part of her plan at all. Indeed, her unexpected appearance was, in the beginning, a complication. But now that 'Mrs Ridgeway' knew about her, things had become altogether different, and merely re-inforced the reason why the settling of scores was so important.

Mrs Broadbent was the kindest and sweetest of women. She took in the occasional paying guest at her small cottage on the outskirts of Belper, and the modest amount she charged helped her to make ends meet and supplemented her meagre savings, now that she was retired from the asylum where she had worked. When asked if she would like to help a mental patient with short-term lodgings, she was more than happy to assist.

Considering how she had been shunted from pillar to post, Marion settled into her new environment very well. She would sit and study Mrs Broadbent when her hostess talked to her about this and that, but mainly the conversation was about the latter's nursing days. Then, one day, Marion asked, 'Can we go for a walk, Sister?' She was making an association between Mrs Broadbent and Sister Agnes.

'Oh no, my dear. I wasn't a sister,' answered Mrs Broadbent. But the association was set in Marion's mind, and as the hostess quite liked the ring of 'Sister' preceding her name, she went along with the charade. 'Very well, Marion! Sister Broadbent would love to go for a walk with you.' Marion produced an adorable smile.

The next two days were heartening to see: a kind old nurse, dutifully re-playing the days when she had assisted the people in her care. And as for the patient, she delighted in the attention lavished on her. The hours they'd spend playing pat-a-cake and I spy. Then, it all changed, with a series of coincidences.

First there was the incident of the knock on the door.

'Well, hello, Dr Robertson. What a surprise,' Mrs Broadbent had said.

Hearing the name brought an instant reaction from Marion, listening in the room. Her eyes were suddenly ablaze with fear. She clutched her arms tightly into her body, remembering the needles.

The person who had visited Mrs Broadbent was, however, not the Dr Robertson Marion associated with her old asylum. Instead, he was merely a young junior doctor who had been sent to enquire whether Mrs Broadbent still held some photos of the Derbyshire Royal Infirmary. The former nurse remembered the young doctor well and listened as he explained that he was involved in the compiling of an archive for the hospital. Mrs Broadbent was invariably the one people turned to when they needed to research the history of the hospital. She had worked there since it opened, some twenty-two years earlier. Indeed, she had some papers dating further back than that, from when the old infirmary was still in existence.

'Well, do come in, please, doctor. I'll have a look to see what I can find,' she said. Walking through the small hall into the dining room, she called out, 'Marion, this is a young doctor I used to work with at the hospital.' Then, she stopped. 'Oh, she's gone. How strange!' She called out again, 'Marion! Marion! Where are you?' When no reply was forthcoming, the young doctor could clearly see she was anxious, and he now felt he was intruding.

'Listen, Mrs Broadbent. Why don't I leave the matter with you? If you manage to find any photographs we could use, perhaps you'll keep them to one side. I'll drop by next week,' the doctor suggested.

Mrs Broadbent seemed preoccupied, and concerned as to where Marion could have gone. 'Er … well, er … yes. Please do that, Doctor. I'm sure I'll be able to dig out something for you.' She saw him to the door and then returned, flustered, to the dining room.

'Marion! Marion!' she called again. This time, a face full of fear started to appear from behind the sofa. 'Oh there you are. I wondered where — My dear girl, whatever is the matter?'

From then on, although Mrs Broadbent tried constantly to reassure her, she couldn't help but notice that Marion was anxious about something. But of course, she had no idea what the cause of her guest's anxiety was.

The second incident that triggered a response from Marion occurred whilst the pair were out walking.

The day had started like any other, with a breakfast of porridge and oatcakes, which Marion loved to flip over on the griddle suspended on the fire. Then she would help Mrs Broadbent make the beds. After that came her favourite task: taking the crumbs and carefully placing them on the dovecote. She had only been doing this for four days, but already the doves nesting inside didn't seem frightened by her presence. Each morning and early evening, she would quietly approach the wooden box, gently cooing all the while. Once up close, she'd look through the hole and coo again. The birds' heads would bob about from side to side, and, if she were lucky, she would get a coo back in return for her efforts.

Mrs Broadbent smiled and held out a coat for Marion. 'I thought today we'd go by the canal, and then down over the railway siding and back via the meadow. What do you think, Marion?'

Marion had no real perception of which place was where, but gave her usual smile. Today she appeared almost chatty. 'That sounds nice,' she said. It all seemed perfectly normal until she added, 'Will there be a table? … Buzzzzz!'

'That's all finished with now, Marion. We've talked about this before. Come now,' Mrs Broadbent rebuked, but in a manner that only twenty years of dealing with the mentally ill could teach you.

Once over the canal bridge they had to stop at the railway tracks to allow a goods train to pass. The engine and first few wagons passed with Marion chugging away in time to the sound of the train. Suddenly, her expression became serious and she stared at the next set of wagons passing her by. They were full of coal, and painted on the side, in big bold letters, were the words: THE WARSOP MINING COMPANY

Marion had the briefest of flashbacks. Lord Ranskill was standing in front of her, ranting. His face was so vivid. It was going redder and redder and coming closer and closer. Then, as if he'd exploded, the image of him went and she was once again looking at the last wagon chugging by. Startled, she pulled away from Mrs Broadbent's hand and began running away, first across the line and then left towards the meadow.

It was a full twenty minutes before Mrs Broadbent finally discovered Marion, huddled against the trunk of a large oak tree. She simply held out her hand and said, 'Come Marion. We'd better be getting back, or you'll be late giving the doves their crumbs.' Marion's face lit up and, as if nothing had happened, she grasped the open hand and began walking.

That night, Mrs Broadbent was sitting reading a book, by the fire. Marion entered and put their cups of hot milk down on the small table between the sofa and the chair. She looked in the mirror, but saw herself differently from the way she usually did. She stroked her flaming red hair.

'I expect we'll be hearing from Mrs Ridgeway quite

soon, Marion,' commented Mrs Broadbent.

'Who am I?' Marion simply replied.

Chapter 11

The little room below stairs was barely big enough to seat two people in comfort, let alone three, but Mr Dowling insisted they discuss matters here. As he saw it, if their visit wasn't for official business with his lordship, then there was no reason to be upstairs. Tom had hoped he would be able to visit the library again and take another look at the book that had intrigued him on his previous visit. However, he accepted that he'd have to settle for just asking questions.

Dowling was a busy man and, although always pleasant, he acted in accordance with the principle that time was not for wasting. He was certainly capable of matching Elliott in ensuring a conversation got straight to the point.

'Well, gentleman. How can I help you?'

'It's not so much me, Mr Dowling, but the professor here who's curious about something,' Elliott answered, whilst still trying to find the best position for sitting on a chair that wouldn't stop squeaking.

'Curious about what, Professor?' Dowling asked rather bluntly.

Tom instinctively sat up straight, suddenly feeling

like he was at an interview. 'Er … yes, well … I was merely wondering about a book I saw in the library when we were here last. More accurately, I want to know who last read it?'

'You will forgive me, Professor. It is a library. People pick up and move books all the time. And despite what you may think, butlers don't know everything that happens in a household.'

Tom gave a wry smile of appreciation at Dowling's sarcastic humour before re-phrasing his question. 'Very well, could I ask then …' but stopped, being thoroughly distracted by Elliott's chair, which, no matter what he did, wouldn't cease its squeaking.

'I'll stand, Tom,' offered Elliott apologetically.

'Are all the family readers of fiction, Mr Dowling?' Tom continued.

Dowling gave the question a moment's thought. 'Well, my observation would be: certainly not his lordship; but definitely Master David; and on one occasion I saw Lady Matilda reading a book. Although I doubt it would have been fiction.'

'Lady Matilda?' enquired Tom.

'She is the earl's sister. No longer resides here, sir.' Despite Tom raising his eyebrows in curiosity, Dowling had no intention of explaining why.

'Master David, is he a meticulously orderly person?'

Dowling was quite baffled as to the relevance of the question, and so too was Elliott, who continued to say nothing but remained very much intrigued. Eventually Dowling gave his answer. 'It is not really my place to comment, sir. But I will confirm that 'orderly' and 'Master David' are not words that readily go together.'

'And Lady Matilda?' Tom wanted to know.

'Oh very organised,' Dowling replied in a tone not exactly sarcastic but indicating his indifference to the woman.

Tom could see that Dowling was tiring of his enquiries but persisted with one last question. 'Does Master David play much music from the operetta *El Triste Matador*?'

Even Elliott had to look baffled in response to the question.

'I am sorry, Professor, but I truly wouldn't have a clue. I couldn't tell you the difference between operetta, music hall or a sea shanty!' Dowling said, unable to comprehend any relevance to the book.

Elliott was relieved when Tom's peculiar questioning of the butler ended. Apart from his feet beginning to ache through standing, he was beginning to feel quite nauseous at the strong smell of cheese coming from the adjoining storeroom. Once outside, he soon perked up and the two men began the long walk down the drive to the hall's entrance gates. Elliott began to rack his brain, then he suddenly remembered.

'*El Triste Matador*. Of course! That's where the music comes from,' he said. 'But what's that got to do with the book? And Master David?'

'Do you not know the story?' Tom asked, as if it were a commonly known fable.

'Well, no, not really. Isn't it meant to be a bit macabre?'

Tom had read the book when he was a student and certainly remembered it for its gore, but perhaps more for the fact that the subject matter was considered very controversial and the book was ultimately removed from the library. He started to explain to Elliott.

A hundred yards further on, nearing the fountain structure, Elliott had to interrupt. 'Oh, Tom! Enough, please. It fair turns my stomach. Why would Master David want to read about such things?'

'It could be just morbid curiosity, but I'm guessing there's more to it.'

'I can't honestly see that Lord Ranskill would have chosen it for his library.'

'He most likely didn't. But I know a man who would have it in his collection of books.'

Their conversation was diverted as they came to the new fountain. Since their last visit, work had progressed rapidly, and the fountain was now a most impressive feature nearing completion. There was no disputing that it was a triumph. For all the earl's failings, nobody could doubt his ability in architectural landscaping. He himself had provided the drawings that were going to ensure the view from the library would be spectacular. The lavish structure in delicately carved stone superbly framed the beautiful gardens beyond.

'These lads of yours, Mr Elliott. Been a damned marvel, I can tell you,' announced Arthur Wallis, the groundsman. He was standing next to Mr Earnshaw, the master stonemason. Beside them, strewn on a makeshift table, were all the relevant technical drawings and associated paperwork.

'Well, I'm glad they've been of use, Mr Wallis. They're not all wrong 'uns really, given half the chance. Perhaps I can get you to write a few references. It always helps when trying to present another side of them in court.'

'Absolutely, sir. Just let me know when.'

Tom left Elliott to chat some more with Mr Wallis, whilst he studied the plans and exchanged pleasantries with the stonemason. It was only a matter of time before he caught sight of the small photograph pinned to a sheet of paper. It was the same photo, showing the elevation of the house, that Sister Agnes had seen at Rosterhay Asylum. Like her, he immediately recognised the woman posed in the foreground as Marion. He was quite shocked. 'Who is this woman, sir?'

Mr Earnshaw took a look at the woman he was pointing to but only murmured vaguely, 'I've no idea, I'm afraid. Mr Wallis may know.'

'What's that,' asked Mr Wallis, having had one ear on their conversation.

'The lady in this photo. The gentleman here asked who it is.' He handed over the picture. An inquisitive Elliott peered over the shoulder of Mr Wallis to also have a look. He opened his eyes wide and looked over at Tom in surprise. He too recognised the woman as Marion.

Both Elliott and Tom were even more surprised when the groundsman gave his answer, which was quite definite. 'Oh, that's …'

~~~

Being an accomplished horse rider from an early age, Matilda could easily match any male rider in the saddle. Horses were her passion. The aunt had never married, despite the fact that she had once been an attractive woman with many an admirer. For the most part, she desired, and indeed had sexual encounters with men. But she constantly struggled with her true sexual identity. On occasion, her preference could quickly turn towards
~~~

other women; and when it did, she would take trips far away from Haddington. Now in her forties, she tried to maintain her looks and figure; but her love of the cook's pastries meant she was always fighting a losing battle, and this fuelled her jealousy of Louise whenever the younger woman paraded herself in a beautiful gown.

Matilda was a complex character. On the one hand, to the world, she was the socially adept Lady Matilda, hosting bridge days and indulging in society gossip. But, behind the façade, she could be cruel and calculating. She liked nothing more than to trap a fly in her room and skewer it with a hat pin, watching it suffer and wondering just how long it could survive. Her intentions towards Louise were fast becoming similar.

Many a time, Louise witnessed Matilda's volatility first hand. One moment, the aunt would be happy and content, lavishing gifts and affection on Frederick and baby Edward. Even, occasionally, on Louise. The next minute, the scene was all darkness and Matilda resumed her role as queen of vipers, becoming as vindictive as it was possible for a person to be. Matilda epitomised the lonely woman past her prime and desperate to show society that she was not yet beyond a proposal of marriage. What surprised Louise was the man the aunt saw as an appealing proposition: Dr Robertson. Quite why Matilda felt this way would mystify most women, as the doctor lacked any alluring traits.

There had developed between Matilda and the doctor a friendship which was driven by a mutual interest in brutality and the macabre. She was fascinated by his theories about experiments with humans that would produce a future world of hybrid beings, a project through which he sought acclaim as a medical pioneer.

For some time after Louise's arrival, Matilda had shown some tolerance of her nephew's wife's fiery nature, accepting that they were equally antagonistic to each other. Then, a defamatory article about the Warsop family in *The Yorkshire Post* raised her suspicions as to who the anonymous writer might be. Indeed, her suspicions were well founded, for Louise was the contributor. Knowing that its origins would be impossible to trace, Louise had written the piece one day, out of sheer boredom and devilment. She was more than capable of lighting a fire under Haddington and then demurely enquiring where such scandal could possibly have come from.

Following the appearance of the Yorkshire Post article, the conversations between Matilda and Robertson about Louise, which had hitherto been guarded, suddenly became more open in terms of hypothetical scenarios. And always the outcome was the same – the suffering and demise of the outsider!

Chapter 12

If there is one occurrence that captures most of our emotions, then it has to be when a young child drops their ice cream. Cecil was absolutely horrified when he turned back from watching the brightly coloured fun train pass by, only to find his delicious scoop of vanilla had plopped into the sand. His first reaction was to pick it up and attempt to clean it off. But the task was hopeless, and deep down his upbringing told him it wasn't an option. Then came his despair. The little face, which only seconds earlier had been full of excitement, was now fit to burst with equal amounts of disappointment and anger.

His brother Henry was in fits of laughter, whilst Ann and Mary tried desperately to conceal theirs. Cecil wanted to hit his brother and then, out of jealousy, take his ice cream off him. He puffed and sighed, wondering what to do next. Tears welled up in his eyes. To add insult to injury, a seagull had landed and was ready to peck away at the free meal. He looked over to his mother, who just couldn't hold her laugh in any longer. He burst into tears. The humiliation of it all!

'It's not funny!' he blubbered.

Mary, still able to restrain her amusement to a slight

giggle, went to console him. 'Ah, bless him,' she said and gave him a hug. 'No, don't laugh,' she admonished Ann and Henry. But, eventually, her own laughter had to come out. She lifted up Cecil's chin. He finally succumbed to the infectiousness of it all and began laughing himself. The range of emotions was soon complete as his eyes lit up with delight when Mary suggested, 'Come on. Let's go and get you another one.' Although the ice cream stand was a good fifteen minutes' walk back down the seafront, Mary was happy to make the trip.

It was the hottest day of their holiday so far, and they decided to take a break before tackling the walk back. Sitting on the bench, Cecil commented, 'Phew! It's hot, Mary.'

'Hot! This is nothing. Let me tell you about hot, young man. When I first went to the Arabian desert …'

'That Mesopots place?' he interrupted. Cecil still struggled with pronouncing the word.

Mary smiled. 'Yes, it's Mesopotamia. Well, it was Aden actually. Is that easier to say?'

Cecil was more than happy with that and licked at his ice cream before shuffling back on the bench in readiness for Mary's explanation. 'I would say today is about 75 degrees Fahrenheit. Now over there, at this time of year, it's at least 100 degrees Fahrenheit.' She thought she'd also provide a bit of dramatic effect, and added, 'It was so hot in the mornings we could place a tin lid on a stone in the sunshine and fry our eggs.'

'Blimey!' said the attentive Cecil, before putting a question. 'Do you think they'll send Henry and me to war there, Mary?'

His question brought home to her just how much of a possibility that might be, certainly for Henry, should the war carry on for many more years. However, she painted a much more optimistic picture to Cecil. 'Oh, I would hope things will be over long before then.'

'You had a brother over there didn't you? Will you tell me about him? Though we're not supposed to ask because mother says it may upset you.'

Mary gave a warm smile and drew him in close. 'Nonsense. I'd love to tell you about him. His name was Walter.'

'Was he like Tom?'

Mary raised her eyebrows, 'Er, well. Not exactly. He was a bit of a mischievous one, Walter, but loving and caring all the same, just like Tom.' She took the locket from around her neck and placed it in his hand. 'It's a long story, and one for when you're a bit older. But you see, unlike you and Henry, Walter and I didn't grow up together. But we did each have a half of this locket which our mother gave us. And this locket was the reason for me going all the way to Mesopotamia. So I could find him and we could see each other again.'

Already Cecil was enthralled.

Mary looked out at the sun dancing on the sea and she drifted into imagining Walter again, as she sometimes did, particularly when the sun shone. Eighteen months had now passed since Walter died in his beloved land, but the memory of him never faded for her.

Watching a small brother and sister arguing on the beach made her wonder about his two twin children and their mother, Iza. What had become of them? She felt a guilt that she hadn't attempted to track them down and offer them a life in England, although, to do so would have involved nothing short of a military exercise. Mary had to be content that they were in a country and culture that they knew, and that Macca, Iza's father, would be more than able to provide for them all. Also, this was what Walter would have wanted. She was sure about that.

Sometimes, when she imagined him, Mary would visualise scenes which had obviously never happened, but which brought her comfort. It was like her opening the same book, only each time the chapters could be written differently. For example, today Walter and Mary could have been the children on the beach.

'Mother! Tell him! He's doing it again,' Mary protested, as once more Walter flicked sand high into the air and watched it rain down on her head.

'Oh, Walter. Stop teasing, please,' said Lucinda, taking Mary on her knee to brush through her gorgeous dark wavy hair. Mary, in return, took her mother's hand and studied the beautiful rings on her fingers. Then she looked into her mother's deep brown eyes and touched her lovely olive skin. Never once did Mary ever visualise Lucinda as being anything other than a beautiful and caring woman.

Cecil broke her concentration. 'Father says Walter was really good at sailing.'

'Yes, he was. And won awards for it too,' Mary responded with pride. She began to visualise yet another new chapter in their shared past.

In the hard, driving rain, she grumbled to herself at being dragged to watch her brother compete in the yacht race. Still, she showed her support. 'Go on Walter! Go on!' she screamed at the yachts way in the distance, believing completely that Walter was in the lead as the yachts rounded the marker buoy.

'Think he'll win?' said a voice, from next to her.

'Walter!' she gasped. 'But you're supposed to be ...'

'No! I came off the water an hour ago. Sorry, I meant to have told you. It was just the one race I was in.'

'Walter. You made me come all this way to watch you ... in this lot, and you're only in one race!'

Walter beamed that smile of innocence, as only he

could. 'Under here,' he said, and held his coat over their heads. He squeezed her in and kissed her drenched hair. 'Thanks for coming, sis.'

What could she say?

Mary snapped out of her imaginary story and listened to Cecil chattering away about engines. '… and they have 42 bhp, you know.'

'Really?' Mary asked, with a smile.

As they were walking back, Cecil asked a very unexpected question. 'If you were my auntie, what would that make baby Lucinda? I can't remember.'

'A lucky girl, my dear, because she'd be your cousin.'

Cecil thought deeply as he held Mary's hand and they pretend marched along the front. It was another few minutes before he asked, 'Could I call you Auntie Mary and Tom Uncle Tom?'

Mary felt quite emotional and squeezed his hand. 'If you like. Of course you can.'

'Yes. And then I can tell everyone about my Uncle Walter.' Cecil revealed his motive instantly, being as forthright in his words as his father. Mary laughed, realising there could be no mistaking that Cecil was a chip off the old block.

Finally, they arrived back, much to Ann's relief. They had been gone a good forty-five minutes. 'I was just about to send out the search parties for you,' she joked.

'I'm really sorry, Ann. We stopped for a little rest and got chatting,' Mary explained. 'Lucinda not been any trouble?'

'Never murmured.'

'Lucinda is going to be my cousin,' announced Cecil proudly.

'Is she now?' responded his mother.

'Yes, and I'm going to call Mary, Auntie Mary.'

Ann looked over to Mary and shook her head in playful anticipation. 'Dare I ask?'

Cecil addressed his next remark to his brother but he was still within earshot of his mother. 'Mary's told me …' He stopped and corrected himself. 'Auntie Mary's told me all about Walter. That makes him an uncle. We have a hero in the family, Henry.'

Ann's shoulders dropped and she let out a sigh of exasperation. 'Oh no! What's he been asking?'

Mary placed her hand on Ann's shoulder to reassure her. 'It's absolutely fine. I've loved every minute of telling him.'

Ann continued to look apologetic.

'No, honestly, I have,' Mary insisted.

An eventful day was rounded off with a trip to the harbour. This was mainly for the benefit of Henry, who was desperate to see the size of the fish that returning holiday fishermen were bringing ashore. Engines were all well and good, but fishing, now that was a proper hobby!

Ann and Mary took a well-earned rest and sat on the harbour wall, whilst the boys gawped at the prize cod being carried off the boats by proud fathers.

'I wonder how Robert and Tom are getting on?' Mary asked.

'Well, if Lily is still sick, and I know anything about my husband, there'll be a sink full of dirty pots waiting to greet us. Not to mention, in my case, an unmade bed and a bedroom floor full of screwed up clothes. Still, we live in hope of equality one day, eh!' Ann replied, with a wink.

Mary, also knowing her husband, found it difficult to disagree with Ann's assessment.

'Thanks for inviting us. We've really enjoyed ourselves,' Mary said.

'You're more than welcome. Anytime, Auntie Mary!'

Both women laughed. All things considered, it had been a most enjoyable day.

Chapter 13

Following her explosive row with the earl, Louise had gone back to her room, knowing that Frederick would ultimately return like a scolded puppy, trying to justify his father's behaviour. She was in no mood to listen to any of it, and certainly didn't wish to witness his pleading for reconciliation. Still seething from the whole episode, not least, her husband's pathetic stance in it all, she turned the key, not caring a fig where he would spend the night. Just as long as it was not in their bed.

Next day, Frederick was conspicuous by his absence and Louise stayed in her room most of the morning, brooding. It was unthinkable to her not to feed her own baby, but she knew there was no way that her father-in-law would give an inch on the matter. Equally, she was not going to wallow in self-pity any longer. 'If it's a game he wants, then he can damned well have it,' she snapped, and went to ring the bell.

A knock on the door signalled Crecia's arrival. By now she'd heard all about the argument from the staff below stairs and, having not heard from her mistress all morning, she opened the door with apprehension. 'Yes, Miss Louise?' she enquired anxiously.

She needn't have worried, for Louise appeared to be in buoyant mood. 'Ah, Crecia. Come in. How long have we known each other?'

Crecia shrugged her shoulders. 'Er, five-a, maybe six years.'

'And in all that time, have I ever asked you to deceive for me?'

Her maid could instantly think of one occasion. 'Well, er … There was —'

'Yes, yes. Apart from that incident,' Louise interjected, knowing her maid was remembering the time at the theatre. There, she'd been asked to advise a very boring Mr Kentmore during the interval, that Louise had been taken ill and had had to leave very suddenly.

'Will you help me, Crecia?'

'Of course-a, Miss Louise.'

'Bless you.'

Louise then requested Crecia to find Edith and bring her up to her room. Edith was the young woman from the village who had been employed as her wet nurse.

'Oh, Miss Louise. No sparks-a fly … please!'

Louise laughed. 'I promise you.'

Edith's knock on the door could not have been more feeble. She really didn't wish to face Louise. It was only because Crecia pushed her into the room that she was left without any alternative. She stood there with her head bowed, fully anticipating her ladyship's resentful words. Despite Louise's assurance that she wouldn't create an uncomfortable scene, Crecia wanted to leave the room; but her mistress insisted she stay to listen.

'Are things so bad that you can't look at me, Edith?' Louise asked.

Edith eventually raised her head. 'I know your feelings, m'lady. And I truly feel terrible. I don't know what else to say. I'm sorry.'

Louise smiled at her warmly. 'Dear girl, I'm not angry at you! You're merely doing what you were employed to do.'

Edith breathed a huge sigh of relief, and so audibly that Louise couldn't help feel the plight of her situation.

'I'm told you too have a son, Edith? Not much older than baby Edward?'

'Yes, ma'am.'

'And can I enquire who cares for and feeds him whilst you stay here?'

Edith's head dropped down again. 'The poor nurse,' she answered, with acute guilt in her voice.

Edith's situation was typical of that of a single new mother desperate to earn enough money to keep herself and her child out of the workhouse. Often, the mother's only chance of doing this was to deprive her own baby of her milk, and instead offer it to a well-to-do new mother through providing the services of a wet nurse. Such duties would entail boarding at the family's house, whilst the wet nurse's own baby would be cared for elsewhere. If she were lucky, this would be with a member of her own family. If she were unlucky, then she would use a poor nurse or if she were desperate, a baby farmer.

'How much does Lord Ranskill pay you for your services, Edith?'

'Five shillings a week plus board and lodgings, m'lady.'

Louise walked slowly around the room before presenting her solution. A solution that meant both women would come out winners, and there would be only one loser - the Earl of Ranskill. It was a prospect most appealing to Louise. 'Well, ladies. I have a proposition for you,' she stated and began to explain. 'I will pay you another two shillings a week, Edith.'

Crecia's lifted her forehead in surprise and just a hint of jealousy. Until Louise proposed, 'For you, Crecia, a new dress.'

'Sorry, I don't understand, m'lady,' Edith said, 'Pay me extra to do what?'

Louise asked Crecia to fetch her own cloak and bonnet. On the maid's return, she gave her mistress the most confused look, but duly handed them over. In turn, Louise handed them to Edith and told her, 'You should arrange for your son to be brought to the entrance gates each morning and evening. At those times you will wear this cloak and bonnet and, as if you were Crecia, you will make the journey to the gates. I want you then to feed your baby until his belly is full.'

'But, m'lady! … What if I'm found out?'

'Then you'll be dismissed, but you have my word, Edith. I will cover any shortfall in your pay.'

'And you, Miss Louise?' enquired Crecia.

'I simply lock the door and blissfully breast feed my child, the same.'

'It's-a brilliant!' Crecia cried.

'Well?' Louise asked Edith, who looked terribly nervous but excited at the same time. She took a moment longer to think over the plot.

'It is most kind of you, m'lady. Yes, I will do it.'

'Excellent … Right, all we need to do now is find a reason for Dowling to believe you need to go out each morning and evening, Crecia. And for the next six weeks!'

'You leave-a him to me, Miss Louise. I sort-a the penguin.'

~~~

Although Louise's act of rebellion against her father-in-law was clever, crafty, and would prove to be most
~~~

effective, it was still all a game to her. A battle of wills. The earl's and Dr Robertson's plans however, were anything but a game. Their scheming had only one aim: to destroy the young woman.

Robertson calculated carefully how he would crush her. He knew Louise was popular in society circles, respected by the local villagers and clearly admired by the staff – not least by Mr Dowling, who saw Louise as the catalyst for change at Haddington. To bring Louise to her knees, therefore, Robertson would first need to dispel the notion that she was a Lady. She needed to be seen as nothing more than a reckless society gadfly and an unfit wife and mother. The warped doctor had all the necessary means at his disposal to achieve this.

Ranskill was uneasy with his friend's suggestion of where to start. It would mean embarrassment for him and endless gossip: things he could not abide. But he was eventually convinced it was the price he would need to pay. Louise had to be humiliated.

Haddington Hall was rarely the scene of dinner parties. However, to recognise the Warsop Mining Company's successful opening of a new colliery, a lavish celebration was planned. With over fifty guests and dignitaries invited, it was highlighted as the social gathering of the season. Just for a brief moment, the house was transformed back to its glory days, to a time when laughter had radiated from its very foundations.

Louise was stunned by the prospect of the proposed occasion. The mere idea of the family resorting to having fun was almost too much for her to absorb. Her father-in-law would have to wear a smile on his face for the whole evening! Well, that was beyond even her imagination. She wasn't expecting it, so she wasn't surprised that she was never consulted on anything to do with the party, and was left out of even the most mundane of arrangements.

The dinner party, when it came, was indeed a splendid affair. Ranskill saw it as one more opportunity to show his society peers the success of the family business. It was a pity though, that they would also see the strange behaviour of a family member.

After dinner the guests mingled and chatted. Louise was on comfortable ground, sweeping from one conversation to another and always with charm. The less than charming Dr Robertson then made his move, forcing himself beside her as she looked around for her next engagement with a guest.

'A successful evening so far, Lady Warsop,' he said, holding two glasses of champagne.

Louise was surprised, to say the least. His smug face came closer to hers. She wanted nothing more than to hit it, but decided she would play the part. Moving back slightly to avoid his disgusting breath of rich red wine and cigar smoke, she remarked, 'Yes. I have to hand it to the earl. It's a fine soirée.'

'One hears Master Edward develops well under his nurse,' the doctor remarked, wanting to twist the dagger.

'Indeed he does,' Louise said, only half able to conceal her smile.

'And, no doubt, when his nanny is on board, he'll —'

Louise knew this was going to be the next stage in her father-in-law's interfering ways. She was quite prepared and interrupted, 'Oh, Dr Robertson. There will be no nanny, I can assure you of that. Please report that back to his lordship.'

Robertson's eyelid began to flicker as his expression hardened. 'If I may give you some advice, Lady Warsop.'

'If you feel you must.'

'Conformity is invariably the best policy.'

'Or docile obedience is an absolute requirement. Perhaps that is more what you are trying to say, Doctor!'

The hard look on Robertson's face now turned into a snarl. Even with all he intended, he had been prepared to hold out an olive branch. But Louise had no intention of grasping it.

'Very well. I did try,' Robertson said. His body stooped even lower as he muttered further into her ear. 'You would do well to remember which stone you choose to dislodge. For if it falls, it could crush you.'

'And, Doctor, you'll do well to remember, that if you can't be kind, please have the decency to be vague.'

Although their swords had clashed, the doctor was prepared to withdraw, not in defeat, but merely to stand aside and watch Louise fall onto the dagger he had prepared for her. He handed over the glass of champagne and politely bowed his head to signal farewell. 'Lady Louise.'

Thinking she had got the better of him, Louise sipped her drink and made a beeline for her husband, who was talking with Captain Armstrong and his wife. It wasn't long before she had turned the conversation away from military matters and more towards the light-hearted topic of the theatre, much to Mrs Armstrong's relief. Taking another sip of champagne, she indulged the couple with a description of the latest touring show that she and Frederick had recently seen.

Dr Robertson in the meantime had returned to the earl's side and waited for his evil plot to take effect. He was skilful enough to know just how long it would take, and had used just the right amounts of barbiturates and opiates to obtain the desired outcome.

First, Louise began to giggle. She knew she was doing so but couldn't seem to help herself. Next came the most raucous laughter at Frederick's comments, which had no humour in them at all. He glared at her in astonishment, which only brought from her a muffled snigger. Louise then gave a hiccup and laughed again. 'Oops! I dooooo beg your pardon.' By now she had started to sway from side to side. Frederick grabbed hold of her arm.

'Louise! Please! Whatever is the matter with you?' he said, in a tone that could be considered polite yet firm. Captain Armstrong gave a smile of embarrassment. His wife clearly did not know how to react, and just kept looking around at the other guests, who by now, had turned to see where all the hilarity was coming from.

Dr Robertson was beside himself with anticipation. Ranskill simply wished he'd never agreed to his partner's idea of humiliating Louise. He closed his eyes, hoping the scene would be over quickly. It wasn't.

Just as Robertson knew would happen, Louise started to hallucinate. She stared wildly at the different animal tails that began protruding from the vents of the gentlemen's dinner jackets. Again she laughed out loud. Suddenly the faces of the guests began to change into those of animals, like something from *Alice in Wonderland*. She was mesmerised by her fantasy, watching animals dancing outrageously. Breaking away from Frederick's grasp she attempted a dance with Baron Helmsley – the zebra!

The earl was, by now, alternating between acute embarrassment and rage. 'I do apologise!' he kept saying to guests around him.

Eventually, Louise set eyes on her father-in-law. She stood on the open dance floor and broke out into another fit of laughter, pointing and mocking, 'A baboon!' Nobody seemed to know what to do, other than to gasp in amazement.

Grinding his teeth, Ranskill looked over to Robertson. 'Do something!'

Louise's vision suddenly turned sinister as she watched a huge spider coming towards her carrying her baby. Her eyes dilated in fear. 'No! No! Get away from him,' she screamed and ran towards Robertson. Trying to grapple with him, she started to plead with the crowd of onlookers. 'They're trying to take away my baby. My son! They're stealing my son! Help me … Somebody … Please!'

The doctor promptly slapped her hard across the face, shouting, 'Lady Louise!'

She stood there in a trance, holding her face, then turned to Frederick. 'Did you see that, dear? A spider has just hit me.'

Finally, she wobbled and fainted. The cruel first part of Louise's downfall was over.

Chapter 14

Watching Elliott and Tom discussing things in the study was like observing a couple of barristers in court. Back and forth went the questions and answers. However, quite who was acting as the prosecutor and who was the defence was sometimes unclear as they debated social influences on crime. Certainly, Elliott could take the high ground in citing lack of morals and drink as being the root causes of many a downfall. Tom, however, could easily present a good case for conditioning.

What was needed to avert a stalemate was a diversion. It came in the form of a voice from the corridor. 'Hello, Mr Elliott!' And much to the delight of both men, the voice rang out without a croak.

After knocking discreetly, Lily popped her head round the door. 'I hope you don't mind, Mr Elliott, but I used my key to let myself in,' she said.

'Lily! How are you?' cried Elliott, in delight. Although he was genuinely pleased to see her looking well again, he was also unable to disguise the fact that five days without a cook and housemaid was taking its toll.

'You look a whole lot better, Lily, I have to say,' added Tom.

'I am. Very much so, Professor Sharpe. Well, I'll just put my case in my room and then I can make a start with catching up on things,' Lily announced chirpily, before smiling appreciatively to Elliott. 'Thank you for your understanding and, of course, my pay whilst I was off.'

'It was never a thought to do anything different, my dear,' replied Elliott, much to Tom's amusement. He gave Lily a wry smile and a wink. At that, her head disappeared back behind the door, only to reappear seconds later.

'Have you had dinner? Or would you like me to prepare something?'

It was like watching two children opening their presents on Christmas morning. Their expression was full of anticipation. After four consecutive nights of fish and chips, their faces lit up at the prospect of a hearty meal, although their disappointment was soon apparent, as Lily suggested, 'How about if I did you some fish and chips?'

'That would be different, eh, Robert!' Tom joked. Elliott's look was priceless.

~~~

Suitably fed and watered, the two men again retired to Elliott's study. It was a small room but appeared somewhat larger due to the spacious bay window overlooking the
~~~

garden. In the corner was his desk, stacked high with folders and papers, which always appeared to be on the verge of toppling over. When they did, he simply started another pile. Next to the open fire was a large bookcase holding a vast array of books, mainly non-fiction, about court procedure, criminality and probation. Never did they seem to have any logical order to them. However, like any man who practised organised chaos, Elliott could, if asked, immediately lay his hands on a specific book. Over most of the dark parquet wooden floor was a square carpet, and on it stood two armchairs, a coat stand and a sideboard that Ann absolutely forbade her husband to fill with clutter. Hanging on the wall was a much-prized, framed photograph of the first probation officers' conference that Elliott had attended, in London.

Elliott stood by the bay window and lit his pipe. In recognition of Tom's disapproval of the habit, he compromised by opening the top window, which at least allowed some of the billowing smoke to escape. He plunged down into his chair behind the desk.

'Well, Tom! All in all, another eventful day?'

'Sheffield certainly still holds its mysteries, that's for sure,' Tom replied, as he attempted to rearrange the tulips in a vase on the sideboard. But no matter what he did they wouldn't stay upright, and kept drooping. Eventually, he gave in as his friend gave him a strange look.

'Have you quite finished?' quizzed Elliott.

'Sorry!' offered Tom, before deciding to sit in the armchair. 'So, do we go to the police?'

Elliott puffed on his pipe. 'And tell them what, Tom?'

'That we've discovered who Marion is, of course!'

'But we don't know that for certain,' Elliott responded. 'In all probability you're right. But we've only seen a photograph. How do you think it would sound, stating that we've recently met a woman called Marion – though we don't believe that's her real name? And that we believe she might be linked to the mystery at Haddington Hall – though we can't be absolutely sure. Then we end by telling them that we've no idea where she is now.'

Tom immediately jumped in. He held his hands wide open to support his words. 'Remember, we're not the only ones to have seen her. Sergeant Drake and most of the constables in the police station could testify.'

Back came Elliott with a logical reply. 'Again, testify to what? There's no evidence to say she is who we think she is. And besides, this matter was never investigated as a crime, as I recall. It's certainly a very intriguing mystery, Tom. But there's no misdemeanour apparent.'

'Are you saying we just leave it?' Tom huffed, and waited for a response. However, there was a good pause before he got one. Elliott was far too busy concentrating on lifting his thumb on and off the tobacco in the bowl of his pipe, whilst sucking furiously on the mouthpiece, in a desperate attempt to keep the thing lit. Eventually, a cloud of smoke spread out in all directions.

'No. All I'm saying is that we need to be careful how we approach things,' Elliott answered at last.

The two men spent the next ten minutes discussing the ins and outs of the matter, both agreeing it was worth further investigation. Tom, in particular, couldn't stop thinking about Dr Robertson. Whilst there was no real evidence to support his feelings, his sixth sense told him that his old adversary was involved in some way. To try and prove it, he needed to find out more about Robertson's whereabouts and his career after he'd left the Derby Royal Infirmary. As Elliott was busy in court the following day, he decided he would look up an old friend at the hospital who, he was sure, would be able to help him. Meantime, he had an idea to present, 'Perhaps, we should get the press involved.'

The suggestion met with a look of disgust from Elliott. His impression of the press was that they were only one up from a sewer rat. Many a time they had published complete lies about people under his care, in articles intended only to scaremonger. It didn't take any words from Elliott for Tom to deduce his friend's thoughts on the suggestion.

The grandfather clock in the hall suddenly chimed

the hour. Elliott instinctively pulled out his pocket watch to check its accuracy, whilst, right on cue, Lily appeared. 'Would you like me to make you a nightcap, Mr Elliott?'

'Yes, please, Lily. The usual.'

'Professor Sharpe?'

'What have we on offer? Maybe a whisky?'

Lily gave Elliott an uncomfortable look. She knew his thoughts about drink but was conscious that there were bottles of spirits kept for guests. Tom could see her unease. 'Perhaps just a small dash in some hot milk, instead,' he said, not wishing to offend Elliott and feeling it was a compromise.

As they drank, Elliott remarked, 'Well, here's to a goodnight's sleep – if I'm lucky.'

Tom hadn't broached the subject of Elliott's dreams since their conversation at the breakfast table. This, despite the fact that he was aware of Elliott shouting out again in his nightmare the previous night.

'These sudden nightmares, Robert, they concern me.'

Elliott tried to pass them off as nothing but couldn't ignore Tom's insistence they discuss them further.

'Let me try to make sense of them for you.'

'Very well,' Elliott finally agreed. He couldn't see how Tom would be able to help, but was prepared to talk about them further. In truth, he was becoming more and more worried by his nightmares. Always their content was strange and harrowing. And always Canon Brockwell was present.

'Will you let me hypnotise you?' Tom asked, knowing full well what Elliott's response would be.

'Tom. You know I don't go in for all that mumbo jumbo.'

'But I also know, Robert, that you won't talk freely about them with me. Even more so if they contain the sort of thing I think they do. Hypnotising you would simply allow me to talk to your subconscious, that's all.'

Elliott took a deep breath and considered the proposal. In the end, he held up his finger. 'If you promise not to breathe a word of this to anyone. And certainly not to Ann!'

Tom agreed, but had to make a quip. 'That exciting!' He quickly returned his expression to one of seriousness, as he realised Elliott's appreciation of his humour had reached its limit.

As Tom had suspected, his friend was not the easiest of patients to hypnotise. To get him to relax was a task in itself, let alone getting him to study a swinging pocket watch. There was an obvious resistance in Elliott to being taken under – to the point where Tom couldn't see how he was ever going to get him to succumb. Then, at last he saw a brief flicker of Elliott's eyelids so began asking him repeatedly to relax, and to focus only on the watch. Elliott had stopped his cynical remarks. Tom was convinced his friend was nearly there. At last, Elliott's head toppled to one side.

'Tell me about your dreams, Robert,' Tom started.

It seemed to take forever to get an answer and Tom began to wonder if Elliott was actually under his influence or whether he'd just fallen asleep. Then, without warning, Elliott sat upright and gave an apathetic shrug. 'I just go to places. See things … nasty things.'

Suddenly he became frustrated, and his gestures animated. 'Why does he want me to witness these horrors?'

'Who, Robert? Who wants to show you awful things?'

'Canon Brockwell, of course!'

'Is it the cage disaster? Is that where Brockwell takes you?'

Elliott sighed. 'And elsewhere.'

Tom could see Elliott was uneasy and troubled. He allowed him time to settle again before continuing his questions. 'Where else does he take you?'

'You should know. You were there!' Elliott said, then paused. 'You surprise and disappoint me, Tom.' He took another long pause before asking bluntly, 'Why? Why would you do such a thing? You cut the wire. You killed those men.'

Tom was taken aback. The last thing he was expecting was Elliott rounding on him with an accusation of murder. He thought for a moment about how best to handle things. Soon, he was remembering a strange case he'd once witnessed, where a patient of his was convinced that he was always following him, holding a knife, ready to kill him.

'Robert, whatever you're seeing isn't real. It's just your mind that's responding to death.'

Tom suspected Elliott was in a state of guilt about Canon Brockwell; that somehow he felt a responsibility for not being able to prevent his death; that despite what he had learned about the canon's perversions, he felt he should have helped him; or at least allowed him to be brought to justice with dignity. That was Elliott's way. Tom also thought that these feelings must have lain dormant for all this time. Now, something had happened to bring them to the surface, and Elliott was allowing Brockwell to enter and control his subconscious mind, associating loved ones with bizarre situations. He'd certainly seen this type of situation with drug addicts who were hallucinating, but he couldn't understand what acted as the trigger with Elliott.

'These nightmares, Robert, are just a way for you to deal with the horror of Brockwell. He's not there, except in your imagination. You must tell yourself that. Do you understand?'

Elliott opened his eyes and reached over for his pipe. 'Is that it?'

Tom realised that, although it was most unusual without a prompt, Elliott had quite suddenly come out of his hypnotic state. He looked over to his friend and smiled. 'Yes, that's it.'

'Well, have you learnt anything?'

'You can't remember telling me?'

'All I remember is somebody talking softly to me.'

Tom had seldom witnessed such a blasé reaction by someone coming out of hypnosis. Without doubt, this would keep him pondering Elliott's crisis for some time to come.

As the grandfather clock chimed the half hour, the two men bid each other goodnight.

~~~

Elliott was nervous, his hands unusually clammy. Should he read another chapter of his book or lie back and try to get to sleep? He attempted another few pages, but realised he was reading the same paragraphs over and over and not retaining any of the information. Trying to keep his mind occupied, his thoughts turned to the
~~~

problem of Marion. There was much to contemplate. Did she have a past with any of the deceased? If so, was that past turbulent? Maybe she was seeking revenge. Was she in fact mentally ill or just clever at deceiving people and perhaps an accomplice to murder? More importantly, who was the supposed relative who had just turned up and taken her away? With each presumed answer came another question.

Elliott mulled each question over again, trying to find a motive. Coming up with nothing he'd not already considered, he allowed his attention to drift and then focus on the day ahead. It was the day of William Doherty's appearance in the magistrates' court. He knew the proceedings would be brief. Due to the severity of the charge, the case would be referred to the Assize Court. Nevertheless, Elliott was to be called to give an opinion and began to go over in his mind whether he had all the necessary information. Whilst Elliott's assessment of Doherty would be carefully considered by the magistrates, he knew there was no chance it would stop Doherty being committed for trial. Elliott's heart sank at the prospect.

As on the previous nights, he started to perspire and feel woozy. Suddenly, he had trouble focusing his thoughts. Then his eyes closed. All he had feared might happen again when he did eventually fall asleep was about to be realised.

This time, the dream didn't start with him seeing Canon Brockwell in the chair in his study. Instead, Elliott was walking alone down a darkened street. He looked up at the house ahead and started to cross the road. Out of the shadow of a shop doorway came a voice. 'Ah, Robert! I thought you were never going to join me.' Brockwell stepped out into the moonlight. 'Come,' he continued, and held out his hand to lead the way.

Elliott stopped and hesitated as the house came more clearly into view. 'This is the lying-in house. The house Mrs Hart used for —'

'Let's call it entertaining,' Brockwell finished for him.

'Why have you brought me here? I've no desire to see anything in there.'

'Oh, everyone likes to see themselves having fun, Robert.'

'And what exactly do you mean by that?' Elliott hissed.

Brockwell just gave a sickening smile and walked on.

Elliott held his eyes closed for a split second and sighed in exasperation. When he opened them, he was shocked by what he saw – himself, lying naked on a bed, a young woman struggling pitifully underneath him. He turned his head away in shame. Brockwell grabbed hold of his face and forced him to look at his own image.

'See!' Brockwell spat. 'You're no different to any of us. We all succumb to the temptations of a young woman's flesh.'

'No! No!' Elliott cried.

Elliott stared at the image of himself in horror. The young woman begged him to be gentler in his motion.

He tried to move forward, wanting to pull his body off the woman. But it was as though Brockwell had rooted him to the spot. The canon just laughed. 'Evil you,' he chortled.

The door to the bedroom suddenly opened. Two figures entered. Bizarrely, it was Brockwell, accompanied by Ann. Seeing her husband, Ann gasped and held her hand to her mouth in shock. Turning around, she buried her head in Brockwell's shoulder for comfort. Then she fled the room.

'No, Ann! Please, this isn't me,' Elliott shouted. He turned to address Brockwell, 'Please tell her …' But Brockwell was no longer next to him.

'She now sees you for what you are, Robert,' Brockwell said, smugly, from the doorway.

'Why do you do this to me?'

'Like I told you – revenge!'

Elliott stood with tears rolling down his face. The image of himself and the woman on the bed had now gone.

'What should you do now, Robert?' Brockwell mocked, and he held out his hand towards Elliott. In the open palm was a revolver. 'You could always end it here.'

Elliott stared at him, contemplating the possibility.

'You see the dilemma now. Can you ever face your wife again? What will people say? No, I can't believe it. Not Mr Elliott!'

Reaching out his hand, Elliott picked up the revolver.

~~~

Just as on the previous nights, Tom was awakened by the noise. This time, it wasn't Elliott's screams that woke him, but the sound of his continuous sobbing, the haunting sound of a man beside himself with remorse.

He entered Elliott's bedroom and saw the disturbing sight of his friend trembling and holding two fingers against his head. Gently, Tom took hold of Elliott's hand and moved it away from his temple. 'Robert. Just relax,' he said softly.

Tom was anxious. He wanted to wake his friend slowly. In his studies of dreams, he had read of people being awoken dramatically from a nightmare, only to suffer a heart attack at the shock.

Elliott heard only a muffled version of Tom's words. Brockwell's voice was competing to give him instructions.
~~~

'No, listen only to me.'

But Elliott was coming out of his dream cycle of sleep, and Tom's words were becoming the more dominant ones. 'Can you hear me, Robert?'

'Damn you!' blasted Brockwell.

Elliott awoke with a jolt and opened his eyes. It was Tom who was looking at him, but all Elliott could see was an image of Brockwell overlaid on Tom's face. Elliott drew his head back and then launched it forward, headbutting Tom, and immediately rendering him unconscious. Blood began to trickle from his guest's nose, as he lay sprawled on the floor next to Elliott's bed.

Eventually realising what he had done, Elliott got out of bed and attempted to resuscitate his friend. With little space between the bed and the wall, he decided to drag Tom by his arms into the centre of the room. Just then Lily appeared, having been disturbed by the commotion. She looked over in amazement at her master dragging Tom's lifeless body. Elliott, in turn, glanced up at her and was lost for words.

'The church play?' she asked dimly.

What could Elliott do but nod his head in agreement.

Chapter 15

Dr Robertson's first plan had achieved its goal. Talk of Louise's odd behaviour was everywhere. Even the staff couldn't help but begin to think there might be a problem with Louise's mental stability. All gossip was ably stoked by Matilda, who switched wickedly between the concerned aunt and the fork-tongued snake. Articles soon began appearing in the newssheets describing Louise as 'a lady in crisis'. For the earl, it should have been the epitome of embarrassment, but he soon saw the benefit of the outside world casting him as the anxious father-in-law. What better opportunity for him to begin to make decisions on the future of his grandchild than during his daughter-in-law's time of distress.

Louise knew exactly what was happening, and for the first time truly felt the hatred directed towards her. Most women would have buckled from the start; but Louise had a fighting spirit which knew no bounds. What she would need to do, however, was be more on her guard with Robertson. The drugging of her drink made her realise that there were no limits to the depths to which he would stoop to get his own way.

The problem, on the other hand, was that Louise

just could not stop playing the rebel. In many ways she courted her own downfall and played into Ranskill's and Robertson's hands over the following weeks.

Husband Frederick had now taken the path of least resistance, choosing to avoid any discussion with his wife of their ongoing problems. On the rare occasion he did attempt to dictate how things should be, Louise was more than a match for him. Invariably, he would end up getting flustered, banging his fist on the table, only for Louise to bang hers even harder, demanding that he retract any unkind words. He simply couldn't compete with her skill for turning the argument.

The final straw came when the family went to spend a weekend at Wenderley Park, the home of Brigadier Mountford. The occasion, predominately a gathering of the landed gentry and high ranking military men, was to discuss the increasing risk of war in Europe. On the Saturday evening, they were to be honoured by the presence of the Prince of Wales.

The evening had passed off without incident and ended with dancing, where Louise showed her talents in the ballroom, much to the dismay of her father-in-law and Dr Robertson, who seemed to have been tagged onto the Haddington party as an afterthought. Louise was unexpectedly approached by the Prince. He stood before her, held out his arm and addressed Frederick.

'Lord Warsop will forgive me if his charming wife favours me with a waltz.'

Frederick gave his bow of acceptance and placed Louise's gloved hand on the Prince's arm. 'Your Royal Highness,' he said and bowed even lower.

The earl was plunged into more resentment as Louise gave him a gleeful smile. He leant towards Robertson to remark, 'Playing to the gallery like some bold as brass actress. There is a limit to my patience, Anthony.'

On the dance floor, the effervescent Louise soon had the Prince smiling.

'So, Lady Warsop. How are things up in Yorkshire? As cold as one remembers?' the Prince enquired.

'Are we talking about the weather or the family, sir?' Louise jovially asked in return.

It wasn't long before the men retired to the library for brandy and liqueurs, whilst the ladies finished the evening chatting in one of the many lounges. At the prospect of being drawn into a dreaded game of cards, Louise made her exit under the pretence of an oncoming migraine. At least back in her room she could call on Crecia to have a normal conversation with her.

Some forty minutes later, Louise was brushing her hair by the dressing table when Frederick returned, looking once more like a whipped dog. He didn't say anything, just fumbled as he removed his ceremonial sword. Finally, he pulled at the fingers of his white gloves and threw them onto the bed.

'Should I assume from that there is something wrong, my dear?' asked Louise very calmly, whilst continuing to arrange her appearance in the mirror.

'Yet again, it appears we are in disgrace.'

'Oh, is that all? I thought it must be more serious.'

Frederick began unbuttoning his tunic and getting undressed. 'It would help matters if you weren't so gregarious, Louise.'

'So that's it. Father is displeased because the Prince did me the honour of inviting me to dance with him. Well! Had he been wearing a ball gown, he too might have been favoured!'

Struggling to remove his boots, Frederick gave the look of disapproval he usually assumed when his wife became flippant. But Louise wasn't finished with her comments. 'Sorry, I forgot. There is no levity where father is concerned.'

'Please, Louise, let's not quarrel. I've had enough arguing for one day,' replied the forlorn Frederick.

'You need to stand up to him. It isn't right. It's unjust!'

'Father is just, well … father.'

'And father is not happy unless he is rendering others unhappy!'

Louise sighed in exasperation. She watched her

husband stumble around the bed wrestling with his boot. 'Oh Frederick, did you never once disobey him? Would you not, for just one time, like to play the mischievous son, the black sheep? Give him a run for his money?'

Frederick, now dressed only in his long johns, stood there, perplexed at her suggestion. 'You really don't have the slightest idea, do you?'

Louise stood and picked up his sword. She held it towards him. 'Here! Leave it outside on the landing - all night!'

'Are you raving mad? I am an army officer. My sword is sacred. To lose one's sword would wreck one's career,' Frederick replied, in his most serious tone.

'Then if you won't do it, I shall.'

She opened the door and placed the sword on the landing.

An astonished Frederick immediately went towards the door, intent on retrieving it. Louise blocked his way and playfully teased him. 'It will be most safe, I'm sure.'

'Louise, don't be foolish. Let me pass.'

'But think, Frederick. Not only to defy father, but also to flout army regulations! Does your hand not sweat at the thought? Come, let me feel your heart beating in anticipation.'

'You are quite mad!' said Frederick, before finally losing patience. 'I really can't see the humour in your antics.'

'Oh dear, so glum … Very well, let no woman come between a man and his beloved sword.' She stood aside and opened the door to allow him onto the landing.

Behind him Frederick heard the door click shut, and then the alarming sound of the key turning. He went white with dread, knowing exactly what childish games his wife was capable of. Hastily he retrieved his sword and tried the door. Sure enough, it was locked.

'Louise, what on earth are you doing? Open up, this instance.' In desperation, he furiously rattled at the handle. 'Louise, Louise! Open this door.'

'Do you promise to leave your sword?' Louise shouted, as their conversation continued on either side of the locked door.

'This is preposterous. For heaven's sake, I'm in my under garments. If anyone were to see me!'

'Yes, I dare say they would giggle.'

'Will you open the door?'

Louise was suddenly having fun with the whole episode. She teased him further by offering a way out of his predicament. 'Tell me you love me first.'

Frederick snapped back, 'This is no time for the frivolities of the bedroom.' He paused before attempting, 'You will open the door and I, in return, will agree to forget your little game.'

'My dear, you are in no position to negotiate … Tell

me you love me!'

'I will do no such thing.'

'Then the door will stay firmly bolted until you do.'

'Louise, I warn you. I shall break the door down.'

She laughed. 'And risk an inquiry from the Brigadier. So, you do have some mischievous spirit, after all.'

Frederick took a moment to think about the situation. It was obvious that Louise wasn't going to relent without him playing her little game. If his panic was to end, he needed to succumb. He cleared his throat and mumbled, 'Very well. I love you.'

Louise heard him well enough but was quite unreasonable in prolonging his agony. 'I'm sorry, my dear. I didn't quite hear you.'

Closing his eyes in desperation, he shouted, 'I said I love you. Do you hear? I love you!'

What Frederick hadn't realised was that three men had rounded the corner of the landing and were standing in surprise, watching a man dressed only in his long johns, holding a sword and talking to the door. Brigadier Mountford let out a polite cough. Frederick spun round in shock. In front of him, accompanying the brigadier, were his father and Dr Robertson. If ever a hole were to appear and swallow him up, now would have been a good time.

'A budding thespian amongst the family, George,'

chuckled the brigadier, before politely walking on with Robertson, leaving the earl to deal with the situation.

Ranskill, alarmed at seeing his son in such embarrassing circumstances, could barely speak.

Frederick tried explaining, 'It's just Louise having a bit of fun, father.'

With a face like thunder, his father simply stated, 'Bring that woman to heel, Frederick, or I swear I will disinherit you from Haddington!'

~~~

There was nothing jovial about the long train journey back to Yorkshire. It was over three hours of stony silence inside the carriage. The tense atmosphere could be cut with a knife. Every so often, Ranskill would lower his newspaper, glare disapprovingly towards Louise, and then snap his paper back in front of his face. Louise knew her antics had gone a step too far for her father-in-law, but she was really past caring. Occasionally, she decided to add fuel to the fire by looking up from her magazine and smiling demurely at Dr Robertson. He never returned the gesture. His thoughts were now intensely concentrated on the next phase of his plans – her alienation.

Finally, back at Haddington, she walked in the
~~~

gardens with Crecia, who pushed baby Edward in his pram.

'Miss Louise, I worry for you!' her maid began. 'I see only hate in their eyes. You must be careful. They plot more and more against you,' she added, and looked up to the window where Ranskill and his partner peered down at them.

'I'm well aware of their intent, Crecia. But as long as I have baby, I am safe,' replied Louise, although, for the first time, Crecia could sense anxiety in her mistress's voice. Frederick was due to return to his regiment in a couple of days' time. And whilst he was no real help in protecting his wife from the coldness of the family, at least his presence shielded her from the barrage of caustic words that was likely to erupt once he was gone. Louise knew it would soon be open warfare again. Constantly watching over her shoulder was gradually wearing her down.

Walking across the lawn towards the summer house, the two women were greeted by David, who was returning from a walk across the meadow. Louise's face lit up. Apart from Crecia, he was the only one she could trust, and she looked forward to the times when they could talk openly with each other.

'Ladies,' he said, tipping his hat.

David, like his brother, was very handsome.

Standing six foot tall, he looked every bit the dashing aristocrat. However, there was never anything snobbish or conceited about David. At just turned eighteen, he was the most reasonable, thoughtful, caring, and above all, trusting individual. Louise found it hard to believe that somebody so tender could originate from a man so cold and horrible.

Crecia quickly felt she was in the way and tactfully suggested she return to the house with baby Edward.

'I hope I wasn't intruding,' said David, gently.

'Not at all,' Louise replied. She slipped her arm through David's. 'Come, let's walk a while. Let me tell you all about the weekend at Wenderley Park.'

'So, was the secret military gathering exciting?' he said, mocking the establishment.

'I'd describe it as eventful. But I dare say your brother and father might choose a different word!' Louise smiled, and with the flush of innocence she'd mastered so well.

'Louise, I dare not even ask!'

Ten minutes of her recounting the tale left David with tears of laughter rolling down his face. He loved the spirit of his sister-in-law and could only imagine how much his father would have disapproved.

'Oh, David. Who is going to laugh with me when you return to your posting?'

'Please, don't remind me,' he responded, turning

serious. 'I hate the Army.'

As was the tradition in the family, David had been thrust into the military as soon as he was old enough. But he was the most unsuitable soldier and had proved a great challenge for his training officers. Whilst David was athletic, brave and hardworking, he constantly confronted conformity and brought upon himself many a trivial charge for insubordination. The army though, had taught him a sound knowledge of mechanical engineering. There were two things David was passionate about: firstly playing the violin, which he'd studied from an early age, and secondly engineering, which he excelled at.

Louise had long suspected David's sexual preference might not be for women. Not that he was in any way effeminate. In fact, there had never been a hint of him being that way inclined, in all the conversations she had had with him. Also, it was never a thought offered by her husband. But Louise had a sixth sense and felt now was the right time to confirm if her suspicions were correct.

'David, may I ask you something?' She pulled her arm more tightly into his. 'It is rather personal and I don't really want to pry but —'

'Yes I am,' David interrupted. He smiled sweetly at her. 'Well, that is what you wanted to know, isn't it? Whether I'm homosexual?'

'Well … yes, it was actually,' admitted Louise.

'Does the fact offend you?'

Louise pulled up and looked at him with surprise. She was not perturbed at all that David might have such preferences, for she had met many homosexuals during her time living amongst students in Europe and had enjoyed their company.

'No, I'm not offended. What relationships you have are your private affair. As long as you are happy, then it doesn't matter to me in the slightest,' insisted Louise.

David gave her a peck on her cheek in appreciation of her understanding. 'So now you can see my battle ahead with father?'

'Does he have to know? You know the consequences.'

'I won't live a lie just to please father.'

She took a sharp gulp of breath and let out a loud sigh in anticipation of the fallout of that conversation.

'I'm not afraid to confront him with things,' insisted David.

Again, Louise took another deep breath. 'Then could you do it on a day when I'm out in the village?' she playfully asked.

In the meantime, she was pleased that she had him as a friend, an ally and a confidant.

'You know your father and Robertson want me out of the family.'

David took a moment to respond. Eventually, he

pushed his flowing dark silky hair up and away from his forehead. 'Yes, I fear you're right.' Then, unusually for him he started to get quite angry. 'Why doesn't Frederick do something? He should stand up to them.'

She stopped, and cupped his face in her hand. 'Bless you. But I think we both know that isn't going to happen.'

'They cannot be allowed to get away with it. You must always tell me things, Louise. Let me help you.'

She gave him one of her appreciative smiles, full of sweetness, and they turned around and headed back to the hall. Once again she slipped her arm through his. 'Don't you worry for me. I will be absolutely fine.' Deep down, they both knew that was wishful thinking.

Suddenly, David started the strangest conversation about Germany and how he admired many of the German people's ideals. In turn, he described with frustration his disillusionment with the British government, especially its failure to take seriously the rising tensions in the Balkans.

'Quite an opinion,' Louise stated. 'And is this your view, or merely what you read?'

'Through reading, but also through talking to Kurt.'

Louise couldn't help wondering just what sort of partner her brother-in-law would choose. Would he be as handsome as David? As caring and sensitive? The endless images rolled over in her mind. However, Kurt was not

David's lover, as she thought. Kurt Mueller was a man whom she would discover was very much a heterosexual, a charmer and, equally, a very dangerous man.

Finally the pair arrived back at the entrance to the hall, only to find Dowling hurriedly trying to make his way over the gravel forecourt towards the rear of the building. He carried a bundle, wrapped in a sheet.

'Dowling!' Louise called out.

The butler had no alternative but to stop.

'You seem in a rush.' She then saw the bundle in his hands. 'What are you carrying?'

'I'd prefer you didn't see, Lady Warsop.'

'Dowling, I insist you show me.'

Hesitantly he opened the blanket. 'I was hoping I could clear things away before you came back.' From inside the sheet he revealed the mutilated carcass of Millie, her dog.

Louise gasped in horror. Then she buried her head in David's shoulder and began to sob.

'A fox?' David asked.

'Oh, this was no fox, sir. That much I know. These are the deliberate slashes of a knife.'

Louise lifted up her head and turned to look at Dowling, then upward to the window, where she knew somebody would be looking down. That somebody was Dr Robertson.

Chapter 16

When presented with an interesting mystery, Tom often became obsessed by it. Certainly, if the puzzle had been anything medical, it wouldn't have taken him long before he had found a logical explanation for things. So, although playing the detective was something altogether different, he decided to use the same principles as in his medical problem-solving: firstly understand the symptoms; then systematically work through the possible root causes and discount those that didn't fit. He knew the symptoms all right – a society lady had gone missing, and had now been discovered, seemingly mentally ill. The question was simply: why? What had happened to her?

First he needed to learn more about the circumstances behind her disappearance from Haddington Hall. Surely this would have been reported extensively in the newspapers. The city library was the practical place to go and find out. Tom requested an armful of printed matter from the archives and, sitting at a large reading table, began trawling through it.

One after another, the newspapers all told the same story: *Lady goes missing under mysterious circumstances*. What fascinated Tom was the gossip about why this might have happened. The common picture seemed to be one of a lady in crisis, possibly as a result of drug abuse, unhappiness, an affair or some other scandal. But nothing he read seemed to have much substance behind it and, as Elliott had previously stated, there was never any mention of a crime being committed. He carried on studying the papers, although he was becoming a little bored with reading the same facts dressed up in different ways. Putting a newspaper down on the table, he squeezed his tired eyes with forefinger and thumb.

Trying to focus once more, he looked down across the endless columns until, just when he was on the verge of calling it a day, his eyes caught sight of the words: *Dr Robertson*. This was the single thing he had been looking for. Tom drew his chair further into the desk and leant over eagerly to read on. The allusion was short but it proved a link with Robertson.

'Dr Robertson, a physician to Haddington, had earlier that evening reportedly administered a sedative in an attempt to calm her ...'

He jotted down the page number, newspaper name and date on his small notepad and approached the librarian on the desk. 'Thank you very much for your help, my dear. I hope you don't mind if I leave them there,' he said, pointing back towards the reading desk. 'It's just I have a train I must catch.'

The woman behind the desk looked beyond Tom to the pile of papers strewn everywhere on the table, then gave him an unimpressed glare. He attempted an innocent smile in return, but the woman was having none of it.

'Sorry!' Tom gestured, and dashed to the door.

He had completely underestimated the time he would need to get to the railway station to catch his train to Derby, and ended up running the last fifty yards of the journey like a man possessed. He made it with literally seconds to spare. As the train pulled out of the station, he threw himself down on a seat in a compartment and attempted to regain his breath.

Derby was an hour's journey from Sheffield, but the route passed through some lovely scenery, and Tom sat in a window seat taking in its beauty. He drifted in and out of daydreaming until, in what seemed no time at all, the train was pulling into the city's station. As with Sheffield station, nothing appeared to have changed since he was last in Derby. He had no trouble remembering where the taxis queued up.

'The Royal Infirmary, if you would please, young man,' Tom instructed the driver, who was leaning out of his window and drawing on a cigarette stub which was barely visible between his fingers.

'Of course, mi duck. Jump in,' replied the driver,

and flicked the tiny white butt a good five yards into the distance. No matter how much Tom tried to understand the local speech, he found a man referring to another man as 'Mi duck', quite strange, but nevertheless, humorous.

'It's refreshing to see a young man who hasn't been conscripted yet,' Tom casually commented, as he positioned himself on the rear seat. It was only when he looked up and saw the young man's face in his rear view mirror that he realised how inappropriate his words were. The left side of the face was terribly scarred. The man attempted a smile.

'I'm so sorry. How stupid of me not to think …,' Tom said. Through his experience of seeing such injuries, he realised that the young man must have been retired from service, most probably after suffering horrific shrapnel wounds from a grenade. He wished he could rewind time a few seconds and start his conversation again.

'No problem, sir. You weren't to know,' replied the ever cheerful driver. 'Me getting Jerry's lot, saves someone else.'

Tom gave him an apologetic smile and sat back in admiration of the man's philosophical approach to his tragedy. On alighting from the cab, he gave a sizable tip. 'Keep the change, please, with my best wishes.'

The driver looked down at the coin in his hand and said chirpily, 'That's most kind of you, sir!'

Entering the hospital's administration building immediately brought back memories of his time spent there. They weren't particularly happy memories: those were reserved for his days practising as a surgeon in Sheffield. Perhaps it was also due to the fact that the place instantly reminded him of Dr Robertson. He recalled that here, in this very area, the pair had rowed terribly.

His thoughts were broken by the voice of his old friend and member of the Board of Governors, Dr Richard Johnstone. 'Tom, my dear fellow. How are you?' called the doctor, holding out his hand.

Tom smiled and grasped the hand. 'Richard! It's good to see you again.'

Having not seen each other for over three years, the two had much catching up to do. They stood talking for a while, before the doctor offered Tom the more comfortable option of chatting in his office.

Eventually, after discussing just about every other topic, Tom broached with his friend the real purpose of his visit. He decided not to go into too much detail, just in case his theories were way off the mark. He felt it would perhaps be better for him to simply mention the news of Dr Robertson's death and suggest that, in order to help a friend with a financial matter, he needed to know what became of the doctor after he left Derby.

Dr Johnstone, however, was no fool. He remembered

quite distinctly the way the two had behaved towards each other. There had to be more to it than this. 'Oh, come now, Tom. You're going to have to come up with something better than that!'

Tom sat back in his chair. He was never any good at lying. 'Very well, Richard.' He took a pause before explaining his true concerns.

Dr Johnstone listened patiently to Tom's ideas before asking the most logical question, 'And you think Robertson was involved in her disappearance?'

'That's just it. I don't know. It's a sixth sense. A theory I can't get out of my head. But you remember him, Richard. You know, more than most, just what he was capable of.'

The doctor, who had been Chairman of the Board at the time of Robertson's hearing, couldn't disagree. 'All right. How can I help?'

One thing that seemed clear to both men was that Robertson wouldn't easily have found work in another hospital, and certainly not as a surgeon. At best, he could have set up as a general practitioner somewhere, but even this wouldn't have been easy. Unless, of course, he practised in the dark underworld, outside of any regulatory control. More likely, thought Dr Johnstone, that Robertson had ties somehow with the Earl of Ranskill, as Tom seemed to be suggesting. Though quite what these ties would be, he couldn't think.

Tom's friend's surmise was quite accurate. For Robertson's and Ranskill's history went back a long way.

During his time serving in Africa, Ranskill had suffered an accidental bayonet blow to the back of his knee. The severe wound left his tendons damaged, and when the wound healed, he continued to be plagued by excruciating pain. On his return to England, he sought the view of a consultant surgeon and was told that it was highly unlikely that surgery would cure the problem. In fact, the opinion was that operating could do even more damage, and might even lead to him losing the use of his leg. Ultimately, the consultant refused to take the risk. However, a young doctor training under him at the time saw things quite differently. The doctor was none other than Anthony Robertson.

Robertson boldly made contact with the earl and requested a meeting to offer his theory and, more importantly, the opportunity for an operation. Now suffering daily agony, Ranskill finally made his choice and went under Robertson's knife in an out-of-the-way surgery known to the young doctor. The operation was a total success. As a consequence, an unlikely friendship was formed, and the young doctor was asked to advise on medical matters for the earl's new mining company.

Although Robertson had become a respected

surgeon in York, he finally settled in Derby in 1908. Throughout his career, he maintained his friendship with the earl and continued to advise him on changing medical legislation. Ranskill was very impressed by his friend's aptitude for business, including his ruthless ability to save money. To exploit this skill further, Ranskill offered Robertson a non-executive position on his board of directors. After Robertson's dismissal from the Derby Royal Infirmary, the disappointed surgeon decided to concentrate his efforts on business and was soon rewarded with being made the Warsop Mining Company's Director of Operations. But, more important to the earl, was that the man had skills in other areas that he had every intention of utilising.

Tom was eager to learn of Robertson's past and candidly asked his friend about where Robertson had worked prior to arriving at Derby.

'I can't honestly remember without looking at his notes,' admitted Dr Johnstone.

It was inevitable that Tom would raise his eyebrows in anticipation of finding out.

'Tom!' started Dr Johnstone, '… if I let you look at his file, you must give me your word that any information you use will never have come from me or this hospital.'

Tom smiled appreciatively. 'You have my word, Richard.'

Reading the file, it didn't come as much of a surprise

to Tom when he discovered that Robertson had initially trained in psychiatric medicine and started his career working in drug therapy at Rosterhay Asylum, near York.

~~~

Conscious that he needed to take the 4.38 train back to Sheffield, Tom kept secretly checking his pocket watch whilst talking to Dr Johnstone. Eventually, he stood up, gave his friend a firm handshake, said his farewells and set off towards the hospital entrance. Looking at the time on the large clock in the foyer, he realised that it must be wrong. Then he had the disturbing thought that perhaps it was his timepiece that was running slow. Fumbling for the watch and not really looking where he was going, he bumped into a man. The small box of photographs the man was carrying tipped all over the floor.

'I'm so sorry. I simply wasn't looking where I was heading,' said an embarrassed Tom, and he bent down to help collect the photographs together.

'It's all right, sir. Accidents happen. Don't worry, I can manage.' Just then the man realised who had bumped into him. 'It's Mr Sharpe, isn't it?'

Tom looked up. Whilst he never forgot a face, he was hopeless with names. 'I recognise the face but please forgive me …'
~~~

'I used to attend your lectures when you were surgeon here, Mr Sharpe,' the young man offered.

Tom studied the man's face hard. Eventually he began to place him. He wagged his finger. 'Paul …? No, Peter …?'

'Peter Robertson, sir,' said the man, putting Tom out of his misery. It was the young doctor who had visited Mrs Beaumont in Belper, enquiring about photographs for his archive project.

'Of course! I remember you. Well, how did you do?' Tom asked.

'Oh, I passed last year, Mr Sharpe. Now a fully qualified doctor.'

'Good for you,' replied Tom, continuing to pick up the photos. He stopped and studied one.

'They're for an archive project I'm doing,' explained the young doctor.

'I see.' Tom flicked through a few more of the photos. Again, he stopped and studied one. 'Mrs Beaumont. Goodness me, this takes me back. I wonder how she's doing?'

'Very well, sir. It was she who loaned me all these. She's retired now and lives in Belper.'

Tom would have been happy to continue the conversation but was more interested in the correct time. 'What time do you make it, Doctor?'

'4 o'clock, Mr Sharpe.'

It was as Tom feared: his pocket watch was running slow. Now he needed to find a taxi quickly.

'I'm sorry but I must rush for a train. Please remember me to Mrs Beaumont when you see her again, won't you, Doctor,' Tom said, by now halfway out of the main entrance doors.

The 4.38 train was packed almost to capacity. Tom wandered up and down the corridor looking inside each of the compartments in the hope of finding a seat. Eventually, he came across one, which was occupied on one side by three businessmen. On the other side, an elderly lady was sitting by the door and a soldier in uniform had taken the middle seat. Tom made his way in and took the seat by the window. He leant his arm against the glass and rested his head on his hand, relieved at being able to sit down at last. By now, the train had reached its first destination, Belper.

Shortly after pulling out of the station, the carriage door opened and in walked the guard, requesting tickets. Each passenger handed their ticket over for checking and clipping. Tom fumbled through his jacket pockets, trying to remember where he'd put his. Eventually, he found it, hidden between a small stack of folded papers, and handed it over to the guard, trying to steady himself as the train slowed and rumbled over the cross rails of the sidings. Looking out of the window, Tom couldn't believe his eyes. He'd only been talking about her no more than an hour earlier, and now there she was, standing at the railway crossing. What was even more bewildering was the person she had with her. 'Mrs Beaumont! … Marion!' Tom shrieked.

As usual, the women were taking their afternoon stroll and had stopped to watch the train pass by, before continuing on over to the meadow.

The women looked up to see Tom half standing with his hands placed on the window. He then stood upright and insisted, 'I need to get off.'

'I'm sorry, sir, but we've passed the station. The next stop will be Chesterfield,' the guard tried to explain, as the train began to pick up speed again.

Tom began to clamber over the outstretched feet. 'No, you don't understand. I need to find two women I've just seen out there.'

His pleading brought only a sarcastic remark from the soldier, 'Yeah, you and me both, mister.'

Tom begged, 'Please! Let me off.'

The guard prepared himself for a scene. 'Please, sit back down, sir. No one can alight now until Chesterfield,' he insisted.

Unusually for Tom, he began to let his emotions get the better of him. Stupidly, he pulled at the emergency cord. Within seconds, the train was screeching to a halt. Bodies lunged backwards and forwards. The guard clung desperately to the luggage rail. Tom stumbled over the soldier's feet and fell in front of him. A kit bag suddenly tumbled from the rack above and caught its owner on the back of his neck.

'You idiot!' shouted the angry soldier, looking at Tom, who was kneeling before him. He pulled back his fist and then let it fly. Tom flopped. In the space of less than twenty-four hours he was out cold once more.

<div align="center">~~~</div>

Elliott looked at his watch again and began to wonder where Tom had got to. It was now gone eight o'clock and he could have sworn that his friend had said he would be back around seven. Elliott shrugged and decided the delay was most probably caused by some sort of technical fault on the line. But as nine o'clock approached, his curiosity was beginning to turn to concern. Then the phone rang.

'Oh, hello, Mr Elliott. It's Sergeant Drake from the station. I'm sorry to disturb you at this hour but ...'

Elliott was surprised to hear Drakes's voice. Very rarely was he called upon at nighttimes. He assumed the sergeant needed something urgently. 'Yes, Sergeant. What is it?'

'I'm afraid to tell you that I have Professor Sharpe in custody,' said Drake, with just a hint of smugness in his voice.

Elliott didn't wait for an explanation; instead, he simply stated, 'I'll be right down.'

When Elliott arrived at the station, Drake began describing to him how Tom had been held in the guard's carriage until the train arrived back at Sheffield. Then, he had been handed over to the police. The constable had charged him with improper use of the train's emergency communication chord and, consequently, Tom was brought into custody.

Elliott was shocked to hear the news and knew the penalty for Tom could be a hefty fine and a magistrates' court appearance. 'Very well! Open his cell. Let me have a chat with him,' he requested of the sergeant.

Drake obliged, clearly enjoying the predicament the professor found himself in. Not to mention the fact that it wasn't very often he could say that he had got the upper hand of Elliott.

Nursing a swollen lip and cheek, Tom looked up at Elliott and gave an apologetic shrug of his shoulders. Once Drake had disappeared, he began explaining the day's events and finally the train incident.

'I'm so sorry, Robert. It was just a moment of madness. I don't know what came over me,' Tom concluded.

Elliott had listened attentively. He stood up and let out a sigh. 'You are aware that this could mean you having to go to court?'

'Yes. And if that's what comes of it all, then I only have myself to blame.'

Pinching his fingers across his top lip, Elliott deliberated. 'Right. We'll have a word with Sergeant Drake,' he said at last. 'Let me do the talking, Tom.'

Drake strutted back into the cell on being asked by Elliott.

'Sergeant Drake, Professor Sharpe has clearly acted foolishly and is most sorry. So much so that he intends to write to the railway company with his apology and offer to make a donation of two pounds to the company's benevolent fund. Then I believe that should be the end of the matter.'

Tom's eyes opened wide in surprise at the amount suggested, but he carried on playing the regretful detainee when he saw Elliott's stern look.

'Oh, I'm not sure that would be possible, Mr Elliott,' replied a gleeful Drake, who knew the law in such circumstances and, moreover, always relished it when the middle classes got a taste of justice. Elliott also knew that Drake had the authority to drop the charge if he wanted to. The sergeant just needed some encouragement.

'On being questioned by the magistrate, Professor

Sharpe, I trust you will be mentioning your treatment whilst here in custody,' Elliott announced, and moved towards Tom, before studying his swollen lip. 'Quite a blow, Professor.'

Drake immediately puffed out his chest. 'Now wait just a minute, Mr Elliott. Are you suggesting that …'

'I'm not suggesting anything, Sergeant Drake. I'm merely thinking that if you do elect to press charges and I'm called to give an opinion, then I can only mention my observations and recount what the professor here tells me,' replied Elliott with skilful ease.

'But it's a downright lie, and the professor knows it!'

Elliott shrugged his shoulders with indifference. 'When the professor's before the bench, I do hope, for your sake, Sergeant, it isn't chaired by Mr Braithwaite. However, I suspect it will be. It was he whom you upset when in court last time, was it not?'

Drake remembered the incident very well and didn't wish to be reminded of his contempt of court episode. 'I suppose your proposal is a fair compromise. And, really, who needs all the paperwork, eh?' he suggested, knowing that, once again, the probation officer had thwarted him.

At the charging desk, Drake got Tom to sign for the return of his possessions and handed him back his wallet, a bag of small change, his notepad, and a tongue depressor.

'Thank you, Sergeant Drake, for your understanding,' offered Tom.

'Goodnight gentlemen,' replied a resigned Drake, before accompanying them to the door.

Chapter 17

With every passing week, Louise felt her alienation more and more. Whilst she had baby Edward to dote on, Crecia to talk to about the pettiness of her squabbles with the family, and David to confide her concerns in, she longed, simply, to feel truly loved. Or perhaps, more accurately, to feel the act of love again. There was a void in her life that began to consume her every thought. As she lay in bed at night, she wondered just where her life was heading. As much as she felt she could fight against the cruelty of her father-in-law and Dr Robertson, she asked herself what would ever change? Did she want to stay in a life of continual coldness, waiting for Frederick to return occasionally, exercise his matrimonial rights, and leave again, with her likely pregnant with another child, maybe two? She needed more, resolved to have more, but couldn't see where it would come from. That was until one morning, when a meeting would totally change her life.

Coming down the grand stairs looking for Dowling, Louise was startled by the sudden opening of the double entrance doors. She stopped and watched as the earl, Robertson and a rather strangely dressed man entered the hall, followed just behind by David. As was usual, her father-in-law simply ignored her, whilst Robertson gave her a hostile glare, a look which Louise now always felt was a precursor to his planning something horrible for her. The strange man, on the other hand, stared at her with fascination. Who, she wondered, was this stranger who was allowing his eyes to consume her from head to foot.

'Ah, Louise! Allow me to introduce you to Kurt Mueller,' announced the friendly voice of David.

At this, Ranskill finally looked up towards Louise, gave a guffaw, and carried on walking with Robertson to the study, leaving David and Mueller to follow.

'Kurt, this is my sister-in-law, Louise,' announced David.

Gliding down the stairs and holding out her arm, Louise welcomed the visitor. 'Pleased to meet you, Mr Mueller.'

His piercing blue eyes never strayed from hers. He clicked his heels together and taking her outstretched hand, he bowed courteously. 'Lady Warsop,' he said, in his clipped German accent.

'Mr Mueller is the engineer in charge of sinking the new pit shaft. He's from Germany,' continued David.

'So I can hear,' pronounced Louise, before greeting him in his native tongue. 'Guten Morgen, Herr Mueller. Wie geht es Ihnen?'

'Danke, gut … You speak German well, Lady Warsop,' Mueller replied.

Before Louise could respond further, Dowling appeared and stated, 'His lordship informs me there are some things to bring in from the car, Mr Mueller.'

'Yes, of course. I will show you,' answered Mueller.

With the German guest outside, Louise wasted no time in giving her opinion to David. 'Absolutely ravishing! He's quite a catch, dear David,' she whispered.

David began to laugh. 'No, no, Louise. You misunderstand. He's merely the one I told you about – the one who tells me all about his homeland.' He sighed in playful disappointment. 'So handsome though, I have to agree. But alas, a man with an eye firmly for the ladies.'

'I see,' said Louise, watching Kurt and Dowling come back towards them. She gave Kurt her best smile and remarked, 'It looks cold out.'

Mueller lifted his eyebrows and gave her a fleeting smile, forcing the dimples to appear in his cheeks. It was an expression that he used well, and which had charmed many a woman into his bed. 'Is it not always cold in England, Lady Warsop?'

'Oh, please, do call me Louise,' she replied, completely charmed.

'Father has arranged for Kurt to stay at Haddington for a while,' David explained.

'Has he indeed! Well, I look forward to talking with you again, Mr Mueller. David tells me that you have fascinating stories to tell of your country's culture. I spent some time studying in Berlin myself. Perhaps we could share our experiences.'

It was an innocent enough statement, but an astute listener might have picked up a double entendre.

Seeing Dowling clearly struggling to support the many maps and plans in his arms, Louise suggested, 'Well gentlemen, please don't let me intrude further if you have a meeting.'

As the men walked towards the study, Louise couldn't take her eyes off Kurt. Everything about him intrigued her. She flushed with excitement at the idea of their meeting again. Kurt turned back, again gave that fleeting smile, and then continued staring at her for a few seconds as he walked on. All the while, Louise felt he was undressing her in his imagination. She drew her hand across her breasts, as if to protect her modesty. But there was nothing reserved about what they both really wanted from each other.

~~~

In the study, Ranskill handed a whisky to Robertson and then began pacing the floor, as he invariably did when he
~~~

was concerned.

'Something is on your mind, George. I can tell,' remarked Robertson, placing himself in a chesterfield wingback chair.

The earl seemed not to be listening, but rather to be looking out of the window, over the vast garden. He was, however, merely pulling together his thoughts before answering. Eventually, he turned to address his friend. 'Mueller. I'm not sure I trust him, Anthony.'

'Because he's German? Or because you don't think he's up to the job?'

Ranskill threw back his drink in one gulp. 'Oh, there's no man finer at sinking a mineshaft, on time and on budget. That much I'm certain of. No, it's where he's from.'

'Oh, come now. When have we ever let national sentiment interfere with business?'

'You know his men's anti-English feelings. They could be doing anything down that shaft. I'm hearing things from the men at Treeton, Anthony. Things I'm not comfortable with.'

Robertson leant forward and clasped both hands around his glass. 'You're thinking they could be planning some sort of sabotage. Is that it?'

'It's feasible!'

'Granted,' acknowledged Robertson. 'But you're

forgetting that we have David's talent for engineering. Why do you think I wanted him involved in the project with Mueller? He'll be able to sniff out if there's anything wrong with the design and the brickwork. We just need to delay his military activity for a while and have him working on site.'

Ranskill let out a sigh. 'It may not be that easy.'

'That's your department, George!'

'David and Mueller. Where have they got to?' Ranskill wondered aloud, whilst beginning to clear enough space on the desk for the technical plans.

'Still talking with your ever delightful daughter-in-law, no doubt.'

'Yes, no doubt,' replied Ranskill in a contemptuous tone. 'Speaking of her, how are things in your department?'

Robertson just gave a devious and chilling smile.

~~~

'Oh, Crecia, I swear I felt disrobed in seconds. I can't even bring myself to imagine how he would touch me,' swooned Louise, as she flopped onto her bed like a smitten schoolgirl. Crecia raised her eyebrows at the thought, but knew her mistress well. She knew that it was only a matter of time before the emptiness of Louise's marriage to Frederick found her looking elsewhere for
~~~

attention. And, having now seen Kurt for herself, she could clearly see the attraction of the man.

After each time she met Kurt, Louise fell further into a web of entangled feelings. On the one hand, she found the German arrogant, chauvinistic and insensitive. On the other, she desired nothing more than to kiss him, to feel the power of his arms around her, to allow him to take her and do whatever he wished with her body. At night, she would fantasise about him, imagining what would happen if, by chance, he were to appear in her bedroom. Her body tingled at the very prospect, however unlikely. But, with her fantasy, came an increasing desire to make it happen. Her thoughts began to turn more and more into a desperate expectation. Soon she was trying to engineer situations where the possibility could become reality.

Kurt, of course, wanted her and knew a sexual encounter would ultimately take place. But he had long since perfected the art of flirting outrageously one moment, then skilfully reining himself in and appearing uninterested the next. The situation was driving Louise to the point of obsession: a charade that poor Crecia was the brunt of whenever a disappointed Louise returned to her room, exasperated. But Crecia was the most loyal of servants and always went along with her mistress's desperate attempts to manufacture opportunities for meetings.

Then disaster struck. Frederick returned on leave!

Now, not only would her plans have to be curtailed, but Louise would have to endure lovemaking with a man she no longer loved. No matter how much she tried, there was no desire there for her husband. To think of Kurt was the only way she could tolerate him. As for Frederick, he had no idea of his wife's misery, but merely went about the act of intercourse like one of his barrack room inspections: it had its purpose.

For five long days, Louise attempted to turn the tables on Kurt. At every opportunity, when they were all together in company, she would act like an attentive puppy towards Frederick, overtly showing him as much affection as etiquette would allow. It was a situation that her husband was completely unable to comprehend, never suspecting that he was being used as a pawn in Louise's childish game. By the end of his leave, all he understood was that his return to the army was the only way he could escape his wife's smothering performance.

With Frederick securely dispatched back to his regiment, Louise now had every intention of playing hard-to-get with Kurt. However, her resolve lasted little more than a day. After dinner on a particularly hot summer's evening, Louise decided to get some fresh air and walked alone to the summerhouse. There she sat and closed her eyes, listening to the chorus of birds singing their evening song. She was oblivious to anyone being there until the evening sunlight suddenly touched her eyelids. She opened them and there he was, standing in the doorway.

Slowly he closed the door and used his foot to drag a chair in front of it. She watched as he walked towards her, the last ray of sunlight disappearing behind his body. Neither spoke. Towering above her, he held out his hand. She took it and he effortlessly pulled her towards him.

Her heart raced in anticipation of what might happen. But she knew only too well what would happen. It was more a question of how they would do it. Clasping her face in his hand, he held her steady and kissed her. It was hard for her to breathe with the force of his lips on hers. Then, he released his grip and she finally felt the tenderness of his mouth. They pulled apart and gazed at each other intensely. It was always his eyes! Those exciting, fierce, dark blue eyes that ignited something deep within her. She leant forward and held him tight as they kissed again. This time they came together slowly and with a passion she had never thought possible.

He struggled to pull the braces off his shoulders, as they pressed more tightly into each other. Eventually, he managed the task, as they relinquished their kiss. Still no words were spoken. He allowed his trousers to fall. Pulling open her blouse and rolling it down over her shoulders, he kissed her neck, her chest bone and, finally, he kissed her breasts - slowly and softly. Anybody might have being watching through the window, but Louise was past caring. All she wanted now was the ecstasy of feeling him within her.

The act, when it came, took her breath away. Never before had she done it standing up. He lifted her dress. She wrapped her arms around his neck and moaned with pleasure at the experience that followed. Her eyes closed. This was not about love: this was sheer lust. He held up her leg; her eyes then opened wide; she gasped! Her head rolled from side to side in abandon. Eventually, she could hold back the sensation no longer. Her legs shuddered. Whilst it might have seemed like an eternity to her, in reality, it was over quite quickly. Gently, he allowed her to slide to the floor.

'More!' she whispered.

~~~

As for Matilda, her relationship with Robertson lacked any element of romance or sensitivity. The simplest gesture of affection from her was lost on a man who could easily ensure that a romantic encounter had all the appeal of a wet fish. Once, when she attempted to put her hand over his, she was rebuffed with such an
~~~

uncomprehending glare that it should have turned her to stone. Still, Matilda continued to be obsessed with the doctor, when any other woman would have run a mile to avoid his company. Always, after receiving his callous rejections, she would vent her frustration by riding one of the horses so hard through the grounds of the estate that the poor creature would be exhausted.

Like Louise, Matilda couldn't help feeling attracted to Kurt. But unlike Louise, she never got more than a pleasant smile from the German when she attempted a flirtatious manner. One day, after suffering yet another humiliating snub, she took Louise totally by surprise when she sank down heavily opposite her on a sofa in the library, sighing, 'What is it about them?'

Louise dropped her book into her lap and looked around, assuming Matilda must be speaking to someone else – someone who had suddenly appeared in the library without her noticing. Eventually she realised that Matilda was engaging her in conversation. 'I'm sorry, but I really have no inkling of what you're talking about.'

'Men of course!'

Louise looked at her aghast.

'Let's talk. Woman to woman,' Matilda suggested to the stunned Louise.

'Matilda, have you been drinking?'

'Oh, I know we rarely see eye to eye. But perhaps we

should make a little more effort to be friends,' Matilda stated, as if her past coldness toward Louise were a mere triviality.

Just what was the queen of vipers up to, Louise wondered. Whilst she knew Matilda could easily swing from one emotional state to another, never before had she offered the hand of friendship. Louise wasn't convinced. 'Matilda, our relationship would need the attention of a skilled surgeon before we could become friends,' she retorted.

'Very well!' snapped Matilda and stood up. 'As so often, dear niece, I find your humour most tiresome.' With a condescending shrug, she strutted out of the library, leaving Louise to wonder what on earth their exchange could possibly have been about. Could Matilda herself, for once, be feeling snubbed? And if so, just how would she take her revenge?

~~~

Never before had Louise made love so often. Sometimes it was tender, on occasions it was rough, but at all times, for her, it was passionate. Whether in the summerhouse or the meadow, she would always meet Kurt with excitement roiling within her. Nothing else that was happening in her life seemed to matter, just so long as she
~~~

could have the feelings he aroused in her. If she lived to be a hundred, and never made love again, Louise would be content knowing that she had experienced true sexual fulfilment.

The ever faithful Crecia was the couple's trusted look out and would send out a convincing cuckoo call should danger come near. If they were in the summerhouse, Kurt would slip away through the small hatch door at the rear, leaving Louise sitting on a wicker chair reading her book, a blanket covering her from the waist down. In the meadow, it was not quite as easy. However, their chosen spot was always near bushes large enough to provide Kurt with a quick exit if necessary.

After five weeks of a glorious summer, the realisation of her stupidity began to dawn on Louise, and she became mired in guilt. Soon, as she lay under Kurt, she was feeling not wonder and passion, but only sadness at how tawdry and pathetic it had all become. She vowed to herself that it had to stop. And stop it did; but not before Aunt Matilda's suspicions of an affair had been aroused. It was the aunt's conviction that there had been an affair that was to allow Robertson's future plans for Louise to progress rapidly.

Only twice did Crecia have to play the cuckoo: once when a young gardener went in search of some tent poles in the summerhouse; and then on the fateful day when

Matilda decided to take a stroll in the garden. The discreet Italian maid would watch carefully in all directions, always smiling at the moans and groans she wasn't meant to hear, but did. However, today was different. The sounds coming from the summerhouse weren't ones of lovers at play. Instead, they told her that relations between Louise and Kurt were becoming unpleasant.

Crecia had never liked or trusted Kurt, and Louise's cries of discomfort merely confirmed her distaste for him. She closed her eyes and held her hands over her ears. It was only when she looked up that she realised there was somebody there. It was Matilda, and looking as sour as usual.

'Where is Lady Louise?'

Poor Crecia froze. What should she say? Should she just lie and hope that the aunt would accept her explanation that she did not know where her mistress was? But a lie wasn't needed.

'No … please stop, Kurt. You're hurting me!' cried Louise from inside the summerhouse.

Matilda's eyes opened wide in astonishment, but she said nothing. To Crecia's horror, she headed straight towards the door; but her way was immediately blocked.

'No. You can't go in!' Crecia bravely insisted and stood fast.

There was just enough time for the couple to

scramble to their feet. A startled Louise tried to make sense of what she needed to do. Luckily for the pair, they were both fully clothed. Matilda pushed at Crecia's small frame and easily brushed her to one side. 'Out of my way!' she shouted. And pushing down on the handle, she flung open the door.

Louise pulled Kurt towards her and held her hands up to her face. 'No … Please stop, Kurt. You're hurting me!' she protested. Then, quite casually, she moved away and went to pick up a pencil resting inside an open notebook lying on a table. 'Yes, that would be most effective, Kurt. After that I think she might … Oh! Matilda. Hello.'

'Louise! What's going on?' the aunt demanded to know.

'Going on?'

Matilda was dumbstruck at Louise's response of innocence.

'You surely don't think …?' Louise said. 'Really, Matilda … Kurt is merely helping me act out my writing,' she added, quite calmly but firmly.

It was nothing short of a brilliant foil. Yes, outrageously unbelievable, but there was nothing Matilda could do to disprove Louise's explanation. Louise knew as much, and consequently she played out her charade to a conclusion.

'As ever, you've been a marvel, Kurt. You will be able

to make it again tomorrow, I hope.'

Kurt smiled. He couldn't believe anybody could come up with anything so simple, yet so undeniably effective. 'Of course, Lady Warsop,' he replied and made a hasty exit.

Louise turned towards Crecia, who was agog. 'Don't worry, Crecia. I don't really mind Aunt Matilda knowing about our secret acting.' She turned to Matilda to finish. 'So protective of me, bless her.'

Matilda was seething inside with rage. She couldn't abide the fact that Louise always had an answer for situations that should have left her humiliated in front of people. She looked her adversary directly in the eye and spat out, 'Don't think for one minute I believe any of your twaddle. Trust me, dear Louise, your little games will come to an end.' She promptly turned around and made her way out. On the other side of the doorway, she stopped and grabbed Crecia by the chin, staring deeply into the young Italian's eyes. 'And you, my girl, won't always be around to protect your precious mistress.'

Chapter 18

If something needed saying, then Elliott wouldn't mince his words. Even though Tom was in his thirties, he couldn't help feeling like a chastised schoolboy after his friend's assessment of his foolish behaviour on the train.

'I know. But a guinea, Robert! I don't know how I'll explain it to Mary,' Tom moaned.

'I think the split lip will take more explaining,' Elliott said, with a touch of humour in his voice.

Tom touched his lip gingerly, then looked at Elliott, who now had a wry smile on his face. 'All right, you win,' Tom conceded.

The two of them had returned home for an early lunch and were sitting down at the table waiting for Lily to appear with their food. When she did, she couldn't help but notice Tom's lip and swollen cheek and stopped to stare. 'It does look so realistic, Mr Elliott. I can't wait to see this play of yours.' Neither man had the heart to spoil her illusion.

'Right! Well, I need to drop into a solicitor's later, Tom. Fancy a trip? Keep you out of mischief, an' all,' Elliott suggested.

Tom smiled in appreciation of Elliott's continued

teasing, 'Yes, all right.'

Really, all Tom wanted to do was get to the bottom of the mystery of Mrs Beaumont and Marion being in Belper. Elliott knew as much and, in truth, he himself was very much intrigued by what Tom had discovered. The mystery was certainly worthy of more investigation.

'Perhaps you could find out where this Mrs Beaumont lives and then, tomorrow, we could pay her a visit. What do you think?' Elliott commented, knowing it would perk Tom up a bit.

His proposal had the desired effect. Tom pulled back his shoulders and sat up straight in excitement.

'Yes,' he agreed, before giving the suggestion a moment's consideration. 'But I would say it would be better to go and visit Rosterhay Asylum first. Let's see what information we can glean about Marion, and Robertson's association with the place.' He then had an idea. 'Tell you what! We could stop off in Scarborough. Surprise the girls and the children.'

Elliott felt the most chilling sensation suddenly come over him. He shuddered at the horrible split second vision that had just passed before him. His face went white and a hollow feeling hit his stomach. Then, as quickly as it came, the feeling passed, and he felt calm again.

~~~
~~~

Ann normally had the patience of a saint, but sometimes, with Cecil, this was tested to the full. Standing outside the small gift shop on the sea front, she watched her son agonising over his dilemma. Eventually, she cried, 'For goodness sake, Cecil, just make a decision. It's either a red one or a blue one.'

She turned to Mary and sighed. 'I ask you! Who'd believe choosing a spade could be so difficult?'

Mary just laughed. 'I can't possibly think who he takes after.'

Finally, the decision was made. Cecil pulled the red spade from the large tub and handed his pennies over to the old man sitting by the door. Strolling back past the tub, he stopped and viewed the blue one again.

'Cecil! … Out,' his mother demanded.

Soon it was off to the beach again but not before Ann and Mary had viewed a couple of shops themselves. Ann handed over a saucy cartoon postcard to Mary and assumed an expression of naughty surprise at the double entendre. Mary giggled and bit her lip. 'I don't know how they get away with it.'

Outside the next shop they sorted through a shelf of hats. 'Oh, that's pretty, Ann,' Mary said, gently rocking Lucinda in her pram, and watching Ann try a hat on. It wasn't long before the pair were deeply engrossed. Henry, meantime, was getting bored. He asked his mother if he and Cecil could visit the fishing tackle stand across the road in the harbour.

'All right,' Ann agreed. 'But just be careful and watch over your brother.'

Cecil threw his spade against his shoulder, pretending it was a rifle, and started to march alongside his brother.

'It's a spade, Cecil,' Henry tutted in disgust.

Henry was soon in deep conversation with the stallholder about the latest fishing rods and reels. He all but ignored Cecil, who was parading up and down the pavement and occasionally wandering onto the steep, slimy steps that led down to the deep water of the harbour.

'Seen anything you like, Henry?' asked Mary, suddenly appearing beside him.

'This one's fantastic,' Henry replied.

Mary looked at the price ticket. 'Phew! It ought to be.'

'Where's Cecil, Henry?' Ann interrupted their conversation.

Henry looked quite guilty. 'Er …?'

His mother grasped the situation straight away. 'I told you to watch over him!' She looked around, but Cecil was nowhere in sight. 'Where did you last see him?' she asked, a hint of panic beginning to enter her voice. Henry had to admit that it was on the steps going down to the water.

Ann's look of anxiety turned to one of horror. She stared at the water lapping against the steps and harbour wall. Mary rushed to her side and held her hand.

'Where is he?' Ann cried, her eyes darting in every direction, but always returning to the water.

'We'll find him, don't worry,' Mary tried to reassure her.

But Ann's panic was beginning to turn to hysteria. She broke loose from Mary and ran up and down shouting, 'Cecil! … Cecil!' Soon she was screaming his name.

Henry dropped his head and began to sob. The realisation of what might have happened suddenly hit him.

Mary went to comfort him and held up his chin. 'Henry. We need you to be the man of the family right now. Take care of Lucinda, while your mother and I go and look for Cecil.'

A forlorn Henry wiped away his tears and nodded his head in agreement.

By now people were stopping, curious at the sight of Ann running backwards and forwards shouting her son's name. A small crowd began to gather.

'What's he look like, luv?' asked a woman, placing her hand over Ann's. Ann was trembling and could only blurt out, 'He's … er … he's —'

Mary interjected, 'He's dressed in a white shirt and charcoal trousers. Eleven years old, with blond hair. His name is Cecil.' She began to take control of the situation, directing various couples from the crowd where to begin searching.

'Don't cry, luv. We'll find him,' a man said to Ann. But all Ann could do was look down at the steps.

'Was he playing on the steps?' asked the man. Ann didn't answer. 'Did he go in the water?' the man insisted.

'I don't know!' Ann screamed.

Stripping off his jacket and boots, the man ran to the steps. Clambering down them, he looked hard into the water. He couldn't see much in the murkiness. Then he thought he saw something moving and launched himself into the depths. By now, about twenty people had gathered. Speculation spread through the chattering crowd like a gust of wind. Soon all eyes were on the water.

The man surfaced and gasped for air. He shook his head, spluttering, 'I can't see.' A bold young soldier began to strip off his uniform and make his way to the steps, ready to jump in and search the water.

There can be no more upsetting sight than a distraught mother having to contemplate the possibility of her son having drowned. In Ann's eyes there was nothing but fear. She stared at the water in disbelief. Mary held her tightly.

A body pushed to the front of the crowd and asked, 'What's happening?'

The answer was direct and to the point. 'A young lad has drowned.'

A bewildered face looked up, 'Oh dear!'

All attention suddenly turned to the small figure dressed in a white shirt and charcoal trousers and now holding a blue coloured spade. Sighs of relief began to ring out.

'Here he is!' shouted a man, pulling Cecil forward.

The sheer joy on Ann's face. The relaxation of her tense shoulders. She nearly fainted with relief. Tearfully, she held out her arms for Cecil to run into. Mary stepped back to allow them to embrace.

Henry slowly walked forward, expecting to face a stern lecture. It would happen later but, for now, his mother simply looked at him and lifted up her arm, gesturing for him to join the cuddle.

Mary wiped the tears of joy from her eyes and held onto the handle of her pram. Now she could breathe again. The burden of anxiety lifted from her heart.

~~~

At the assizes, Elliott was most often the only advocate for the poor. If he felt a defendant was innocent – or even
~~~

if he felt the man or woman was guilty – providing he had some hope of a better future for them, he would use his experience to urge leniency. However, when dealing with a charge of murder, as was the case with William Doherty, he knew that his chances of influencing the judge would be limited. What was needed was a philanthropic solicitor and Elliott knew just the man – Mr Cooper of the firm Briggs, Stock and Cooper.

As usual, Tom was impressed at just how skilfully Elliott went about persuading Cooper to represent the young and delinquent Doherty. Given his knowledge of the evidence the police would be bringing, Tom knew that the task of gaining an acquittal for Doherty would have been a challenge even for an Old Bailey barrister, let alone for a man more frequently associated with legal representation in financial and inheritance disputes.

'And do we know who is undertaking the prosecution?' Mr Cooper asked Elliott.

'I don't, I'm afraid but I can find out for you.'

The stocky Mr Cooper leant back in his chair and ran his hand across his flabby cheeks. 'Erm … Most probably Wilshaw and Moate, given that it's a mining case.' He drew his lips to a point. 'They're good, Robert, very good. Still, I like a challenge,' he said, and leant forward again. 'Leave it with me. I'll have young Dobson look at things and I'll be in contact.' Like Tom, Ernest Cooper was always keen to dabble in areas of his profession that he hadn't initially trained in.

The three men stood up and shook hands, and Cooper escorted them out of his office towards the outer door of the impressive Georgian building the firm occupied. As they passed through the outer office, his secretary called over to a woman sitting on a chair, 'If you'd like to go through now, Mrs Ridgeway, Mr Cooper will be with you shortly.'

Mrs Ridgeway got up and nodded politely at the men as she passed them.

Each of the men acknowledged her in turn, with Tom giving her one of his broad smiles. She for her part kept looking at him rather longer than was usual for a passing stranger. Once outside the building, Tom remarked, 'Did you see how she looked at me? It was as if she knew me.'

Elliott shook his head playfully, then pulled a handkerchief out of his pocket and gave it to Tom. 'Probably on account of your alluring lips.'

Tom pulled up and, looking bemused, felt his lip. What he had failed to realise was that his broad smile had split it open again and blood was trickling down his chin.

Back in Mr Cooper's office, the well-dressed Mrs Ridgeway sat graciously on a high-backed chair. Beside her on the floor was a large bag.

'Well, Mrs Ridgeway. Your phone call was most intriguing. How can Briggs, Stock and Cooper be of assistance to you in your matter?' asked Mr Cooper, easing himself into his chair and trying not to show too much of his oversized stomach.

'I'm told your company has had some success in affairs involving miscarriages of justice, Mr Cooper,' she said.

The pleased partner drew himself up and proudly replied, 'One likes to think our reputation precedes us. Yes, I would say we have.'

'Then I would like you to represent me,' the woman before him explained.

'Represent you in what way exactly, Mrs Ridgeway?'

At this, Mrs Ridgeway leant over to the bag on the floor and pulled out quite a bulky file, tied up with string. 'Everything is in here, Mr Cooper,' she said, placing the file on the desk. 'I'm sure you'll find it fascinating reading. It's the whole truth.'

Ernest Cooper was seldom presented with a case with any great mystery and, therefore, was most eager to open the file. However, his manner continued to be that of the consummate professional he was. 'Very well, Mrs Ridgeway. I shall take a look in due course and advise you of my fee. You are aware that disputes of any kind can be costly?'

'Oh, I think that will be the least of your worries, once you have read the contents of the file, Mr Cooper,' was Mrs Ridgeway's reply, as she stood up and offered him her hand.

Somewhat surprised at the sudden ending of their interview, the solicitor struggled to quickly lift himself out of his chair, but eventually managed it and shook his new client's hand. 'Please let my secretary have your details, so I can make contact with you.'

'I am currently staying outside the area,' replied Mrs Ridgeway. She looked over to the file once more. 'After reading those papers, you'll understand why. Shall we agree that I contact you in a day or so?'

After that, she left. Outside the building, a man was waiting for her in a car.

~~~

An hour later, Elliott and Tom walked through Elliott's front door. On hearing the door open, Bessie, the dog came ambling out of the kitchen, faithfully carrying her master's newspaper in her mouth.

'Bless you, dog,' responded Elliott, bending down to acknowledge his pet with a pat.

It wasn't long before Lily also appeared and asked, 'Have you had a good day, Mr Elliott?'
~~~

'Very productive, Lily. I think you'd agree, Tom.'

His friend had to admit that there had not been a dull moment.

'Any phone calls, Lily?' enquired Elliott.

'Yes, Mrs Elliott rang. She said … wait, I've written it down.' Pulling out a piece of paper from her apron, she read it aloud: 'Mrs Elliott says, "Still having a great time. Nothing of consistence to report …"'

Both men frowned with confusion, until they realised she meant 'consequence'.

'… Going up to Whitby tomorrow for the day. Will try to call you after that.'

'Well, that puts paid to visiting them tomorrow, Tom … Anything else, Lily?'

Ann wasn't one to raise unnecessary alarm by talking about the incident with Cecil. She knew it would be much better to wait until they returned home. By then, she would be able to paint a more objective picture of events. She did, however, offer a comment via Lily that was quite unusual for her, but showed just how much the episode of the day had affected her, and made her concentrate even more on her loved ones.

'Just that I'm to tell you – Mrs Elliott and the boys love and miss you very much. Just like Mrs Sharpe and baby Lucinda love you, Professor Sharpe.'

Two proud men gave a smile of contentment.

Chapter 19

Crecia's actions at the summerhouse had made Matilda see red. The aunt knew that if it weren't for the little Italian, she would have caught Louise and Kurt in the act. As it was, she could now only offer her brother a tale based on suspicions and assumptions. Whilst the earl would have no trouble in believing his sister, there was no way he could banish Louise from Haddington on a charge of adultery without solid evidence. Although, with Crecia, it was a different matter.

At Haddington, it often seemed that cunning and vindictiveness were a sport, and Matilda was adept at both. She had every intention of ensuring that Crecia would pay the price for crossing her. Robertson also saw it as yet one more opportunity to drive Louise deeper into a state of alienation. Without Crecia by her side, he knew he could make things almost intolerable for a woman now teetering on the brink of despair.

But Robertson's plans were beginning to go much deeper than just the destruction of Louise: he was now intent on taking control of Haddington and the Ranskill mining empire. How he would ultimately achieve this aim was a matter for careful planning and evil deception.

What he couldn't anticipate though, was the occurrence of events that he considered as exceptional luck.

Matilda, although oblivious of the fact, had always been pivotal to Robertson's plans. From his point of view, he needed Matilda as the family member he could control and who would make decisions on behalf of the estate – once, of course, he had removed the figurehead of his supposed friend, Ranskill. The trouble was, Matilda had started to become more and more insecure, unstable and, as a consequence, unpredictable. What he thought might aid matters actually had quite the opposite effect.

One evening, Crecia heard a gentle knock on her door, followed by a small note being pushed into her room. Curious, she opened the note and read it.

My dear Crecia,

I ask so much of you, but please, one more time. Meet me at the summerhouse at 9 o'clock. Not a word to anyone!

Louise.

They were unmistakeably the words of her mistress and seemingly written by her hand, or so she thought.

At precisely the requested time, Crecia went to the summerhouse and, in the fading light, gently knocked on the door. 'Miss Louise … Miss Louise, it is me, Crecia,' she whispered. There was no response. Gingerly, she opened the door and walked in. Behind her the door quickly closed shut. Before she could turn around, a cloth came over her head and was pulled tight into her mouth. She tried to scream but it just came out as a muffled cry.

A hand pulled her arms behind her back, rendering her unable to struggle. Then she felt his breath beside her ear.

'Keep perfectly still or I will harm you,' he said.

She recognised the voice instantly. Feeling something sharp pressing against her side, she stopped moving.

'That's better,' muttered the voice of Robertson.

With her dark Latin eyes wide open with fear, she listened as he continued. 'I'm going to give you the chance to go back home to Italy, girl.'

Crecia shook her head from side to side, signalling no.

'Oh! There is no alternative, I'm afraid,' said Robertson, emphasising his determination by pushing the object a little harder into her side.

He pulled her towards the small table and made her kneel. In front of her was a hand-written note, a blank piece of paper and a pen.

'Copy it,' he demanded.

Again, Crecia shook her head.

'If you want to see your family again, you will copy it,' Robertson explained chillingly.

She looked at the letter, written in broken English and poorly spelt.

Miss Louise,

I have sad news tonight with telegram. Father is ill.

He near to die. Am travel on train to London tonight. Tomorrow boat to Spain. And after boat to Italy. I try telephone you.

Crecia.

Robertson forcibly pulled her hand from behind her back and held it in front of her. 'Do it!' he snarled.

Fearing for her life, Crecia picked up the pen and began writing. Robertson grinned to himself as she finally finished and laid down the pen. He pulled her to her feet and once more held her hands behind her.

'She's all yours … enjoy her,' he said to the woman who had been watching quietly and patiently, out of view.

Matilda walked slowly forward and looked into Crecia's distraught face. She smiled and caressed her cheek. 'I've often wondered about you!'

Crecia understood the inference but was powerless to do anything. She watched as Matilda raised a handkerchief towards her nose. The smell on it was so strong. In a matter of seconds she felt she was floating.

Robertson handed over a thoroughly disorientated Crecia to Matilda and left by the door.

~~~

After quietly slipping Crecia's note under Louise's door, Robertson retired to his own rooms. Invariably, these days,
~~~

the doctor would stay at Haddington, taking advantage of Ranskill's hospitality. It was now past midnight. The events of the evening had taken much longer than he'd anticipated, mainly due to the fact that Matilda had become hysterical at what had happened. Only after administering a sedative to her, could Robertson get her calm enough to return to the Hall without drawing attention to their furtive entrance.

Robertson then had to return to the summerhouse and deal with the problem of Crecia's body. What Matilda had been led to believe was just small amounts of chloroform and laudanum on the handkerchief, to ensure that Crecia could not resist her advances, was in reality a cocktail of substances that slowly released its lethal power.

In the darkness, Robertson carried Crecia's small frame to his car. After cramming her into the boot, he drove to the lake beyond the meadow. Stopping under a knot of trees, he moved the body some twenty yards up the shore, where he left it in the shadow of a small jetty. Returning to his car, he retrieved two heavy cast-iron miller's weights, and these he tied tightly to the body – one to the little maid's hands, the other to her feet. Then, he manoeuvred the body into a large sack and tied this up in a business-like fashion. Robertson had done his homework. He knew that, even if the hessian tore or perished quickly and the body fell out, because of the weights tied to it, it wouldn't float to the surface. Careful not to trip on the uneven ground, he carried the sack into a rowing boat, then clambered in alongside it and pushed away from the jetty. Once in the centre of the lake, Robertson struggled to push his victim into the water but eventually managed to lift the sack up enough to slip it over the side. Quickly it sank. Soon the ripples disappeared and the water returned to its former calm. Haddington Lake now held an awful secret.

On reading Crecia's note next morning, Louise stood motionless in disbelief. She read it again. How could this all have happened so suddenly? Why hadn't she been informed? It all seemed so unreal. Carefully, she looked once more at the note. It was definitely written by Crecia. But something occurred to her, something that only someone who really knew Crecia would realise. It was the word 'Father'. In all the time that she had been her maid, Louise had never heard Crecia refer to her father as 'Father'; it was always 'Papa'. Immediately, she sensed something was wrong. Clasping the note in her hand, she went downstairs in search of Dowling.

Discovering him overseeing a workman repairing the faulty grandfather clock in the hallway, she interrupted. 'Dowling.'

'Yes, Lady Warsop.'

Louise got straight to the point. 'Did a telegram arrive for Crecia, yesterday evening?'

'I believe so, ma'am.'

'You believe so. Are you not certain?'

Dowling moved away from the repairman, who seemed captivated by the conversation despite the butler's look of disapproval. Out of earshot, he replied to Louise in a quiet tone.

'Dr Robertson advised me of its arrival. He had just taken delivery of it from the post boy outside. And, as he was going past Crecia's room, he kindly offered to ensure she received it.'

'Were you aware of Crecia's departure last night?' Louise continued her questioning.

'No, I was told this morning, ma'am.'

'So you had no knowledge of her leaving suddenly? Surely, you should have been informed.'

Dowling didn't care for being questioned in front of the tradesman. He gestured for Louise to move more towards the library. 'Lady Warsop, if I may be permitted to say, Dr Robertson very much chooses to ignore household etiquette when it suits him. To please his lordship, I simply accept his peculiarities.'

Louise let out a laugh. 'Oh, Dowling! I do so love your diplomacy. The man's a pompous ass. I think we all know that.'

She apologised to Dowling for taking him away from his duties and began to walk towards the dining room, but not before stopping and asking, 'Would you do me a favour and take a look in Crecia's room? See if you can find this telegram.'

'And if I do, ma'am?'

'Then please bring it to my room.'

Louise entered the dining room to find the family sitting quietly eating breakfast. The earl looked over to the clock and decided he would give his opinion. 'Breakfast is normally served promptly at eight.'

'Then it's a good job, I'm not eating, sir,' Louise batted straight back.

She didn't wait for the look on her father-in-law's face. Instead, she turned to address Robertson. 'Dr Robertson. When exactly were you intending to tell me about Crecia?'

Matilda immediately dropped her fork onto her plate. Struggling to gain her composure, she eventually stood up and stated, 'I suddenly feel quite nauseous, please forgive me.' With that, she placed her napkin over her mouth and made her exit.

David, unaware of what was going on, asked, 'What about Crecia?'

'She's gone, David,' was all Louise responded.

Even Ranskill looked surprised to hear the news.

'It seems that everybody is blissfully in the dark about events, Dr Robertson! Perhaps you could enlighten us all,' Louise continued.

Robertson appeared unfazed by Louise's questioning of him. He'd given careful thought to just how he would explain things. Slowly and deliberately, he lowered his knife and fork, taking the time to dab at his mouth with his napkin. 'Had you been at the breakfast table, I would have explained. As you weren't, I had every intention of notifying you as soon as possible.' His words were effortless and, to everyone except Louise, quite believable. 'On returning to the hall yesterday evening, I took delivery of a telegram from the post boy. It was addressed to Crecia, and as I couldn't immediately find Dowling, I decided to take it directly to her room. I could see when the girl opened it that she was distressed and I could only assume it was bad news. She explained that her father had suddenly been taken very ill and she wanted to return to Italy straight away. I suggested she wait until the morning and then we could help make arrangements for her.'

He paused for dramatic effect and pulled his chair out slightly, which allowed him to cross one leg over the other. He leant his arm over the table and played with his napkin. 'Unfortunately, Crecia wouldn't listen. She insisted she go immediately to the station and catch a train for London. The poor girl was beside herself,' he said, attempting sympathy. 'As I had just remembered that I needed to drive back into town, I simply offered to drop her off.'

'And Crecia never once thought to speak to her mistress,' Louise remarked, mocking Robertson's story.

'I did suggest as much. But you have to appreciate it was late. Crecia didn't wish to disturb you. I did, however, insist she at least leave you a note.'

Louise folded her arms in scorn. 'How very thoughtful of you, Doctor. And, how very convenient for your story!'

Robertson didn't appreciate being challenged. He hardened his look. 'What exactly are you implying?'

'I'm not implying anything, Dr Robertson. I'm merely observing how well everything appears to fit together,' Louise answered, unfolding her arms.

The doctor regained his composure and gave one of his sickening smiles. 'We can all appreciate how much you will miss Crecia. If there is anything we can do, or indeed, any medication I can offer for your anxiety…'

'How touching. I can only imagine how effective that would be, sir!' Louise replied. She promptly turned to walk out of the dining room, but decided to stop at the door and make a cryptic parting comment. 'Papa, Dr Robertson. Always Papa!' Then she made her exit. The doctor thought for a moment, before realising what she had meant.

David eventually stood up from the table, gave his apologies and went in search of Louise. He found her walking slowly through the gardens. 'Louise!' he called. She waited for him to catch up with her.

'I thought I might find you here. Mind if I join you?' he asked.

'Of course you may,' Louise replied and, as always with David, she slid her arm through his and held him tight. She looked so forlorn. Despite all her bravado with Robertson, she was struggling to keep herself together.

'I'm really sorry to hear about Crecia,' David said with genuine sympathy. Louise just smiled in appreciation. It was a troubled smile and David knew it. 'You didn't believe him, did you?'

'Oh, David,' Louise sighed. 'Crecia wouldn't have just gone like that. This is all to do with alienating me from anyone dear. I don't know what he's done to her, but I'm determined to find out.'

'Let me help you.'

'No, David. I must find the solution to this alone … for now at least.'

'Then be careful, sweet sister-in-law.'

He held Louise's hand to his lips and gently kissed it.

Back in the dining room, Ranskill seemed less

than pleased with his partner. Although the pair had tentatively discussed removing Crecia from her position, nothing had been finalised as to how this would happen. Ranskill paced the dining room, becoming more and more annoyed. Eventually, he turned to his partner and warned him, 'Be aware, Anthony. Any future decisions regarding how we proceed with our plans will be made by me. Is that clear?'

Robertson took his reprimand but secretly knew he would do no such thing.

'So, how much did it cost to get rid of her?' asked Ranskill, oblivious of the truth.

'Five guineas.'

Ranskill puffed out his cheeks.

'We won't be seeing or hearing from her again for that, George. Trust me.'

'I should hope not,' Ranskill answered, with relief. 'And now what?'

'Louise will buckle, now she has no allies.'

'I wish I could share your optimism. She looked anything but ready to buckle a moment ago.'

Robertson conveniently chose to ignore his partner's comment. 'As she becomes more depressed, you need to stop her seeing the child. And keep hounding her at all times. That will drive her over the edge and then we shall simply put her in an asylum. After a time, Frederick will quietly file for divorce … on our terms! And that's it – game, set and match.'

It all sounded so plausible but Ranskill didn't appear to be fully convinced. He moved over to the bay window and gazed out, pursuing his thoughts. 'I almost feel sorry for her,' he said, to a shocked and concerned Robertson. The last thing the doctor needed was for the earl to start showing any sympathy or understanding towards Louise. For Ranskill to have a change of heart about his daughter-in-law and allow her to stay at Haddington, was unthinkable to Robertson. He knew he would need to accelerate his plans. At the very least, he could certainly do with Louise being distracted from meddling further in the mystery of Crecia's disappearance.

Two days later, news would come that would help him in his predicament, although, at Haddington, for every problem solved, another would take its place.

~~~

Following Crecia's disappearance, the atmosphere at Haddington became tenser than ever. Everyone was used to a caustic comment suddenly igniting a spark, but normally things calmed down as quickly as they started. Now, when there was an eruption, it was invariably between Louise and Robertson at the dinner table, and
~~~

the resulting fire would burn fiercely.

On such occasions, Kurt couldn't help but admire the spirit that Louise showed in defending herself. Although their physical relationship had ended, he was still impressed by this very feminine woman's ability to fight her corner. It was something he had seldom witnessed back in his homeland. But here at Haddington, he found that, just when he felt tempted to supply a supportive word or gesture, Louise would volley a response back across the table, and one that cut deep into her opponent.

During one particularly unpleasant skirmish, Louise decided to throw down the gauntlet. She couldn't have caused more surprise if she had stripped naked and paraded on the table. Standing up and slamming down her napkin, she cried, 'I refuse to take this bullying anymore!' She turned to her father-in-law. 'Sir, tomorrow I intend finding a solicitor, and I shall seek a divorce from Frederick. Furthermore, I shall be leaving this wicked place with baby Edward.'

The table fell silent. The earl's mouth literally fell wide open. Louise, red-faced with rage, strode swiftly out of the dining room.

David stood up to follow her, but not before he too had his say: 'Why can't you all just accept her? What has she ever done to this family, except tell us the truth about ourselves?'

'Sit down!' Ranskill blasted.

David glared at his father but answered him quite calmly, 'No, father. I will not be party to your cruelty.'

Matilda, rarely in attendance at dinner these days, looked down and fumbled with her spoon. Kurt, for his part, simply suggested politely to the earl, 'Perhaps it is best if I leave you to discuss what is, after all, a family matter.'

Ranskill eventually nodded his acceptance. And Matilda seized the opportunity to leave the table herself, giving her apologies and stating her usual reason of feeling nauseous.

The poor footman, Bennett, who had had to witness the whole affair, remained standing like a statue, his eyes never once moving from their forward stare. Unfortunately, as he was the closest to Ranskill, he was directly in the firing line for his master's sarcasm. 'And I suppose you found that hugely amusing?'

'No, m'lord,' answered Bennett.

'Well, you damn well should have, because they're a joke!' he bellowed in the lad's face, before ordering him to leave.

Ranskill paced the floor, running his fingers and thumb back and forth across his forehead in exasperation. 'Now what?' he asked Robertson.

Robertson didn't answer immediately. Instead, his

face contorted into various expressions indicating the different ideas running through his mind. Eventually, he had to admit he would need more time to consider a suitable solution.

'Everyone clawing at each other's throat. And now, Lady … bloody fearless decides to throw in a grenade. I can do without it, Anthony.'

'I'm sure it's just another of her little games.'

'Games! She seems to be winning, by my reckoning!'

Robertson took the comment, as it was intended – as criticism.

Beyond the door, Dowling wasn't relishing entering the room, but a visitor had arrived and he needed to bring this to the attention of his master. He took a deep breath and puffed out his chest. '*Once more unto the breach, dear friends, once more,*' he muttered to himself.

He hardly had time to close the door before Ranskill was shouting at him. 'Yes, what is it, Dowling? Can't you see that I'm busy? Or perhaps you've come to put in your two penneth, as well, eh?'

As much as Dowling would have loved to give his opinion, his expression never changed from that of the professional, if not long-suffering, butler. 'There's a Captain Greaves requesting to speak with you, m'lord.'

'At this hour!' Ranskill exclaimed.

'Apparently so, sir,' Dowling drawled in response.

'Shall I show him to the drawing room?'

Ranskill thought for a brief moment and made up his mind. 'No, I'd better come.' He pulled down at his waistcoat and adjusted his tie. 'Excuse me, Anthony.'

In front of the double entrance doors, Captain Greaves was standing patiently, his hands crossed slightly as he held a small leather briefcase in front of him. On hearing footsteps, he drew himself up out of politeness.

Approaching the captain, the earl announced, 'Ranskill!'

'Captain Greaves, 13th/18th Royal Hussars,' the captain reciprocated.

'Well, Captain. How may I help you?'

'May we speak privately, sir? And with Lady Warsop present?'

'Of course,' Ranskill replied and gestured towards the drawing room. 'Although, I'm not sure where Lady Louise is exactly … Dowling?'

'I believe I saw her going for a stroll in the gardens, m'lord. I shall see if I can find her,' Dowling offered.

Carefully positioned out of view but just within earshot, Robertson strained to listen to the conversation. If there was one thing the man couldn't stand, it was getting news second hand. Experience had taught him that eavesdropping, whilst against all the rules of good conduct, often allowed him to take an offensive position.

He snarled in frustration as the door to the drawing room closed.

Ranskill poured himself a larger than usual whisky and threw it down his throat in one gulp. Turning to the captain, he simply asked, 'When?' He knew the form well enough.

'This morning, sir,' came the equally short reply.

The doors opened and in walked Louise. 'I understand I'm wanted,' she said.

'Louise. This is Captain Greaves,' Ranskill began.

'I'm afraid I have some bad news, Lady Warsop,' the captain said, taking over the conversation. Louise looked at him with no real perception of what was coming.

'I'm sorry to inform you that your husband was killed early this morning, whilst on a training exercise … I really am terribly sorry.'

Unsteady on her feet, Louise finally buckled and fell.

Chapter 20

No sooner had Elliott put the phone down from speaking with Ann and the boys than it rang again. This time, it was someone he could barely hear at first. Only after a couple of minutes of farce worthy of a music hall routine, did he discover it was a very unexpected caller.

'Hello, Robert, it's Ernest Cooper,' a very distant voice announced.

'I'm sorry, who the trooper?' Elliott asked.

'No. Ernest Cooper!'

'The Loyal Trooper? No, you've got a private number,' Elliott insisted, believing the call was for the local public house.

The caller tried once more, to no avail.

Elliott tapped the earpiece against his hand several times and then began unscrewing it. Finally, he gave it a hearty blow and did the same to the mouthpiece, which thoroughly startled the patient Mr Cooper at the other end of the line.

'Hello?' Elliott enquired.

'Robert?' came the somewhat exasperated reply.

'Ahh! That's better. Yes, this is Robert.' He covered the mouthpiece and explained in all seriousness to Tom.

'Must have been some fluff!' Never for a moment did it occur to him that it had simply been a bad connection.

Having watched the whole episode with a smile, Tom shook his head. There were times when Elliott's failure to cope with the everyday world quite bewildered him. This was a man who was so intelligent and sharp, and was in many ways so practical, yet give him something like a telephone and he was like a puzzled apprentice.

Elliott's conversation was soon back on track, with Cooper explaining the purpose of his call. 'I would very much like your opinion on something, Robert. Could you come to my office tomorrow?'

'Well, yes, if I can help. Is it about the lad, Doherty?'

'That's the thing. I'm not altogether sure. You see, I've just finished reading a file that I have been given, and I've been absolutely astonished by what's in it. To be honest, Robert, I really don't know the best way to proceed. I could do with your expertise.'

'I see. Well, you've certainly got me intrigued. Suppose I come over at half past ten.'

Cooper agreed and the two men bid each other good evening.

Elliott turned to Tom. 'That was Ernest Cooper.'

'So I eventually gathered,' Tom replied. But his gently mocking tone was lost on Elliott.

'He's asked me to his office tomorrow morning. So

I'm afraid, if you don't mind, you'll have to go alone to visit Rosterhay Asylum.'

Tom didn't mind at all. In some respects he preferred it. Sometimes, his friend could be overpowering and certainly he was forthright in his questioning. Tom knew nursing staff better than most, and he felt he would have more success using his own relaxed style than Elliott would have conducting an inquisition.

So, the scene was set. Each man hoped that, by the end of the next day, he would have an important part of his particular mystery solved. But, could it be that simple?

~~~

Rosterhay Asylum was an imposing red brick Victorian building on the outskirts of York that had once been owned by a wealthy wool merchant, before being sold and converted into a workhouse. Some years later, ownership had been transferred to the Diocese, and the building turned into an asylum, which was currently staffed mainly by Anglican nuns from the order of the Sisters of the Charity. A 15-minute taxi journey brought Tom to the asylum, where it had been agreed the mother superior would be available to meet him at 11.30 am. Just before the appointed time, Tom rang the bell at the side
~~~

of the large oak door and waited. Eventually, the door opened and a pleasant faced young nun smiled up at him.

'Good morning, sir.'

'Yes, good morning to you, Sister.'

'How may I help you?' the nun asked, affably.

'I have an appointment to see Reverend Mother Elizabeth at 11.30.'

'Then do please come in,' directed the young sister. 'May I inform Reverend Mother who is calling?'

'Of course, yes, I'm sorry. Professor Sharpe. If you tell Mother Elizabeth that we spoke on the telephone.'

Tom was offered a seat, as the sister gave him another genteel smile and knocked on an office door. He was quite surprised by the volume of the woman's voice that responded from within. 'Enter!' it boomed. The tiny figure of the sister gently turned the large brass knob and disappeared inside. Tom couldn't help thinking it reminded him of many a situation he'd encountered over the years, when a timid nurse had entered the matron's office. Would she come out unscathed, he wondered. Eventually she did, and gave him yet another lovely smile. 'Reverend Mother will be with you shortly, Professor Sharpe. May I offer you some tea?'

Tom nodded. 'Thank you. With just a little milk, please.'

It all appeared so friendly and congenial. Then, the

door opened. The mother superior was as big as her voice. And certainly her face was stern enough to give any matron that Tom had ever known a run for her money. However, once inside her office, Tom found Mother Elizabeth was not quite as austere as her looks suggested. Nonetheless, he became aware of an evasive tone as she started to answer his questions. What was needed was a way of charming himself into her good graces and, looking at the amateur watercolours adorning her wall, he thought he might just have found it.

'That's Malham Cove, isn't it?' he asked, pointing to one of the pictures. 'And ... is that the Tarn? They're very good. Who's the artist?'

Mother Elizabeth looked down bashfully. She blushed slightly before answering, 'Well, it's me actually.'

'No. Really?' said Tom, mustering as much astonishment as he felt he could get away with.

After a further couple of minutes discussing the nun's love of art and painting, Tom knew he had almost broken down her reserve. But to be absolutely sure, he decided to play his master stroke. 'The next one you paint – perhaps you might consider letting me buy it?' The nun was now putty in his hands.

Sitting back in her chair, the mother superior returned to their previous conversation and admitted, 'Yes, Dr Robertson was a strange sort on occasion, Professor.'

Tom seized his opportunity. 'I am surprised that the doctor continued to do clinics here, with all his other business interests.'

'Oh, he hadn't done a clinic here for some time. But he did always come to see and treat one specific patient.'

Tom's eyebrows lifted and the tramlines appearing on his forehead were a sure sign he was in the grip of an idea. Could that patient possibly be the one he was thinking of? Then he became aware of a noise coming from the slightly opened window. Unexpectedly, it all now made sense, as he watched a pair of pigeons cooing on the window ledge.

'Would this patient be Marion, by chance, Reverend Mother?'

'I couldn't possibly discuss our patients, Professor Sharpe.'

'Perhaps I could see your patient then,' Tom chanced.

'That wouldn't be appropriate.'

'Not appropriate or not possible?'

The Reverend Mother reverted to her former demeanour and assumed a stern face. 'I think our meeting is perhaps at an end, Professor.'

It certainly wasn't from Tom's perspective. He had obviously touched on something sensitive and wanted to know what it was. 'It's not possible because she isn't here, is she? In fact, I'm guessing she's been missing for several weeks, perhaps even months.'

The mother superior went to open her door. 'Good day, Professor Sharpe.'

Tom stood up but he had every intention of telling the nun his theory before leaving. He held onto the back of his chair and confirmed, 'I know as much because I've met Marion only recently. Indeed, I know where she is right now. Losing a patient is a serious matter. I trust the police are involved.'

Slowly closing the door, the mother superior sighed in a resigned tone. 'You'd better sit down again, Professor.' Then she explained the whole embarrassing affair of Sister Agnes going missing and taking the patient, Marion, with her.

By the end of the story, Tom had his confirmation of Robertson's knowing Marion from the start; of the doctor's prolonged treatment of her with a cocktail of drugs; and of his refusal to allow any doctor to treat her other than himself. What he didn't have, though, was any indication from the mother superior as to where Marion had come from, because, just like Sister Agnes, she simply didn't know.

That Marion had disappeared from Haddington had always been obvious to Tom. He just couldn't work out exactly what had happened. However, his friend Elliott was about to discover the answer to that question.

<p style="text-align:center">~~~</p>

He wouldn't admit it, but Elliott was becoming obsessed with his receding hairline. Catching sight of himself in the mirror whilst visiting the solicitors' cloakroom, he lifted up his fringe and was convinced that it had moved further up his forehead from where it had been the previous week. He gave a sigh, washed his hands and went back into the waiting area.

'Oh, there you are, Mr Elliott. I was beginning to wonder where you were. One minute you were here and the next you'd disappeared,' said the receptionist at Briggs, Stock & Cooper.

Elliott gave an apologetic shrug of his shoulders and gestured back towards the cloakroom.

'Mr Cooper is available now, if you'd like to go through.'

'Thank you,' said Elliott, making his way over to the office door with its frosted glass panel proudly displaying in bold lettering the words: 'Ernest Cooper, Solicitor'. He rapped firmly on the glass with his knuckles.

'Are you sure you weren't a policeman in a former life, Robert?' joked Ernest Cooper on opening the door. He offered his hand and welcomed his guest in. 'Please take a seat,' he said, and made his way behind his desk. 'How are you?'

'Getting older, Ernest!' Elliott grumbled, still thinking about his hair.

His friend didn't altogether follow Elliott's thread, but he went along with him all the same. 'Yes, it comes to us all I'm afraid,' he replied, patting his oversized stomach and finally sitting in his chair. 'Anyway, it's good of you to come, Robert.'

'Not at all! I have to admit you have me fascinated by whatever it is you need my opinion on.'

The solicitor leant forward and laid his hands down flat on the file on his desk. 'This file contains information and a story that would make a good crime novel.'

Elliott turned his head attentively and waited for an explanation.

'Yes, and I'm baffled what to make of it: whether it's fact or merely a case of somebody playing a game for some reason.' Cooper leant back in his chair and continued, 'That's where you come in, Robert. You deal with criminals all the time. I'm hoping you'll be able to do a bit of digging. See if you can find any rumblings of a deliberate deception.'

'Well, it all sounds intriguing. What information does this file contain exactly?' Elliott asked, casting his eye over to the file, bound in string and tied with a simple bow.

'I have never before divulged confidential

information about a client, but if the information in here is true, then it will be public knowledge soon enough. And if it isn't true, then I want you to have witnessed its existence,' explained the solicitor, untying the bow and opening the file. He went on to ask, 'Are you familiar with Haddington Hall?'

Elliott chuckled, 'Oh, very familiar … Sorry, go on.'

At this, Cooper started to reveal a whole sequence of events, just as Mrs Ridgeway had written them down. Elliott listened agog. He couldn't believe he was being told exactly what had happened at Haddington. All the blanks in the mystery Tom and he had been pursuing were being filled in, one by one, and with the truth, it seemed to him.

Elliott couldn't hold back any longer: he had to interrupt and tell his friend, 'This is just so bizarre, Ernest,'

'I told you. It's like a novel,' reaffirmed Cooper.

'No, no! What I mean is …'

Elliott proceeded to explain to Cooper about meeting Marion in the cells, the photograph, her disappearance and re-emergence in Belper with Mrs Beaumont, Tom's theory of Dr Robertson's involvement. In fact, everything. The two stories that the men were discussing had neatly dovetailed into one.

'So you see, Ernest,' said Elliott, looking over to

the file. 'What that contains is a detailed corroboration of what Tom and I have already discovered. Only we couldn't figure out who had put her into the asylum and why. Now it's clear, and Tom was right all along,' Elliott said, slumping back in his chair. He was truly flummoxed at the coincidence of it all. 'I honestly can't believe it.'

Ernest Cooper was equally amazed. He let out a sigh. 'Well, it appears all that the captivating Mrs Ridgeway has written under her clever cover, is the truth.'

Pondering the situation for a moment, Elliott began tapping the back of his fingers against his other palm. 'Yes, quite a curious case for you.'

Cooper swivelled his chair round and stood up. 'Do I detect some scepticism, Robert?'

'As with all good mysteries, Ernest, the reader only gets to see what the writer wants them to know!'

'Go on.'

'The obvious question is whether Robertson's death is associated with all of it. You've studied the evidence against the lad, Doherty. Do you think he cut that wire?'

Cooper was emphatic with his response, 'No, I do not.'

'My thoughts exactly. So who did cut it? I don't dispute any of the facts in that file but … is there a murderer amongst the people mentioned there?'

'Are you suggesting revenge?'

Elliott shrugged philosophically. 'Revenge invariably drives evil. You've only got to look at the war, to realise that.'

~~~

The meeting between Elliott and Cooper had finished with them agreeing that Briggs, Stock & Cooper should take on the case when Mrs Ridgeway made contact again. Meantime, Elliott wanted to do a bit of digging. There was one comment that the solicitor had made which he thought needed investigation.

Back at home, Elliott was half dozing in his chair listening to his music on the gramophone when the door handle turned and a very enthusiastic Tom bounded into the parlour. 'Well, you can't imagine what an interesting meeting I've had!' he all but shouted.

'Really,' yawned Elliott, stretching out his arms and legs, before painstakingly lifting the needle off his record and carefully putting the arm back on its rest.

Tom got the point. 'Oh, I'm sorry, Robert. Am I disturbing things?'

Elliott rubbed his palms over his sleepy eyes. 'No, no. I was just thinking, come on Elliott, make a move, stop enjoying yourself. Tom will be back any minute and he's going to want to tell me all about his day.'

'Sorry! Shall I get Lily to put the kettle on?' Tom
~~~

offered in recompense, and went in search of the maid.

Elliott watched as Bessie lumbered up and sat beside him. He patted her on her head saying, 'And what kind of day have you had, girl?' Bessie just dropped her head onto the arm of the chair and looked at him with her well-practised stoic expression.

'On its way,' said Tom, coming back into the room and sitting in the other armchair. Bessie got up and ambled over, wagging her tail. Again she placed her head down and gave her best forlorn look. 'Hello, girl! Has old grumpy not taken you out yet?'

Elliott smiled. 'I thought you might like the pleasure, later on.'

Tom was soon eagerly replaying his day and the visit to Rosterhay Asylum. Elliott could see by Tom's sheer exuberance that he had discovered something and was building his account towards a climax. Now knowing infinitely more than Tom did, he decided it would be fun to keep interjecting ideas and highlighting possibilities for what might come next.

'Very well! What exactly have you found out?' Tom eventually asked, conceding that his friend's meeting with Mr Cooper might have been even more fruitful than his own trip. He listened carefully as Elliott explained about Mrs Ridgeway's alias, and the story contained in the file. 'Goodness me!' he kept saying in amazement.

'So, you were right, Tom. Marion is who you thought she was, and your meeting at Rosterhay confirms what happened to her,' Elliott concluded.

'Knowing Robertson, I never doubted that part of the story. But Mrs Ridgeway! I never thought she would turn out to be …!'

'Tea up, sir,' interrupted Lily, entering the room before he could finish. She carried the tray in and placed it on the table. 'Come on Bess! Leave Mr Elliott and the professor to their discussions. Let's get you some dinner,' she said, and waited for Bessie to waddle out of the door before closing it behind her.

After pouring out two cups, Elliott handed Tom his. 'Quite a saga, eh?'

'That it is.'

Elliott knew what the tramlines suddenly appearing on Tom's forehead meant. It was only a matter of time before Tom came to the same conclusion as he had. Continuing to stir his tea, Tom eventually looked up and said, 'But doesn't that raise the question …?'

Elliott cut across him and handed over the sugar bowl. 'You're thinking exactly the same as I did. Was one of them involved in the cage disaster and Robertson's death?'

'Well yes,' admitted Tom.

'And that's why we're going to visit Haddington

again tomorrow. To check on something.'

Elliott went on to explain how Mr Cooper had mentioned to him that his office window looked out onto the High Street and that, after Mrs Ridgeway had left the building, he'd watched her approach a car. The man in the driver's seat had immediately got out and walked round to the pavement to open the door for her. 'Yes, out of courtesy, you'd do that when a lady first gets into the car. But after each time she returns from visiting somewhere?'

'Unless he was in service as a driver,' suggested Tom.

'Or perhaps the butler!' Elliott clarified, with a self-satisfied smile.

Chapter 21

Through her window, Louise watched as two majestic Belgian black horses, each with a plume of black ostrich feathers attached to a braid around its head, drew the glass-sided hearse through the archway and into the courtyard. Inside the carriage, Frederick's coffin was draped in a union flag, and escorting it on either side were two cavalrymen on horseback. Following behind, a cortege of empty carriages pulled up to the entrance.

With a gentle knock on her open door, Matilda stated, 'They're here, Louise.'

Watching for a moment longer, as the servants began to open the carriage doors in readiness, Louise eventually spoke, 'Yes, thank you. I will be down shortly.'

'We must talk … when all this sadness is through.'

Louise didn't respond. She just pulled the black veil down over her face and walked along the landing towards the stairs, before stopping nervously at seeing the servants lined up in the entrance below. Also, waiting for her at the bottom of the stairs was her father-in-law, dressed in full military ceremonial uniform. Breathing deeply, she made her way slowly down the steps.

As instructed, the nanny was waiting with baby

Edward in her arms, his attentive little face watching all the activity. Louise lifted her veil and Edward, on recognising her, held out his arms, wanting his mother to take hold of him. She clutched his tiny hand and stroked his blond, feathery hair to one side. 'Soon my darling,' she said and released his hand. At this, the bewildered face burst into tears and struggled to be reunited with his mother. Dowling gave a nod to the nanny and she quickly turned to take Edward away. Again, Louise breathed deeply, trying to hold herself together.

Lord Ranskill formed a curve with his arm for his daughter-in-law to take hold of, so that he might escort her to their carriage. Not since the day of her arrival at Haddington, when he'd grudgingly kissed her, had Louise had any physical contact with the earl. Not even when Edward was born did he display any sort of affection, such as a hand of congratulation on her shoulder. It all seemed so hypocritical: a blatant show of family closeness for people who had, on so many occasions, observed very much the contrary. But Louise had no strength to challenge any aspect of the traditional funeral arrangements. In truth, had she been her usual self, she would most probably have stunned the family by electing to have a simple service without any of them present.

Stepping into the carriage she caught a glimpse of David, on horseback, acting as one of the outriders accompanying the hearse. How she wished that it could be him sitting opposite her and not his father. At least there would have been some honesty in such an arrangement.

It was a short five minutes' journey to the small chapel nestled beyond the hall and towards the lake. And one that started in silence inside the carriage. Eventually, Louise spoke, although never taking her gaze away from the scene outside the window. 'Well, at least it's not raining.'

'Yes, I suppose there is that,' replied Ranskill. He took a long pause before speaking further. 'Louise, after all this is done, I want to sit down and talk with you.'

'Everyone is so eager to talk with me, it seems,' replied Louise, with a hint of sarcasm.

Unusually, Ranskill did not retaliate. Instead he calmly stated, 'There are obviously things we need to discuss, like arrangements for your future at Haddington. And, of course, baby Edward. We have to ensure his future remains the focus for both of us.'

'Oh, indeed, sir. One must always look out for one's future!'

The rest of their journey was spent in silence, until finally the procession arrived at the chapel. Here, as protocol demanded, the funeral went forward with full military honours, everything being planned to the last detail. Louise sat listening to one eulogy after another and smiled inwardly at some of Frederick's supposed attributes. 'Strong and fearless in the face of adversity,' she repeated to herself. 'Well, I must have been absent on that day!'

~~~

Frederick's death had hit Louise hard. Not because she still loved him, or believed that the purpose of her marriage could have somehow been rekindled. It was the grief of suddenly losing the man who had once been the light of her life, the man who was the father of her child. And despite all of Frederick's failings, she knew that for his part, he had truly loved her. Guilt over her adultery with Kurt engulfed her. Becoming a widow was the final event that had brought Louise to her knees. Apart from baby Edward, she had lost everyone once dear to her. Even David, whom she longed to talk to, had been dispatched back to the army temporarily. All those who now surrounded her were members of a family that she had no desire to share her grief with. She began to take long walks alone.

Ahead of her lay only open meadow: the place where she had known joy, passion and fulfilment with Kurt; the place full of vibrant colour, which she had viewed with fascination when first arriving at Haddington, wondering
~~~

what was beyond; the place where she had walked with Frederick and her dog, Millie, before the birth of baby Edward. And at all those times, excitement had danced inside her and hope had filled her heart. But now, the meadow was no more than a field to her, leading where it might – she didn't care.

In the sky above there were dark, storm-laden clouds. In the distance, a veil of rain headed towards her. The wind, which moments earlier had been gentle and fresh, was soon howling angrily around her. Louise didn't even pull up the collar of her coat. Instead, she just turned her face towards the wind. Tears rolled down her cheeks. She felt the first drops of rain through the flaming red hair that had fallen across her face, hiding the anguish and pain that consumed her. Where had it all gone wrong, she wondered. Where was the life full of optimism for the future; the woman who, from a tender age, had used her dogged spirit to fight against the odds? Quite simply, they had slowly been stripped away, as beauty eventually disappears from a once beautiful face. Lightening forked from the menacing dark autumn clouds, and torrential rain fell, quickly soaking Louise. Finally, she pulled up her collar and began to walk … and walk. To where, she had no idea. All she knew was that she would end up somewhere.

Further and further she trudged, until the impact

of the wind and rain was so strong that she was forced to take what shelter a large oak tree could offer. She trembled as the cold and damp engulfed her body. It then dawned on her that she had no idea where she was; and with the storm showing no sign of abating, a panic came over her. Not that she was concerned for her own welfare any more. It was the prospect of Edward losing not only his father but now, also, his mother that terrified her. The realisation of her predicament, just for a moment, brought back the spirited and pragmatic Louise. To give herself any chance, she knew she had to find somewhere dry. She looked around, trying to get her bearings. There must be some landmark to give her a clue as to her location. But there wasn't. With a sigh, she laid her head back against the trunk of the large tree and closed her eyes.

In the distance, she thought she heard someone calling her name. Opening her eyes, she could barely see through the curtain of rain. 'Louise! Louise!' the voice came again, now louder and clearer. All of a sudden she could hear the thud of hooves pounding the ground. The sound unexpectedly stopped. 'Louise! Louise. Are you out there?' the voice called again.

A relieved Louise stumbled into the open. 'Here … I'm here,' she managed to shout, trembling and at the point of exhaustion. 'Matilda!' she gasped in surprise.

The last person she expected to come trying to find her was dismounting from her horse. Unclipping and removing her waterproof riding cape, Matilda wrapped it around Louise. 'Whatever possessed you to venture out in this weather?' she asked, but not unkindly.

~~~

After the funeral, Louise barricaded herself into her room. Here she could be alone with her thoughts, and she barely left, except to attend to her son, even though he now had a nanny. This was something Louise had had to agree to, in order to save herself from any further conflict, at least until a time when she felt strong enough to cope. She seldom ate any more, and certainly never entertained the idea of going down into the dining room, although hostilities towards her had all but ceased. Even Robertson had been unusually pleasant towards her, but she had no doubt that, as soon as the family's exaggerated display of grief was over, he would assume his position once more as the twisted doctor of malice. And she was right. For despite Ranskill's instructions to suspend their plans for Louise, Robertson was already secretly plotting his next move in detail.

The fly in the ointment though, was Matilda, and Robertson was forced to watch as she suffered an ever
~~~

deepening crisis. She was now racked with guilt over the evil and sordid affair with Crecia – guilt that she couldn't speak of to anyone other than Robertson. And he, of course, had no desire to listen to her remorse and fears. The loss of her favourite nephew simply added further to Matilda's state of anxiety. With each passing day, Robertson became more and more concerned as he watched her seeking solace and wanting to reconcile her differences with Louise. He feared that it wouldn't be long before she would let the cat out of the bag.

It was time to re-evaluate his plans. The one person he thought he could control was suddenly becoming too unpredictable. But he hadn't anticipated that Matilda had plans of her own.

One afternoon, there was a knock on Louise's door. She didn't answer it.

'Please, Louise. May I come in?' called Matilda, in a gentle voice that Louise could never have imagined possible of the aunt.

'I have no desire to quarrel with you, Matilda.'

'Oh Louise, I haven't come to argue. I've simply brought you some food. Please open the door.'

Louise eventually turned the handle, but left the door only slightly ajar. She moved back towards the window and once more stared out at the gravelled courtyard below. Matilda slowly pushed the door open. Standing there, a tray in her hands, she looked over towards Louise, who pulled her shawl more tightly around her shoulders and leant her head against the windowpane.

'You must eat,' Matilda implored.

Louise didn't answer.

'Is everything all right? We haven't seen or heard from you for days.'

'Matilda, we've never spoken civilly to each other. Let's not pretend we're going to start now.'

Matilda felt most awkward, but persevered. 'It's time for change, and I know I have to make the first move … So, may I come in?'

Louise lifted her head away from the glass and looked straight at Matilda. 'Whose suggestion is this?'

'Mine of course!' replied the surprised aunt.

'You and I could never be friends, Matilda,' Louise insisted.

To avoid any eye contact, Matilda dropped her head. 'I realise I've been truly unwelcoming to you since you arrived here.'

Louise could only respond with a huff.

'But I want you to know before I leave Haddington, that I am sorry for my coldness.'

Whilst the aunt might appear genuinely sorry, Louise was not in the least inclined to trust her. She was, however, intrigued by Matilda's comment about leaving

Haddington, so she enquired, 'I don't understand. Why do you say you're leaving Haddington?'

'I plan on staying at Brentwood House for a while.'

Brentwood was a beautiful property nestled in a coastal valley in Dorset that the earl had purchased some years earlier, intending it be used as a holiday retreat, although most of the time it was unoccupied.

'With all that has happened here … First Crecia, and now the terrible tragedy with Frederick, I just —'

Louise interrupted her. 'What about Crecia?' She knew Matilda had never cared anything for any maid, let alone an Italian one. Immediately, she had a flashback to the dinner table and Matilda dropping her fork on hearing the news of the maid's departure. Why, on any occasion when the girl's name was mentioned, did the aunt look uncomfortable and suddenly have to leave?

'What do you know about Crecia, Matilda?'

Clasping her hands together nervously, Matilda eventually regained her self control. 'Why nothing, Louise. I was just meaning it was so sad for you … for all of us.'

Louise didn't believe a word. 'If you have any information about Crecia's disappearance, I want to know.'

Matilda desperately wanted to confess her sins, but she knew that if she did, the consequences for her would be terrible. She was under no illusion as to what Robertson was capable of.

'Of course, Louise. But why would I have any information about Crecia's disappearance?' Matilda asked anxiously before swiftly changing the subject. She stood and smiled. 'I do hope you'll find it within you to accept my apologies.' Next, she looked over to the tray of food. 'And do please try and eat something.' With that, she left the room.

Louise frowned. Exactly what was Matilda up to, she wondered. She could only think that her father-in-law and Robertson had orchestrated the whole thing, but for what reason? Lifting the lid off the plate of food, she looked down at the glazed chicken on a bed of salad and promptly returned the lid. She wouldn't have been at all surprised if the prettily presented plate had contained something truly sinister.

Chapter 22

Tom had no idea how he was going to explain the night's events to Ann. 'How could it possibly have come to this?' he kept asking himself over and over. With all his medical knowledge, should he not have seen it coming? Should he not have had the answers? Well, he didn't.

It was all quiet now – no more shouting, no more desperate pleas, no more thrashing about. He looked up to where the rope had hung just an hour before. He couldn't understand it. If he had only woken earlier, perhaps he could have stopped it. Lily stood there beside him, utterly shocked.

'I suppose we ought to make a start, Lily,' Tom said forlornly and picked up Elliott's slipper which, in the frantic mayhem, had been kicked off his foot and now lay on the floor by the upturned chair.

The evening had been no different to any of the previous ones. Tom and Elliott had sat in the parlour, discussing all manner of things. As usual, it had ended with neither man really winning the debate: but the fun was in trying. At 11.00 pm Lily had brought in their nightcaps and some ten minutes later Tom had said his goodnight and left Elliott to finish his drink. Four hours later, the scene that met Tom in the kitchen was one of absolute horror.

Sitting thinking about nothing in particular, Elliott stretched out his legs, took another sip of his drink and, before he knew it, had started to nod off. Lily, doing her final checks before going to bed, had discovered him snoring away and decided not to wake him. Would it have made any difference? Tom tried to convince Lily that it probably wouldn't have, and that she couldn't blame herself. It was all just a tragic accident.

The nightmare Elliott was soon experiencing felt utterly real. He was deep in a trance-like state, powerless to prevent the events that were happening to him, unable to trigger his natural instinct to wake up. As always, Canon Brockwell appeared, and led him on a bizarre journey. But this time, it was as if Elliott were constantly bringing things to a conclusion. In his vision, he visited the butcher and corner shop and paid his outstanding debts. He then sat calmly at his desk and carefully laid out his last will and testament in full view for Ann to see. Finally, he pulled out of his pocket the little bootie that always accompanied him, kissed it, and gently placed it down on the desk.

'All done?' mocked Brockwell from the armchair. Then he gave his usual sickening smile. 'We can't leave business unfinished now, can we?'

Elliott just stared at him, resigned to his fate.

'Well, it's more than I got, Robert!' Brockwell added with sarcasm.

The scene then changed, and to a place Elliott knew well. It was the vestry and annexe at St Mary's Church, where he'd had his final altercation with Brockwell. Only this time, it was Elliott who was in front of the writing bureau, pulling at each drawer, desperately looking for something. Eventually, he found what he wanted and pulled it out – the hip flask that contained the laudanum.

Elliott was about to attempt the same awful deed as Brockwell had. He turned the key to the annexe room and entered. There she was, strapped to the chair, her face full of fear. The only difference from Brockwell's evil intentions for her was that Mary didn't have a scarf holding an apple in place in her mouth.

'Why Robert? … In God's name, please don't do this to me,' Mary sobbed, watching Elliott unscrew the top on the hip flask.

'It was always how it was meant to be, Mary,' Elliott said, clasping hold of her chin.

Barely able to speak, she wept, 'Robert. You're almost my father.'

Stirring in his nightmare, Elliott thrashed about in the armchair. It was if he were trying to wake up, 'No! Please, God!' he shouted.

But the voice that responded was Brockwell's: 'You *will* do it, Robert. You *will* sin!'

Sinking deeper into his nightmare, Elliott found himself pouring the laudanum mixture down Mary's throat. Then he stood over her waiting for it to take effect. Slowly he took off his jacket.

Outside the annexe room, Elliott heard the desperate banging on the vestry door and voices shouting. Brockwell slammed the annexe door shut. 'I should never have answered it,' he shouted, remembering how it had been. 'Do it! Sin, damn you!'

'No, please, no, I beg of you …,' Mary tried to say, as Elliott moved in closer to her. But she never finished. Instead, her eyes just rolled upwards and her head tumbled to one side.

All of a sudden, the location changed again. Elliott was in his kitchen. Sitting at the table, Brockwell was tying a washing line into a noose. He gave Elliott one of his horrible smiles. 'Oh, Robert! How could you? Not with Mary.'

Elliott was weeping with guilt.

'You're just misunderstood … as I was. But who's going to listen?' Brockwell asked, sliding the knot forward to ensure the noose worked effectively. 'And certainly no one is going to forgive you.'

Brockwell touched the bullet wound at his temple

and shuddered. 'Better that we choose a suitable ending,' he said and threw the line to Elliott. 'It's time for us to meet properly again – in hell!'

Elliott caught the line and looked up to the ceiling, to the hoist housing that held the wooden clothes rail. With Brockwell watching, he slowly took a chair and put it into position under the rail. With resignation, he stood on the chair and began to slide the line through the hoist housing, before tying it into a secure knot. Only when the task was done, did he peer down at Brockwell.

'But you defiled her, Robert. I never got the chance!'

With determination, Elliott pulled the noose over his head and tightened it. His expression contorted, as Bessie started to bark at him. Once again, it was if he were willing himself to awake from his nightmare. But it didn't stop him from finally pushing the chair away and plunging downwards. He came to a stop with an awful jolt.

~~~

It was Bessie's barks that woke Tom. They were distressed barks that signalled something was wrong. Turning on his light, Tom struggled to look at the time. He moaned as he saw it was 3.00 am. The barking continued. 'Damned thing,' he muttered, becoming more awake. His eyes at last adjusted to the light. He threw off his blankets and
~~~

headed out of his room. Bessie's barks were now howls and Tom decided he would have to go downstairs and investigate.

What greeted him as he opened the kitchen door shook him rigid. Elliott, his dear friend, was standing on a chair with a washing line looped round his neck and suspended from the ceiling. At first, he didn't know what to do. It was all so unreal. Then logic took over. Elliott had to be acting out a nightmare, he realised. He'd observed many a patient sleepwalking but never, in all his years of medical practice, had he seen someone so deeply in a trance and ready to do something so terrible.

Tom tried to assess the options quickly, although there was really only one: he would need to hold onto Elliott's torso to stop him falling, and then try to bring him slowly out of his trance. But first he needed to silence Bessie. With every bark she made, he could see Elliott becoming more agitated. It only needed his friend to stumble and it would all be over. 'Shh! Shh, Bess! There's a good girl.'

But Brockwell's voice was all too clear in Elliott's head. 'Do it, Robert … Do it!' the voice cried. Before Tom had chance to act, Elliott cried out in anguish and pushed the chair from underneath his feet. It flew across the floor. His slipper followed.

The whole scene went into slow motion for Tom as

he desperately flung himself at Elliott. He watched as the line tightened round his friend's neck. The face in front of him writhed in agony as he gasped for air. Finally, his body jerked to a halt. Everything accelerated as Tom tried to clamber to his feet. But before he could manage it, Elliott's body fell on top of him, followed closely by half the ceiling, crashing down on them. Plaster, debris and dust engulfed the pair on the floor.

'My God … Robert!' Tom cried, frantically pulling away lumps of lath and horse-hair lime plaster. He uncovered Elliott's red face, with his tongue still hanging out. The washing line had cut deeply into one side of his neck. Carefully, Tom released the crude slip knot that Elliott had tied in haste, and moved it over his friend's head. He felt for a pulse. To his sheer joy, he found one, and it was racing like a piston engine.

~~~

After thoroughly checking over the very fortunate Elliott, Tom gave him the all clear and dispatched him to bed with a strong dose of aspirin. Elliott was exhausted and utterly shocked at what he'd attempted in his nightmare. Even more, he was highly embarrassed. All he could do was keep apologising to Tom and Lily. But Tom was having none of it: instead, he explained that there was
~~~

a rational psychological reason for what was happening to Elliott – he just needed time to analyse everything and begin piecing together all the medical facts. In the meantime, he was adamant that Elliott should remain in bed and rest. It was agreed that Tom and Lily would take it in turns to check on him every fifteen minutes; this despite Elliott's insistence that what had happened was nothing.

With the grumbling patient tucked up in bed, it was time to assess the damage to the kitchen ceiling and begin clearing up the mess. Tom surveyed the scene and puffed out his cheeks at Lily. 'Where do we start?'

Lily took her usual approach to sorting out any type of mess, which was to simply roll up her sleeves and get on with it. However, she drew the line at attempting this whilst dressed in her nightdress and dressing gown. 'I'll just get changed and then, if you wouldn't mind carrying the dustbin in for me, Professor, I'll have things shipshape in no time,' she explained.

Looking around at the dust and debris, Tom wished he could share her optimism. He peered up towards the gaping hole in the ceiling, which exposed the upstairs floor joists. 'Do you know any tradesmen nearby, Lily?' he asked.

'Well, not who'd come out at 3 o'clock in the morning,' she had to admit.

As he continued to gaze up at the ceiling, it became more and more apparent to Tom just how lucky Elliott had been. Had the clothes rail hoist been firmly screwed into the wooden joist instead of into a supporting lath, then the outcome might have been altogether different. As it was, he gave thanks to the lord for small mercies and hoped Ann would see it the same way when she returned home in a couple of days' time.

It wasn't long before Lily had things firmly under control and, once the mess had been cleared up, the strange looking hole in the ceiling didn't look too bad. Tom thought that if he could get the help of a tradesman, he could at least have it all plastered in readiness for painting. But that was something to tackle later. In the meantime, he felt that Lily had done a stalwart job and should finish off, then go back to bed and get some well-deserved sleep. In return, he would keep an eye on Elliott, who was by now, mercifully, fast asleep and snoring.

All the while, Tom had been mulling over just what was prompting his friend's nightmares. He couldn't help thinking that what Elliott was experiencing bore the hallmarks of hallucinogenic drugs, which were bringing about some very disturbing dreams and subconscious interactions. But he knew Elliott was no drug addict or he couldn't bring himself to believe that he could be. He wondered just what was going on.

Lily interrupted his thoughts. 'Would you be so kind as to lift this bucket of water to the sink for me, Professor Sharpe? I don't think I've got any more strength left.'

'Of course,' replied Tom, taking the bucket over to the sink and began pouring out the water. It was then he got a whiff of something that he'd come across before. It was a smell he associated with the vagrants he often treated in hospital after they had been brought in off the streets in a state of hallucination. At first he thought it must merely be a similar type of smell coming from the dirty water emptying down the plughole. But even after he'd rinsed the sink with fresh water, the smell remained. He looked round the work surfaces until his eyes eventually came to rest on a dark-coloured paste in a pestle. He picked it up and held it under his nose. Sure enough, it was what he suspected – the aroma was coming from damp, ground morning glory seeds.

'Lily! Have you ground these?' Tom asked, showing the maid the pestle.

'Well, yes, Professor. They're for ...' She stopped mid-sentence and thought for a moment whether she should continue. 'I shouldn't really say. Mr Elliott would be most embarrassed.'

'And I will be most annoyed, Lily, if you don't tell me.'

Lily looked sheepish but eventually unburdened

herself. 'Very well! I get them from my brother. To grind into a paste and put into Mr Elliott's nightcap of an evening, as instructed.'

Tom lifted his eyebrows in shock. 'You do what!' he exclaimed.

'It's for his thinning hair, Professor. But please don't tell him I told you,' Lily blurted out nervously.

Tom paused for a brief moment before throwing back his head and beginning to laugh with relief. He grabbed hold of Lily's face and kissed her forehead. 'Oh, my girl! If only you knew. These won't do anything for Mr Elliott's receding hair. They're morning glory seeds. What they'll do, once they've been ground and swallowed, is to give a person the most vivid hallucinations.

'Oh dear,' sighed Lily, before vowing: 'That brother of mine! I'll kill him!'

Chapter 23

For a woman like Louise, depression and sorrow could live within her only so long. Her character was all about the joys of life, love, and, above all, finding enrichment through experiences. For the last twelve months, she had allowed herself to be consumed by the negativity of Haddington and a family that cared nothing for her. Now, it was time for her to rise and resurface once more: a woman of happiness. Quite how she was going to achieve it, she wasn't sure, but Louise was determined that she and baby Edward would live life free from darkness and without the stain of sadness so often associated with the Warsop name.

By contrast, the Earl of Ranskill, a man steeped in chauvinistic male dominance, was only prepared to tolerate minimal change in order to maintain his hold on the family heir. He saw accommodating Louise as nothing more than putting on a show for the outside world. As for his business partner, Robertson, a man whose intentions were rotten to the core, time was of the essence. If his plans were to be realised, then under no circumstances could Louise remain at Haddington.

It was David's release from the army and his

homecoming that had been the catalyst for the change in Louise. One morning, on her return from a walk, she stepped through the entrance doors to hear the beautiful sound of a violin coming from the drawing room. Instantly, she knew who would be playing it. Eagerly pulling off her coat and throwing it down on a chair, she rushed towards the open door of the room. She stopped on seeing David standing there facing the window, his back to her. Oblivious, he drew his bow lovingly across the strings of his violin creating the most tender and haunting melody. Slowly, she walked over to him, wrapped her arms around his shoulders and chest, and laid her head against his back. He knew immediately by the smell of her perfume whose touch it was.

'Louise!' he called out, managing to turn around just enough for her to place her finger against his lips to silence him.

'Just play for me a while,' she whispered, and again nestled her head against his back. He repositioned his fingers and tenderly stroked the bow. The resulting gentle sound drifted through the air like a satin sheet slowly falling to the floor. She clung to him and smiled. This was happiness.

In David's company, Louise became her old self. They would spend their evenings together in the library discussing a multitude of subjects. Often they would tease each other with opposing views but always they would laugh. Anyone not knowing their circumstances could be easily forgiven for believing the pair were lovers. David soon recognized Louise's ability to turn an argument round to her way of thinking; and even when discussing an engineering problem, he had to admit there was logic in her opinion.

Often, Kurt would join them and add more contention to the debate. With each passing week, he was becoming more impressed by Louise, to the point where he was falling in love with her. No longer was it about the physical side of love. Now, he desired the whole of her. This was a woman he could admire: a woman he wanted to have as his wife. However, Louise had no more real interest in Kurt.

The German's jealousy of David soon became apparent and their previously friendly working partnership began to falter. Where once they would have discussed technical issues concerning the new pit shaft and worked out a compromise, now, it became a battle of personalities and engineering supremacy. What added to Kurt's frustration was seeing how much Louise adored David and this frustration only increased when he discovered the truth about David's sexuality. Kurt was most definitely homophobic.

Louise and David's closeness also caught the

attention of the earl and Robertson. Both of them still saw Louise as a problem that needed removing, but each man had different ideas of how to achieve this. Ranskill felt he could attain the best result by offering Louise a deal which, no matter how unfair she felt it was, she would ultimately have no alternative but to accept. Robertson, on the other hand, knew that Louise wouldn't entertain any proposition that didn't suit her. And besides, the possibility of her being at Haddington for much longer was making him anxious. With every conversation they had, it seemed she was getting nearer to discovering the truth about Crecia's disappearance.

In the library, Ranskill attempted to make his offer.

'Ah, Louise. I knew I would find you here,' he said with a friendly smile. 'I thought now would be a good time to have a talk with you about the future.' In truth, there was no thought given to whether she was ready or not. Ranskill had merely decided that he wanted to discuss things here and now. Of course Louise knew as much and, therefore, needed to ensure she gave her father-in-law a run for his money.

'This talk, sir. Will it be at me or with me?'

Straight away, Ranskill could feel his hackles rise, but he remained calm.

'Now things are …' He paused for a moment in an attempt to choose the right words. 'Well, back to normal,

I suppose.' Nobody could deliver a forthright assessment of a sensitive matter in such a business-like manner as the earl. Louise was not really expecting anything less. In fact, she was surprised that he had waited four weeks to broach the subject. Her assumption had been that he would do so the very week after Frederick's funeral.

'Yes, it appears everything is back to normal, sir. Time is a great healer, I find.'

Ranskill gave one of his contemptuous looks. Whilst he could compete with the best at handing out sarcasm, he struggled to accept it when it came back at him.

'I will remind you that Frederick was my son. I miss him just as much as you do, Louise.'

Realising that if she allowed it to, their conversation would turn into a game of spiteful tit-for-tat, Louise decided to hold back and just let her father-in-law have his say, after which she would take her leave of him. But she didn't quite anticipate how spiteful the game was.

'I've been thinking. Perhaps it might suit you better to live away from Haddington in the future,' said Ranskill, opting to get straight to the point. 'I'm sure we could find a suitable place.'

Louise was shocked at the suggestion, but was far from averse to the idea. 'Well, I haven't given it a great deal of thought, I have to admit. But, with Edward growing up so fast, maybe it would be good to settle him elsewhere sooner rather than later.'

Ranskill turned his face slightly to one side and assumed an expression that suggested his words had been misinterpreted. 'No, I think you misunderstand, Louise. Edward is the future heir to the estate. He must remain here – at Haddington.'

The fire immediately ignited within Louise and she felt her anger rushing upwards. Eventually she was red-faced with rage. 'Sir! Do you honestly think I would leave here without my child?'

'I'm sure we can come to some arrangement where —'

He didn't get time to finish before she lambasted him with her response. 'To call you unbelievable, would be callow flattery. What possesses you to insult me with the notion that I could abandon my son in favour of a life in a fine house somewhere? And, I use the words "fine house" loosely if you have anything to do with its purchase.'

What had started as a tense conversation had built up, in just a few sentences, to fever pitch. Louise was as near to screaming at her father-in-law as ever she could remember. Ranskill was equally as fired up. Just then, Dowling appeared and discreetly pulled the doors closed. It was a brief moment for them to regroup.

'If, as is blatantly obvious, you want me out of here, I will purchase a house with my own wealth,' Louise insisted.

'Your *bit* of wealth became part of the Ranskill estate when you married Frederick and now forms part of Edward's inheritance, whilst you, dear Louise, are technically penniless. Without my help and charity, you are no better off than a serving girl.'

Louise looked at him with incredulity. 'Then I shall appoint a solicitor and fight you for what is rightfully mine.'

'Yes, do that. If, of course, you can afford one,' Ranskill smugly replied. If there was one thing he was good at, it was ensuring every aspect of his affairs were legally watertight. 'In return for custody of Edward, I agree to pass the title of Brentwood House to you, along with a most generous annuity to live there,' he attempted.

'Oh! I have no problem with Edward remaining here at Haddington … but with his mother! And here are my terms for that: I shall occupy the upper floors, as presently, with the addition of four more rooms to make the apartment more private. And —'

'Who the hell do you think you are?' Ranskill spat with contempt, as Louise continued to lay down her demands.

'Why, Lady Warsop of Haddington, of course. Mother of the future earl.'

~~~
~~~

With Matilda having firmly made herself at home at Brentwood, Robertson re-appraised how he could gain and maintain control of Haddington without her. The only way he thought this possible was to ensure that Edward became the Earl of Ranskill quickly, under the guardianship of his mother. Then, by institutionalising Louise, he could get a court to give him control over the child's affairs. That was, of course, after he'd removed Ranskill, Matilda and David. Their demise, however, would need to be most inventive if the whole thing were to be plausible. Each night, Robertson sat up in his room until the early hours, musing over every possible scenario. What was always obvious to him, though, was that it would all take time to achieve. Except with Louise. With her, the situation was altogether different. And as the earl was again on board with the doctor's plan, events could now move forward swiftly.

~~~

Archduke Franz Ferdinand was dead. Relations between Serbia and Austria-Hungary were in deep crisis. Germany had refused to intervene. By early August, the German Chancellor had declared to the British Ambassador in Berlin that Germany was contemplating war with France. Britain, in turn, had told France it would give her "… all protection in its powers." Europe and Russia were
~~~

teetering on the brink of all-out war.

Nobody was more aware of the delicate situation than Kurt. His contact with his homeland had always been strong and now, through his brother's senior role within the Reich's government, his situation was brought to the notice of the Chief of German General Staff, Helmuth von Moltke. Moltke felt that a German working as a chief engineer in Britain's coal industry was a golden opportunity for espionage. His assistants were encouraged to exploit Kurt's fortuitous position, particularly his encyclopaedic knowledge, not only of British colliery locations and production, but of the steel industry that Ranskill's and other collieries supplied. Instructions were given for a spy to make contact with Kurt and, before he knew where he was, the patriotic German was willingly feeding information back to Berlin.

Anti-German sentiment though, was growing daily in the pits and Kurt knew it could be only days before he and his men would be interned. Knowing this, he managed to get a message to Berlin requesting he be smuggled out of Sheffield immediately and repatriated to his fatherland. The dangerous German began secretly to amass as many technical plans, maps and information documents as he could, in preparation for his proposed rescue. Until then, Kurt continued his skilful charade at Haddington, as a deeply neutral pacifist.

~~~

Once again, her intuition was right. 'Dear David, don't forget I too have known love,' Louise reminded him and smiled broadly. David had a lover. She locked her arm through his. 'I want to know everything about him. Is he tall? Is he broad or thin? What's his name? Will I like him?' she demanded to know. David just assumed a coy expression. 'Louise, please!'

But Louise had no intention of talking about anything else until she knew all there was to know about the man who was seemingly making her brother-in-law the most contented of men.

Since David's return to Haddington from the army, he had worked tirelessly on site at the new pit shaft. Quickly, he won the respect of the men through his technical knowledge and problem-solving skills. And he was never happier than when getting his hands dirty, proving that he was more than just the earl's son. Most impressed was a young shaftsman, Stephen, who rode the tub daily with David, up and down the shaft. The small-framed, fresh-faced youngster, always dressed in a large waterproof coat and hat which half-buried him, watched in fascination as the athletic new engineer gave instructions to hold the tub steady. Then, David would bravely hang over the side to inspect the brickwork and
~~~

take measurements before writing them down in his notebook along with some sketches.

Most days, Stephen wouldn't speak much beyond work-related comments, exemplifying his shyness. That is until the day the tub hoist mechanism became jammed and the pair were left dangling in the shaft for over an hour. 'Well …,' said David, putting his notebook into his pocket, 'So, what do you like doing when you're not at work?'

The acutely conscious Stephen stuttered, 'I love music, sir.'

Their relationship was born.

Having to accept that David wasn't going to expand much more on his lover, Louise squeezed his arm. 'I'm so pleased. Nobody deserves happiness more than you.'

'And you?' David enquired. 'I sense your happiness isn't going to be here at Haddington.'

Louise patted his hand gently. 'No, I don't think it will be. But for now …' She paused briefly, reflecting on her previous conversation with his father. 'Well, let's just say, for now, Haddington serves its purpose.'

~~~

Staff at Haddington Hall would soon be able to tell the story of a night involving great mystery. This was to be an evening where people would speculate about what really
~~~

happened for months to come, perhaps forever. Yet, it started like any other.

Louise, David and Kurt were chatting in the library following dinner. The earl was reading through and signing some documents in his study. Robertson, as usual, had chosen to retire early to his apartment, always seemingly uninterested in conversation. By 8.30, however, things had changed and both Kurt and Robertson were feeling the tension inside them grow. And all because the sun was beginning to set. Which simply meant that Louise would soon be taking her evening stroll.

Complaining of severe indigestion, David had given his apologies and left the library for an early night, leaving Louise and Kurt to talk further.

'You look unsettled, Kurt,' said Louise, observing him constantly looking at his pocket watch and scratching his arm nervously.

'Do I?'

'Yes. Is everything all right?'

Kurt stood up and walked over to the fireplace, gripping a glass of brandy tightly in his palms. He turned back to address Louise. 'Our countries will be at war any day now,' he stated, clipping every word with his heavy German accent.

Louise moved round to face him. 'Yes, if what I read is correct, then, I fear you're right.'

His eyes stayed fixed on hers. Eventually, he walked over and sat beside her on the sofa. Putting his glass on the coffee table, he placed his hands over hers. Louise was quite taken aback but didn't pull away. Instead she just continued to look into Kurt's eyes, which were ablaze with danger.

'If I stay, my men and I will be interned here. It may be only days away. I must return to Germany.'

'But how will you —?' Louise began. But she stopped, suddenly realising that he was trying to say he would be leaving tonight. The look on her face let him know she understood.

'Come with me … Marry me!'

Louise pulled her hands swiftly from underneath his and stood up. He followed and held her arm. 'Marry me, Louise. Let us live in Germany. We can be —'

'No! … Kurt please,' she interrupted. 'How could I possibly marry you? I have just been widowed – and I have a son who is heir to Haddington.'

'The boy belongs here, but you do not.'

Louise's look hardened. 'How could you even think that I would leave my son and flee my country to live in Germany with you?'

'This country is doomed to destruction,' came Kurt's arrogant response. It never took much for him to flip to the nastier side of his personality.

'Like all your countrymen, you're very sure of yourself, but don't underestimate the determination and resolve of this country, Mr Mueller.'

Kurt grabbed at her arm and pulled her towards him. 'I will marry you,' he said sternly and forced a kiss onto her lips. She struggled to set herself free. 'And in Germany!' Louise promptly slapped him hard across his face and stormed out of the library.

Moments later, through the bay window, Kurt watched Louise begin her evening stroll. He looked at the time on his pocket watch, then, up towards the sky, before again allowing his eyes to follow Louise. He grinned and wondered, what if …?

Also watching Louise commence her walk was Robertson. From his window, he looked down and, placing a bottle of chloroform and some gauze into his jacket pocket, he too wondered. Only his thoughts were far more sinister. 'Enjoy your walk, Louise. For it will be the last you take as a sane woman,' he said out loud.

~~~

It was Robertson's snooping and eavesdropping that prompted his decision to act without further delay. He knew that if he left it any longer he ran the risk of being finally exposed as having caused Crecia's disappearance.
~~~

Earlier that morning, whilst walking down the corridor, he heard Louise talking on the telephone. As he always did if he thought himself unobserved, he slithered behind something – in this case a folding screen – and listened in to the conversation, to see if it could benefit him in some way.

'… And you can confirm that the telegram originated in York?' Louise asked. 'I see. Most intriguing,' she continued, in response to Mrs Lucas's answer from the village post office. '… So, if it had come from Italy, it would almost certainly have been transferred via London?'

'Yes, ma'am.'

'Excellent. Well, thank you very much,' concluded Louise, with a satisfied smile, and she replaced the earpiece onto the phone.

Robertson felt uneasy. He knew Louise had been intent on investigating what had happened to Crecia but, with everything that had happened with Frederick, he had thought that she wouldn't pursue it. Placing the telephone back on the table, Louise walked away and towards him. He slid behind the decorative screen and peeped through the panel's hinged fold to secretly watch until, at last, she was out of sight. Only then did he re-emerge. 'How very sad that what you've learnt will be of no use to you.'

That evening, on her walk, Louise took her usual route. Once through the courtyard archway, she strolled along the narrow gravel pathway leading from the fountain, passing the summerhouse, before finally winding back onto the driveway, which was flanked by the meadow to her right. Never on her walks did she feel afraid, simply because never before had anything happened to make her feel so. Even the scurrying of a fox in the bushes seldom frightened her.

Louise was oblivious of what lay ahead on this walk. Hidden and motionless in the large bushes some thirty yards away from her, a pair of menacing eyes peered out through the camouflage of branches and leaves. Cheerfully humming a tune to herself, she approached along the driveway. Ahead of her, the sun had now disappeared behind the hall. She saw a footman in the distance lighting the oil-burning lights around the courtyard, which made her think that in future she would need to shorten her route if she were to beat the sunset. If only she had made that decision the day before.

Hearing a rustle, she didn't think anything of it. The snapping of tinder dry branches did, however, make her stop and look around. The noise stopped but the eyes eerily followed her every move. Walking on, she again heard a rustle and this time thought she saw something large move. Now she was becoming nervous. Her heartbeat began to increase slightly. She quickened her pace. The rustle followed, then stopped.

'Who's there?' Louise said, with a tremble in her voice.

Of course there was no reply.

There was another rustle, only this time it came from behind her. She spun around, but there was nothing there. Totally alone and now afraid, she felt her heart racing frantically. To make matters worse, a dark cloud passed over the rising moon, casting the scene into dark shadow. Only the lights from the hall offered any comfort, but they suddenly seemed so far away.

Another branch snapped. She jumped, sensing it was just feet away. Her chest heaved as she struggled to breathe normally. Again, she spun round, thinking she'd heard the rustle once more. The sense of being stalked like a deer engulfed her. She knew something or someone was going to pounce, but when? How? Rooted to the spot with terror, she wanted to cry out to get attention, but her fear stopped anything coming out of her mouth. Her lips were as dry as parchment, her head pounded with pumping blood.

A slither across the leaves. The fiend was almost upon her. Another rustle.

She followed the sound but saw nothing. In desperation, she cupped her face in her hands and wept,

'Please God, help me!'

Dropping her hands from her face, she gasped in shock. The eyes finally met hers.

'Hello, Louise!'

She was so terrified she couldn't reply.

'Oh dear! Did I frighten you?' said the voice of Robertson, then, he pushed the gauze into her face and manoeuvred himself behind her to hold it forcefully in place.

She struggled with all her might but it was useless. The chloroform she was inhaling quickly rendered her unconscious and, finally, she slumped backwards into Robertson's arms. 'Don't worry, I will make your goodbyes for you,' he said chillingly and began to drag her body away.

Chapter 24

After listening to Tom's explanation about the true effects of ingesting morning glory seeds, Elliott looked up to the kitchen ceiling and had to smile at the absurdity of it all. But touching the deep cut on his neck, he knew that, really, he was a lucky man and inwardly thanked God for sparing his life. He wandered over to the mirror and pushed up his hair. 'I think I'll just accept growing old gracefully from now on.'

Tom couldn't resist. 'Like I said, Robert: at least you have all your own teeth!'

'This age lark will come to you, soon enough,' Elliott replied, with a playful scowl.

Tom patted his stomach. 'Any more of Lily's pies and I think you're right.'

As if on cue, the door opened and in walked Lily, feeling as guilty as ever a person could and hardly able to look her master in the eye. Eventually, she had to unburden herself and spoke at such a speed that she barely made sense. 'I'm so sorry, Mr Elliott. I honestly didn't know they … he said they were … oh dear! … you won't turn me out, sir, because —'

'Lily. Calm down. You're not in trouble. Nobody is

going to turn you out,' Elliott interrupted.

'But it was all my fault. My brother told me they could be used for ever so many ailments.'

Tom contributed his opinion. 'I'm sure they are. But used in the wrong way, then the effect can be … Well, we've seen how dangerous they can be. Let's just say it's a lesson learnt, eh.'

Lily dropped her head and anxiously twisted the tea towel in her hands. 'I really am sorry, Mr Elliott,' she said with genuine remorse, before raising her head and allowing her eyes to meet his.

Elliott just smiled. 'I think we've both been a little naive on this one.' He stood up and walked to beneath the damage in the ceiling. Rubbing his chin with his thumb and forefinger he decided, 'Right, we'd better get our story sorted before Mrs Elliott gets back.' Deliberating for a moment, he suggested, 'I was stupidly standing on the chair trying to hang some clothes when …' But he stopped, catching sight of Tom shaking his head. 'Yes, I suppose you're right. We'll just tell the truth.'

Both Tom and Lily nodded in agreement.

During breakfast, Tom asked Elliott, 'Are you sure you're up to visiting Haddington, Robert? Why don't we leave it until tomorrow and you get some rest today?'

'Nonsense! 'I'm fine,' responded Elliott, as if what had happened to him was a mere accident. 'A couple more of those pills of yours and I'll be as right as a bobbin.'

Tom finished off the last of his breakfast by pushing a piece of bacon around his plate to capture the last of the egg yolk. 'Physically you'll be fine, I've no doubt of that. But we need to examine the underlying reason for the content of your dreams.'

'I'd rather not discuss it, Tom.'

'But I would.'

Elliott put down his knife and fork deliberately and argued, 'It was just hallucinations, as you say.'

Determined his friend wouldn't just shrug off what had happened, Tom wasted no time in offering his theory, whether Elliott liked it or not. 'Hallucinating was the effect of the compound, Robert, but an hallucinogenic state is the physical side of what is invariably troubling the mind subconsciously.'

Making it obvious that he didn't want the conversation pursued, Elliott held up the teapot and asked nonchalantly, 'More tea?'

'No!' snapped Tom, infuriated. 'No, thank you … Listen! If you don't deal with the problem, it will return in another form.'

Placing the teapot down carefully, Elliott then leant back, folding his arms. 'Very well. I'll talk about what you want. What bit do you want to know first? The sick bit or the very sick bit? The bit where I watched myself doing something unspeakable to a poor young woman? Or the bit when I was in the vestry and —' He stopped himself. Some things he just wasn't prepared to confide to Tom. How could he even attempt to explain to him what he was doing in there?

Tom allowed Elliott to simmer down before suggesting, 'The common theme in your experiences always seems to be Canon Brockwell.'

'And …?' Elliott responded forcefully.

'I'm only trying to help, Robert.'

Realising he was becoming far too emotional, Elliott took a deep breath. 'Yes, I'm sorry,' he said, returning to calm again.

'Do you blame yourself in some way for what Brockwell did?'

Elliott took a while to answer. 'I blame myself for not being able to see him for what he was. Then, perhaps I could have prevented some things.'

'Some people have a side to them, Robert, that we just never imagine possible. Brockwell was good at leading a double life. How could you have known?'

Elliott gave his friend an unconvincing look of acceptance. Tom, in turn, pushed home his point. 'Come on! In your profession, how often do you see deception? Always. And it's only with the benefit of hindsight, we think back and say, yes there was that time when … or, of course, now it all adds up!'

'And that's a medical opinion?' Elliott muttered sceptically.

'No. But if you want one … You're transferring his guilt onto yourself. Allowing him to dominate your subconscious. He becomes almost real in your mind, trying to rationalise his behaviour. Eventually, he turns the tables and convinces you that it's *you* doing horrible things. Later you shrug them off, because they're in a nightmare. But if the truth be known, I'd say you're having similar thoughts at other times as well.'

Chewing the inside of his lip nervously, Elliott looked over to Tom. 'Sometimes,' he admitted.

'Look, Robert. There's still so much we don't understand about why the mind does what it does. And for every theorist there'll be a different theory. But you must try to let these feelings go. Free yourself. Accept that Brockwell was just evil and don't allow the memory of his deeds with loved ones to haunt you.'

Elliott sat back. 'Perhaps you're right,' he said with resignation, although inwardly he couldn't help thinking back to when he'd met Mrs Winters, a celebrated spiritual medium, at his church hall several years ago. As much as Elliott was a sceptic about such things, it did unnerve him slightly, remembering her theory that troubled spirits often sought closure by revealing themselves in dreams and visions. Suddenly, the thought crossing his mind made him shudder.

There was a brief silence before Tom smiled and enquired, 'I was thinking, maybe I could —'

'Absolutely not!' interrupted Elliott, knowing exactly what Tom was going to suggest – that he become a case study for his students.

'Just a thought, old chap!'

'Yes, well, let's keep it that way, shall we?'

Half an hour later, the pair were en route for Haddington, in order to quiz Mr Dowling about their findings, and his relationship with the mysterious Mrs Ridgeway. Little could they imagine what else they were about to discover.

~~~

After numerous pulls of the bell cord, the door was eventually answered, although not by Dowling or a footman, as expected, but instead by a maid, and one who was obviously quite flustered.

'Oh, hello, Dorothy! Sorry, I was expecting to see Mr Dowling,' offered Elliott in surprise to the young girl, whom he actually knew well, as he'd managed to secure her a domestic service position some months earlier.

'I'm really sorry, Mr Elliott, but he's busy. I'm afraid
~~~

we have a bit of a crisis,' replied the maid, looking round at her colleague, who was rushing, with a chamber pot in her hand, towards the stairway which led to the quarters below stairs.

'Oh dear! … Anything we can help with?'

'Not unless you're a doctor, sir.'

Elliott looked over to Tom. 'Well as it happens …'

'Yes, I'm a doctor, young lady. What's the problem?' Tom enquired.

'Flippin' everything, sir. Everybody's dropping like flies.'

At that moment, Dowling appeared, asking, 'Who is it Dorothy? Oh, Mr Elliott!' The butler then caught sight of Tom. 'And the professor. Am I glad to see you! Please do come in.'

Both men stepped into the entrance hall with confused looks on their faces. Tom naturally asked, 'Whatever is the matter, Mr Dowling?'

The butler waved Dorothy back to her duties before explaining, 'We have a serious case of food poisoning, sir. His lordship's gone down with it, along with the cook, two maids and Bennett, the footman. And Master David is really quite ill.'

'I see. And what makes you think it's food poisoning?' Tom wanted to know.

'Dr Cuthbert's opinion, sir.'

Tom gave an enquiring look.

'He's the doctor from the village. Looks after the family's medical matters since Dr Robertson's death. He's upstairs with Master David.' He looked over to Elliott and continued, 'They've all come down with stomach cramps and vomiting after eating the venison.'

Squeezing out his chin and bottom lip whilst nodding his head, Tom asked, 'I'm sure the doctor will be right, Mr Dowling. May I go up and see if I can help?'

'Yes, of course. Please follow me.'

The two men started to climb the stairs, leaving Elliott at the bottom feeling quite helpless.

Tom entered David's room to find the elderly doctor standing over the bed and looking pensively at his patient.

'I was wondering if I could give you any help, sir?' Tom asked politely.

The reply wasn't exactly friendly. 'And you are?'

Tom couldn't abide condescension. But if this was to be the name of the game, then he would give some back. 'My name is Professor Tom Sharpe, Director of General Surgery, St Thomas's, London. And you are?'

This obviously had the desired effect. Dr Cuthbert cleared his throat with a stilted cough, embarrassed for his rudeness. 'I'm sorry, Professor. I thought …'

Tom smiled, happy that he'd received an apology. He held out his hand. 'Dr Cuthbert, I understand.'

The grey-haired doctor reciprocated with a firm handshake.

'Well! A bad case of food poisoning, is it?'

'With everybody else, yes. But I'm sure not with the earl's son.'

'Oh! Why is that?' Tom replied and looked over at David. Immediately he knew that something was very wrong. He felt the young man's forehead and watched for a while as David seemingly drifted in and out of consciousness, with a raging fever and the onset of what looked like jaundice. Tom pushed his hand under the sheet and proceeded to feel David's abdomen. He pushed gently. David groaned.

Dr Cuthbert held out a chamber pot for Tom to look into. The dark yellow and cloudy contents instantly prompted him to say, 'Pyuria! Doctor, this man's suffering an acute urinary tract infection.'

'And I think I know the cause,' stated Dr Cuthbert with some apprehension. He lifted the sheet off David and pulled up his nightshirt.

'My God!' cried Tom.

What he saw immediately made him think of the macabre goings on in the book, *El Triste Matador.*

Tom's heart sank. He could only guess at who might have been responsible for what he was looking at.

<div style="text-align:center">~~~</div>

He was the handsome, dashing matador; she, the fiery flamenco dancer. Apart, they were self-absorbed exhibitionists; together, they ignited a passion that could have lit up the streetlights outside the seedy bars of Calla Atocha, Madrid.

El Triste Matador was written by a doctor under the pen name of Fernandez Cruz and was allegedly based on the story of a famous bullfighter, Juan Martinez, and his affair with Rosetta Castel. There would have been nothing unusual about the book, had it not been for a graphic description of surgical butchery which flooded over the pages, and which took the medical profession by storm. In the second year following its publication in 1902, it was reported that the book was outselling the bible in Spain. Several years later, the story received further notoriety when it formed the basis of an operetta. And all because of a nation's fascination with love, jealousy, gore and the ultimate act of revenge!

Married to a surgeon's daughter, Martinez was well known for his torrid affairs, and he played the role of the adored matador to the full, boasting of his sexual prowess in entertaining the many gullible young women who surrounded him when he visited the city's bars and restaurants. It was something his long-suffering wife,

Maria, had grown accustomed to, always hating, but nonetheless tolerating it. That is, until Senorita Castel came on the scene. Then, things were to change, and the once accepting wife was to enter into an act of barbarous butchery to seek her revenge.

Having endured the humiliation of discovering her husband in the middle of an explicit act of love with the more than eager, Rosetta, Maria finally snapped and vowed retribution, not only on her spouse and Castel, but on all the young lotharios who frequented the bullfighting circuit. The disturbed wife soon took to parading her desire for the eager matadors and, once in their bedrooms, would carry out the act of mutilation with cruel efficiency.

Without doubt, the events described in the book were embellished by the author but the details of the medical procedure used by Maria Martinez to achieve her goal were not. It was this gruesome procedure that had gripped medical students across Europe, and none more so than the young Dr Robertson, who was fascinated by the writer's account of the many varied surgical techniques.

Unlike most readers, who would analyse Maria's state of mind, and what drove her actions, Robertson was only interested in how she achieved her intended effect. He would skip whole chapters describing her thoughts and how she lured her victims to their fate. All that concerned him was the procedure and its outcome. And here Maria Martinez excelled, having, from a young age, secretly watched her father perform operations in his private surgery.

As Robertson was a man inexorably drawn to pioneering experimentation, *El Triste Matador* had a lasting effect on him. However, it was at Haddington that he reacquainted himself with the book, after one day seeing it lying on the table. Immediately it brought back memories of his days of experimentation at Derby Royal Infirmary. Even with all his success as the earl's business partner, his desire for surgical experimentation never quite left him.

One evening, Robertson and the earl learned the truth about David's relationship with Stephen from a tenant farmer on the estate, who had come upon them exchanging caresses in his field. Until this point, the earl had had no idea about his son's secret homosexuality. Not that David was reluctant to make his feelings known in his family circle, but he accepted Stephen's pleas not to reveal their relationship, for fear of the inevitable persecution – and the possible imprisonment – that could affect both of them.

Ranskill, in the throes of rage, paced up and down his study, lashing out at the papers stacked on his desk.

He poured himself a large measure of whisky but, no sooner had he taken a sip, than he flung the glass at the fireplace. Robertson watched from his chair, electing not to pass comment.

'I won't bloody stand for it, Anthony,' Ranskill spat at his friend. 'I'm prepared to accept most things in this day and age, but not this!' He again went to the drinks table, grabbed at the whisky bottle and glugged out a shot, before throwing a lump of ice at the small tumbler, which it missed. He cursed and seized the glass. Tilting his head back, he tossed down the drink in one, then grimaced. 'I can't believe it. We just nicely get rid of one problem with her, Louise, only to end up with another.'

Robertson just gave one of his strained smiles of sympathetic acknowledgement – although he was revelling in the fact that the family was being forced into yet another crisis. He couldn't immediately think how, but he was sure he would be able to make the situation work to his advantage.

The door opened and David sauntered in. 'I understand you're looking for me, father?'

Ranskill slammed down his glass on the desk as hard as he dared without it smashing to pieces in his hand. 'I saw Mr Tanner earlier from Huthwaite Farm,' he started, coming straight to the point.

David gave an enquiring turn of his head, but knew

from years of observing his father that a caustic remark was imminent. He was not wrong.

'Yes. He says he's seeing things in his field, like a pair of bloody nancies!'

Immediately David knew what his father was referring to. 'I see,' he said quite casually. And, with a great deal more courage than his brother had ever shown, he stood up tall and never let his eyes move away from his father's.

'I see! I see! Is that all you can say? After dragging this family into the mire with your ...' Ranskill stood back, his face consumed with disgust, trying to think of the most damning words he could use. 'Your deformity of character,' he eventually said.

David reared up, offended and hurt. 'The only deformity of character, father, is yours!'

'Over four generations of Ranskills and never a blemish on our stock. Now on my watch, a ruddy nancy,' Ranskill cried.

'It's called being homosexual.'

'No! It's called being disgusting, unnatural and against God's wishes.'

'Actually, if you read the bible carefully, you'll find —'

Ranskill cut across his son with venom in his voice. 'Don't you dare try and lecture me about the bible.'

David breathed in deeply through his nostrils in order

to maintain his calm. 'Is that it, father. Have you done?'

Raising his hand, Ranskill went to strike his palm across David's face. 'You insolent …'

Catching hold of his father's wrist, David held it tight. 'No more will I fear your hand, sir,' he said, his eyes looking fiercely into the face of a man with whom, he knew, his relationship had changed forever.

'You owe your father some respect, young man,' piped up Robertson, suddenly standing up from his chair.

David looked over to him. 'Keep out of this, Dr Robertson. You've meddled in our family's affairs long enough.'

'Meaning?' replied Robertson, somewhat taken aback by David's hostility.

'You may have hounded Louise out of this family but her words still ring true: "Justice comes to those who wait."'

David left the room, slamming the door shut behind him. Now it was Robertson's turn to be livid. He paced the floor, spluttering, 'Whatever happened to children should be seen and not heard?'

The room fell silent for a moment, with each man pursuing his own thoughts.

'What's the available treatment?' Ranskill asked, out of the blue.

Robertson glanced over, only half listening. 'Sorry.

Treatment? Treatment for what?'

'For his condition. He's still my son, Anthony. If he needs treatment to change his ways, then I'll pay.'

Even Robertson was shocked at the earl's naivety about homosexuality. He laughed cynically. 'You can't just give him a pill and hope he becomes normal, George.' His scornful expression showed his own repulsion and homophobic feelings. 'They are what they are.'

Ranskill dropped his shoulders in disappointment. 'No specialists you know?' he said, in the vain hope there was someone who could wave a magic wand.

'Oh, I could put you in contact with a dozen do-gooding doctors who believe they can treat it with therapy. But it doesn't change them. They convince themselves that they've tried every possible treatment. But they've no real desire to change. They're just worried about social disapproval. There's only one way, in my eyes, to deal with homosexuals.'

Ranskill was listening but not looking at Robertson. Eventually he turned his head and interrupted his friend's gaze. 'And that is?'

Robertson's lip curled at the side, as it always did when he was thinking about anything macabre or sinister. 'Castration!'

The way Ranskill raised his eyebrows made the doctor feel he had to give some justification for his opinion. 'At least that makes them sterile and reduces their sordid sexual desires.'

'Are you seriously advocating that I consider castrating my own son?'

Robertson simply turned away and didn't answer.

'Good God, Anthony! I thought I was ruthless.'

~~~

Returning downstairs, Tom shared with Dowling and Elliott what, even for a doctor, was a devastated look. This soon turned to a well-practised doctor's smile of optimism, but really signalled that all was not as it should be. Whilst Dowling's position meant he should offer only a polite enquiry as to the patient's health, his manner was altogether different. He was visibly anxious and genuinely emotional. Just when he was about to ask whether anything needed to be done, he was forestalled by Tom wanting to know, 'How long has the earl's son had his condition, Mr Dowling?'

Elliott assumed Tom was simply referring to the food poisoning, so was utterly surprised to hear Dowling respond, 'You've seen?'

'Yes, Mr Dowling. I would say it was impossible to miss.'

Dowling puffed out his cheeks, remembering when
~~~

he'd first discovered the truth. 'It will be going on for a year now, sir.'

'I see,' replied Tom, with a frown.

Elliott just had to interrupt. 'Excuse me, gentlemen.' He shook his head with confusion. 'I'm obviously missing something here!'

'Indeed, we both are, Robert. But Mr Dowling here is going to enlighten us. Aren't you?'

Dowling's head dropped.

'… and about everything!' Tom added, much to Elliott's continuing look of bemusement.

'Gentlemen. Let's talk in my room,' Dowling said with resignation. Secretly though, he was relieved that at last he could unburden himself about the whole situation. He held out his hand and indicated the way forward. What he would tell the two visitors was a tale of sadness and, ultimately, one of entangled revenge. For Tom and Elliott, they thought it would finally complete their jigsaw and solve the mystery, however, little could they have imagined just how involved Dowling was in it all.

In his little room, Dowling sat back in his chair. 'As you once said, Mr Elliott, on a visit here, the place seems to lack any soul. You were right.' He drew in a deep breath in preparation of further explanation, 'You see …'

Chapter 25

In the library, David closed the book *El Triste Matador* and slid it onto the table. He found it far from appealing and couldn't really think why he'd ended up reading so much of it. Walking over to the shelves, he tilted his head to view the titles on the book spines. Occasionally he pulled one out, flicked through it, only to put it back, and usually out of sequence.

The large double doors swung open and distracted him from his thoughts. In walked his father, accompanied by Robertson. David turned and gave a nod of acknowledgment but nothing more. Since the argument with his father, their relationship had been one of cold neutrality, with only the briefest exchanges of words or gestures. Neither was quite sure where their relationship would go, but equally, neither would back down on their beliefs.

For his part, Robertson saw the situation as black and white. He considered homosexuality to be a medical problem that only a medical solution could solve. Ranskill, on the other hand, was trying to convince himself that David's sexuality was merely a passing phase, and one that he could grow out of.

As was usually the case at Haddington, a system soon developed where, to avoid conflict, one person would leave the room as the other entered. This particular evening was no different, and David decided to exit the library first. Walking back to his room, he experienced the recurrence of a pain in his lower stomach which had plagued him for weeks. It took his breath away and caused him to pull up. Leaning against the wall, he grimaced. Rounding the corner onto the corridor, Dowling couldn't help noticing David struggling. 'Master David! Is everything all right?' he asked, trying to assist him.

Clutching at his stomach and taking deep breaths, David finally managed to answer the butler. 'Yes, Dowling, I'm fine. If you could just help me to my room, and then I can lie down.'

But David wasn't fine. He was suffering. Once on his bed he continued to writhe in agony.

'I'll fetch Dr Robertson, sir.'

'No!' insisted David. 'I'll be fine.' But then another wave of pain caused him to cry out in distress.

Dowling decided to take matters into his own hands and hurried downstairs to fetch Robertson, who was by now engrossed in the book left out by David. It was one that he remembered only too well. Dragging his forefinger across each line, his eyes began to burn as he stared hard at the text. So intense was his concentration that he didn't even notice the dribble of saliva coming from the corner of his mouth. It beaded before dropping onto the page. Where it landed magnified the start of Maria Martinez's words. He sighed with joy as he read on:

… No more will he be like a man. It feels good. I am content, avenged, and now, I give my gift for all the Calla Atocha to see - a freak! Tonight I have excelled myself. Father would be proud. For not only a castration but a full penectomy, and all in record time!

'Yes! This is what I truly miss,' mumbled Robertson, absorbed in Maria's detailing of her terrible deed.

'Pardon?' said Ranskill from his armchair.

Robertson looked up, confused. 'Sorry?'

'You said something?'

'Did I? Sorry. I must have read something out loud.'

Dowling's discreet knock and his opening of the door disturbed their vague exchange.

'I'm sorry to disturb you, m'lord, but I think Dr Robertson should take a look at Master David.'

'Master David?' asked the bemused Ranskill. 'He's just this minute left us. What's happened?'

'I found him struggling on the corridor, m'lord and —'

Robertson put down his book and interrupted. 'Struggling? With what exactly?'

'I'm afraid I have no idea as to the cause, sir. All I know is that when I left him he was in agony.'

David was still rolling about in pain when Robertson and his father arrived. Immediately, Robertson began checking him over. As much as David didn't want the doctor near him, he was thankful for any medical help.

'And the pain is here?' Robertson asked, feeling around. 'And here? What about here?'

David just nodded in agreement.

'… and does it sting when urinating?'

Again David agreed.

'For how long has it been stinging?'

Clenching his teeth to fight the pain, David confirmed, 'Weeks.'

Robertson almost certainly knew what the problem was, but he had one last question. 'And is there pain in the testicles?' Dowling turned away, more out of discretion than because he didn't want to hear the answer.

David again nodded in agreement.

'Point to where,' instructed Robertson.

Rolling down the sheets, David obliged.

As part of his medical role at the colliery, Robertson always kept sedatives at hand, to be used in the event of an accident. Turning to Dowling, he instructed him to fetch his bag.

Once sedated, David flopped back onto the bed and closed his eyes. Dowling had by now decided it would be more appropriate to wait outside the bedroom. Robertson gave Ranskill his diagnosis. 'He has a severely infected epididymis, complicated by a chronic water infection.'

'And is that supposed to mean something to me, Anthony?' rebuffed Ranskill.

'The tube that runs around the testes. It's massively infected.'

'I see.' Ranskill didn't really understand, but he thought for a moment and then asked the logical question, 'Well, what needs to be done?'

What needed to be done was far different from what Robertson had in mind. But he was driven by his desire to once more pick up a scalpel and experiment. And this time, the writings of Fernandez Cruz's *El Triste Matador* were freshly in his mind!

~~~

The one advantage Robertson had over the earl was his medical knowledge. He knew that David should have been hospitalised and his condition treated first with bloodletting. But would he ever get such an opportunity again? The prospect of being able to operate on the earl's son fitted perfectly with his ambitions. Even before David had slid into full unconsciousness, he was mulling over the options. If he could strip David of his confidence and any feelings of self esteem, then, with Mueller now gone,
~~~

what better way for him to start controlling even more of the business decisions?

Convincing Ranskill to allow him to perform an operation on David was much easier than Robertson could have hoped for, even given his skilled explanation to the earl of the proposed simple procedure. With David now thoroughly sedated, arrangements were made to take him to the Hall's convalescence room. It was here that the earl had established a clinical area for the treatment of his gout.

As he prepared for the operation, his sense of anticipation made Robertson tingle from head to foot. He glanced over to David's limp body, lying unconscious on the table, and felt a rush of excitement. With adrenaline pumping through him, he picked up his scalpel and walked over towards the slender and attractive figure in the prime of life.

Sweat began beading on his forehead. His hands were trembling in front of him. Could he really get away with it? Why not? He had no alternative! David's problem was far worse than they had first thought. But the most convincing argument was that no surgeon would reasonably be able to judge his decision one way or another. And certainly Ranskill would never be able to do so.

All the while, Maria's thoughts in *El Triste Matador*

were echoing in his head.

Tonight I will try a different technique. Well! After all, I do have a record to beat. My theory is good, but alas, it's untried. Dear Juan will be my victim tonight. Bless him, he always did like to beat a record. Or so I'm told.

'Just keep it simple,' said Robertson's rational voice.

'No! show me your skills, Anthony,' Maria Martinez's voice was telling him.

Robertson plunged down with his scalpel. He sighed with satisfaction – nothing made him feel more elated than that first cut!

David remembered little of the night of his tragedy, other than that one moment he was in agony, the next, he had a strange yet comforting feeling of warmth throughout his body. With each breath he took, his pain seemed to dissolve. His eyes grew heavy and he willingly let his head topple to one side. Soon he was floating away into darkness. The only words he remembered were his father's: 'Do whatever you need to do, Anthony.'

When he came round, he found himself lying in his bed but suffering even more awful pain. Nothing made sense to him. What had happened? And why had he awoken feeling so thoroughly groggy? The watery, acidic taste in his mouth told him what was coming. Powerless to stop it, he leant over the side of the bed and vomited. His retching caused only horrific stabbing sensations at the top of his leg. He winced and blew out in shallow breaths until, eventually, the pain subsided. Only then could he drop his thumping head back onto the pillow and sigh with relief. Had he been drugged, he wondered. But his thoughts were interrupted as another wave of pain hit his leg. This time, it shot up across his groin and into his stomach. Screaming in agony, he saw everything around him go fuzzy. His suffering was so bad he passed out.

Some two hours later, David came round again. 'The pain! Jesus Christ, the pain,' he shouted. Through the corner of his eye he could see people in the room. Suddenly, Dr Robertson was standing over him with a syringe. 'All right, David,' he said and plunged the needle deep into a vein in his arm. 'This will ease things.'

David felt a warm relaxing sensation as the morphine-induced euphoria consumed him.

Two days on and David was to discover the reason for his continuing pain. Removing the dressings and bandages, he looked down in disbelief. Standing and facing himself in a full length mirror, he trembled whilst studying his mutilation. Tears built up in his eyes, before they slowly trickled down his cheek. From that day on, David wanted only to block things from his mind, choosing never to speak, only to spend his days obsessively playing the violin, sometimes until his fingertips bled. But the one thing he could never block out were his father's words to Robertson.

<div align="center">~~~</div>

David pushed the doctor's hand away. 'I can do it!' he insisted, pulling the leech off his stomach and throwing it forcefully into the dish.

'Very well,' said Robertson, walking towards the window. 'I had no alternative, David. The infection was spreading.'

David just stared at the last remaining leech, almost full to bursting with blood.

'If I hadn't done what I did, you would have died,' continued Robertson. 'You would do well to remember that. Without me you wouldn't be here now.'

David simply reached for his violin. Placing it under his chin, he began playing the overture to *El Triste Matador*. Robertson knew the music well enough but pretended not to notice, as he made his way to the door of the bedroom.

'Justice comes to those who wait,' David called out.

Robertson stopped but never turned around. 'Try to get some rest,' he said, and opened the door. Once outside, he laid his head back against the wall. For the first time since it all happened, he looked anxious.

<p style="text-align:center">~~~</p>

It was over a month before Ranskill learned the whole truth as to the extent of his son's surgery. After his operation, David simply refused to speak to his father and, whilst Robertson's explanation had always referred to having had to remove a testicle, never had there been mention of anything else. Had it not been for the earl overhearing loose talk between two footmen, it might have been much longer before he found out the real facts.

Filled with rage, Ranskill flung open the doors to his study and strode in like a man possessed. 'You bastard!' he screamed.

Robertson, the person the statement was aimed at, nearly jumped out of his skin with shock. He had no chance to do anything else before he was being pinned against the wall.

'Why?' Ranskill demanded to know, staring into his face. Robertson could see the venom in his eyes. He felt that if one tiny drop of a tear landed on his skin, it would eat through and paralyse him instantly.

'George! Please. For heaven's sake, calm down,' Robertson pleaded, with the servile and pitiful look he so often used to avert the earl's outbursts.

'I asked you why?' said Ranskill, squeezing his forearm slightly harder against Robertson's throat.

'I've no idea what you're talking about!' Robertson managed to shriek, before another flex of his attacker's arm almost cut off his breath.

'David! … Why?'

'I had no choice.' The doctor's voice was barely audible; in response, the pressure from the forearm was reduced just enough for him to continue. 'Trust me. There was honestly no alternative.'

Ranskill drew back his other arm, formed a fist and let it fly at the wall. It thudded down right next to Robertson's head.

'George! Good God, man. What's wrong with you?'

Releasing the pressure on the doctor, Ranskill dropped his arms and walked away. Although fury was still raging in him, he tried to be rational. 'Why didn't you tell me exactly what you'd done?'

Robertson was now able to think – or at least to get his excuses in order. 'Because I knew it would destroy you, George. Then, as time went by, and with David not wanting to discuss it, I thought … foolishly I admit, I thought that it was maybe for the best that you didn't know. Being told all the details would just have made the whole thing harder to accept for you.'

An endless stream of reasons as to why he had taken the action he did poured effortlessly out of Robertson's mouth. So convincing was he that Ranskill almost ended up apologising for doubting him. Eventually though, he steeled himself and spat out, 'If ever I find that you have lied to me, in any way, Anthony, I swear I will kill you!'

~~~

'And were you told anything?' Tom eventually asked Dowling, after he and Elliott had attentively listened to the butler's account of the night David was brought back to his room.

'Well, only that Master David had needed surgery,' explained the butler.

'But not the details of what had happened?'

'I'm the butler, Professor. I think I remember telling you, I don't get to know about everything that happens here at Haddington,' came Dowling's retort.

Tom allowed the lines across his forehead to even out before responding. 'Oh! But I think you do, Mr Dowling… You know more, much more.'

Until this point, Elliott had kept quiet, leaving Tom to ask all the questions, mainly because they were medical ones. However, he decided he couldn't allow Tom to totally dominate things and he wasn't prepared for the conversation to be side-tracked into a tit-for-tat. 'So when did you learn the truth about what happened?' he asked Dowling.
~~~

'It was a couple of days into his recuperation, sir. Master David rang the bell, so I went to see to his needs. But I found him sitting naked on the bed, sobbing his heart out. Naturally, I enquired what the problem was and, of course, offered him his dressing gown.' As always, Dowling was the model of discretion and placed great emphasis on the words 'of course'.

'Go on,' encouraged Elliott, after acknowledging Dowling with a nod.

'He stood up, gentlemen, and looking in the mirror he said, 'Look what the …" Dowling paused and coughed politely. 'I won't use his exact words, only that he said, look what the hell they've done to me.'

'And that's when you saw that his genitals had been removed?' asked Elliott bluntly, sparing the butler the need to go into great detail.

'Yes, sir,' replied Dowling, dropping his head forlornly.

'And did you ever enquire why?'

'Mr Elliott! There are some things one doesn't ask one's master.'

'Did you ever presume why, then?' Elliott rattled straight back.

Dowling breathed in deeply. 'I think Master David was the victim of Dr Robertson's knife, purely for his pleasure. That and …' He paused as he always did when presented with an awkward situation. '… That and the fact he was punished for … I believe the modern term would be "batting for the other side".'

'David is homosexual?' Elliott said, with some surprise. But mostly he was seeking clarity. He had little time for expressions with hidden meanings.

'Yes,' confirmed Dowling.

Tom's look showed he was convinced. 'I'm almost certain you're right, Mr Dowling. That the young man endured unnecessary surgery. And undoubtedly *El Triste Matador* was the reason for it all.'

The butler drew his eyebrows together and assumed a very confused expression.

'It's a book and an operetta. One that, if you remember, I saw in the library and asked you about,' explained Tom.

The prompt enabled Dowling to agree. But really, he didn't have a clue what it all meant.

Elliott was intrigued by something Dowling had said. But before quizzing him, he first needed to stand up. The numbness in his buttocks told him that sitting so long in an uncomfortable chair had finally taken its toll. 'You said earlier that David spoke to you. Yet when we came to speak to the earl and saw him playing the violin, you said he couldn't speak,' Elliott pointed out, desperately hoping his numbness would not bring on pins and needles.

'No! I believe I said that he *wouldn't* speak, sir.' Dowling replied, being quite sure about what he'd said. Elliott just nodded in recognition of his misunderstanding.

Tom interjected, 'It's quite normal, Robert, after enduring a trauma such as this, to simply withdraw. I see it a lot with the badly war wounded, particularly those who have been disfigured. They feel worthless, and they drive all their anger inwards. Not to speak is their way of dealing with the situation. We call it aphasia voluntaria.'

'Do you now! Well, thank you for educating me with your wisdom,' replied Elliott, with just enough sarcasm to remind his friend he was being patronising. Returning his attention to Dowling he asked, 'Do you believe Master David knew that Dr Robertson was responsible for his tragic circumstances.'

'Of course. He just didn't have enough evidence to prove his operation went far beyond anything that was necessary.'

By now, Elliott had picked up a rubber band from the desk and was rolling it back and forth between his forefinger and thumb. He stopped abruptly, turning his head to meet Dowling's gaze. 'But he had enough reason to want to see Dr Robertson dead!' he said, before returning to rolling the band in his fingers.

Dowling took a moment to answer. 'Even with all

that has happened to him, I couldn't believe Master David is capable of murder.'

'How about Mrs Ridgeway? Or Marion? I would say they had good reason for wanting Dr Robertson killed.'

With an uneasy twist of his shoulders, Dowling stated, 'I'm afraid I've no idea what you are talking about, sir.'

Elliott smiled. 'Why don't you arrange for a pot of tea, and then you can tell us all about it.'

The thoroughly defeated Mr Dowling offered no resistance. His deep sigh was enough to signify the relief he felt that the burden on him could at last come to an end. 'Yes, I think I would like to do that, Mr Elliott,' he said, leaning forward and standing up. 'I really would like to do that,' he reiterated, and left the room.

'What?' said Tom, looking at Elliott, who was wearing a smug expression.

'Well, can't you see?'

'See what?'

'I thought it would be obvious by now.' Elliott offered another smug smile. 'No?'

Tom had to concede he had no idea and shook his head.

Elliott winked at him. 'We call it intuition, Tom,' and he proceeded to explain.

Chapter 26

What else could she have done? The temptation was just too great! As soon as she saw the large backside of her husband, bending over the bucket, she knew she wanted to give it a good hard slap.

Ann put her finger against her lips to silence the giggles of Mary and the boys and furtively tiptoed forward. At last, she was near enough and pulled back her hand: three, two, one – smack! 'We're home!' she shouted.

The totally startled recipient shot upright. 'What the bloody hell …?' and turned around. It was hard to tell who was the more surprised, Ann or the tradesman. Immediately she clapped her hand to her mouth and muffled a gasp, realising the man was not, as she had assumed, Elliott. Her look of absolute shock was equalled by those of Mary and the boys. Eventually, though, Mary burst into a fit of laughter.

'I'm so, so sorry. You see … I thought you were my husband,' Ann explained in huge embarrassment.

Finally over the shock of it all, the tradesman joked, 'Don't worry, luv. The pleasure was all mine!'

Ann's face went a deep crimson colour. Cecil,

some way down the path, began milking the humorous situation for all it was worth, until his mother gave him a glare. Then, she turned back to the man, who was holding a trowel. 'I really am sorry … Forgive me, but who are you?'

'I'm the plasterer, sweetheart,' replied the affable tradesman.

'Plasterer? Plastering what exactly?' asked Ann, thoroughly confused.

'I'm mending the kitchen ceiling.'

'R-i-i-ight! drawled Ann, giving him a look of even more confusion until, eventually, she had to exclaim, 'What's he done?'

By now, Mary was standing beside Ann wondering whether Tom was involved in some way. Ann sighed and shook her head playfully. 'Come on, Mary. Let's go and see just what delights await us.'

Once inside the kitchen, the women saw Lily on the floor busily trying to clear up the blobs of plaster, which the less-than-tidy tradesman had allowed to drop everywhere. They both let their eyes drift upward towards the ceiling, before opening them wide in surprise at the half-plastered hole.

'Oh, Mrs Elliott! … And Mrs Sharpe! Hello. I thought you weren't coming back until much later,' said the guilty-looking maid.

'Lily, what on earth is going on?' Ann simply wanted to know.

'Ah, well … you see!' She paused and sighed. 'Perhaps it is best if Mr Elliott explains things.'

Ann was emphatic with her response, 'No, Lily. Let's hear your version.' She looked over to Mary and joked, 'Somehow I think it will be more accurate, and certainly quicker!'

Whilst Lily's words may well have been accurate, they certainly didn't make a great deal of sense to either Ann or Mary. Poor Lily set off nervously, like a Bren gun, moving swiftly back and forth with her story. '… And I heard a scream and a thud … I couldn't find my dressing gown but when I did … well, I went downstairs. It was all my fault because of the paste, you see. Mr Sharpe was on top of Mr Elliott and there was a rope round his neck – Mr Elliott's neck, that is. Bessie was barking. I thought it was all for his play but there was rubble and plaster everywhere. Then —'

An alarmed Ann interrupted, 'Lily! For goodness sake, slow down.' To her relief Lily stopped and drew breath.

'Right,' continued Ann, 'Let's start again shall we. Slowly, from the beginning. You heard a scream and a thud …'

Both Ann and Mary listened in amazement to the

saga, which became much clearer once they had got Lily to backtrack and were able to ask her a myriad of questions. By comparison, the episode with Cecil at the seaside suddenly seemed to pale into insignificance.

'And where are Mr Elliott and Mr Sharpe now?' enquired Ann, shaking her head in disbelief.

'I believe they were going to Haddington Hall, Mrs Elliott.'

'Haddington Hall!' exclaimed Ann in surprise. 'What on earth have they gone there for?'

~~~

Time seemed of no consequence to Elliott or Tom as Dowling continued his story. To say they were engrossed was probably an understatement. Eventually though, the tale did reach its end, and with it came an offer from Tom that he would help all he could with David's situation. For his part, Elliott agreed that, if he could exert any influence in the matter, he would do so.

Walking home they had much to discuss, not least the question of exactly what they should do from this point. Eventually they rounded the corner into the avenue where the Elliotts lived.

'Well Tom, just enough time to make sure the plasterer is all done and dusted and everything is neat
~~~

and tidy. Then the girls and the children should just about be back,' said Elliott, blissfully unaware that they had actually caught an earlier train.

'Indeed. I'm sure Ann will hardly notice it at all.'

'Listen. I've being giving this nightmare thing and what happened some thought. Perhaps we could play it down somewhat with Ann. You know, not to worry her.'

Tom raised his eyebrows, reminding him that it had all been agreed.

'No, I'm not saying we don't tell the truth, just not make such a song and dance about it, that's all. I'm sure if I have a quick word with Lily, she'll do the same.'

With a smile, Tom replied, 'Let's see how it goes, eh.'

When Elliott opened the gate, he looked surprised to see the plasterer still mixing plaster. And his look soon turned to one of horror when he heard Ann call out to Cecil, playing ball in the garden, 'Watch my plants, please!'

Catching sight of his father and Tom, Cecil immediately dropped his ball and ran up to them, cuddling each one in turn. 'Hello, father.' The strength of Cecil's embrace around his waist told Elliott just how much he'd missed him whilst they had been away, although it wasn't long before all that was forgotten and the child was asking the more important question of what had happened to the kitchen ceiling.

'Oh, it was just a small accident with the clothes rail, that's all,' Elliott said, swiftly dealing with the question, before leading them into the house.

Inside, Ann was busy in the hall, sorting through some shoes that the boys had conveniently dumped in a pile, when Elliott announced, 'Hello!'

With a hearty smile, she walked over to him and gave him a loving embrace. Even after eighteen years of marriage, their love had never dulled. And, as they held each other close, it more than showed.

Ann held out her arms to Tom. 'Good to see you again, Tom,' she said, following it with an embrace.

Tom reciprocated her tender squeeze saying, 'Don't worry, I've looked after him well.'

Arching her back, she looked at him with a sceptical but playful expression. 'Mmm, yes, so I'm hearing!'

Whereas the Elliotts' reunion was subtle and discreet, Tom and Mary's was one of sheer elation. On hearing her husband's voice, she bounded out of the parlour and unashamedly wrapped her arms around Tom's neck and kissed him. 'Oh, I've so missed you, darling,' she murmured, before attempting to whisk him straight into the parlour to see Lucinda. However, she stopped, quickly realising that in her excitement, she'd not even greeted Elliott.

She reached out and clasped his hands. 'I'm so sorry,

Robert. How utterly rude of me.' And gave him a tender peck on the cheek. 'It's lovely to see you.'

Finally standing alone with her husband, Ann cuddled him and looked up into his eyes. 'Hello, husband.'

Elliott gave her a smile. 'Hello, wife.'

It was their silly little ritual, but one they had had ever since getting married. Then he winked, which simply told her he was glad she was back home safe and sound.

The moment was interrupted by Cecil, who marched past them and up the stairs with his spade against his shoulder. 'It's my rifle, father,' he said to a rather baffled Elliott.

'Ah, I see. Well, they'll certainly see you coming with a blue one,' commented his father, willing to humour his son.

'It was a red one. But that's a long story for later,' interjected Ann, before swiftly changing the subject. 'As is the story about my kitchen ceiling, I'm told.'

'Ah, that! Well...'

It was the best Elliott could offer before Ann started to lead him towards the garden. 'I'm all ears, dear!' she said, with mock sternness. Of course, she knew that it had in fact been a serious and disturbing situation, and one they would discuss in depth when the time was right. But for now, she was happy to listen to her husband's insistence that it was all nothing.

Later that evening, with all back to normal, both couples were sitting relaxing and chatting in the parlour.

'So, what's all this about Haddington Hall?' Mary asked Tom, intrigued by the place.

Tom glanced over to Elliott. 'I'll let you begin, shall I?'

~~~

She remembered exactly which shops in the city centre Dowling visited on his day off: normally the barber and the tailor, occasionally the pharmacist, but always the ironmongers located next to the police station. Here, the butler would invariably indulge himself in studying the latest gadgets to find their way onto the High Street. Even in the hard times of war, there would be something new to take his interest. She watched him through the window, absorbed in conversation with the shop owner. At last, it appeared he was done, and she adjusted her hat in readiness for their meeting.

'Hello, Mr Dowling,' she said discreetly, her hat tilted down to obscure her face.

'Oh, hello,' replied Dowling out of politeness, but not having any idea whom he was talking to. All he could really see was the brim of her hat casting a shadow onto her face. Slowly she lifted her head. His eyes then opened wide in amazement. 'Good lord!' he cried.
~~~

She took hold of his arm and gently drew him aside on the crowded street. Pulling down the brim of her hat once again, she spoke softly. 'Mr Dowling, please do not call out my name. I cannot make myself known just yet. Simply refer to me as Mrs Ridgeway. Will you do that?'

The utterly bemused Dowling eventually nodded his head in agreement. 'But … Why? How did —?'

'I will explain everything,' interrupted the woman. 'if we could just go somewhere quiet.'

Dowling, still reeling from the shock, finally found his words. 'Of course. The car is parked just over there.' He looked at her face. It was how he remembered it. 'I honestly can't believe it —'

'Ahh!' A finger pressed against his lips as he was about to say her name. 'Mrs Ridgeway, remember,' she reminded him.

He had a hundred questions he wanted to ask her, but he sat patiently listening to the woman beside him as she told her almost unbelievable tale. 'So you see, Mr Dowling, who else could I trust to help me?' she concluded.

A good half an hour had passed and all the while he had duly noted everything that he was being asked to do. There were documents to find, photographs to take from albums; in fact, there was so much expected of him, he truly wondered if he would dare to do it all – whether he could do it all! The final request, however, unnerved him more than anything else.

'Tell me you will do it, Mr Dowling. You must know that it's the one thing I need more than anything else,' Mrs Ridgeway said, almost pleading.

'Very well,' the butler eventually conceded. 'I'll see what I can do.'

In the time remaining to them before they parted, Dowling explained various items of news from Haddington, not least the death of Dr Robertson and the tragedy that had befallen David.

Putting a hand of appreciation over his, Mrs Ridgeway thanked him and they agreed to meet again at the same place in three days' time. Then she had gone. Just as she had appeared from nowhere, she had now disappeared to nowhere.

At their next meeting, Dowling duly waited by the car, his eyes scouring the street for the brimmed hat. The trouble was, they all looked the same. A glance here, a mistaken smile at some lady there. He sighed in exasperation, only to be tapped on the shoulder.

'You've brought him?' enquired the excited Mrs Ridgeway.

'Ahh, there you are!' said the surprised Dowling. 'Yes, I've brought him, ma'am. Although against my better judgement.'

Looking into the car where a little figure was fast asleep on the seat, she held her trembling hand to the window, her fingertips finally making contact with the glass. Raw emotion flooded through her body in an unstoppable wave. She held her other hand across her mouth. Tears started to cascade down her cheeks, until she began openly to sob with joy.

Dowling gently opened the door, carefully picked up the small child and laid him against her shoulder. The little mite hardly stirred in his sleep. 'There you go, Miss Louise,' he said, instinctively using her real name.

'Mother's here, my darling sweetheart, mother's here,' her choked voice said, before she rested her lips against his little angelic face. How she had dreamt of this moment. Cupping her palm around the back of his head, she gently rocked him. 'Mother's here.'

It had been such a long time.

~~~

Such a long time had, in reality, been just over eighteen months, during which time Louise had been forced to endure so much heartache. Not to mention a marriage, and worse. As she once more stood at the gates of Haddington, she was pregnant again. All the doing of yet another man she had grown to despise – Kurt Mueller.
~~~

Ironically though, had it not been for Mueller, the life intended for her by Dr Robertson would have been far more tragic and would perhaps already have ended. If nothing else, she had to thank him for saving her from Robertson. But the thing that saved Louise most of all was her body and her beauty! Once she had been drugged, on the night of her abduction, it was the warped doctor's intention to drag her straight to his car, but instead, his sick desires got the better of him and he pulled her into the bushes.

Fortunately for Louise, Robertson's caresses got no further than her breasts, but only because he was disturbed by Mueller, who approached up the drive.

'Louise!' Mueller shouted in confusion, wondering where she could have gone. She should have passed him by now. He had waited for her at the end of her route, having every intention of trying to convince her again to accompany him back to Germany. But, with the reconnaissance aircraft due to arrive in the meadow at 9 o'clock, he was more than prepared to take a different tack if necessary and force her at gunpoint to leave with him. He wasn't to know that he would discover Louise unconscious, and that Robertson would already have prepared the way for him.

Mueller was on the verge of giving up his search and making his way towards the meadow, when he heard a rustle as Robertson moved about on the dry leaves. 'Louise?' he called.

Robertson froze. The German was the last person he was expecting to see. In fact, he hadn't anticipated seeing anybody. He cursed his stupidity in allowing temptation to get the better of him. What could he do? There was nothing he could do, other than keep perfectly still and hope that Mueller would not investigate further. Mueller, however, was not easily dissuaded. It all came to a climax when Louise let out a faint moan. Robertson desperately fumbled in his pocket for the chloroform-laden gauze, but it was too late.

'Louise?' shouted Mueller again, before parting the foliage to discover Robertson. 'Doctor!' he said in surprise. Then he saw Louise's helpless body. 'What …?' he started to say, as Robertson spat out in rage, 'Get away!'

Mueller, whose athletic build was more than a match for any man, had little to fear from Robertson, who, with his pathetic frame, was now attempting to adopt a threatening stance. Though Mueller had a revolver, he simply lunged at Robertson and dragged him away from Louise's body. Crouching over the limp figure, he felt her pulse. It was beating. Then he saw the unbuttoned blouse and looked around in disgust at the doctor. Had it not been for that glance, he would almost certainly have joined Louise unconscious on the ground. Robertson was coming straight at him, wielding a large broken branch.

It didn't take much for Mueller to disarm his weak attacker and fling him to the ground. Now pointing his gun, Mueller contemplated whether to shoot Robertson, who had immediately assumed a position of surrender and was pleading pathetically for mercy. He knew the doctor was nothing more than a coward, always a bully, and now a fiend. Why shouldn't he do it, he thought. Mueller had only ever tolerated the man out of a desire to keep working. Now he was leaving, why should he care anymore? But, whilst Mueller was devoted to his country, and would happily spy for her, he was not yet ready to kill. He formed a fist and pulled his arm back. As the drone of the approaching aircraft engine was heard, he told Robertson, 'In Germany she will know happiness with me.' Then, he thrust his fist forward. Robertson's head wobbled like an unsteady coconut at a fairground stall, before falling backwards. He was out cold.

Mueller picked up Louise and put her over his shoulder. Ten minutes later, she was being strapped into the seat of a Golte plane and heading for a new life she had not wished for, in a country she had no desire to be in. And with a man she would never forgive for what he had done, not least for the fact that she had been ruthlessly parted from her son.

Perversely, when Robertson regained consciousness,

he quickly realised that, although Louise's disappearance had not been what he had planned, it nonetheless had achieved the desired goal – to remove her from Haddington. And, moreover, what better excuse could there be to convince people of her instability? The woman had become a traitor. She had callously left her son and family to abscond to Germany with her lover.

~~~

'Oh, dear lord. That is so sad,' said Mary, pulling baby Lucinda closer into her for extra protection.

She looked over to Elliott and Ann on the other sofa and frowned. 'But … if Mrs Ridgeway was really Louise, who then is Marion?' she exclaimed.

Ann gave that look which only being married to Elliott could have developed. 'How long have you known Robert, Mary? Do you honestly think he would make the story straightforward?' She patted her husband's knee playfully. 'I suspect we've barely started yet, eh dear!'

'Is Marion this Matilda woman?' asked Mary, hardly able to take much more suspense.

Elliott pulled the pipe from his mouth. 'If you didn't know all the facts, you would certainly think so, wouldn't you?'

Both Ann and Mary let out a heavy sigh. Tom smiled
~~~

at Elliott's teasing.

'No, Lady Matilda never returned from the family's house in Dorset. Dowling told us that, unfortunately, she took her own life last year.'

'Then, *who* is Marion?' Ann demanded to know, having become just as intrigued as Mary.

Rising from his seat, Elliott walked deliberately to the door, like some Scotland Yard detective might strut around a crime scene. 'It was Tom here who discovered who she was … from a photograph.'

'Who the heck is she?' Ann again demanded, getting just slightly annoyed with her husband's game. But Elliott wasn't done yet – not by a long way. 'You'll have to excuse me one minute,' he said, and left the room.

The two women's sharp intake of breath made poor Bessie draw back her ears and open one eye in apology. Invariably, hearing a tut or a huff whilst she was lying asleep meant she'd done only one thing!

Mary turned to Tom. 'Who?'

'I wouldn't dare steal his thunder!' Tom declared.

Chapter 27

If Dowling was amazed at his re-acquaintance with Louise, he was utterly bewildered at meeting Marion. Was it all coincidence? Perhaps it was fate. Certainly Dowling liked to think the latter, for he had loved her!

Louise would soon discover it was both, as well as being an inconvenience, although one that in fact worked to everybody's advantage.

The odd-looking motorised police carriage had drawn slowly to a halt in front of them. Out of the rear door stepped a young constable, followed by a bedraggled woman dressed in a lemon coloured dress covered in dirty black marks. Her tousled red hair was pulled up into a crude sort of bun and loosely held in place with pins. Dowling's mouth fell open in astonishment as she was escorted onto the pavement in front of him.

'Excuse me, sir,' said the policeman, indicating that Dowling was blocking the way. But the confused butler simply continued gazing at the woman. She stared back, her eyes full of emptiness, although somehow they yearned for help in telling her story.

'No, it can't be!' muttered Dowling, wanting to hold out his hand and tenderly touch her face. 'Surely it can't

…,' he began, but stopped, mesmerised by his thoughts of her past beauty. The woman gave him a lovely half-smile.

'Yes, it is, isn't it?' he asked in hope.

But the woman just smiled again and puckered up her lips. 'Coo, coo.'

Even after all this time, he knew it was her.

'Are you all right, Dowling?' asked Louise, looking at the man, who seemed to have been transported to another world. For a split second, he had. He was back in a world and a time when things were different – different ways and different points of view. In that world, she had touched his heart. As one unhappy, and too often alone, she had shared with him her feelings … and more! He had simply adored her and always wanted to hold her. Now those memories were stored in a tiny compartment in his mind, only to be revisited very occasionally.

'I'm sorry, ma'am. You were saying?' said a melancholy Dowling to Louise.

'I was asking if you were all right? You appear so engrossed with that woman. Do you know her?'

Dowling looked towards the police station door, through which she had been taken. Eventually he replied, 'Yes, Miss Louise, I think I do.'

Seeing his expression of restrained sympathy, which she knew only too well from her own times of sadness, she suggested, 'Why don't we take a walk through the park, Mr Dowling? Then you can tell me all about her.' Referring to him now as 'Mister' somehow seemed to fit with Louise's idea of how she saw her future. Dowling, however, looked slightly uncomfortable.

The story that Louise heard that afternoon thoroughly shocked her for several reasons. Not least was the idea that Dowling could have had such a romantic side to his nature. Secondly, she was horrified that a woman with such a privileged past could now be held, dirty and unkempt, in a police cell. Both of them thought it, but Louise was the first to say it: 'I feel quite sure that Robertson will have had some part in all this.' It was something they were determined to find out.

~~~

Armed with a plan of action, two days later, Louise and Dowling walked into the police station and enquired whether an unfortunate and confused woman had recently been brought in.

'And who might you be?' said the ever charming Sergeant Drake.

Louise wove the sergeant a tissue of lies and presented them perfectly in an outstanding, if not lengthy, performance as Mrs Ridgeway, who had returned from
~~~

Scotland to find that her poor delusional sister-in-law had gone missing again.

'She was wearing a lemon coloured dress at the time of her disappearance, Sergeant,' Louise concluded, in a very broad Scottish accent.

The rather dubious Drake asked, 'And what would they be calling this sister-in-law of yours, Mrs Ridgeway?'

Louise's prompt answer showed Dowling that she had not lost any of her skill for volleying back a response. 'Well, dear,' she said, looking at Dowling. 'We've just about had them all, haven't we? Which one do you think she will have used this time?'

Dowling entered into the deception, and into the spirit of his role, with perhaps a little too much enthusiasm. 'Ermintrude, is my guess!'

Louise scrunched up her nose slightly and rolled up her eyes. Drake decided he would refer the matter to Detective Hollins, as he was already in the cells where the woman in question was being kept.

Whereas Drake might have needed further convincing, Detective Hollins was putty in Louise's hands and, after listening to her theatrical endeavours, he quite willingly escorted her and Dowling to the right cell. The short walk was an experience that each had no desire to repeat. Louise clutched her handkerchief tightly to her nose and hoped the smell would only be temporary.

Dowling constantly cleared his throat, wondering how on earth anybody could work in such conditions.

The detective stopped and drew down a hatch. Louise gestured for Dowling to look first. He did so, before turning and nodding to indicate it was the person they were looking for. 'Why exactly has she been brought here, sir?' he asked.

The whole situation, as it was known, was explained and Detective Hollins ended by giving his opinion, 'If I'm perfectly frank, I think it's merely a case of her being in the wrong place at the wrong time.' Then, pushing a key into the lock, he gently opened the door. 'I am sorry.'

Louise lifted her head showing her confusion.

'For her illness, Mrs Ridgeway. It must be awful to see your loved one like this.'

Looking at the poor woman sitting on the solitary bench, Louise felt the guilt of her lies consume her. It suddenly occurred to her that she was looking at somebody who must indeed be being missed by someone. And more saddening was the thought of the nightmare she must have endured if Robertson had been involved in causing her plight.

'Would you have any idea why she might have been on the Ranskill Colliery spoil heap?' asked Detective Hollins, holding the door open, in order that Louise and Dowling could enter.

'Who knows what goes through her mind, sir. But I'm sure whatever it is, the colliery somehow has an association for her,' replied Louise, thinking more and more that Dowling was right.

'I'll leave you to chat with Marion for a while then, eh?' offered the detective.

Louise smiled appreciatively. Dowling walked ahead of her into the cell. Studying the woman, he felt a sadness wash over him. Was it really her? His mind raced back in time once more. The image of her was so vivid. Her voice speaking softly to him. Gathering his composure again, he realised that he might just have got it all wrong. 'Hello,' he said with a pleasant smile, expecting her to respond. Nothing was forthcoming.

Reaching out his hand, he gently placed it on her shoulder. 'It's me, John.'

His words brought no reaction from Marion other than a polite, 'Hello, John.'

Dowling knew instantly from her voice that he was right. He knelt down before her and took hold of her hand. 'You remember me? John, John Dowling.' Her lack of recognition made his heart sink with disappointment.

Marion's eyes slowly traced the contours of his face. Brief flashbacks of him, literally a second long, were triggered somewhere deep inside her mind, but always they were contrasted with other images that meant nothing to her. In the silence, he allowed her fingers, black with grime, to explore his distraught face. The tenderness of it all made Louise put her hand to her mouth and gulp back the tears.

'Yes, it's John,' Dowling repeated, feeling the back of her fingertip run down his cheek. She moved her face towards his, and all the while, her eyes stared at him curiously. Closer and closer her face came. Eventually, she opened her mouth. 'Coo, Coo,' she whispered, and then turned away.

Dowling dropped his hands in despair. 'Oh! Isabelle. Whatever has happened to you?'

Chapter 28

Ann looked over at Mary, who was simply speechless, her mouth slightly open in amazement at the tale Elliott had just told them. On this occasion, Ann had to admit her husband had excelled himself in maintaining the drama and suspense right until the end.

'Well, I've got to hand it to you, dear, I didn't see that coming,' she said to him.

Elliott gave a slight bow of his head in recognition. 'Quite a story, the whole thing, isn't it?'

Mary was horrified. She just couldn't believe that something so awful could have gone unnoticed for such a length of time. 'To keep someone hidden and drugged for over ...' She began trying to reconcile the timeline. '... nearly twenty years! It just beggars belief. How devious and evil can a person be?' The disgust and anger in her voice were growing with every word.

Tom sighed, 'Knowing Robertson as I did, I would say he was as evil as they come.'

The questions continued. Ann wanted to know, 'So, was the Earl of Ranskill involved in it all?'

'That's the bit we've yet to establish, dear,' interrupted Elliott, answering for Tom.

'Well, I'm sorry, but I hope this Dr Robertson's death was a painful one,' said a thoroughly emotional Mary.

Elliott brought it all back to a sobering level with just one comment. 'The trouble is, Mary, nine other men also suffered a painful death in that tragedy.'

She couldn't have felt guiltier. 'You're right, Robert. Sorry, I wasn't thinking.'

~~~

The question of what to do next preyed on Elliott's mind. The information he and Tom now had certainly answered many questions, but some remained - one being, should they get further involved, or leave it to Ernest Cooper, the solicitor, to deal with everything from this point? After all, he was probably best placed to identify the legal implications of it all. The trouble with Elliott though, was that he couldn't leave anything unresolved. And, more importantly, he'd seen on too many occasions how those with money and position closed ranks to evade justice. He knew that the earl would be able to buy the best legal representation in the country.

Alone in the parlour, with his favourite record playing on the gramophone, Elliott sat back in his armchair and took another puff on his pipe. I wonder, he thought, as a cloud of smoke slowly drifted upwards.
~~~

It was what Mary had said that had made him think about things again. 'Umm!' he muttered and sank deeper into his chair. Of course, it wasn't long before he was up on his feet and beginning to pace the floor. As was his custom when deliberating, he turned at each end of the room with the precision of a soldier, all the while tapping his finger against the bowl of his pipe. His tight frown signalled that he was in the middle of some enormous puzzle and wouldn't be content until it was solved. With another draw of his tobacco, he plunged the room into an obscurity of smoke.

His concentration was broken by the door opening. Tom walked in but pulled up swiftly and began wafting his arms furiously, in an attempt to clear the low hanging veil of grey. 'Good grief! Are you in here, Robert?' he spluttered.

Elliott did not appear concerned. He was far too preoccupied with a theory. The resulting explanation was, to Tom, quite bizarre, starting somewhere in the middle and appearing to assume that he was a mind reader. Fortunately for Tom, his friend eventually began to make sense, when he stated, 'Mary was right. It beggars belief that someone could be hidden away for all those years.'

'Oh, I don't know. Royalty have been doing it for centuries and getting away with it,' replied Tom cynically.

Elliott gave enough of a wry smile to imply he shared Tom's view.

'No, there's more to it, Tom. When you went to this Rosterhay Asylum, did the Mother Superior say exactly how long Marion, or Isabelle as she really is, was a patient there?'

Tom thought hard. In the end, he had to admit that Mother Elizabeth hadn't given any time period because he simply hadn't asked. He'd just assumed that Marion had arrived there straight after she went missing, as suggested by his research at the library. Then he smiled, realising he must be right, 'Ah, but if you remember, Robert, I said that a newspaper had reported that *Dr Robertson gave her a sedative to calm her down.*'

'I've no doubt he did. But did he do it on the actual night Isabelle was abducted? My suggestion is …' Elliott began to explain his theory, which was, in fact, incredibly accurate.

~~~

For the young Isabelle, married life with the earl at Haddington had deteriorated into something that even Louise would not have imagined possible. Ranskill spoke to his wife in a tone scarcely different from the one he used when speaking to his staff and he treated her little differently. It became standard practice for him to criticise and humiliate her in front of other people; and worse was
~~~

his willingness to strike her behind closed doors. All the staff knew from his bellowing and her screams what was going on, but nobody ever dared say anything for fear of losing their job.

At just turned twenty one years old, Isabelle was as unhappy as it was possible to be, and with two young children whom she had no real instinct to mother, she sought any type of attention she could get. Above all, her real desire was for physical reassurance, rather than for sexual adventures. She simply wanted somebody to hold her, to comfort her, and to make her feel like the young and vibrant woman she once had been. That somebody became Dowling, who, against his better judgement, succumbed to her open invitation to supply the affection she so desperately needed. There was perhaps nobody who could identify more with the feeling of loneliness and the longing for love than he could.

Dowling, however, unlike Isabelle, could not accept that their relationship was never to be. He fought hard to convince her otherwise but their brief involvement became like a carriage trying to go in two different directions. Unfortunately, the only possible destination was one of disappointment for the butler.

Having given Isabelle comfort and helped to restore her self-confidence, Dowling was soon dropped from Isabelle's affections, as she turned her attention to finding a ticket out of Haddington. That ticket was eventually handed to her by a young and dashing American executive, whose company had sent him to England to assist in the completion of an equipment deal with the earl. During the single week he spent at Haddington, a tempestuous relationship quickly began between Isabelle and himself.

Isabelle's self-belief soared yet higher and, after a little too much wine at dinner one evening, she became like a phoenix ready to rise and take flight. The result was a dramatic argument with Ranskill, the fury of which spilled out from the bedroom, onto the stairway, and eventually downstairs and into the drawing room. The stunned earl, unable to control his wife, quickly gave instructions for her to be calmed through sedation. All of this was watched by his anxious American guest.

The following morning, not only was Isabelle gone but so was her lover. However, there was nothing sinister about their disappearance. It had merely been a case of her packing a bag and secretly leaving Haddington Hall in the early hours. Allegedly, no one saw or heard them leave, not even the duty footman, it seemed. But in reality, he had lied, not wishing to admit to having fallen asleep on duty.

For the next eight years, Isabelle lived an affluent life as Mrs Jack Wagner in the city of Richmond, Virginia. But, as at most periods of Isabelle's life, tragedy was not far away, and she was eventually left in substantial debt when her husband's business dealings went seriously wrong. Waking one morning, she found a note saying he would collect her later that week. He never came.

Penniless, and soon homeless, she decided her best option was to return to England. There, at least she could try to re-establish some sort of relationship with her estranged family. She made one last plea to her friends to lend her enough money to pay for a passage back to her homeland. With no help forthcoming, the reality of how she would have to earn that ticket quickly dawned on her. By the winter of 1907, when Isabelle finally stepped on board the ship Carpathia, bound for Liverpool, she was nothing more than a third class passenger, and a broken woman. All but disowned by her own family, Isabelle attempted contact with the only person who, for the sake of their children, she felt might help her get back on her feet – the Earl of Ranskill. How wrong she was! And after a meeting with Dr Robertson, acting on the earl's behalf, her fate was sealed.

Turning the corner of the street back to her miserable lodgings one day, she was shocked to see the doctor standing in front of her once more. He gave her one of his sickly smiles and held a gauze to her face.

~~~
~~~

'So do you think she may well have gone to America, as the rumours suggested, and then returned at some stage?' asked Tom.

Elliott sighed and went to sit down in his chair. 'Oh, I don't know, Tom. It's just a thought.'

Taking the seat opposite, Tom was intrigued by his friend's theory and keen to expand on it further. 'And one we need to check out.' He then looked rather philosophical, 'Although it can't change the fact of her current state.'

'Why do you think Ranskill and Robertson kept her institutionalised anyway? Surely, with their capabilities, it would have been quite easy to just do away with her?'

'Robertson's sick mind, I'd say. The chance to experiment on her with drugs.' Lifting his eyes and glancing over to Elliott, he finished, 'That and other things behind closed doors.'

Elliott passed his hand over his forehead, before squeezing his eyes tightly with forefinger and thumb. 'Good Lord, Tom! Just what kind of world are we living in?'

'It's not the world that's the problem, just the people in it,' Tom replied.

Chapter 29

All three men were sitting patiently waiting when the knock came on the door. On being given instructions to enter, the efficient-looking, if slightly dour, secretary turned the handle and stood to the side of the half-open door. 'Mrs Ridgeway has now arrived for her appointment, Mr Cooper,' she said in her stern, professional tone.

'Ah, yes,' replied Ernest Cooper. 'Please show her in would you, Miss Denton.'

Normally Cooper would always check his pocket watch to ensure the time was as shown on his calendar, but today he was most anxious, and instead he fumbled with his waistcoat, trying to disguise his large stomach. He stood up in anticipation of his client's entrance. Elliott and Tom followed his lead and did the same.

This time, after a small, more discreet knock, the door opened wider. 'If you'd like to go through now, Mrs Ridgeway,' suggested the secretary. Louise strolled in wearing a dark coloured suit, with a raised and lightly defined waist to the jacket. Even with all the restrictions of wartime on fashion, Louise knew exactly how to show her figure to advantage and make the most of what there was available to buy. She held out her hand to Cooper. He gently took hold of it.

'How lovely to see you again, Mrs Ridgeway. Do please take a seat. Allow me to introduce you to two gentlemen, who I think will be very useful in assisting in your case.'

With the formality of introductions over, Louise looked at Tom. Touching her chin, she joked. 'And you look altogether different without the blood, Professor Sharpe.'

Remembering her strange look at him at their first, brief meeting, Tom gingerly touched his lip. 'Of course, yes!' he smiled.

Poor Cooper didn't have a clue what it all meant, so he just coughed politely. 'Well, if we could get started.'

Starting first entailed Cooper pulling at the string tied round the file and opening it carefully. Taking his notes from the top of the pile, he remarked, 'In all my years of legal practice, I don't think I've come across anything quite as intriguing … or so concerning.'

'Concerning, Mr Cooper?' said Louise.

'Concerning on numerous accounts, Mrs Ridgeway —'

Louise interrupted, 'Perhaps we should now dispense with my alias. Obviously I am no longer Lady Warsop. But I've no desire to use my more recent surname, Mueller. So, please would you call me by my maiden name, Coberwell?'

'Very well,' replied Cooper. 'Miss Coberwell, I am firstly concerned as to whether your true motive has been one of seeking revenge, or whether your aim is to seek justice.'

Louise did not appear disconcerted by his question. She calmly moved her handbag a little further down her lap and replied. 'The intention was both, Mr Cooper. To exact revenge on Dr Robertson and also to make sure that the earl got his just desserts. However, my main motive has always been to be reunited with my son, Edward.'

Louise's answer could not have been more direct, and she saw the eyebrows of all three men rise at her response.

Elliott interjected, in a voice that would accept no nonsense, 'Miss Coberwell, by exacting revenge do you actually mean murder?'

Staring into space, Louise was clearly remembering Robertson. Eventually she turned to give Elliott her reply. 'With all that I've suffered at the hands of that man, killing him was very much on my mind when I returned to England, but I can assure you that somebody else beat me to it!'

'And would you know who that was?'

Louise gave a pleasant and seemingly genuine smile. 'That's something I honestly don't know, Mr Elliott.'

Cooper lowered his glasses and began turning

over several sheets of paper in the file. 'When reading these documents, Miss Coberwell, I could see nothing that would convict the Earl of Ranskill of having any involvement in the terrible events we are talking about. You don't need me to tell you of your father-in-law's influence. He will amass quite a formidable legal team to contest any action we try to bring against him.'

Laying down his glasses, the solicitor pushed back in his chair. 'At the very least it will be a lengthy, messy battle.' He paused and breathed deeply. 'And a very costly one.'

Louise immediately argued that there would be more than enough money available on winning any lawsuit. However, Cooper felt himself bound to put the facts squarely to his rather naive client. 'I am afraid that to acquire the service of barristers, we would need a sizeable amount of money upfront for fees. Do you have those kind of resources, Miss Coberwell?'

Of course she didn't and Cooper suspected as much. Louise dropped her head slightly, in noticeable disappointment. The room fell silent. It was Tom who, having sat through the whole exchange so far as an observer, made a suggestion. 'You mentioned earlier that your main motive was to get custody of your son again?'

'Yes,' Louise answered, unsure what Tom was suggesting.

'And after, do you have aspirations to return and live at Haddington?'

'No, Professor!'

'Then it's clear to me that we should try a different tack altogether, Mr Cooper.'

The somewhat startled solicitor sat upright at Tom's sudden change of tone and forthright manner. 'Well, er … yes … of course we should,' he said but then had to ask, 'What exactly *are* you suggesting, Professor?'

Tom rose from his seat to explain, 'It's my experience when dealing with businessmen …'

Elliott adopted a droll expression. His chest rose and fell with an inward sigh, as he feared his friend was about to offer his usual medical analogies. Cooper folded his arms in preparation for his enlightenment. As for Louise, well, she was just happy that, at last, there were people genuinely interested enough to want to help her.

~~~

At 3.05 pm Ranskill strode confidently through the doors into the premises of Briggs, Stock and Cooper. Standing and looking around at his surroundings, he abruptly stated to the secretary, without so much as a glance, 'Ranskill. Appointment at 3 o'clock.' Miss Denton was shocked at his rudeness. Although quite used to impolite
~~~

– even pompous – clients, she had never encountered one so arrogant as the man now staring at her with impatience. She could feel anger building up inside her, but was far too professional to show it. Instead, she got up and knocked on Mr Cooper's door. Opening it, she repeated, with a ceremony that bordered on mockery, 'His lordship, The Earl of Ranskill. Your three o'clock appointment, Mr Cooper.'

Ranskill walked past the secretary and into Cooper's office without giving her another look. Once inside, he was surprised to see not only the man whom he assumed must be Mr Cooper, but also Elliott and Tom. 'So, Cooper! What is so important that it can't be dealt with by my solicitors?'

Ernest Cooper remained calm and stood up slowly. He was determined that the earl would not dictate the pace or content of the meeting. He gestured with his hand towards a chair. 'Please take a seat, Lord Ranskill.' Turning towards Elliott and Tom, he spoke further, 'I believe you are acquainted with Mr Elliott and Professor Sharpe.'

Ranskill grudgingly gave a nod of his head. 'Time is money. Can we get to the point, Cooper?'

'Lord Ranskill,' replied the solicitor, doing his utmost to stay calm, 'a cooper is one skilled in making and repairing barrels. I am not such a person. Nor am I in your employ. I extend you the courtesy of addressing you by your title. Kindly treat me in the same way.'

Ranskill was not used to being challenged about his manner and certainly didn't like it. Nevertheless, he had to admire the solicitor's firmness. 'Very well, Mister Cooper. Shall we get to the purpose of your asking me to your office regarding Dr Robertson?'

Placing his hand on the file on the desk in front of him, Cooper began his explanation, being careful to make sure he only implicated Dr Robertson in any wrongdoing at this stage. The earl sat attentively assessing every word of the allegations that his ex-business partner had abducted Isabelle and Louise. If it was not news to him, he certainly appeared to play the part of a shocked man well, occasionally lifting his eyebrows in utter surprise, giving a frown here and there, and interjecting a useful tut when appropriate. In truth, he was genuinely shocked, very shocked. He had always believed what Robertson had told him – that he had killed them both! As for the story of Louise absconding with Mueller to Germany: that was just something that the pair had concocted to cover her disappearance.

Why had Robertson lied to him, he wondered. The answer was simple: with Isabelle, just as Tom had suggested, the doctor wanted to experiment on her with drugs, and to fulfil his sexual desires. With Louise,

Robertson never did tell the earl about the debacle of her abduction, deciding that, for as long as Ranskill thought he was complicit in a murder, he had the advantage over his partner.

Eventually, the earl regained his composure and decided to play devil's advocate. 'But of course, Dr Robertson is not around to refute any of this.'

'No, I grant you that,' replied Cooper.

Ranskill thought for a moment. 'Well, I'm not sure how I can help you but I'm happy to provide whatever information I can.'

Leaning forward, Cooper again placed his hand on the file. 'The trouble is, Lord Ranskill, the documents in here state that you were party to it all.'

'What!' Ranskill bellowed and stood up. 'How dare you even insinuate that I could be involved? It's outrageous! Have you forgotten whom you're addressing?'

The reaction was nothing short of what the three men had anticipated, although they hadn't imagined it would be produced with quite as much gusto. Ranskill slammed his hand down onto Cooper's desk. 'This file! The stories it contains are lies. Where did it come from? No, don't answer. Save it for my lawyer.' He moved in closer to Cooper. 'I'll see your practice destroyed for this, Cooper. Do you hear me? Destroyed!'

Elliott had witnessed enough of Ranskill's outburst

and stood up to face him. 'The facts were provided by somebody you know well. And also verified by my and the professor's investigations.'

'Oh, were they now, Elliott?' spat out the earl. 'Well, I should like to see this person and give them a piece of my mind.' He moved towards the door.

'As you wish,' stated Elliott. 'Tom, perhaps you could ask Miss Coberwell to come through now.'

Ranskill froze like a statue. The blood in his face drained as quickly as the fear in his stomach rose. Slowly he turned. The side door to Cooper's office began to open. Then, the woman he never thought he would meet again was suddenly standing before him.

'Hello, father-in-law,' her voice said.

Ranskill was too stunned to respond.

'Why don't you come back and sit down, sir. Professor Sharpe has a proposal for you,' said Elliott.

As white as a sheet, Ranskill returned to his seat. It was only then that Elliott's words fully registered with him. Proposal? That surely meant that they didn't know he had colluded with Robertson in plotting the women's deaths or, at best, he thought they didn't have enough proof. 'What is it exactly that you mean by a proposal?' he asked.

'The options are really quite simple, Lord Ranskill,' explained Tom. 'As yet, we don't know the full extent of your involvement in all of this, and with Dr Robertson gone, we probably never will.'

It was as Ranskill thought. A smug feeling engulfed him.

'However, if you decide to fight all the allegations, there will be one hell of a circus. The press will have a field day. And believe me, Mr Elliott here will ensure the police investigation will be a most thorough affair. Furthermore, I will use all my powers in the medical profession to bring evidence forward. The effect on your business, reputation and social standing will be immense. Not to mention, of course, the financial cost of it all. Or … you can agree to Louise's demands, which, as I see it, are most reasonable. And more than you deserve.'

Realising he was snared, Ranskill started huffing and puffing. Scraping his tongue along the back of his lower teeth he stared hard at Louise, before diverting his glare back at Tom. 'And what terms might they be?' he asked contemptuously.

Cooper stood up firmly, wanting to regain control of the conversation, and needing to ensure there would be no ambiguity. 'In return for her silence, my client will take full custody of her son, Master Edward, and thereafter, will reside at Brentwood House, with an annuity to be agreed.'

'No! he is a Ranskill and will remain at Haddington,'

cried the earl.

Cooper simply ignored him and continued, 'With regard to Isabelle, your estate will provide all necessary funds to ensure that her future needs for care and comfort are met.'

Rising to his feet, the earl marched towards the door and grabbed the handle.

With Ranskill half out of the door, Cooper made things clear. 'I will give you three days to agree terms, Lord Ranskill, after which, if there is no settlement, my client will take this file and approach the press.'

'I will not be dictated to by you, her or anyone!' Ranskill bellowed.

With a whoosh of air, the door to Cooper's office slammed firmly shut.

~~~

On his return to Haddington, Ranskill thundered through the entrance doors, his face filled with rage. Anything or anybody that got in his way was likely to come up against either his fist or a severe bout of verbal abuse, perhaps even both. Luckily, there was nobody between him and his study. However, a large vase was not so fortunate and it went crashing to the floor.

In his study, Ranskill went immediately to his drinks
~~~

table and placed his hands at either end. 'I am the Earl of Ranskill. Nobody will tell me what to damn well do!' Feeling his temper rise again, he lifted the table and flung it upwards. The resulting carnage of broken decanters, glasses and bottles of spirits was spread across the wooden floor. Dowling, who by now was in the hall probing the mystery of the smashed vase, went into the study to investigate the sudden noise. 'M'lord, is everything all right?'

Ranskill was standing in front of the fireplace, his arms outstretched across the mantelpiece. 'No, Dowling, everything is not all right. There's no bloody whisky! Get me some.'

'As you wish, m'lord.'

'Oh, and Dowling. Get him to stop playing that wretched, mournful music or I'm likely to —'

'I'll see what I can do, sir.'

The music to which Ranskill was referring was coming from the drawing room. It was David playing *El Triste Matador.*

The earl dropped into his armchair, suddenly feeling light-headed. His brow began to bead with sweat. Taking deep breaths and mopping his forehead, he tried to relax. Eventually, he thought he was back to normal and tried to stand up, only to experience an odd tingling down the side of his arm. He felt weak. Sitting back down allowed him to regulate his breathing. He knew what was coming and braced himself for the pain of an angina attack. He also knew he needed his pills. Fumbling inside his pocket he was unable to locate his small pillbox. Panicking, his eyes began darting across the room. Where could it be?

A slight creaking sound made him look back at the door. It was David.

'Ah, David. Thank God.'

David said nothing, just stood with his violin and bow loosely hanging in his hand.

'My pills. I need my pills.'

His son never moved. There was no real expression on his face, no appearance of concern.

'David, please. Help me find my pills!'

After what seemed an eternity, David did begin slowly to walk towards his father. He said not a word until, once near him, he saw the pillbox on the bureau. Picking it up, he walked towards the chair. 'Here it is, father,' he said and started to open it. To Ranskill's horror, he opened it right up, turned it upside down, and allowed the pills to spill out across the floor.

'No! Noooo!' cried his father, clutching his chest, which felt like it was carrying the weight of an anvil. He gasped for air and attempted to stand, only to stumble and fall to his knees. Looking up he pleaded in desperation, 'Help me!' Seeing a pill lying in front of him, he reached out. But the shadow of a foot came over it. Soon it was being ground into powder on the floor. The once mighty earl pathetically tried to scoop it to his mouth. Rolling over, he slurred, 'Ple-e-ase!'

David picked up his violin and looked down. 'Do whatever you need to do, father.' With that, he walked away. Outside the door, he met Dowling returning with a new decanter of whisky. 'I would leave him, Dowling. He's on the telephone and it looks like he may be a while.'

Two hours later, the Earl of Ranskill was pronounced dead, having suffered slow and painful heart failure.

Chapter 30

It was reminiscent of the last time they had all stood on the platform of Sheffield railway station. All that is, excepting Tom, whose last experience here was one of a swollen lip and being escorted to the police station. However, the Sharpes were going back to London, and there the incident would soon be forgotten, although not their visit as a whole. That would be remembered as an eventful and, ultimately, a very happy time by Tom and Mary.

Ann wanted to cuddle Lucinda one last time, but 'little Miss obstinate' as she had affectionately become known, was anything but amenable and struggled furiously. All the baby was interested in was where the strange sound was coming from, as the steam engine released its pressure. 'Very well, back to mother then,' Ann said, handing over the lively bundle.

'Oh! I was rather hoping you'd say she could stay with you here in Sheffield a little while longer,' Mary sighed in jest.

'Don't tempt me!' replied Ann and wrapped her arm around Mary. 'It's been an absolute pleasure having you all to stay. And thank you for coming to Scarborough.'

She held up her hand to shield her words: 'Much better than if grumpy guts had gone.'

Mary kissed Ann on her cheek. 'Now you know you don't mean that. I love him dearly and so do you!'

Ann looked over to Elliott, deep in conversation with Tom and oblivious of the fact he was being talked about. She smiled fondly. 'Yes, Mary, I'm afraid I do … very much.'

Henry's voice broke her moment of reflection. 'No, it wasn't a zeppelin, Cecil, it was just a cloud,' he said, shaking his head in disgust at what he saw as his brother's sheer stupidity.

Ann looked curiously towards the sky and decided to tease. 'Oh, yes, I think I can see it too, Cecil.'

'Mother, it's a cloud!'

'Oh, Henry! Where's your sense of adventure?'

Henry looked as if he'd been slapped with a wet fish.

'See what I mean, Mary. Like father, like son,' Ann concluded.

A smile quickly returned to Henry's face when Mary asked him to look for something wrapped in her bag. He pulled out the large book-shaped object and looked confused.

'For your birthday next week,' explained Mary. 'I saw you looking at it longingly in Scarborough.'

'Oh wow! Thanks, Mary … I mean Auntie Mary.'

'And for you, Master Cecil,' continued Mary, before handing Lucinda over to Ann, 'One of Auntie Mary's very special … kiss and cuddles.' She promptly chased Cecil playfully along the platform. 'Ooh, I love you,' she said, after finally catching him and holding him in her arms.

The words 'I love you' were all too familiar on the platform, particularly these days, as soldiers travelled to London before going on to meet their regiments. With doors opening and closing, kit bags and battered suitcases being loaded, lovers said their final goodbyes. The guard shouted again, 'All aboard now!'

Tom held out his hand to Elliott. 'Well, old chap. We'll say our goodbyes.'

Giving a firm handshake, Elliott replied, 'Hey, not so much of the old, eh? Listen, I've really enjoyed your company, Tom. Thanks. And I hope your stay has been useful to you.'

'I think I'd call it an education, Robert!' answered Tom, drawing his face into a smirk. 'I'm just sorry I can't stay for the conclusion. You will let me know the outcome as soon as possible.'

'You'll be the first to know.'

The guard blew his whistle. Tom clasped his friend's hand a little tighter. 'Goodbye, Robert! And remember what I said about Brockwell. You need to find a way to stop his memory affecting you.'

Elliott simply shrugged off the issue. 'Oh, I'll be fine.'

Before he knew it, Mary was standing in front of him, arms outstretched. They gave each other an embrace. For him, it was like a father saying goodbye to his daughter. The strange and comforting feeling of holding her tight, the flutter in his stomach, the ache of sadness that she was leaving. Then, he had a flashback to the moment when, all those years ago, the nurse had confirmed that Amy had died. His hand instinctively clutched his daughter's little bootie in his pocket. Even after all this time, the memory remained so vivid. Eventually, the image was gone and he was looking at Mary. 'Take care my sweetheart,' he said and kissed her forehead.

With a huge puff of smoke and steam, the 11.40 am train to London St Pancras pulled out of the station.

~~~

That night in the parlour, it all seemed so quiet without their guests. Even Bessie wandered around aimlessly, wondering where the man had gone who gave her endless bits of food. Eventually she settled on the rug, but cocked her ear up at the slightest indication that he might have returned. 'Yes, I know what he did, girl, but they're not good for you,' said Elliott. Bessie dropped her
~~~

head forlornly between her paws, as if she understood every word. Perhaps she did.

Ann smiled from behind her cross-stitch. 'Bah humbug!'

The rest of the evening Ann and Elliott talked and adjusted back into their usual routine. Ann was quite surprised at how unusually chatty her husband was, and decided now would be the right time to tell him the story of Cecil's escapade at the harbour. However, by the time she had finished, it came across as little more than a humorous incident. Ann had learnt over the years to always put her slant on things and to tell her husband only what he needed to know. This way, a crisis or argument was invariably avoided.

'You haven't forgotten we said we'd visit Elizabeth this Sunday,' Ann said, changing the subject.

Elliott frowned. 'I'd rather not, dear. Can't she come here?'

'It's not the same. It helps if we visit and treat it all as normal.'

'But it isn't normal. It can never be normal,' Elliott insisted.

'She needs our support, Robert. Whatever he did was absolutely nothing to do with her.'

Elizabeth was their friend and the wife of the deceased Canon Charles Brockwell. Since his death and all the revelations about him, she had had an extremely difficult time. Unsurprisingly, learning about the evil things her husband had done as he pursued his double life, had brought her almost to the point of a nervous breakdown. More recently, her physical health had begun seriously to deteriorate. People whom she had thought were her friends suddenly disappeared and, had it not been for Robert and Ann, she might well have already been in her grave.

Mention of the visit allowed Ann to ease into the conversation her other concern. 'Tom reckons the Jewish faith has a good way to deal with it.'

'Deal with what?' replied Elliott, who had returned to reading his newspaper and was only half-listening.

'Feelings of guilt. Jews apparently imagine casting breadcrumbs into a flowing stream of water. Each breadcrumb represents a sin and the flowing water washes them away.'

Elliott slowly dropped his newspaper. 'Ann, I don't have feelings of guilt about Charles Brockwell's sins. It was just the paste Lily prepared that made me have hallucinations, that's all. It isn't a problem.'

'Robert, if trying to hang yourself from the kitchen ceiling isn't a problem, then I don't know what is. Talk to me about him. We've never really spoken about Charles since … well, it happened.'

Elliott's expression said more than any words could have.

'He was a friend for a long time, Robert. And it's only natural for you to think as you do. You feel let down. We all do. But what good is it going to do, you carrying the burden of his sins like this? Accept that we didn't truly know him at all. There was nothing you could have done to save any of those unfortunate women or babies. Accept that was what he was!'

The deep sigh from her husband cut across her appeal.

'You have to, dear. Otherwise, it's going to paralyse you – emotionally. His memory will keep haunting you. Then who's won?'

For Elliott though, acceptance was one thing; putting the theory into practice was another.

~~~

There were several things Elliott needed to do before the whole affair of Haddington and the pit disaster could finally be laid to rest. All would prove to be emotional events.

First, he met with Detective Hollins and Sergeant Drake at the police station and, once more, began telling his long story. His narrative left both men lost for words.

'So, you see gentlemen, in my opinion, William
~~~

Doherty is no more guilty of cutting that wire rope than you or I,' Elliott concluded.

Detective Hollins, standing with a mug of tea in his hand, looked towards Drake and at last gave his opinion: 'Well, Sid, it looks like we'd better look out for our jobs in future, eh? Two men from outside the force solving a murder! What will the inspector say to that?'

Elliott took the comment in the spirit it was meant.

'Right then, Mr Elliott, we'd better pay this person a visit and see what they have to say for themselves.'

A car of any description, let alone a police car, was a rarity in the old village near the colliery. Elliott knew the meeting would be fraught enough without an audience so, to prevent villagers unashamedly opening their doors and gawping, they parked some way away and took a ten-minute walk to Wood Lane. Eventually, they arrived at the row of back-to-back terraced houses and knocked on the door of number 87, which had an immaculately washed stone step. A woman holding a baby responded to their knock.

'Good morning, madam,' began Detective Hollins. 'Can we have a word with Mr Dawson please?'

'Which one?' enquired the woman, quite logically as there were two who lived there. 'My husband or my son?'

Elliott confirmed, 'Your son.'

'What's it about?'

Elliott inclined his head slightly to indicate that prying eyes were now looking at them all from across the street. 'Perhaps we could come in and discuss it?'

Looking over Elliott's shoulder at the nosey neighbour, Mrs Dawson gave a hesitant smile and pulled open the door. Once inside, the three men were invited into the kitchen, which was full of drying nappies. In fact, it seemed as if there were nappies everywhere: some by the fire; some on clothes horses; some on a ceiling rack; some even on the backs of chairs. If something could be hung on it, then a nappy was drying on it.

The woman handed her crying baby to a shocked Sergeant Drake and attempted to clear away some laundry. 'There's some men here to see you, luv,' she said, appearing to speak to someone, although neither Elliott nor the detective nor Drake could see exactly where that someone was.

Eventually, a man stood up from behind one of the clothes horses.

'Mr Dawson?' asked Hollins.

'Yes.'

'We'd like to have a chat with you if we may.'

'But who are you?'

'We're from the police.'

'Oh Lord, no! He's not in any sort of bother is he?' asked the alarmed mother.

Looking as uncomfortable as ever a man could holding a baby, Drake handed back the crying infant to its mother. 'Why don't you go through to the parlour, Mrs Dawson, and sort the bairn. We'll give you a shout when we're done.' It didn't take long for her to realise that what they had come to see her son about was indeed serious.

Elliott moved to collapse another clothes horse and leant it against the wall, trying to create a little more space. 'I think you know why we're here, young man.' His voice was authoritative but reasonable. There was something about Elliott's manner that made people look at him with respect, but also with an expectation they would be heard fairly.

'About the cage disaster?' the young man's voice stuttered.

'Yes it is, Stephen,' Elliott replied, with a resigned expression on his face.

It was always about the obvious for Elliott. Once he knew of David's homosexuality, all that was needed was some further questioning of Dowling to reveal who his lover had been. Then, he simply had to decide which one was capable of murder. Whilst there were certainly enough people at Haddington with a motive to want to kill Dr Robertson, there were only two people who possessed the required technical knowledge of the engine room operation and the winding ropes: David and Stephen.

Stephen was shy and nervous, and the more he tried to explain, the more he stammered. Elliott placed his hand on the lad's shoulder to help calm him. 'Take your time. Just tell the detective how it was.'

Feeling the encouraging pressure of Elliott's hand, Stephen relaxed somewhat and continued. 'I heard David had had an operation. Then I found he didn't want to see me any more. I couldn't understand why. When I did get to see him, at first he just seemed to have lost interest in me. Then, suddenly, he got angry, as if he hated me for some reason. I asked him to please tell me what I'd done. Then he just went crazy and started to take his clothes off. All he kept saying was, 'Look at what he's done!"

'By 'he', he meant Dr Robertson?' asked the detective.

Stephen stared into space, remembering the occasion. He began to sob. Then a fierce anger rose up in him. Wiping away his tears, he raged, 'Yes, I mean Robertson. That evil bastard of a man had mutilated David. He'd destroyed him! David was saying it was the end of our love.'

There was really only one question left for Hollins to ask. 'Stephen, did you cut the wire rope and make the cage plunge down the shaft?'

Stephen looked at each man in turn before simply answering, 'Yes!'

<div style="text-align: center;">~~~</div>

Anticipating that, for Louise, being reunited with her son would be an emotional ordeal, Elliott suggested that she become reacquainted with Edward, now a boy of nearly two, in stages. Their first meeting took place at the church on the estate.

Being driven by Dowling into the grounds brought back mixed emotions for Louise. Gazing through the window, all the memories came flooding back one after another. Tears rolled down her cheeks as she remembered. She didn't even attempt to wipe her tears away, even when Dowling looked back at her in his mirror and their gaze met. It was a fact that, here at Haddington, Louise had endured, and learnt to accept, sorrow for far too long. Without doubt, what she'd experienced had now made her who she was – a woman able to survive. However, as the car turned to bring the hall into view, she held her hand over her unborn child and vowed she would find happiness again, a life full of laughter, joy and love.

Approaching the church, she clasped her hand over her mouth, seeing Edward walking hand-in-hand with his nanny and dressed in a finely tailored, buttoned blue coat with a velvet collar. Louise stepped out of the car and stood watching her little boy do a hop and a skip, with no comprehension of just whom he was about to meet.

The nanny bent down. 'Edward, this lady is your mother.' The poor child didn't really have a clue what that meant. All he could see was a woman in front of him openly sobbing. Bemused, he lifted up his innocent, rosy-cheeked face towards the nanny and said, 'Why is she crying?'

~~~

Since the earl's death, David had shown no inclination to take the reins of the family business, refusing to meet or talk with any of the company executives. With regard to Haddington Hall, he showed little more interest, and mostly looked to Dowling to give directions on estate matters. This he did, as much as his position would allow, but it wasn't long before the Warsop dynasty was like a rudderless ship.

Accompanying Ernest Cooper and Louise to break the news to David was, for Elliott, something he couldn't quite predict the outcome of. How does someone react to being told that his mother, whom he's never known, has just reappeared but is mentally ill? Also, how would he take the news that Louise had returned, a woman whom he'd previously trusted and adored, but who was now labelled a traitor to her country. It would be a case of doing the best they could. In the end, however, it
~~~

was Louise who took it on herself to explain the whole situation to David.

Standing in the hallway she trembled with anticipation. Half of her wanted to race into the drawing room where the music was coming from and, as she'd previously done, wrap her arms around his chest and simply hold him. The other half of her just wanted to cry as she opened the door and saw him. He looked so different, so gaunt and thin. There was none of the fine open look she remembered him for, instead, there was just a man playing a tune full of beauty and soul, with emptiness and sadness etched on his face.

Gazing out of the window, he continued to play his violin until he caught sight of Louise's reflection walking slowly towards him. Turning around, his arm dropped to his side, the bow falling to the floor. She reached out her fingertips and touched his hand. Tenderly, their fingers entwined. With her other hand she cupped his face and finally spoke, 'Oh my dear, lovely David. Whatever have they done to you?'

Chapter 31

Haddington Hall, 2014.
Extract from the Heritage Guided Tour

'… And now we enter what was the library. If you look up to your right, you will see a portrait of Louise, painted by Sir James Shaftsbury in 1920. After the death of the third earl, in 1916, Louise returned to live at Haddington Hall and, as is evident from the photograph on the far left of the cabinet, she was heavily pregnant carrying Andrew, the last Earl of Ranskill. At the time, there was great debate as to who the father was. It still remains very much a mystery! If official sources are to be believed, then the father was George's second son David, which is what is recorded on Andrew's birth certificate. However, more likely, it was the German mining architect, Kurt Mueller, whom we learned about earlier. This was a great scandal at the time and, if nothing else, it certainly made a good story.

Another great mystery in Haddington's history was the true identity of a mentally ill woman you'll see in many of the photos on display. We know that she was called Marion and lived in an apartment in the east wing of the house but, other than that, we know little more about her. There was speculation that she was, in fact, David's mother who disappeared to America when he was very young. However, others think that this is nothing more than an intriguing tale. It is more likely that she was simply a friend of the family to whom they showed considerable charity.

It was in the years after the First World War that Haddington enjoyed its most lavish and, some would say, its happiest times. Without doubt this new era was influenced by Louise. Many articles written about Haddington during this period state that laughter and joy could be found in every corner of the hall.

In the spring of 1919, Louise married David in All Hallows Church, located within the grounds. Some of Louise's diaries which have survived show us that their marriage was very much one of love and, before we move towards the drawing room, perhaps I could just read you one of Louise's diary entries:

My past has been about sadness, abuse and manipulation. I felt compromised in my innermost being. Now my life is all about happiness again.

Once I thought I knew everything about love, but now I realise that all I'd ever really known was the fulfilment of my sexual desires. Today I understand true love. My heart aches as I watch the clock, waiting for him to return.

Damn this thing called love – for David has only been away on the pheasant shoot for two hours!

~~~

The Countess of Ranskill

by

Sir James Shaftsbury
~~~

Coming Soon

Follow Elliott and friends in the next mystery
of the Entanglement Series...

Deceit

For progress and sneak previews visit
www.chrisbrookes.info

For book clubs and writing groups

Chris is always keen to discuss his writing with groups and, wherever possible, will try to attend an invitation to speak. For availability or simply to discuss further please make contact: **enquiries@chrisbrookes.info**

Test Readers

Normally Chris will invite test readers to assess a new book or script as he writes it. If you would like to be part of a story's evolution, from concept to completion, and willing to spare a little time in order to give objective feedback, opinion and comment, then please visit **www.chrisbrookes.info**

Read on

For a preview of book one in the series available through bookstores ISBN: 9781782999089

ENTANGLEMENT of
FATE
BOOK ONE OF THE MYSTERY SERIES

Chapter 1

Street Arab

Sheffield, England, Winter 1912

Past midnight was no time to be running over the wet, slippery tiles of the city's terraced rooftops, trying to apprehend a criminal; and particularly not one who moved over the ridges with the agility of a cat. But such was Constable Reynolds's challenge, as he struggled through the shroud of rain, soaked in a sulphurous stench.

The sound of muffled clicking on the roof tiles overlaid the never-ending thud of foundry hammers in the distance. They were strange, random clicks with no rhythm, the sort that would annoy anyone who liked order and pattern. The noise stopped for a moment, then began again, becoming more and more audible. Finally, it had a beat – click, click, clunk. Through the veil of lashing rain, Reynolds caught sight of a slim, bedraggled figure, running and balancing with ease, his heavy hob nailed boots clicking against the slates.

The figure stopped to catch his breath and looked back at Reynolds struggling behind him, the flickering light from the constable's torch bouncing erratically round. In the back alleys beneath, dogs began to bark in disharmony at the sound of indistinct police whistles, whilst on the street, a dozen policemen grouped together, all fighting to keep their faces out of the biting cold wind, half-heartedly moving their torches back and forth to throw a dim light up to the rooftops. Three nights this week they had been called out to catch the man they now dubbed the Street Arab. Each time, they had failed. One minute he'd be up on the roof, the next at the bottom of a drainpipe two hundred yards further on than you'd believe he could be.

As the rain eased and bright moonlight broke through the clouds, the Street Arab drew back to hide in the shadows until, once more, darkness could give him cover. He pushed his drenched black hair away from his youthful, swarthy face with its dirty half-grown beard. His dark sunken eyes glared out in anguish as he wedged himself flat in the gully, well hidden between dormer and roof tiles.

Least impressed this night was Sergeant Drake, a portly man who constantly ran his fingers through his thick handle-bar moustache. For him, this nonsense had to stop once and for all. And stop it would, by fair means or foul. He was determined that this 'toe rag', as he called him, would see the inside of a cell. He looked upwards and bellowed out to the rooftop, 'Reynolds!' There was no response. 'I can't see a thing. Where the bloody hell is that lamp?' he demanded. Finally, a constable handed him a heavy-duty torch, which he fiddled with until at last it came on, flooding the rooftop with light.

'Reynolds! Can you hear me? Where are you?' bawled Drake, becoming more and more agitated.

A sorry-looking character finally appeared above; trying to balance over the roof ridge, one hand waving about, the other desperately trying to focus his torch.

'I'm here' responded the thoroughly dejected Reynolds, as Drake's torchlight finally picked him out

'Well! Where is he?

'Er...he's gone, sarge'

'Gone! What do you mean he's gone? Where the bloody hell to?'

'I don't know, he's just…well, disappeared as usual.'

'Disappeared as usual. Lord, give me strength,' the sergeant spluttered, ready to burst at any minute. He looked towards his group of men, all now utterly miserable, and singled out Jenkins. Pointing towards the house door, he said, 'Go in there and ask them, nay, tell them, you need access to the roof from their dormer.' Jenkins obliged, thankful for any opportunity to get out of the wind even for a couple of minutes.

The Street Arab, meantime, dared not move, knowing

that any minute the light of the sergeant's torch could pan across and pick him out. But, equally, he realised that only back on the ridges would he have any chance of escape. Suddenly, with a forceful push of his hands, he was back on his feet again and running. Immediately half-a-dozen torches moved in the direction of the noise. A voice shrieked, 'Look, there he is!' Drake's light easily exposed him, clambering to the ridge.

He reached the apex of the roof and started running along it, only to pull up abruptly. In front of him was the end of the terrace. Beyond, only the gable of the next line of houses, but not before a twenty-foot gap. He surveyed the drop. 'Dear God, at least forty feet,' he reckoned. Looking up again, he saw the drainpipe and considered if he could make it, all the while conscious Reynolds was closing in on him from behind. He knew he could double back and easily bypass him on the ridge, but he couldn't be sure there weren't more policemen further down the roof.

His decision was suddenly made as the dormer window opened and Jenkins crawled awkwardly out onto the roof. It would now have to be the jump to the pipe, however daunting. His eyes opened wide with anxiety, 'Jesus Christ!' he thought, taking another look at the drop. Blood pumped through every part of him. His body tingled. Gently he rocked back and forth, ready to propel himself across.

'It's now or never. I won't be caught,' he said to himself. That much he was determined about: he wouldn't go back to that hell!

'The toe rag's only going to jump,' Drake exclaimed, looking upwards. The next moment the Street Arab was in the air, arms outstretched. Faces below looked up agog at what he'd just done.

A grimace showed the pain as he thumped hard into the pipe. Pain was something he was all too familiar with; but this was in a league of its own. He pulled back to see the damage – a bracket crushed hard into his torso, the wind taken out of him so badly he couldn't even utter a moan. He tried to make sense of what he needed to do next, but all he understood was the need to cling onto the pipe.

Drake flew into a rage. 'No! No bloody way! He's not escaping this time.' Frantically he hollered out instructions, 'You, up that pipe! You lot, get in every house with a dormer and get on their roof! Come on, run!'

His directions, however, weren't needed. The Street Arab was going nowhere. His only possibility was to hold onto the pipe. The pain in his chest was now so severe, he was on the verge of passing out. Finally, he had to concede and slowly slipped down the pipe towards his waiting captors. Only harsh treatment awaited him on the ground. He was frog-marched in front of Drake, who circled around him, like a hyena waiting to attack its prey. Without warning, he unleashed a punch to the man's stomach. The captive's head slumped; his body flopped like a puppet suddenly without strings. Drake pulled up the bowed head by the hair. 'Right lad, your game's done,' he said, and pushed the head back down forcefully, as if it were on a rag doll. 'Get this scum to the station!' He spat out the instruction to his men.

For the Street Arab all pain was gone – the darkness of unconsciousness fell over him.

Chapter 2

The Enigma

The police station cells held no comfort for detainees. They were dark, cramped and, above all freezing cold. The walls were so riddled with damp that any paint had disappeared long ago. In the still of night, only an intermittent flicker of light from a duty constable's lantern offered any small hope of discovering where the sound of scurrying came from, although the occasional scream from a prisoner signalled a rodent's presence was closer than was desired. Certainly not the place for one fearful of rats.

Robert Elliott, accompanied by a young nurse, waited patiently to be led down to the cells. Elliott was undeterred by such conditions. During his seventeen years as a police court missionary, he had become accustomed to even the most atrocious of prison cells. As he saw it, the inmates' futures were his primary concern. Reform of prison hygiene was for the politicians and statutes.

The young nurse, Mary, on the other hand, was horrified. It was all she could do to prevent herself from retching at the vile smell of urine and faeces that suddenly hit her as Drake opened the corridor door.

'Are you all right, Mary?' Elliott enquired.

Clutching a handkerchief to her face, she nodded, although the draining of colour from her cheeks suggested otherwise.

It struck Elliott as slightly strange that Mary should react in such a way. After all, as a nurse, surely she was used to these things. But perhaps it was understandable in one so young and not conversant with the harsh reality of detainment. Perhaps it would have been prudent to offer her some insight into the reality of police cells before asking her to assist him.

His job consisted of a weekly visit to the men and women awaiting prosecution in the courts. After an appearance before the bench, if the charges were trivial enough, the magistrates would release defendants into Elliott's supervision. Then, with church mission support, he would offer them help towards a new beginning.

However, this night was somewhat different. The request was, simply, to offer his account of a detained man who was reportedly deaf and mute. The case seemed intriguing, but with no real experience of the deaf, he had invited Mary to sign for him.

Mary O'Driscoll was indeed well suited to the task, having given much of her spare time to helping in the mission's school for the deaf. Over the last year, she had become very proficient in signing, to the point where she now taught the techniques to parents and schoolmistresses.

Mary forced herself to regain her composure and followed Drake and Elliott along the corridor, her nostrils, at long last, becoming accustomed to the awful stench. Elliott stopped at intervals to look through the cell door hatches.

'With the men, it's generally idleness, drink or gambling that causes their detainment, Mary,' he explained.

'Really, Mr Elliott.' Her tone sounded more apathetic than sympathetic.

He opened a hatch to reveal a young lad eagerly scratching his name on the wall with a rusty nail.

'And with the lads, it's evil home influence, lack of discipline, and above all lack of worthy companions and friends, that lie at the root of their misdoings.'

'I see,' replied Mary, a little more enthusiastic.

Elliott pulled up by a cell from which a woman prisoner shouted abuse and obscenities. He spoke with despair. 'As for the women, it's most often prostitution or theft following abandonment that brings about their undoing.' He gestured to her to look through the hatch. She reluctantly accepted and braced herself for what depravity she might see. Her instinct proved right.

A ragged old woman was sitting on a pile of filthy sacks, and smiled to expose her blackened, decayed teeth. Mary offered a delicate smile in return, half through pity, half through revulsion.

'Want to see, do you, luv?' said the woman.

'See what?' Mary enquired innocently.

Without hesitation, the old woman whipped up her threadbare skirt and started to urinate. Mary, aghast, slammed the hatch shut. The old women laughed hysterically and shouted, 'What's a matter, luv? Never seen an old gal pissing?'

Mary leant her head back against the wall for support, the horrified look on her face giving evidence of her sheltered upbringing. As a nurse at the city's hospital, she had witnessed some crude scenes, but nothing quite as vulgar as this. She turned to look at Elliott for reassurance, but saw he was now some way down the corridor. She quickened her pace to catch up with him.

Elliott saw she was flustered. 'Are you sure you're all right, my dear?'

With her soft Irish lilt, she told him, 'Yes, I'm fine.' Then she thought for a moment before finally taking a stand. 'Well no, actually I'm not fine. You see...quite frankly, Mr Elliott, I find them disgusting.'

'Sometimes the path we're on is not the path we took

by choice. Remember, Mary, let one not judge another without first knowing their plight.' Elliott's words were spoken effortlessly for her consideration.

'But can't anything be done for her?'

'Sadly, some people are beyond any help I can give them, my dear.'

Drake stopped by a cell. 'This is him, sir, our mute. The Street Arab as the men here call him.'

Elliott gave a slight frown of confusion.

'Because he's dark. Has Arab looks, you see,' Drake explained, and drew the hatch up. 'Hardly moved he hasn't for two days. Just crouches there.'

Elliott couldn't altogether see the Arab link as he looked through the hatch. For him the thin shaft of street light from a tiny barred window only showed a prisoner with a dirty, unshaven and anguished face, crouched in a corner, holding his stomach. Drake pulled out his large set of keys to unlock the door and swung it open to reveal the box of a cell. It was nine foot by six at best, Mary guessed, as she surveyed the contents – or more to the point, the lack of them. Her heart felt for the poor wretch inside.

'The slop, Sergeant,' Elliott shouted, meaning for Drake to remove the bucket. Even without Mary, Elliott wouldn't have been prepared to conduct an interview with that present. As Drake took out the bucket, Mary wondered how many hours a day a prisoner had to suffer such indignity.

'And perhaps a chair for Miss O'Driscoll?'

'Of course, Mr Elliott,' Drake replied, being forced to acknowledge that a visitor should at least be afforded a chair.

Elliott walked slowly into the cell, taking careful note of the man still crouched in the corner. He took his cane and gently moved the man's head to one side. A graze was instantly obvious, high on his cheekbone. He allowed the man's hair to fall and cover it.

Drake returned with two chairs.

'Has this man been beaten?' Elliott offered the question without looking at him.

'Injuries sustained whilst resisting arrest, nothing more,' an indignant Drake answered.

'So, the man is violent?'

'No, I didn't say that. Just plays up a bit, that's all. Probably on account of him being hungry.'

'And why would he be hungry?' said Elliott, keen to understand. He turned to look at Drake and continued with authority, 'You know, sergeant, it's against the rules to deny a prisoner food. So again, why would he be hungry?'

Mary flinched at the sudden and unexpected change of tone in his voice.

Drake pulled up his large frame, wanting to show disobedience. 'Look, Mr Elliott, I need to know who this man is. I thought a day without food might bring him to his senses, help him find his tongue and all.'

'And has it?' The sarcasm in Elliott's voice cut Drake straight back to size.

'Well, no, but...,' Drake protested.

Elliott didn't allow him to carry on. 'No, exactly!' He ended the conversation abruptly. Drake swept out of the cell, the door shutting firmly behind him.

Mary gingerly took a seat, trying to avoid the prisoner's gaze. And why wouldn't he want to fix his eyes on her? A young woman in her early twenties, about five foot six, and beautiful, some would say stunningly so; but by any judgment she was very pretty. Mary had features you couldn't help but look at with interest. Her dark hair was swept up at the back and tucked under a nurse's cap, but enough was left exposed to show that when let down, it would be long, silky and wavy. Even in the dim light, her olive complexion was flawless. And finally: her eyes! She had eyes that few women could fail to envy – large, deep brown, dreamy eyes with never-ending depth, set under perfectly formed eyebrows.

Even with all the hopelessness of his situation, the Street Arab still found enough vanity to gently stroke down his tousled hair. Finally, he released Mary from his stare and let his head fall forwards.

'Are you ready to start then, Mary?' Elliott broke the silence, whilst taking off his cloak and gloves.

'Yes, I'm ready, Mr Elliott.'

Elliott raised the man's chin with his cane, making him look again at Mary. She began to sign in earnest as Elliott spoke. 'Good evening, young man! My name is Robert Elliott and I am a police court missionary from the Court of Assize. This lady here is Nurse O'Driscoll. She helps at the deaf school and will be able to sign for us. Do you understand?'

There was no response from the man, who just gawped at Mary. She signed once more as Elliott repeated, 'Do you understand?' The man averted his gaze, until the cane made him look at her again. 'Mary, please ask him his name.' Still there was no response. 'Perhaps then, he could state his age.' Mary signed the question at a slower speed but to no avail.

'I'll try a different sort of signing, Mr Elliott,' she offered.

But she wasn't given time. The man was up on his feet in seconds. Mary gasped, clearly shocked at the swift transformation in him. She pushed back in her chair, frightened, as he approached Elliott. Suddenly, he opened his mouth wide and began frantically to push his fingers in and out. Elliott remained totally undeterred –

no flinching, barely a blink. He just watched the being before him continue to gesture with ever-growing animation. The whites of the man's eyes were yellow and terribly bloodshot.

Elliott was no stranger to witnessing odd behaviour. His years of observing the criminal classes had exposed him to many an uncomfortable situation. He'd been threatened with all manner of things, anything from knives to jagged tin cans, once even by a wooden leg! But, strangely, he had never been physically attacked by anyone. Not that you'd want to try, weapon or not. For Elliott was an imposing man, well over six foot, with broad shoulders. Even in his forty-eighth year, his torso was still relatively 'v' shaped. His pleasant, dignified face remained authoritative as the prisoner carried on his vigorous miming. Time and time again he pushed his fingers in and out of his mouth.

'Ah! I see. Yes, I understand. You're thirsty.' Elliott acknowledged the game. He walked to the door and banged it with his cane. 'Constable, some fresh water if you will.'

The cell door eventually opened and a young constable dutifully stood there with a jug of water. Mary, now calm, looked at Elliott with interest as he took the water and offered it to the man. 'Here. Water, just as you asked… Well, why hesitate? Take your fill.'

Suddenly, the mute man swiped the jug to the floor and made a dash towards the door, only to be thwarted as Elliott swung out his cane to trip him. Next minute, Elliott was towering over the sprawled body, his cane posed aloft ready to beat him.

'No! Please, Mr Elliott, no,' Mary screamed.

'My patience has been tried. Sign me your desire,' demanded Elliott of the mute. The man, accepting defeat, retreated to a corner of the cell and sat hunched up, visibly protecting his stomach, docile once more.

'Perhaps he just wants some food,' Mary suggested.

'I dare say he does. But I want him to sign and tell me so,' came Elliott's swift reply.

Gently she lowered herself in front of the man and began to sign her words at quarter speed. 'Are you hungry? Do you want food?'

Elliott rolled his eyes upwards in frustration. To his mind, what was needed was a quick cuff across the ears and some tough talking. However, patience came over him.

Mary dropped her hands with marked disappointment as the mute yawned.

'I'm sorry, Mr Elliott, but he doesn't seem to understand anything I sign. I've tried all the different ways I know.'

'Yes, quite the mystery isn't he?' Elliott replied, now

convinced it was all an act. He knew just how tough life was on the city streets. To survive was a constant battle for many an able person, let alone the disabled or afflicted. For a deaf and mute person to have any chance, he would need to understand at least some sign language.

Elliott picked up his cane, 'Come, Mary, it seems I have wasted your time.'

'Oh,' Mary replied, rather surprised at the abrupt end to things. 'I feel I've let you down,' she said, waiting for Elliott to attach his cloak.

'Nonsense, not at all, my dear.'

There was sympathy in her voice as she asked, 'What will become of him now?'

'Oh, he'll be remanded here while I make fuller enquiries. That will take a few weeks. Then, of course, he'll go before the Bench.' He drew his prognosis out, like a Shakespearean actor '...who will, no doubt, adjourn for an expert view. I'm afraid he may be here some time, Mary. But don't you go fretting now. These situations always work themselves out in the end. Right, let's see if this constable can find us a nice cup of tea,' he finished.

The constable snapped to attention, having been totally engrossed in the mute's whole charade – without doubt, the best bit of entertainment he'd seen in this station for a while.

'Wait!' A voice suddenly shouted out from behind

them after the cell door slammed shut. They turned to see the man's face at the hatch peering out. 'All right! You win,' he said.

The constable was beckoned to reopen the door and Elliott strolled back into the cell. Mary, totally perplexed, followed. 'Well, well, a mute suddenly to speak. Isn't that a miracle, Mary?' Elliott sarcastically remarked, circling around the man.

'My name is Walter...Walter Stanford. I'm twenty six years. There, happy now?' concluded the man, speaking in a condescending manner.

Elliott huffed his disapproval. 'Such remorse from one who chooses to waste my time.' Then he continued with authority, 'You would do well to remember who is in a predicament, my lad!'

Walter considered the comment before he again went and crouched in a corner of the cell. Mary, now thoroughly intrigued, again took a seat on the chair, as Elliott moved steadily round the cell.

'Well, Walter Stanford, you'd better explain yourself,' Elliott announced.

'I just thought it a prank, that's all. A chance to have the authorities baffled. Give them something to fill their wooden heads with,' replied Walter.

'You obviously have a low regard for authority.'

Walter didn't answer, realising now that Elliott had

the measure of him. He suddenly grimaced with pain and held his stomach.

Mary decided she would join in the inquiry, 'You hold your stomach all the while. Are you...?' She didn't get time to finish her words before Elliott interjected.

'...From around these parts?' He had no intention of suffering any more play-acting.

'Nearby – Ecclesfield,' Walter replied, as his pain subsided.

'Yes, I know it...and whom do you want me to notify you've been detained?'

'Nobody!' Walter shook his head. 'Please, no... I don't want my folks to know I'm here.'

'And why is that?'

'Let's just say I've brought enough worry to people. Whatever trouble I'm in, I'll deal with it alone. I always do.'

'You're no stranger to trouble then?'

'No.' Walter deliberated for a moment before continuing, 'I suppose I ought to tell you, it will come to light anyway...' But he couldn't finish. Another stabbing pain appeared to strike his stomach, this time totally winding him.

'Please, Mr Elliott. Allow me to take a look at him,' Mary pleaded, convinced there was something wrong.

Elliott sighed but conceded, 'Very well.'

She knelt by Walter, desperately hoping it wasn't a trick. Placing her hands on his soiled shirt, she slowly pulled it up to expose a massive bruise covering the width of his chest and tracking down to his navel. She drew back to allow Elliott to see. 'This man is injured, Mr Elliott.'

She replaced his shirt gently. He looked into the deep pools of her eyes.

'It's not good, is it?' he said, pulling his hand back over his stomach. She offered him a half smile in acknowledgement. Again, he winced and then began to cough. Suddenly he was barking uncontrollably. Blood splattered from his mouth.

'He needs to be seen by a doctor!' Mary shouted. Walter slumped into unconsciousness. 'Without delay!' she insisted.

Then the drama was all over. Just as quickly as it had started, it ended. Elliott watched as Walter was dispatched to hospital, Mary at his side.

The quietness allowed Elliott to ponder on what to make of the lad, and how he would offer any meaningful opinion to the courts. As he paced the cell in deliberation, his eye was suddenly drawn to an object on the floor. In the dim light, it gave off just enough of a twinkle for him to investigate further. Bending down, he now made it out. It was a chain and locket, or rather half a locket, slightly dented in one corner but otherwise well cared for. On the inner side was a red velvet lining. Fumbling around the floor, he searched for the other half; but there was nothing to be found.

He studied the locket and thought it looked familiar, but couldn't really think why. Finally, he concluded that most likely, it was somebody's little trinket which Walter had stolen and since damaged. He wondered whether, when he came to interview Walter again, he would be able to find out the rightful owner and return it.

The locket's plain and simple design was in complete contrast to the complexity of its secrets.

Chapter 3

Strange Sensations

A clock on the wall of the hospital receiving room showed 11 o'clock. Everything was ready for the following morning's surge of members of the public seeking any available medical help. Matron Hanson flicked over the pages of the large register on the lectern-type bureau, her bony finger moving down over the columns, checking for the slightest mistake.

'Ah, matron, matron! Just the person.' A refined voice broke her concentration. 'Sorry! Did I make you jump?' he carried on, devilishly, knowing the answer.

'Oh, Mr Sharpe,' said the shocked matron, her hand fixed firmly over her heart.

He proceeded to look around the desk, turning up papers, then discarding them, much to the matron's annoyance. 'Is it something in particular you're looking for, Mr Sharpe?' she asked, putting the papers back in order.

'My notes for tomorrow's lecture.' He continued, rifling through more papers on the desk 'They're somewhere round here, I'm sure.' Thomas Sharpe was a brilliant general surgeon, arguably one of the best outside

London, but alas, he was also perhaps the least organised where paperwork was concerned.

The matron couldn't take any more, her orderly world suddenly violated. 'Mr Sharpe! Please!' she exclaimed, then added calmly, 'If I may be allowed to assist you.'

Then, once again, her calm was shattered as, without warning, the double doors to the room burst open with a bang. Through them rushed a policeman pushing a trolley. On it lay Walter, still unconscious. Behind followed Mary, looking somewhat dishevelled after the night's ordeal. The matron, her eyes wide open, breathed deeply, before looking down at Walter, then at Mary, who had blood spatters on her uniform.

'Nurse O'Driscoll, what on earth...'

'I'm sorry, ma'am, I can explain,' Mary answered, knowing full well she was going to be in serious trouble. Being in uniform outside work hours was bad enough and very much against regulations; but to bring a patient in off the streets, no matter how ill or injured, was always taboo and considered a severe breach of protocol.

'I'm sure you can, nurse...at 8 o'clock in my office,' the matron curtly concluded.

Tom Sharpe, however, saw things differently; he only saw a patient in need of help. He felt Walter's neck for his pulse and checked the beat with his watch until, finally, he frowned and began to circle the man, surveying every inch of him. Taking his pen, he slowly parted a soiled, blood-stained shirt and quite casually remarked, 'Acute haemothorax.' Then turning Walter's head to one side, he touched a trickle of blood in the side of his mouth and rubbed it between forefinger and thumb, testing its consistency, 'Erm...possibly with some damage to the gastrointestinal tract or spleen. Very well, to the theatre with him then, please, nurse.'

'But Nurse O'Driscoll is not on duty, Mr Sharpe.' Matron tried to explain.

Tom looked over to Mary 'No, neither am I, dear... shall we?' He gestured the way forward. 'Oh, matron, would you be so kind as to call Doctor Belling and tell him he's required in theatre.' Matron Hanson gave him the sort of glare only she could.

It wasn't unusual for a nurse, even a probationer, to find herself assisting a theatre surgeon in an emergency. Often, junior nurses found themselves witnessing the most gruesome of surgical procedures, with no real experience. Mary, however, did possess enough medical knowledge to know what was to come. It was the level of her own involvement that she was quite unprepared for.

'Come on, Mr Belling,' Tom muttered, scrubbing his hands harshly with carbolic soap and glancing at Walter, who now gave the occasional moan. Drying his hands, he announced his intention. 'Right! We can't wait any longer. You'll have to administer the anaesthetic, nurse.'

'Me!' Mary responded incredulously.

'Unless you can see anybody else.' Tom declared.

'But Mr Sharpe...I...well...I haven't any skills in such matters,' she answered with trepidation.

'It's quite simple,' he said, handing her the leather bag and face mask. 'Don't worry; I'll talk you through it step by step.' He then proceeded to cut away at Walter's shirt and inspected the bruise, 'Erm, quite a trauma... all right, mask on...and a gentle squeeze.' He carried on, 'What did you say happened to the poor chap?'

Mary, desperately trying to make sure she followed his instructions precisely, blurted out, 'Did I...I mean, I didn't...oh, I'm sorry. Mr Sharpe, would you mind awfully if I were to just concentrate!'

He smiled generously and began to hum out a melody as he unravelled a tube. 'Another gentle squeeze now...Feel his pulse...Right. Now hum with me.'

Mary looked at him perplexed but nervously began to join in as instructed. 'That's it...can you feel it beating in time?' he asked. She nodded in agreement. 'Good, then just let me know if it begins to race or fade.'

With that, he picked up his scalpel and started to talk to himself. 'About here will do.' He made a small incision into the side of Walter's chest. Blood immediately began to spurt out. He plunged the tube quickly into the hole, allowing the bright red liquid to feed through and drain into a bowl on the floor. 'Everything all right at your end, Nurse O'Driscoll?' His comforting tone made her visibly relax.

The sudden sound of hurried footsteps towards the theatre caused Tom to joke, 'Ah, it sounds as if we have the charge of the light brigade, nurse. And just as we were doing so well together!'

'I'm terribly sorry, Mr Sharpe...' Doctor Belling said, as he entered the theatre and rolled up his sleeves in readiness for action, 'Seizure on Vickers Ward, I'm afraid.' He took over from Mary, administering the anaesthetic without any acknowledgement of her efforts. Tom carried on calmly with the operation, not once looking up at Belling.

'Perhaps, well done Nurse O'Driscoll might be appropriate in the circumstances, Dr Belling!' he sarcastically remarked, not being one to suffer bad manners and lack of recognition.

'Yes, of course, absolutely...well done, nurse!' Belling humbly replied and nodded to Mary, although inwardly he seethed that he should be openly embarrassed in front of a mere nurse!

It took another fifteen minutes of all his surgical skill before Tom was finally able to suppress the additional bleeding in Walter's stomach. Relieved, he began to stitch him up, 'Swab please,' he said, holding out his hand. But nothing was forthcoming. He looked up at Mary, 'Nurse, a swab please!' Mary stood next to him in a trance-like state, her eyes wide open and her gaze fixed straight ahead.

Belling called out sternly, 'Nurse O'Driscoll, will you...,' but Tom interjected, raising a palm to silence him.

'Miss O'Driscoll, is everything all right?' he asked, thoroughly intrigued. Getting no response, he waved his hand in front of her face. 'Where are you, nurse?'

Finally, Mary replied, 'I'm here,' her eyes still firmly fixed forward.

'And where is here, exactly?' Tom enquired.

'In the theatre of course.'

'What, in between me and Doctor Belling?'

'No, by the sterilising equipment.'

Tom looked at Belling, offering a raised brow. Belling in return gave only a shrug of confusion, for the equipment was at the other end of the theatre.

'He's going into arrest,' Mary said coolly.

Tom again looked over to Belling, who felt Walter's healthy pulse, 'His heart rate is absolutely fine,' he concluded. Tom glanced over to the clock. It read 11.50.

'What time is it on the clock, Miss O'Driscoll?'

'11.55.'

'Not 11.50? Look again,' he instructed her.

'No, definitely 11.55,' she added.

Tom was now utterly beside himself with

excitement. For all his skill as a surgeon, his passion was for neurosciences and the unexplained workings of the mind. Mary's trance-like behaviour was research material of the highest order.

She moved away and sat in a chair.

'What is going on, Mr Sharpe?' Belling begged.

'She's having some sort of out-of-body experience,' Tom explained.

'A dream?'

'Yes, effectively.'

Suddenly Belling cried out, 'I'm losing his pulse!' Frantically he moved his fingers over Walter's neck and tried to locate the pulse point. 'No, it's gone.'

'Amazing...absolutely damned amazing!' Tom muttered and promptly thumped down hard on Walter's chest before bracing his hands together and starting to push up and down in an effort to resuscitate him. He looked over to Belling. 'Anything?' Belling just shook his head.

'He doesn't die.' Mary spoke out and walked over to Tom.

Tom carried on pumping, until Belling confirmed there was still no pulse.

'No, Mr Sharpe, don't give up! He does make it,' said Mary.

Tom looked into her eyes, which were firmly fixed on him.

'Please believe me,' she requested calmly and with conviction.

If nothing else, Tom realised he was witnessing something unique; and he did believe her. Again, he clasped his hands together and began to pump away at the limp body of his patient, to the utter frustration of Belling, who rolled his eyes in disbelief.

'This is utterly ridiculous,' Belling said, taking no trouble to hide his contempt for his superior – who carried on regardless. 'There's nothing, Mr Sharpe, absolutely nothing,' he added, feeling for Walter's pulse one more time.

Tom glared intently at Mary. With all his bravado, he couldn't now help but begin to feel that Belling would be proved right. 'When, nurse? When?' he called to her anxiously.

Mary walked away and slumped deep into a chair. 'Do trust in me, Mr Sharpe,' she answered and gently closed her eyes.

'Come on! Come on, damn you!' Tom shouted at Walter, still pumping furiously.

'Am I honestly expected to witness anymore of this nonsense?' huffed Belling.

~~~

Want to read more?
Available through bookstores ISBN: 9781782999089
~~~